Anne O'Brien is a *Sunday Times* bestselling author and has sold close to a million copies of her books globally. Anne gained a BA Honours degree in History at Manchester University and a Master's in Education at Hull, living in East Yorkshire for many years as a teacher of history. Today, she lives with her husband in an eighteenth-century timber-framed cottage in the depths of the Welsh Marches in Herefordshire. Her novels are meticulously researched, spellbinding in their retelling and frequently feature a woman teetering on a knife edge at a pivotal point in our nation's history. *A Marriage of Fortune* is her fourteenth novel.

Visit Anne online at www.anneobrienbooks.com.

 anneobrienbooks
 anne_obrien

Also by Anne O'Brien

The Virgin Widow
Devil's Consort
Queen Defiant
The King's Concubine
The Forbidden Queen
The Scandalous Duchess
The King's Sister
The Queen's Choice
The Shadow Queen
Queen of the North
A Tapestry of Treason
The Queen's Rival
The Royal Game

ANNE O'BRIEN

A MARRIAGE of FORTUNE

ORION

First published in Great Britain in 2023 by Orion Fiction
an imprint of The Orion Publishing Group Ltd
Carmelite House, 50 Victoria Embankment
London EC4Y 0DZ

An Hachette UK Company

1 3 5 7 9 10 8 6 4 2

A CIP catalogue record for this book is
available from the British Library.

ISBN (Hardback) 978 1 3987 1114 3
ISBN (Trade Paperback) 978 1 3987 1115 0
ISBN (eBook) 978 1 3987 1117 4
ISBN (Audio) 978 1 3987 1118 1

Typeset at The Spartan Press Ltd,
Lymington, Hants

Printed and bound in Great Britain by Clays Ltd,
Elcograf S.p.A.

MIX
Paper from
responsible sources
FSC® C104740

www.orionbooks.co.uk

To George, as always, with my love. And with gratitude for his perseverance when living with me and the chatty women of the Paston family for yet another year.

*Do your duty now, and do not make me send you
any more messengers about these matters...*

Margaret Mautby Paston to Sir John Paston, 1469

*...if we lose that [Caister Castle] we lose
the fairest flower of our garland...*

Margaret Mautby Paston to Sir John Paston, 1472

One word of a woman would do more than the words of twenty men.

Margery Brews Paston to her husband John Paston, 1481

The PASTON FAMILY

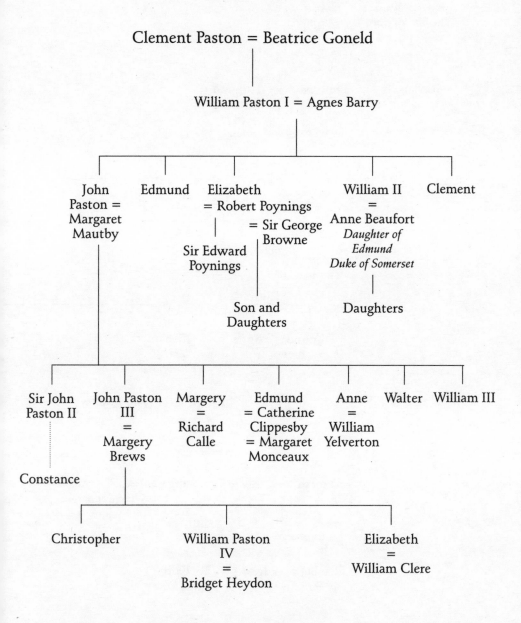

Clement Paston = Beatrice Goneld

William Paston I = Agnes Barry

John Paston = Margaret Mautby	Edmund	Elizabeth = Robert Poynings = Sir George Browne	William II = Anne Beaufort *Daughter of Edmund Duke of Somerset*	Clement

Sir Edward Poynings

Son and Daughters

Daughters

Sir John Paston II

John Paston III = Margery Brews

Margery = Richard Calle

Edmund = Catherine Clippesby = Margaret Monceaux

Anne = William Yelverton

Walter

William III

Constance

Christopher

William Paston IV = Bridget Heydon

Elizabeth = William Clere

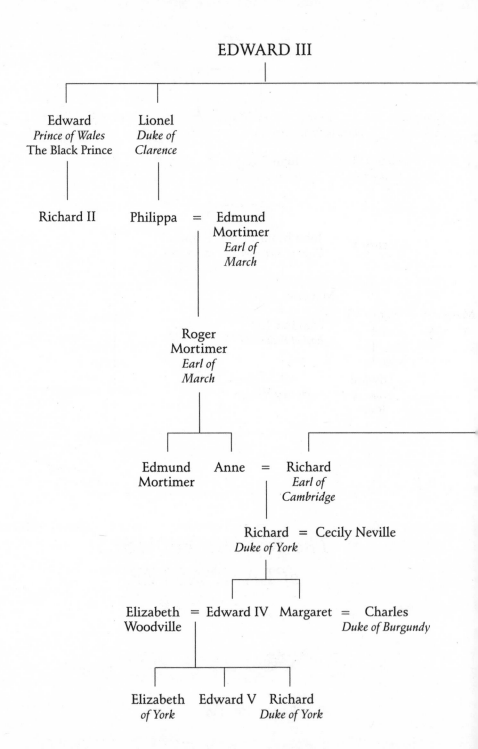

EDWARD III

Edward
Prince of Wales
The Black Prince

Lionel
Duke of Clarence

Richard II

Philippa = Edmund Mortimer
Earl of March

Roger Mortimer
Earl of March

Edmund Mortimer

Anne = Richard
Earl of Cambridge

Richard = Cecily Neville
Duke of York

Elizabeth Woodville = Edward IV

Margaret = Charles
Duke of Burgundy

Elizabeth
of York

Edward V

Richard
Duke of York

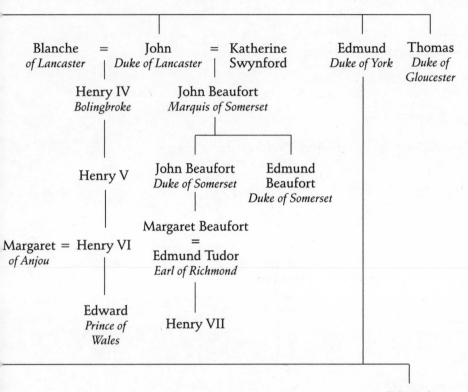

| Blanche *of Lancaster* | = | John *Duke of Lancaster* | = | Katherine Swynford | | Edmund *Duke of York* | Thomas *Duke of Gloucester* |

Henry IV
Bolingbroke

John Beaufort
Marquis of Somerset

Henry V

John Beaufort
Duke of Somerset

Edmund
Beaufort
Duke of Somerset

Margaret Beaufort
=
Edmund Tudor
Earl of Richmond

Margaret = Henry VI
of Anjou

Edward
*Prince of
Wales*

Henry VII

Edward
Duke of York

The ROYAL HOUSES
of LANCASTER
and YORK

PROLOGUE

MARGARET MAUTBY PASTON

Why is it that an unsuitable marriage can all but tear a family apart? My children, in spite of all the care I lavished on them, to instil in them a sense of duty, are becoming a wound to my heart.

My neighbours in Norwich say that I have enough trouble heaped on my new silver platters with the fate of Caister Castle, that the siege and loss of such a notable possession is the greatest calamity that could befall us. I will not refute it. To hold on to Caister, a castle which seems to be desired by every warring family in the land, not least the mighty Duke of Norfolk, is becoming far beyond Paston means. But in my frequent moments of despair, I might reply that the failure of my children to make desirable marriage alliances is threatening to hack all respectability from beneath Paston feet.

Our attaining some semblance of gentry status as castle-holders is recent.

My children, without any help from our enemies, might wilfully destroy the whole edifice.

My two eldest sons, Sir John and Jonty, with unfortunate, but truthful reputations for dalliance, are incapable of bringing a successful marriage proposal to fruition. Bestowing kisses and promises is a weekly occurrence; signing a marriage contract is anathema to both of them.

But it is my daughters who cause me anxious hours and sleepless nights. One estranged from me; the other infused with an unsettling dose of disobedience. These marital missteps might prove an even greater cataclysm to us than the loss of Caister Castle.

That is not all. I have a sister-in-law struggling to hold on to her children's inheritance, amidst all the horrors of treason and hostile relatives. Will she accept Paston help? Not willingly. She is as intransigent as any Paston.

Once, I was considered to be a woman capable of good humour. Laughter is now no longer a recognisable element in my life. Joy is a distant memory. How have I become so morose and manipulative, like a spider sitting in the centre of its web, spinning endlessly to keep the family protected?

I can fight to hold on to a castle under threat. And I will do it.

But in the name of the Blessed Virgin, what do I do with errant daughters, to bring them safe-returned into the Paston fold? I could never have believed that Margery and Anne, my once-compliant daughters, could cast our family into such a maelstrom of social censure. I believe it now.

CHAPTER ONE

MARGERY PASTON

The Paston House in Norwich, Autumn 1467

I was given the task of helping him to collect up the documents
appertaining to rents owed to us in Norwich. My mother was
short of money and our tenants, as ever, slow to pay, and so must
be chivvied with a visit. He took them from the coffer where
they were stored, passing them to me. I looked at the street named
on every document and placed them in order of distance from
our Norwich house. He handed me another. Our hands touched,
his fingers just brushing mine. Not deliberately, for he had too
much honour for that, and knew that it would not be appropriate
for him to make so intimate a gesture, yet with that briefest of
contacts he turned his head and we regarded each other. The
sorting of documents was abandoned.

How often had our hands touched in such a manner, how often
had our eyes met in concern or laughter or merely acknowledging
our existence, before sliding away. That morning, it was different.
Slowly, he stood, taking the document from me, taking care not
to touch me again.

He was taller than I with a shock of fair hair that had fallen
over his forehead. There was dust on his hands and the cuffs of
his well-worn houppelande, fit for nothing but a morning's hard
work amongst the Paston documents, but he was dressed with
his customary neatness in well-cut russet wool as befitted a man
of professional rank. I studied his face with deliberate courage,
refusing to allow my gaze to fall away in case it expressed too

clearly the thoughts that raced through my mind. What did I see? The fair skin, pale brows, straight lips that rarely smiled. His eyes were clear and grey, always alert and assessing. This was Master Richard Calle, bailiff to the Paston family, the most highly trusted man in our household.

'I think the task is complete, Mistress Margery. My thanks for your help,' he said, his voice cool and calm as always, even when under duress from a recalcitrant tenant. 'I will arrange a visit to those in arrears. If you would be pleased to inform your mother that all is in hand.'

But today I did not wish to speak of rents and business. 'What do you think of me, Master Calle?' I asked.

I thought that he sighed, just a mere exhalation of breath. I had never been so forward, so provocative, but now I was almost twenty years of age and had acquired a Paston mind of my own. It was difficult not to, living in close proximity to my mother and grandmother, both women with a will as strong as the iron lock on the abandoned coffer.

Master Calle did me the honour of not pretending to misunderstand my question, or being shocked by it.

'I cannot say, Mistress Margery.'

'Why can you not say?'

He placed the document carefully on the table with the rest, turning away from me, yet he answered.

'I must not say. It would be highly ill-advised for me to speak what is in my mind.'

'That is no more of an answer,' I replied, concentrating on the skill of his hands as he deftly rerolled a number of documents. They were long-fingered, broad-palmed, and I wished that I might feel the touch of them again. Would he never take my hands in his, as a lover might do with his beloved?

'Because what I might think of you must not be, Mistress Margery. As I must not ask what you think of me.' A single line developed between his brows. 'It is wrong of you to ask me.'

I allowed an awkward silence to develop after this statement, waiting to see if he would break it. When he did not, I ventured a mild reply.

'We have known each other a long time, Master Calle.'

'I am aware.'

'For many years. Since I was a child.'

'Yes.'

'Do we not know each other well?'

'Yes. As well as any member of your family knows its bailiff.'

Ah. But there was the crux of the matter. I continued my pursuit of him.

'I think that I may say that we do not dislike each other.'

'We may say that.'

I walked round to stand in front of him. Now there were tiny lines of disquiet beside his mouth.

'Would I be a good wife to you, Master Calle?'

This time it was Richard Calle who paused, as if in astonishment that I should ask. Then:

'No!'

It was an explosive answer, his voice not quite as level as it had been.

'Why would I not? I only ask that you answer me truly, Master Calle.'

His expression remained severe, giving me no indication of what might be in his heart.

'Then yes, if it is truth that you want. You would be the perfect wife.'

My throat dried, my own heart gave a sharp beat.

'Would you, then, be a good husband for me?'

This time there was no hesitation. Denying his usual care, he had picked up one of the documents again, his hands clenched around it, creasing the legal agreement between Paston and some unknown Norwich citizen.

'No. And no. I would not. And do not ask me why not. You know well the answer without my spelling it out for you.'

Now there was anguish in his eyes, in the twist of his mouth, but I would show no mercy.

'I want to hear you say why you will reject what I think has grown between us, unspoken. I wish it to be unspoken no longer.'

'But why, Mistress Margery? Of what advantage would it be, other than to bring heartbreak for both of us?'

It was not a comfortable question. It was full of despair.

'A whim?' I replied. 'A desire to know that a man might admire me?'

'I am too old for you.'

'That is not it.'

'No. But it does not weigh well in the balance of why I am no husband for such as you.'

'Then why are you not a fit husband? Speak truly, Richard Calle.'

'My family is not appropriate for a marriage between us.'

'Why not?'

I would make him say what I knew was in his mind, because it was in mine, too. Was it not in the mind of every member of the Paston family, so strongly rooted that they would never even consider that I would see marriage with this man? I would have someone speak it aloud, even though I knew that his reply could indeed break my heart.

The ravaged document was finally cast aside.

'Margery, you know full well why not.' And he proceeded to destroy the pleasure I experienced in hearing him call me simply Margery. 'I come from a family of shopkeepers. What do they say of us? Selling mustard and candles in Framlingham. My brother is not even a merchant but merely a seller of commodities. What would a Paston say to that? You have your feet planted firmly on the edge of becoming a reputable gentry family with a castle to your name and Sir John Paston betrothed to the Queen's cousin. A Paston daughter does not marry a bailiff, a man in employment, a son of a shopkeeper. A Paston daughter does not wed an employed man without land, a man for the past year without income since your family is in dire financial need and I have had no payment. What have I to offer you? You would be sneered at by the notables of Norwich. You would not be invited across their threshold or to eat at their table with a husband such as I would be. What would your mother say? What would your grandmother Mistress Agnes say? They would damn me for my presumption, and probably you for your recklessness.'

'But I know all of that…'

'Of course you do. You also know how important marriage in the family is to Mistress Agnes: prestige and income and land. Do I need to remind you of the sufferings of your aunt Elizabeth? Of course I do not. The story of your grandmother's failure to find her a husband with enough money to please the Pastons is legendary. Your aunt was beaten and whipped because she could not attract a suitable betrothed. Look at me, Margery.' He spread his hands wide at his side. 'I have no security in money. I have no land. I have no connections to help me take a step up the social ladder, other than through my employment.'

'I know all of that,' I repeated, for indeed I did. None of it was new to me. 'And yet…'

'I do not denigrate my skills,' Richard Calle said. 'I know my own worth, and particularly to your family. I am the perfect bailiff, hardworking and loyal. I can be trusted with any task, to handle any amount of money. Would I thieve from my employer? I would sooner become a beggar in the gutters of Norwich. My relationship with your tenants is excellent. But that does not make me a suitable Paston husband.'

Bitterness coated those final words, sharp as the aloes with which my mother dosed us as a purgative. It was damning and all true. There was no way forward.

'Even if I want you,' I said.

I watched as the muscles of his throat constricted. Never had I been so outspoken, unless it was on my knees to plead that my dreams for the future might be realised. It was one thing to beg the Blessed Virgin's indulgence, it was quite another to speak my yearnings out loud to the man I wanted.

'Even if you want me, Margery.' Richard Calle remained adamant, yet I sensed that beneath his unyielding demeanour his self-control was becoming compromised. 'You know that what I speak is honest. I have a care for your reputation. And, before God, for my dignity, too.'

I turned my face away in an anguish that matched his.

7

'So I will be sacrificed for your dignity.'

'Not entirely.'

'Then why?'

How stern he remained despite my challenge. 'You don't want me. You don't need me. Months from now you will realise that to offer yourself as my wife would be the greatest mistake of your young life. Instead, you will wed a man who will give you wealth and honour.'

'But will I love him?'

'That is not important. As you well know.'

I looked down at my hands that were clasped around the beads of my rosary, although there were no prayers in my mind. Only grief and impending loss.

'Then you will reject me.'

'Yes. My dear girl, I must reject you. I admire your courage in speaking, but I cannot accept the offer of your love, even though it is an invaluable gift.'

'Even if I weep for it?'

'Even if you weep.' He stretched out a hand as if he would have touched mine and then let it fall. 'Oh, Margery, in God's name do not ... It breaks my heart.'

'But mine is broken, too. I beg you to reconsider, Richard.'

I deliberately called him by his given name.

'I cannot. I will not. I am a servant. That is enough. It will be easier for both of us if you do not seek me out. I regret that you should ever have fallen in love with me.'

He walked away, pausing at the door as if all had still not been said between us, but if that were so, any such intention on his part was brutally rejected. With an obvious firming of his shoulders, he lifted the latch, closing the door quietly behind him, leaving me with a pile of unsorted rental agreements and an outpouring of despair. Just as he had closed the door on any possibility of love between us. A door that I had deliberately, heedlessly, opened. I had offered myself to him and he had refused that offer. I should have felt humiliation, but it was not that that made me sweep the documents to the floor in a surge of temper. It was desolation and regret that he should reject me for finer feelings. I could not doubt that he was a man of honour; every word he had spoken about his own position in the world had been unquestionably true, while I had been ungracious. My mother would have been horrified if she had heard me. My grandmother would probably have beaten me, as she was used to beat my aunt Elizabeth when displeased with her. I did not care. I loved him and nothing would change that.

I opened the door to find him still standing there in the shadowed passageway, his back to me, his face turned towards the wooden panelling. With the courage with which he had graced me, I placed my hand flat against his shoulder.

'What would you say, Richard, if I told you that my heart is full of love for you?'

'I would say that your heart is mistaken.'

Now he walked away, turning into the hall. He did not look back.

I had no doubts that he loved me, too.

Which did not soothe the hurt at his rejection.

I had known Richard Calle all my life, it seemed. How old was I when he first came to join our Paston household as our new bailiff? I was a child of no more than six years, while he was a man full grown with much experience. Tall and fair, lithe and graceful, unlike my brothers, who were dark and strongly built, he was there in all my memories. As I grew older, he took my notice. He sometimes gave me tasks to do, to fetch and carry, sometimes even to write lists at his dictation, for I had been well taught by my mother to wield a pen. He said that I was a most capable and loyal daughter. It pleased me and made my heart grow warm. It seemed that he had a care for my happiness within a family that was ever busy. When he offered his grave smile to me, I felt reassured and of value although I could have no complaint in my upbringing.

When I was a little girl, I recalled being the recipient of much love in our Paston household. When I was ill, Mistress Margaret, my mother, sent to London for a pot of treacle, a costly medicinal paste, including the flesh of a roasted viper, taking twelve years to age and credited with curing everything from inability to sleep to the mortal effect of poison. Not that I suffered from either, and I could not recall what had urged my mother to pen a letter to demand its immediate sending. The concoction had a curious aroma and a lingering taste that was not altogether pleasant but, despite my childish resistance, I was dosed and I was cured. I recall my mother's embrace when I recovered.

I also remembered a new girdle, purchased for me at my mother's request in London. I think it was to celebrate the day of my birth. It was cunningly stitched with an intricate fastening, and much admired although it was now too small for me to wear and was folded away, perhaps for use by my own daughter in the future. There was never any doubt that I was a beloved daughter of the house, even if my father was a distant figure and infrequently at home.

It was a comfortable life despite the legal disputes that engaged my father and my brothers. We were a family on the rise, and I was expected to marry well. If I found love, or even affection with my husband, who would be chosen by my father and mother, I would be a fortunate woman. I was told that plans had been made for me when I was a child of six years, but they had come to naught. One was to a ward of my mother's cousin, Sir John Fastolf, the man who had willed his whole inheritance to us, including Caister Castle. It would have been an excellent match, but it seemed that we were not sufficiently important. We might be related in cousin-ship but money and status meant everything. It mattered little to me. I never met the boy who might have been my husband.

I remember travelling to London with my mother to visit my father when he was incarcerated in the Fleet Prison for the third time. My mother was worried for his health and so made the long journey to encourage him and dose him in equal measure. My brother Jonty told her, in a moment of levity, to allow me to kneel at the Rood at the north door of St Paul's and St Saviour's Abbey in Bermondsey while we were there, to pray to the two saints that I might find a good husband. My mother was in a gentle mood when she found my father in robust and argumentative health and so allowed it. She knelt with me for a time, I suppose offering prayers for my father's release. I prayed for a husband.

My mother would not have approved of the man for whom I

offered prayers. She would have rebuked me most severely, but she would have failed to change my mind. How could it have been possible? I had fallen in love.

What did I know of love? Nothing, except that to be in the vicinity of Richard Calle gave purpose to my days. I woke in the morning with the anticipation of seeing him, speaking with him, spending time with him, even if we only passed in a corridor. Some days he was absent on estate affairs, but I knew that he would return. I went to my bed aglow with the knowledge that he had a work-room in our own house where I might find him unless he was abroad about Paston business.

Why did I love him? I could not say. It was no single event that had struck me with enchantment as it might in the old stories. It was no single thread in a tapestry where a knight meets his lady in a magic forest. Instead, it had crept up on me, day by day, a stealthy hunting to capture my emotions, until I could not imagine living without him.

Did he feel the same?

I thought that he did, although nothing was said between us, nor were there any overt gestures that could be misconstrued. Did we not both know that any words of affection spoken between us would have been a matter for censure which might cost me my freedom and him his position?

We loved and yet we did not love.

Until that day when I declared my love for him and he repulsed me. From that day there was an awareness between us that careful distancing could not hide. What my mother would say if she ever suspected, I could not bear to think of it. I trod lightly, as guilt ran hand in hand with desire, and fear of discovery.

CHAPTER TWO

MARGERY PASTON

The Paston House in Norwich, April 1469

My mother sent for me to come to her chamber where she sat with a new sheet of paper before her and a pen in hand. It was her custom to dictate most of her letters, but this one she had decided to write for herself. She had already dipped the pen into the little carved ink-pot with its domed lid. I noticed that no strips had been torn from the full sheet of fine-quality paper that she was about to use; the letter must be appertaining to some matter of importance. I curtsied, expecting an errand to complete.

I had no intimation of what was to come.

Instead of writing, she put down the pen, the ink drying in the warm air. Spring had come early to Norwich, and my mother's chamber, its windows ajar, was full of birdsong and the scent of blossom on the early plum tree. Her expression was severe but not out of the way. She was calmly in control of her daily affairs, as I awaited my instructions.

My mother steepled her fingers together. In her youth she was esteemed a striking woman with fine features and dark eyes. She was handsome still, despite her predilection for confining her fading hair in a short hennin made of dark broadcloth, or in a linen coif. I did not think either flattered her, but Mistress Margaret would care nothing for that. Her hands were fine and capable, her fingers well used to wielding a needle or a pen, or any household implement that demanded her attention. She was forty-eight years old and as neat and healthy as she had always been.

'Margery,' she announced, 'I am arranging for you to be boarded out, to go and live in the house of some noble lady in London. I am writing to your brother Sir John to see what is possible.'

My heart slowly sank as I took in what seemed to be a banishment for me, knowing better than to question why. Not that it was out of the ordinary for young women of a gentry family to be boarded with one of higher consequence. My younger sister Anne was living with the Calthorp family, cousins of ours, to learn the ways of a family of good repute. But why was I to be sent now? And where would I go? I waited for an explanation, if my mother chose to give me one.

'You do not seem surprised,' she observed, her eyes resting on my face.

'I am astonished,' I replied. 'I thought that I was beyond the age to be boarded out.'

My mother shook her head. 'Your aunt Elizabeth,' she explained, now chill as a puddle of ice, 'was sent to be with Lady de la Pole when she was considerably older than you are, and benefited much from it. And she found herself a worthy husband in Sir Robert Poynings.'

So now I knew. All that was unspoken was clear.

'Where will I go?' I asked.

My mother's reply was prompt; she had given it careful thought. 'It is in my mind that the Duchess of Oxford or the Duchess of Bedford might take you. Both are women of high repute. It would be good for you to see something of Court life. Sir John will ask if either would be willing. It would be excellent for your education of how to manage a larger household than ours.'

'Will it be soon?'

How biddable I sounded, when everything within me lurched with horror.

What did she see as she looked at me? Not a copy of herself, for certain. Instead, a self-effacing young woman of twenty-one years with a quiet demeanour although capable of a direct, grey stare. I did not think that I possessed the indomitable spirit that was my mother's when faced with challenges in life.

'It will be soon indeed, if Sir John can arrange it.'

Not once in all that interview was Richard Calle mentioned.

Yet why should my manner towards him be the cause of my mother's decision? There had never been any inappropriate behaviour between us, nothing that could rouse any degree of suspicion. I tried to remember if I had ever appeared too close to him, too willing to keep his company. I could not. There had been nothing, not even a hint of intimacy that Father Gloys our priest could find distasteful. Our priest was always watchful over possible sins, but there had been nothing to watch after that one painful conversation over the rent rolls. No gifts, no innocuous posies left by my door. If I entered a room, Master Calle made an exit, but not so quickly as to draw attention to us. He was polite, courteous, protective of my reputation and his own. The old easy association of bailiff and daughter of the house had gone, replaced by a coolness, deliberately cultivated.

Yet I was being sent away.

Another thought crept into my mind. If my mother had her suspicions, would they cast Richard off? I doubted it. He was far too valuable in these troubled times. But they would send me away, the elder daughter, effectively separating us for ever, and a sudden terrible sense of hurt assailed me, that Richard might prefer such an estrangement. It would remove him from a deplorable situation. As Father Gloys would preach, where there was no temptation there would be no sin.

'Forgive me if I have displeased you,' I said to my mother.

'You have not displeased me. I do not think that you ever could.' Pushing back her stool, she stood, abandoned the pen and moved around the table to take me in her arms. It was a warm embrace when she kissed my cheeks. 'You are my dearest daughter. I know that you will do well for the family. You will discover a husband who will bring you and the Pastons honour.'

A final dry salute to my forehead and she returned to her seat. Dipping the pen, she began to write. 'I will inform you when our request has been accepted. I swear that you will enjoy the experience. It was one that I never had.'

The spasm of guilt in my throat was unbearable. My mother was doing this for love of me. I was betraying her.

I did not have long to wait. April was still bringing us mild sunshine and sharp showers when my anxieties leapt into fevered life. My eldest brother had been busy indeed on my behalf, in the household of his new patron, the Duke of Oxford. My mother had clearly spurred him into action.

'The Duchess of Oxford will be pleased to receive you,' my mother informed me with a falsely casual air, passing me in the scullery as I entered from the herbarium, shaking the rain drops from a fistful of soft herbs for our cook. I knew that she had been lying in wait for me. 'Sir John will arrange the travel as soon as may be.'

To me it seemed like a death knell, an exile from which I would never return.

'Do be careful, Margery,' she admonished. 'Your skirts are drenched.'

An exaggeration, since I had wrapped myself in a length of coarse frieze to prevent the fine wool being spotted, but obediently I brushed the drops away while the only thought that came to me, supplanting the need to deliver the sage and rosemary to the waiting cook, was that I needed a kindly voice to plead my cause for staying in Norwich. My brothers surely would be the obvious source of aid, but that idea did not linger long. Sir John was too wrapped up in life at Court, his wooing of Mistress Anne Haute and his reputation at the tournament. Mistress Haute was cousin to the Queen, thus taking precedence in Sir John's schemes above an unimportant sister. Nor were my other brothers any more likely wielders of a chivalric sword on my behalf. For all my life they had treated me with a shallow affection, to be smiled upon or brushed aside as their interests took them away from home. I was merely a sister to be wedded to a man who would bring esteem to the family. They would do their best for me, of course, but now Jonty was beguiled by estate problems; Edmund, the most self-sufficient, was still completing his legal training at the Inns of Court. Walter and Willem were just too young. No help there.

I was destined for the household of the Duchess of Oxford.

Having seen my future determined so swiftly, I must tell Master Calle of my imminent departure, but he was not here to be told, nor would it be wise within our walls. All I knew was that I had no wish for him to return simply to be informed that I was no longer part of the household, nor would ever be. It would seem to me to be a cruel parting.

I curbed my impatience behind a screen of perfect silent obedience, finishing the storing of my possessions for travel. There must be an opportunity. It must be soon. All I had to do was find a means to waylay Master Calle somewhere in the town where we might achieve some privacy. It would entail a deceit, a sleight of hand, but it could be done.

Yet what could he do, even if I told him?

Nothing. Nothing at all. Still, I would make our parting a personal one, and since it was the twenty-third day of April, I knew where I would likely discover him in Norwich. It might take me a little time to hunt him down, but he would be there with the merchants and traders who found the opportunity to celebrate St George's day. Richard Calle was not a member of the prestigious order of St George, as my father had been, but he would have many acquaintances who were. I would start with Dragon Hall in Old Barge Yard, where the merchant members met before their procession to give thanks in the Cathedral.

It was a busy environment with much coming and going, but I waited outside while within I knew that our Lord Mayor, who owned the Hall, would be laying out his best woollen cloth for inspection, the finest worsted wool, as well as his recent imports from the Low Countries, which he would hope to sell to his fellow merchants. I stepped back into the shadow of an adjacent building and set myself to wait.

And there they came, the members of the Order of St George with their gold rings imprinted with a fierce dragon. And finally, to the rear, there was Richard Calle, emerging from the Hall with a group of associates, still deep in conversation. I watched as they spoke, as they listened to him. One clapped him on the arm as he prepared to depart, for he would not be part of the procession. He might be from a family of shopkeepers in my mother's eyes, but he was a respected member of this community. In this company I became aware of his quiet authority, the respect in which he was held.

Richard Calle pulled on his gloves, straightened his low-crowned beaver hat so that it sat level with his brows and turned as if to return to the Paston House from where I knew he would set out to visit some of our nearest manors beginning with Hellesdon, at present a scene of trouble. His thigh-length cotehardie did not have the quality or the style of the garments of his associates, but it was a worthy garment, with fur at cuff and neck, in a deep viridian green that drew the eye. He wore no jewels, for he would not have the income to purchase any such, although the incised leather of his belt came from one of the best Norwich craftsmen. I knew that it was. My mother had given it to him at the New Year's gift giving, a sign of her appreciation.

I moved to step beside him, my maid in seemly company, as she had been all along.

'Master Calle.'

When he turned his head, I could read no emotion in his expression unless it were a polite interest beneath the moment of surprise.

'Mistress Margery.'

We were still well within earshot of a group of guild members.

'I have a message from my mother,' I announced. I was well practised in my delivery, full of confidence, as if it might be an errand upon which I embarked every day.

'Then you must deliver it.' He bowed to me, and then in fare-well to his associates. 'You must excuse me. This will be a matter of Paston business which I must not neglect. It must be urgent if Mistress Margery has been sent to summon me.'

'The Paston Captainess will have heavy work for you, Master Calle! To which distant manor do you ride this week?' came a cheerful voice from the crowd.

There was some laughter, some comment on Mistress Margaret Paston holding all on a tight rein as he led me from the crowd to a quieter spot by the wall. Many there would know me, but I had a maid and a most acceptable reason for meeting with him. I handed over a folded sheet which might have been a note from my mother. He took it, opened it, and perused the blank sheet with careful interest. I knew that he had done all he could to preserve my good name if anyone chose to gossip.

'You should not be here with me, mistress.'

I would not apologise. My maid was out of earshot.

'I need to tell you this. They are sending me away. We cannot have this conversation at home with duplicitous Father Gloys listening at the door. Or my mother. They are sending me to complete my education with the Countess of Oxford.'

Richard Calle drew in a breath before he replied. 'It sounds to me to be an excellent plan for your advancement, mistress.' So formal. So cool. He frowned a little, smoothing the letter between his fingers as if he were still reading the blank page. Then he looked up, his gaze searching. 'Why are they sending you away?'

'My mother will not say.'

He looked away towards the massive bulk of the Dragon Hall behind us.

'Have you told your mother?'

'Told her what?' I would push him to say it.

'About your feelings for me.'

'And about your reciprocation? Of course not. Besides, what is there to tell? We have exchanged no embraces, no promises. Yet she will part us.' I felt frustrations building inside me. And not a little anger.

'It will be for the best,' Master Calle stated.

'Is that all you can say?'

'You know what I will say. I have said it all before. You will enjoy the visit. You will meet new people. You will meet a man of whom your family will approve. See it as an opportunity that few young women are given.'

'I cannot.'

'Then I will see it for you. And wish you Godspeed.'

My anger was now blisteringly hot, but I kept it banked down. 'I know that you are directed to visit Oxnead after Hellesdon. When you return, when you next set foot in the Paston house, Master Calle, I will be gone and you will never see me again. My aunt Elizabeth never returned to Norfolk after her sojourn in London, and I suspect neither will I. I presume that you will not care.'

'If that is how it must be, then I must thank God for the chance for advancement offered to you. My thoughts on it are of no relevance.' He tucked the misused piece of paper into his sleeve and bowed. 'Good day, Mistress Margery. It would be wrong of me to escort you home. Your maid will see that you are safely returned. I have had a care for your reputation this morning. It would be good if you did so too. You do not need gossip to sully your good name.'

He bowed again, beckoned to my maid and smiled at her. He had not smiled at me. He might have protected my name but he had also quite thoroughly rejected me. This was not care. This was not love. I had been wrong in believing that Master Calle had any interest in me whatsoever.

'Good day, Master Calle. I wish you well in finding a bride of your own, worthy of your love. I regret having troubled you with my own sentiments, which you found to be without value.'

It was as if he could not escape from my presence quickly enough, turning his face from me so that I might not intrude in any thoughts that he failed to hide. The last I saw of him, he was striding in the direction of the Cathedral, swallowed up by the shadows cast by Dragon Hall.

It only took twenty-four hours. Indeed less. News of our meeting had come to my mother's ears by the following morning. Why had I believed that I could escape notice in the centre of Norwich where the market stalls were thronged and the cloth merchants out in force? Who had seen me, taking enough note that it must be carried to my mother's door? I knew not and my mother was not saying. I was summoned once again, my mother making no pretence at writing or being engaged in manorial business.

Rather, she stood before the fireplace, arms folded in a formidable challenge.

'I hear, Margery, that you met with Richard Calle in town yesterday.'

I considered denying it. But only briefly. Why lie when my mother's many informants would have told her the truth of it? How foolish I had been in believing that I could meet with Richard so publicly without it being noted. That I had done so had been a measure of my desperation.

'Yes.'

'Why would you find a need to do that?'

'I wished to say farewell before I go to the Duchess of Oxford.'

I quickly discovered that there was a limit to which I was prepared to tell the truth when my mother was glowering at me.

'There was no need.'

There was ire in her reply, and in her eye.

'I wished to do it. It seemed a courtesy that was necessary.'

My mother pinned me with an accusatory eye. It was no surprise that she did not believe me. I wished that I had told her the truth from the beginning.

'I hope that you do not have inappropriate feelings towards him. It will not do.'

'He is a man of honour.'

'He is a man of no substance.'

'I cannot accept that.'

Lips pursed in disapproval, she surveyed me as if I were a tenant who was up to no good.

'It seems that your affections are engaged, however strongly you might deny it. Have you no sense? If you think to persuade your brothers to support you in such an ill-considered match, you are mistaken. They will never do it. Put Calle out of your mind. A liaison with this man would be detrimental to our position in Norfolk society. I will not have the Pastons become the subject of gossip and innuendo. You will wed a man who will bring into the family valuable manors and wealth. If he has a title, all the better. When you are in the Duchess of Oxford's household, there will be every opportunity for you to meet such a man.'

There it was: the reason for Paston daughters being treated with such lack of compassion in the choice of husband. Land, income, status; they were paramount. But of course this was something I had always known. I could not plead ignorance.

'I do have an affection for him,' I confessed. 'He has been kind to me all my life.'

My mother's arms fell to her sides where I could see that her hands had curled into fists. Not that she would ever use them against me, but still, there was no softness in her.

'He will have no affection for you, if he knows what is best for him.'

My blood was running cold at what was clearly a threat.

I risked a challenge of my own.

'You were compassionate to my Aunt Elizabeth in her unhappiness. Why do you not give me the same consideration?'

It was as if, in recalling Aunt Elizabeth's terrible sorrows, I had struck out at my mother.

'Enough, daughter. Yes, I had compassion for her, particularly when your grandmother, Mistress Agnes, beat her to break her will. Your aunt did not find it easy to attract a reputable husband. What your aunt did not do was set her eyes on a man of inferior standing. She knew what was due to our position in Norfolk society. You have incriminated yourself by your behaviour yesterday, my daughter. It is now clear. You and I can no longer live together at ease until you have learned respect for those with a care for you. You cannot leave this household and Norwich soon enough. I will help with your expenses, pay for your escort, and arrange for you to travel as soon as the end of this week and Sir John can meet you in London. Meanwhile, until then, you will not leave this house.'

All my fears welled up. I took one step towards her, but no more. There was a terrible chasm appearing between us.

'Please do not send me away,' I begged. 'Master Calle will never wed me. He has no ambitions to do so.'

My future was looming before my eyes, far from Norwich, far from Richard. My heart hurt with such pain from Richard's rejection of me and my mother's cold determination. *You and I can no longer live together at ease.* Had she truly condemned me with those words to a life far away?

'I cannot risk it,' she said.

'Richard knows that you will never permit it. His loyalty to you is without question. I beg that you will not punish him, or send me away because—'

'Margery!' she silenced me. 'Say no more. My mind is made up. No, I will not punish Master Calle for a sin that he has not yet committed. But it will be better for all if you are no longer in this household.'

My fate was sealed. My mother did not style herself Captainess of her household for nothing.

'And if you think to meet with my bailiff beneath this roof before you leave, then you will discover your mistake. He will be overlooking affairs at our manor of Oxnead until you have gone.'

Which I already knew. I inclined my head as if in acceptance.

'I am sorry, Mother, that you find my company not to your liking.'

'You have become a grave worry to me, Margery. You are my daughter and my affection for you has not altered, but your reputation must be above reproach if you are to make a good match. I cannot risk your clandestine meetings with my bailiff. You can no longer stay here. Now go to your chamber.'

I walked from the room. Outside, waiting, as if he too had been summoned, was Master Richard Calle. He must have heard the tenor of the whole exchange, even if muffled by the closed door.

I looked at him. What he read in my face I could not guess.

Help me.

My mouth shaped the words but there was no sound. What could he possibly say in reply? I fled in despair, abandoning dignity. All I was aware of was the great sorrow within me. Richard Calle had rejected me and my mother was sending me away. Would my mother dismiss him after all, however useful he was, in a fit of pique? If she did, it would be my fault.

I could not forgive myself if he lost his employment because of my carelessness.

Our household met as was habitual for supper, when all ate

together around the table – my mother, Father Gloys, giving thanks for our blessings in grim tones, my younger brothers and I, and Master Calle. It was an uncomfortably silent affair yet a relief that our bailiff still ranked as one of our household.

Next morning, I found a note pushed under my door, on a corner of paper torn from a larger sheet. It was brusque, written in haste.

> Margery,
> I will come to you tomorrow afternoon when all are from home. If you do not wish to speak with me, do not answer your door. I will understand if you do not wish it, but I pray that you will not shut me out.
> RC

A note that I folded again and again, running my nail along the folds as I considered the repercussions. My response to such a plea could well dictate the path I would take for the rest of my life. To concur would allow me to step into the arms of the man I dreamed of as my lover; to reject would blight that chance of love for ever.

CHAPTER THREE

MARGERY PASTON

The Paston House in Norwich, April 1469

A soft brush of knuckles came against my door. With no hesitation I opened it and allowed Richard Calle to step in. My mother was engaged in business in the city, Father Gloys with her, while the silence told me that my brothers were elsewhere. This was the only chance that I would have, and I would take it.

'I know that I should not be here,' he said. 'And so do you. This is even more dangerous to your reputation than your meeting with me in a street.'

I closed the door and fixed the latch. We would not be disturbed.

'What did my mother say to you? She obviously did not dismiss you from Paston employ.'

His mouth twisted into a wry approach to a smile, before settling once more into grim resolve. I still knew not his purpose here.

'The Captainess was as business-like as you would expect. She made no mention of our meeting. She had presumed the matter settled and we would both be dispatched in different directions. A most practical answer to the problem. As you know, your mother rarely sees the need to explain.'

'And so the matter is settled.' My reply was similarly unemotional. Richard had not been punished, but I had. 'I am to go to London on Friday with my family's blessing. As you said, better for me and for you.'

I was in no mood to be compliant. When Richard Calle,

astonishing me, took my hand and pressed his lips to my palm, the first time such a symbol of any feelings had passed between us, I snatched it away. But then I closed my fingers over my palm as if to hold the salute close for ever. It must be enough. He could not step between me and my mother. My future was laid out and Richard had no part in it; as my mother had warned, my brothers would not support me.

'Is this farewell?' I asked. 'Then it is said and done. It was not worth your coming and risking crossing my mother's path.'

'No, it is not farewell.'

I tilted my chin. I was in no mood to be amenable. 'I understand you not.'

Richard's face was as colourless as the wax candles.

'When your mother gave me the papers to take to Oxnead, she informed me that you were leaving to go to the Duchess of Oxford's household, presuming that I did not know. She said that she expected you to remain there until a marriage was negotiated for you with a man of some significance. It was done in what might have seemed a casual comment. We both knew that it was not. It was a warning to me to keep you at a distance, to make no attempt to contact you. I must not harm your reputation in any manner that would undermine Mistress Margaret's plans for you.'

'At the Dragon Hall, you told me that it would all be for the best.'

And how he had wounded me.

'I was wrong.'

'I still do not understand you. Nothing has changed between us since you wished me Godspeed.' The bitterness at such a rejection dripped from my words.

'Everything has changed. Jealousy. Envy. Call it what you will. I do not think that I am strong enough to let you go to another life and another man in marriage.'

Which effectively silenced me.

'I would claim that I am a man of honour,' Richard said. 'I should leave now, before this can go on any further, yet that is not what my heart tells me to do. I have watched you grow from a girl into a woman, seeing the beauty and intelligence blossom in you as maturity has claimed you. You have touched my mind and my heart, and it has been the greatest obligation on me not to show it. But now I must. Now I must speak of it, or abandon you to a different life. That is not what I want. I want you to spend your life with me, not separated by distance and legalities.'

It took my breath. Richard Calle had never been a man of extremes. 'Richard . . .'

This time, when he took hold of both my hands and placed them palm to palm between his own, I did not resist.

'I know what I ought to do. I know what honour dictates. My fear is that to achieve my own desires, I will hurt you. And yet I cannot allow you to go to London and be snapped up by a man who has no thought for your virtues, only for the value of a Paston alliance. You once asked me what I thought of you,' he said.

'There is no need to say it.'

'There is every need. It would be rank dishonesty in me if I did not speak. I was wrong not to do so over the documents — those you swept onto the floor in a fury.' His smile was full of self-mockery.

'I know that you mean more to me than I do to you,' I observed carefully.

'I am not saying that.' Sliding his hands up my arms, he curled them to clasp my shoulders and he drew me close, placing his lips on mine. Soft as a feather. Warm as a promise. 'You deserve to know the truth. You own my heart, and I cannot bear to let you go, even though you are not mine to claim.'

I thought about what he was saying, needing clarity as my heart leapt in joy and fear beneath the confines of my gown.

'Are you certain of your love for me?' I asked.

'There is no room in me for doubt. But what of your feelings for me? You are very young to speak of lasting love.'

'Yet I will speak it. I have loved you for as long as I remember.' Then the joy drained out of my emotions, leaving me empty. 'But it is all hopeless, Richard. I see no future for us.'

For one moment, the length of a heartbeat, he hesitated, as if making up his mind over a contentious financial dispute. Or an issue that could destroy us both.

'Then hear me. There is one way out of this turmoil, if we are sure that we seek marriage. If you are certain, Margery.'

Abruptly, he stepped back, as if allowing me a little space in which to make a decision that would alter the whole of my future.

'Are you saying marriage? Sir John will forbid a marriage even if my mother does not,' I said.

'Of course he will, but I will not take you as my mistress. Do you think that I would so dishonour you?' His denial was harsh. 'We can take matters into our own hands.' His voice became low and intense, as if arguing a legal case, as he forced me to think, to come to a difficult conclusion. 'The one path out of this labyrinth is for us to step aside from the demands of your family and pledge ourselves to each other with a vow. A vow that will be binding on us, and on all who might try to destroy it. But it will need courage and fortitude. Your family will be reluctant to support us, and I fear that you will suffer more than I. But I think that we cannot go on like this. It is unkind to you, and a terrible weight on my soul. I would that our love was out in the open for all to witness.'

And I knew it. He was a man of pride and dignity. To skulk in corners was not in his nature.

'If this is too heavy a decision for you, Margery, then you must say that you cannot make it. I will not force you against your will. If you tell me to leave, I will go. But if you will give yourself to me then I will take you as my wife. I will swear my love and commitment to you for all time.'

It would turn my world upside down. I could not believe it.

'Why would you do that now?' I asked.

'Because to lose you is more than I can contemplate. I love you.'

He had actually said the words that I had so longed to hear.

'I will love and protect you until the day of your death or mine. I will uphold your good name before any man. I will give you security and, I trust, happiness. We will make a life together.'

There were so many questions to ask.

'Can I make you happy?'

'Yes.'

Here was my dream unfolding before my eyes.

27

'Can we wed without my family's permission?' For here was the crux of our dilemma.

'Yes. We can make a marriage *per verba de praesenti*.'

I knew of such a binding, a private exchange of vows, legal enough but one that was so unsavoury in the eyes of the Church. Had not my eldest brother Sir John engaged in just such a marriage with Mistress Anne Haute? It was a scandalous matter not much spoken of in our household, but it lingered there like a dark storm cloud. Sir John and Mistress Haute were legally wed but it had gone no further than that, my brother regarding it more as a betrothal than a marriage to celebrate with feasting and good wishes. What Mistress Haute thought I did not know, but my brother Jonty whispered that so far the legal commitment had not been physically consummated between the fine sheets on Sir John's bed, so nothing was certain. Yet if it were true, if such a union without priest or family in evidence was good enough for Sir John, then why should I not tread the same path and wed Richard without priest or family to give permission or blessing?

There was one worry in my mind. What a man might do might be considered anathema for a woman. And Sir John had wed a lady of unquestionable birth, cousin of the Queen of England. Richard's lack of social standing was the source of the whole problem between us.

'Is it legal?' I asked with a frown, still unsure.

His smile was troubled but his laughter soft. 'Thus the sister and daughter of lawyers. Of course it is legal. If we make a vow and pledge ourselves, it cannot be broken. It will stand before a priest and the whole panoply of the Church. It will, in truth, be a legal marriage.'

Did I dare? Would I challenge the Pastons and the weight of Church tradition? Was I intrepid enough, valiant enough, to take a step so outrageous? Surveying my interlinked fingers, I considered the strength of my courage. Was my love for this man enough to make me as brave as a woman leading troops into a battle? Surely with Richard beside me I could take a step along this path with all its scandal and dangers. I looked up to find him watching me, solemn and silent, so that I might make my own choice.

'Then let us do it,' I said.

Still Richard Calle offered me a chance to escape. 'It is on my conscience that I should not encourage you, if doubts assail you.'

'I need no encouragement. I am not assailed by doubts.'

'Are you sure, my dear Margery? It is a desperate choice to make.'

'I am sure, dear Richard.'

So it was done. Such scandal between a Paston daughter and a mere bailiff, such as no Paston would ever accept.

We stood before the one small window where much of the sun was obliterated by the overhang of the adjacent buildings. Sir John would have made his declaration to Mistress Haute in a far finer chamber at the royal Court, I was sure of it. But this was Richard and I. This was to be our future. The shadows did not bother me at all. Hand in hand we made our vow.

'On this day I take you as my wife, Margery Paston. May God bear witness to what I say in His presence.'

'On this day I take you as my husband, Richard Calle. May God bear witness to what I reply in His presence.'

He smiled down at me. I smiled at him. I felt no different, and yet I knew that nothing would be the same again. I should have been nervous, anxious, listening for footsteps in the house, but I was not. I had a husband who would protect me and love me.

'We cannot be parted by the law,' Richard said.

'But they will try,' I sighed.

'Yes, they will try,' Richard agreed, 'but we will fight to hold on to what we have pledged this day.'

It was important, Richard said, that we make good our vows through a union of our bodies, and so I turned back the coverlet on my bed in wifely fashion. Richard deftly unfastened my clothing piece by piece until all that remained to me was my shift. Then it was a matter of stripping off his own clothes.

I was virginal, shivering with trepidation; he was gently thorough. I had much to learn and much pleasure in the learning of it. On that afternoon with the dust motes golden around us, we became man and wife. For me initial discomfort was transmuted into a moment of deep pleasure. I smoothed my fingers over his shoulders and down his arms as he lay drowsing. He was mine and I his. How sleek his muscles, how fair his hair where it curled against his neck. How marvellous his ability to awaken every inch of my skin into glowing delight.

'How does a bailiff come to have as many scars and wounds as this?' I enquired, running my nails delicately along a scar on his hip, my confidence a matter of astonishment for me.

'Easy enough' – he smiled into the pillow – 'when working for the Pastons. You have some pugnacious tenants who resent calls from their bailiff. It has been necessary for me to learn to use a sword and my fists.'

'Then I must be grateful that you have fought off the enemy so successfully.'

'Unfortunately, I cannot use a sword against your mother.'

For an hour, no more, no less, we existed in a world that was not real, a time alone within the curtains of my bed where all was privacy, and I could know the joy of physical love. Nor did Richard appear in any manner disappointed by my naïvety. Here was a haven where we pretended that all would be well.

'Where will we live?' I asked.

A moment of practicality when desire settled and reality took hold.

'I know not,' Richard admitted, expression suddenly bleak. 'I could rightly be accused of acting without responsibility. I expect that I should be whipped through the streets. But I swear I will rent us a house.'

'We could go and live at Oxnead,' I suggested.

'Your grandmother would stand at the gate and bar the way to us with a halberd.'

'I am afraid she would.' Oxnead belonged to Mistress Agnes, given to her as her jointure on her marriage to Justice William Paston. 'You could, of course, persuade her to relent. She might take us in as homeless travellers.'

Of course, it was ridiculous fantasy, as we both knew.

'It would take the Clap of Doom to persuade your grandmother to take any step against her ranking in Norfolk society. You need a home of your own. And you should have a dowry from your family.'

'Will they give me one?'

'I doubt it. And you should have a jointure.'

'Do you have the money for such?'

'No.'

Yet nothing could quench our happiness in each other. It fit as close and warm as a new glove made from the finest Norwich leather.

'What now?' I asked as he rose and began to don his discarded garments.

'Your mother must be told.'

Richard handed me my chemise, helping me to pull it over my head as he sat on the edge of the bed. 'We do what we should have done in the first place. What *I* should have done. I love you beyond reason, Margery, but we have made a hard bed for us to lie in. We must tell your mother, your brothers.'

'Not yet.'

'We cannot keep it secret. We must tell them.'

Oh, I was a coward indeed, immature in my happiness. 'Let us enjoy it before the storm breaks.'

'But soon it will surely break. If we live in deceit, it will be all the worse. If we confess now, there is a chance that we will eventually be forgiven.'

'Do you believe that?'

'No.'

It was the truth, and gnawed away at any fleeting contentment.

'What will be the worst that can happen?' I asked, pulling my long sleeves into seemly array.

'You will be sent off to London at the end of the week as your mother has planned. Our marriage will be denied or simply ignored, and I will be cast adrift to find work elsewhere. We knew that this might be a consequence of our vow exchange.'

'And I am not a brave woman.'

He helped me rebraid my hair and pin it beneath a plain coif.

'You were brave enough to give yourself to me as my wife. You are brave enough to face this. They will disapprove. They will be angry. I expect they will vent their anger on me. But they cannot undo what we have done.'

I nodded. 'Then I will tell them.'

For a moment he held me close, then lifted my chin so that I must look at him.

'If you think I will allow that, you have a low opinion of your new husband. I will speak with your mother tomorrow.'

'Why should I not stand at your side? It was as much my decision as yours.'

'Mistress Paston will not see it in that light. In truth, neither do I. She will say that I should have repulsed what was a youthful infatuation. She will condemn me for my lack of integrity. What I will not allow is for Mistress Margaret to put all the blame on your shoulders. I will tell her and then we will see where our future might lie.'

Richard would beard the lion in his den. It had to be done. Whatever worries gnawed at my mind like a starving rat, there were two truths. I was wed to Richard. My mother must be told and she would disapprove most vocally. Was I not as much to blame as Richard? My mother had enough worries, managing to scrape together a mere six or seven marks to keep the household afloat for a few weeks as rents grew more and more difficult to squeeze from our tenants. She was even contemplating selling the malt that she had been holding back until the price rose. She was growing pale with the strain. How would she react to knowing that Richard and I had taken a step so abhorrent to her? Richard was in her employ, having no financial resources of his own to bring to this marriage. It was not only his lack of status that would cause my family to shudder with horror.

Fleetingly I gave a thought to my younger sister Anne who was boarded with the Calthorp family, whom I had not seen for some little time. Her boarding with our cousins was for a financial consideration; Sir George Calthorpe was pleased to allow Anne to live with them and be useful in the household as well as providing her with an education in a gentry family. It was my mother's wish that she remain with the Calthorps until a husband could be found for her. If I thwarted my mother over the matter of marriage, would Anne be the one to suffer, pushed into any alliance of value to the Pastons? Yet I rejected the qualm of guilt. The Calthorps, a most superior family, would surely cushion Anne from my mother's scheming, discovering the perfect match for her while she was under their roof, and she would be happy.

Without doubt, love had rendered me thoughtlessly selfish.

CHAPTER FOUR

MARGERY PASTON

The Paston House in Norwich, April 1469

Richard told my mother of what we had done, seeking her out in the parlour set aside for business in our Norwich house. He would be protective of me, and forthright in his demand that our marriage be recognised. I waited in my own chamber, unable to sit, pacing the floor as my future with Richard was decided below.

I left my door ajar.

All was quiet except for the soft murmur of a long conversation. Perhaps Richard and my mother, against all our fears, had discovered some level on which they could agree. We might face disapproval but the Pastons were not a family for airing their grievances aloud. All would be kept well hid under silence, as if tucked under a costly Norwich blanket. We would be wed with a priest making it fully legal. Richard, his arrears paid for Paston work, would rent a house in Norwich. We would live there. He would continue to be Paston bailiff and we would raise our children.

Was this fantasy?

What a bittersweet memory of requited love to be absorbed in this chamber, if I had the mind to do so. But now the air was heavy with anxiety and mischief.

Time moved on. Yes, enough time for my mother to have come to terms with our decision. She had another daughter, my sister Anne, whom she would wed to a man of consequence. Walking to the window I noticed inconsequentially that one of the servants had dusted away the web and the spider that had been witness to our vow-taking. Such a transitory thing. Would our love be the same?

Then I heard my mother's quick step, her voice as she opened the parlour door into the hall. It was sharp, disbelieving. I stepped out of my own room to hang over the balustrade to watch from above. There below me in a strange foreshortening was my mother with her linen coif, habitually worn indoors, her straight shoulders, her sharp nose, and Richard in his business-like houppelande, his hair neat around his ears, cap and gloves in hand, a leather satchel beneath his arm, as if they had been discussing the lack of rents from Boynton and Haynsford.

My mother's voice rose in outrage. 'I do not believe you. I do not believe that my daughter would play a part in this travesty of what is acceptable. She would not.' Marching through the hall, she wrenched open the door that led out onto the street. 'I wish you to leave.'

Richard still stood below me. I could not see his expression, but his voice in reply was measured.

'Mistress Paston. If you would reconsider.'

'Reconsider? What is there to reconsider? I will not.'

'We are speaking of your daughter's happiness,' Richard said.

There she stood, on the threshold, as if she cared not who heard. The last time I had heard her voice raised to such a degree was when she discovered that Sir John had disobeyed his father, leaving home to run away to Court, leaving most of his belongings and a lame horse for our mother to pay for.

'We made the vows that created a matrimonial bond, Mistress Paston. It cannot be denied, by you or by the Church.'

From my vantage point I could see, even at a distance, the anger that enveloped my mother, painting bright colour on her cheeks.

'Why did you not come to me first?' she demanded.

How courteous he remained beneath the attack. 'I knew that you would disapprove.'

'So why do it?'

'I love your daughter. You had arranged to send her away.'

'Love! When did love figure in a marriage of our sort of people?

It is a matter of family negotiation over money and land. You have neither of those. For a woman, it is a matter of dowries and jointures. Can you provide my daughter with a jointure that will be pleasing to me? Of course you cannot. You inveigled my daughter into a relationship that she should never have even contemplated. Was she raised to think so little of this family? It is my opinion that you misjudged her words, Master Calle, thinking her infatuation was a stronger emotion. And now her reputation is all undone, and we have a scandal on our hands.'

There it was, all neatly arranged as if it were a list of those unpaid rent arrears.

'There was no misjudgement, mistress.'

'I will ask my daughter myself.'

I saw Richard hesitate, just for an infinitesimal moment, before he raised his head to meet his employer eye to eye in a challenge to her authority over me. 'It will make no difference.'

'She will tell me the truth.'

Again there was the slightest pause, in which Richard made his decision.

'We did not only make vows. We consummated our love, Mistress Paston. Legally, Margery is now my wife.'

I watched as my mother all but flinched at this terrible pronouncement.

'Where? Where did this happen? And when?'

'Here, Mistress Paston. Yesterday. In the late afternoon when all were away from home.'

My mother's fury rose to immeasurable proportions. 'God damn you for this, Richard Calle! You would dishonour my daughter, you would dishonour me, under my own roof!'

A dread silence hung in the space below me. When she spoke again, my mother's voice was soft and low with venom.

'Skulking in shadows! What terrible shame you have heaped on me.'

'There will be no shame, Mistress Paston, if you accept that the marriage is true. There will be talk, but it will not be a lasting source of irritation if you accept that your daughter is now Mistress Calle.'

Did he never lose his temper? Admiration took my attention for the briefest of moments, until my mother stepped back from the open doorway.

'I will never accept it! Get out, Master Calle. I do not want to see you cross this threshold into my house again.'

Which made me run down the stairs to stand with him. I placed my hand on his arm and faced the wrath. Did I still not fully realise what I was taking on? I had not seen the half of it. Foolish as I was, possibly naïve, beguiled by the captivating emotion of love, I had not truly foreseen the depth of my mother's antipathy.

'Indeed you must not, Mother. Richard is my husband.'

The venom was now directed at me.

'Is it true that you made vows together?'

Concentrating on the legality or otherwise, she was more concerned with what we had said rather than what we had done.

'Yes.' I might as well confess all. 'And we have had physical union.'

'It is what you have said that is the true danger. I will not have a man so duplicitous beneath my roof.'

'My brothers will support me. They value Richard's work for them.' I was not convinced, but it was worth an argument.

'They will do no such thing.'

'Richard has worked hard for the Pastons. How valuable has he been to you? Will you now deny him as being not good enough to wed a Paston daughter?'

'I'll not deny it. But he is not the man for your husband. It will not be tolerated. How hard did we struggle to raise ourselves from the peasant mud of Clement Paston and his bondswoman wife? You and your marriage to a shopkeeper's son would drag us back there.'

I raised my chin, despair encroaching like a spring tide, chilling my flesh.

'You cannot keep us apart. I will go with him, with or without your permission.'

But Richard silenced me with a hand to cover mine. 'This is not the way, Margery.'

'There is no way,' my mother said.

'We will find one, for in God's sight we have done no wrong,' Richard replied. 'We will pray to God for justice.'

'Justice.' My mother's stare was as keen as a leather-worker's bodkin. 'I suppose that there were no witnesses to your taking of vows.'

'None.'

I saw a smile of satisfaction warm my mother's face.

'As a man with considerable legal knowledge, you realise the weakness in your position.'

'I do, but I must trust in the Paston desire for fairness and honesty. And compassion.'

By now we both knew that it was an unlikely outcome, but we would continue with the charade. Richard bowed to my mother, kissed my hands.

'I will deal with this, my wife. I will come for you. Do not be downhearted; be brave, as I know you can be. The law will stand for us and I will claim you.'

'Why should I not leave with you now?' I asked. 'If I am your wife, why should I not walk out into Norwich at your side?' Instantly, I regretted the appalling innocence of my question.

His reply made all clear. 'Where would we live? We must obtain formal legal recognition of our marriage since Mistress Paston rejects it.' He smiled and bowed over my hand, as graciously as Sir John, or even Jonty, would show respect to the woman who had engaged his affections. But beneath his composure I felt the hard tension through his fingers. Was he wishing he had never done it? I could not add to it. I managed a smile.

'Go with my blessing, Richard. I will wait for you.'

With this promise held close in my heart, I allowed him to go, standing forlorn at the open door, unsure of when I would see him again. How could he fight against the wrath of my mother? She took my arm in a strong grip and pulled me back, shutting the door against any further sight of him. I felt as if my last hope was vanishing into the streets of Norwich. I felt like a prisoner in what had been my own home.

★

38

I was left alone to face the wrath of my mother.

The extent of it shocked me. Was I not her daughter? Did she not have any vestige of love left for me?

'How could you? How could you conduct yourself with such despicable secrecy for all the citizens of Norwich to gloat over? For discover it they will. Servants talk. It will spread through the market like wildfire, to entertain all with nothing better to do than enjoy my discomfiture and the discrediting of our family. I can already hear the neighbours delighting in our shame. I can see them sneering behind their hands, even though they will say nothing to my face. Did you not think ...'

The accusations rolled off her tongue, her features tight with fury, her lips thin and twisted in sour condemnation. I had no reply that she could find acceptable. We had said all that needed to be said and I would not express regret at what we had done.

'You know the precipice on which our family stands. Your father's grandfather was a serf, a bondsman, tied to the land. He had no property of his own, nor could he inherit. His wife was equally low-born. It was your grandfather's education that took him into the law as Justice William. He laid the foundation of our family as it is today. He wed an heiress, your grandmother, as did your father when he married me. Both Agnes and I brought property and distinction into the family. The Mautbys were one of the foremost families in Norfolk. I am connected with families of high repute. And you have wed an upstart from Framlingham!'

'Do we not have status enough?' I asked. 'My brother is a knight. We own a castle. Uncle William wed Lady Anne Beaufort. How would my marriage undermine such a progression?'

'I'll not argue against it. But when our enemies turn on us – as they do with remarkable frequency – what is it that they use in the courts? That we are bondsmen and our inheritance of property is illegal. For that reason Paston daughters must marry well. I despair.' Her teeth all-but snapped together before the diatribe continued. 'And if you were going to tell me about Wulfstan de Paston who came over with the Conqueror, do not bother. Your father and

I made that up when he was in the Fleet. The King might have accepted it, but it is as much a mockery as your marriage.'

She ran out of words, and I could find none.

I was sent to my chamber. I was to spend much time there.

Letters were sent out immediately to summon my brothers home.

In all of the two weeks until my brothers arrived in Norwich, I heard nothing from Richard. If he wrote to me, the letter was intercepted. If he came to the door, he was repulsed. I did not even know that he was still in the town. I wondered who was carrying out the estate work for my mother. I could not imagine her being willing to employ Richard at the same time as she barred the door to him. All I could do was wait, my hopes dying a little each day. I had never felt less married, less secure in my future.

I grew to know the interior of my chamber as well as my own features in my looking-glass.

Then here was come Sir John and Jonty, indicative of the horror engendered by my action, that they should both manage to be under the same roof at one and the same time. Since I was not actually locked in my chamber, I planned on an ambush of Sir John, head of the family. If he would support me, his opinion might just hold weight. I sat on the stair while he sent his horse to the stable and waited for him to enter, hoping that my mother would remain occupied elsewhere.

'Sir John!'

He looked up. His expression was not accommodating, but neither was it unfriendly. Here was the Court gallant, his short jerkin moulded to his figure, woven in the finest blue cloth. His low-crowned hat was embellished with an ostrich plume that moved seductively as he strode in. It was anchored by a gem that glittered in the light. But I had no time to waste on his all-pervading interest in what might attract a woman's eye.

'Come up,' I hissed.

He came willingly enough, leaping up the stair with his usual swagger to sit beside me, hat and gloves in hand. The fur-trimmed length of his sleeves swept the stair as he leaned forward, elbows on thighs. He did not even notice that the fur had collected dust and a grey cobweb, which should have warned me. If my brother was disregarding of the pristine state of his garments, his mood must be awry.

'What have you done, little sister?'

'I have wed the man I love. And my mother will not accept it.'

'Richard Calle.' He scowled at me. 'I don't have to tell you that it was a bad misstep.'

'Tell me instead that you do not know what it is to love someone and wish for marriage.'

It was at the heart of much family gossip, how Sir John had met Mistress Anne Haute. He sought her hand in marriage, and she and her family were in agreement as far as I knew. She was no heiress in her own right, but her connections were impeccable. Not that my mother was particularly favourable towards it. Her advice was always for my brother to secure his inheritance before taking on a bride. She suspected him of lack of commitment.

'My situation is quite different,' Sir John said, unusually stern. 'And to do so in such a manner. A vow taken without a priest.'

'Which you would never do, of course.'

Sir John and Mistress Haute had exchanged just such a vow while dancing at Court, so Jonty said. If this vow was binding, then so was mine. I was surprised to see flags of colour along his handsome cheekbones.

'Our situation is quite different,' he repeated as if that was an end to the matter.

'I do not see that it is.'

'Mistress Haute's court connections are beyond question.'

I felt inclined to seize the ostrich feather from his cap and snap it in half.

'And Richard Calle's are not.' How calm I remained. 'I understand. But a vow is a vow, is it not? When do we meet your new bride, brought home to your family? Was there a priest to officiate when you and she took your vow to be man and wife? I think not, if what Jonty says is true. If you and Mistress Haute are legally wed, then so are Richard and I.'

The flush deepened. 'You have caused a scandal, sister.'

41

'But if you will speak for me, it will become less so. My mother will listen to you.'

'We'll see.'

He rose and clattered back down the stair, taking the hat and the offending feather with him. I was not hopeful. Sir John's apparent good humour was often an illusion to mask his own problems. Had I surprised some secret here, between my brother and Mistress Anne Haute? Certainly, he had hopped swiftly around my question. I wondered if the unknown Mistress Haute was suffering the same opposition to her marriage per *verba de praesenti* as was I. But then if her cousin was the Queen of England, the royal hand could probably unlock many difficult doors for her. There was no one to unlock mine. Sir John's departure left me wishing I could meet his almost-legal wife who might cause a scandal as great as my own.

CHAPTER FIVE

MISTRESS ANNE HAUTE

The Royal Court in the Palace of Westminster, May Day 1469

Admiring the slide of my new silk gown against my skin, I watched Sir John Paston weave his self-indulgent path through the chattering groups of Court gallants and their ladies at this May Day celebration in the Great Hall. He paused to speak with any Woodville adherent he could find, the Woodvilles holding the reins of preferment and gold coin, particularly singling out my cousin Sir Anthony Woodville, Lord Scales. They were tournament associates of long standing. There they stood, laughing together, probably sharing memories of fierce battles and exchanges of blows.

Eventually, Sir John Paston would find his way to me. I hoped that he would appreciate my crimson brocade, neck and hem trimmed with dense sable, as much as I did. Had I not chosen to wear it to remind him that I was a woman of inestimable value? As I had donned the intricate wires and gauze veil of a butterfly headdress over my fair hair.

I was not a Paston. I had hoped by now to be Dame Anne Paston in the eyes of the world, wife of Sir John Paston. My lineage was important for any man seeking an advantageous marriage. Not that I had ever imagined it to be thus as a child from the Kentish Haute family of minor landowners. No great magnates or aristocrats here. Our change in fortune came overnight when my first cousin, Elizabeth Woodville, had married King Edward IV. She had now been the crowned Queen of England for four years.

Thanks to my mother's family, I could begin every conversation with the momentous words: 'My cousin the Queen...'

Yet I was still without a husband. That is unless I managed to win this battle of wills with Sir John Paston, although why it had become a battle I could not fathom, I was beginning to fear that I would always lack one. I was five and twenty years old and to my mind it was more than time that I had a marriage formally recognised. So did my family fear it, all of my four sisters and four brothers were tied into promising matrimonial ventures. I was the exception to the Haute rule of daughters making advantageous matches.

Sir John had seemed to me to be the perfect remedy to my situation.

I had met him at Court some years ago, when he showed no interest in me, a tournament filling his thoughts, and then again in Calais, where we had furthered our acquaintance to more effect. And what a strange acquaintance it was, difficult to decipher. A relief from boredom. A flirtation. An eye to future ambitions. Sir John saw me as the key to opening an essential door at Court, into the presence of the King and Queen. He needed a patron, a sponsor to help him ward off his enemies who had an eye to possessing Caister Castle that his family had inherited from Sir John Fastolf. And I? I needed a husband, and was of the opinion that Sir John had the ambition and a panoply of skills to make a name for himself. As well as that inestimable charm.

Was this a love match? He sent me poems that he did not write himself, he gave me gifts that he did not buy. I knew in my heart that his courtship was based solidly on self-interest. He gave me a little battlemented castle in gold picked out with jewels to pin on my bodice, an inheritance from the Fastolf jewels. His inheritance of Caister Castle filled his mind to the detriment of all else. And yet I did not question that he had an affection for me, even a species of love. Why would he go to the trouble of seeking me out if he did not? Why would he exchange a binding vow with me? I did not believe that it was all a matter of self-interest to achieve a path to Queen Elizabeth's favour; Sir Anthony Woodville could pave that particular path for him. Sir John's kisses, exchanged when we could find a bare corner of privacy in this busy Court, spoke of a passion that could illuminate my own.

Ah, but did I love him? I was loathe to admit it, but the room brightened as with the lighting of a hundred fine wax candles when he entered it. I was also aware that candles, even of the best wax, could be quenched by a blast of cold air. Sometimes I thought myself incapable of love. Sir John's neglect could be just such an icy blast. Unfortunately, a woman of my situation could not be so fastidious that she would not wed unless her emotions were fully engaged. Sir John Paston, a man who could so easily win friends at Court, would be as useful to me as I to him; dependence on my family was not a situation that appealed to my pride. I sought marriage with him. Was I not aware that the slide of his fingers over my wrist filled me with desire?

The question was: would I achieve a marriage with this man? Would he ever claim me and introduce me as his wife? We had exchanged vows, a marriage of sorts but legal for all that, *per verba de praesenti*, without a priest. Or was it merely a betrothal? Would we ever make it a regular union, to be announced to the Court? I knew his fair words. The man to whom I believed I was wed, albeit not in the full light of day, was known for his love of women-kind. Handsome and flirtatious, he was a great favourite at Court.

And now all hung in sumptuous abeyance, much like the fur-enhanced hanging sleeves that he so favoured to draw attention to himself. It was not beyond all probability that he had simply changed his mind. Some men changed their minds as often as they swapped their doublets. Sir John was a notorious lover of what he wore to catch the eye.

'Sir John,' I curtsied before him, my lashes demurely down-swept, 'I am delighted to meet with you at last.'

It had taken him a good quarter of the hour to work his way across the room to my side. He offered me a flourish of a bow, hand on heart.

'Mistress Anne. You cannot appreciate how strongly my heart beats on seeing you here. When we are apart, I cannot forget the quality of your beauty. It disturbs my sleep.'

I smiled winningly. It was a pleasing compliment. I might not be as celestially fair or as singularly elegant as my cousin Queen Elizabeth with all her golden beauty. My brows might not arch with the same perfection of careful artifice, but I knew that I could claim to be a woman worthy of notice, for there was a strong resemblance through our mothers, who were sisters. Sir John, tall and dark, broad of shoulder and slim of hips, with the physique of a fighter in the tournament, disturbed my sleep too but I would not tell him that. He had quite enough conviction of his own worth without my adding a new layer of praise.

'If your heart responds so violently,' I replied demurely, 'why have you been absent from Court, and from me, for so many weeks?'

A line etched itself between his brows. 'Forgive me. I have much to preoccupy me. My manors are under attack. My manors are always under attack!'

'Then you must tell me.'

The line grew deeper. It hurt that he would tell me so little of a matter that made him frown, but I could not force him. Instead, I devised rapidly how to bring him back to good humour.

'Then tell me of your desire to be in my company. I yearn to hear of your love for me. I have felt the lack of it.'

The deep furrow instantly smoothed itself out, as I had known it would, leaving Sir John charmingly receptive to my request.

'And so you shall. I desire it above all things. You know that all my emotions are yours to command. But first, come and make me known once more to your cousin the Queen. It is some months since I bowed before royalty. She may have forgotten me.'

'No.'

He tilted his chin. 'No what?'

'First you woo me. Then, if I am satisfied, I will take you to the Queen.'

'How can I resist offering a paean to your beauty?' Sir John's smile stirred my blood as might the fall of a shooting star in a summer night. So did the touch of his lips on my palm as he captured my hand. And then came his sweet wooing, captured in verse.

'Sweet mistress, come today,
Dear as my heart to me,
Come to my rooms; this Day of May,
They're as fine as fine could be.'

I parted my lips to reply to such an invitation with un-maidenly enthusiasm, to accept, but Sir John placed his fingers gently there, stopping me. 'Hush. I have yet to tell you the best of it.'

'I have cushioned every chair,
I have draped the rooms and blent
The flowers scattered there
With fresh-cut herbs for scent.'

I was taken aback by such an unexpected offering. 'How can I refuse?'

'But listen. There is more:

Beloved, leave delay,
Eagerly let us embrace,
I would die with you away,
Here is love's time and place.'

A little silence fell between us. Then, 'Do you take me to your rooms now, or is this an invitation for the future? You know that I will accept.'

'Tomorrow and tomorrow and tomorrow, my dearest Anne. Never doubt that I love you.' He folded my hands, palm to palm, between his. What devilment there was in him. 'Have I done enough to earn your gracious reintroduction to the Queen?'

And I was willing to be seduced.

'I believe that you have, for now. Have you ever recited that verse for another lady?'

'Never. You wrong me, mistress! The sentiments are all for you.'

I pinched his wrist as I laid my hand there and appreciated the gleam in his eye. Did he love me? In his own way I thought that he did, but I was under no illusion that he loved my royal

47

connections more, and would squeeze from them as much benefit as he could. I must make the most of his presence before he found yet another excuse to take his leave of me or direct his flattery of me into other channels. As he quickly proved before we had even approached the Queen. He wasted no words over it.

'Would you, my dearest Mistress Haute, consider asking your cousin the Queen if she will plead the rightness of my claim to Caister Castle with her lord the King?'

Of course. I should have known that was in his mind.

'I will consider it, Sir John,' I replied equably.

'And you will tell her that the Duke of Norfolk is about to snatch it from under my nose.'

'I will tell her. I expect that she knows already.' What other could I say? I would do what I could. I wondered who had written the poem with which Sir John had wooed me. I would have wagered my finest gilded shoes that it was not Sir John Paston. Nevertheless, he was the only man to quote poetry to me and I would not deny him the right to do so.

I carried out my promise, Sir John having departed on some legal matter that demanded his instant attention, and the Queen summoning me to accompany her from the gathering. I asked the question before we stepped down from the dais on which she had been seated. She laughed softly, her finely plucked eyebrows lifting, and pointed across the crowd to where a group of well-dressed men were in close discussion, heads close together, as if in some secret scheming.

'Who do you see over there?' she asked.

I assessed the group, all expensively garbed, some young in enthusiasm, some old in years and experience. The man I was looking at was younger than most, yet full of confidence, his dark hair allowed to curl beneath a flat-crowned felt hat, a sapphire jewel glittering on its brim.

'The Duke of Norfolk,' I said.

'How many friends does the Duke have around him?'

'Numerous.'

'Do you see my lord the King as one of their midst?'

'Yes.'

There was King Edward, fully engaged in the conversation, gesturing dramatically with both hands. I knew what she was going to say. Indeed, I need not have asked the question in the first place.

'Tell me, Cousin Anne. Is Sir John Paston one of their number?'

'No. He is not there.' They were all men of high title.

'Whose friendship does my lord Edward value most?' Cousin Elizabeth asked. 'The Duke of Norfolk or Sir John Paston?'

'I think the answer is clear enough.'

'Then so is my answer to your request.' Her grip on my arm was friendly but firm. 'Sir John must fend for himself in some matters. I will not speak for him against the friendship of the Duke of Norfolk.'

She smiled to soften her refusal, her extravagant butterfly head-dress fluttering in a sudden draught from the high window behind her. It was not unkindly said, merely a lesson in practical high politics. I would tell Sir John of my failure, if he did not guess it already. I could not be his route to royal preferment when the King needed the most powerful English families on his side. I was sorry for it. It would have pleased me to help him win his heart's desire.

CHAPTER SIX

MARGERY PASTON

The Paston House in Norwich, April 1469

We met, all standing around the table where, so many months ago now, Richard and I had placed those rent rolls in careful order before I thrust them onto the floor. We were not grand enough to have a muniment room, but this was as close as it got, with chests and coffers and piles of ledgers, and an all-pervading aroma of dust and old ink that teased the nostrils. Today the writing surfaces were swept clear of business. I was the matter under discussion. The stools had been pushed back against the walls. This was not to be a meeting where comfort would have its day.

The welcome to my brothers had been brief. There was no ale, no well-wishing. If I had ever held out any hope that one of them would come to my aid, that hope too died an instant death. Sir John cast me to the wolves.

'This is your doing.' Sir John glared at his brother, at whom his accusation was directed. 'Why did you not arrange a marriage for her? She is twenty-one and of an age to have a husband. Also of an age to be aware of any personable man who comes to the house. Why did you not keep an eye on her? I could not from London, but you could. She should never have had the freedom to know Calle so intimately, much less make vows with him.'

Jonty's reply was suitably acerbic. 'Calle has been in and out of our houses many times over the past decade. How should she not get to know him? I could point the same finger of blame at you.'

I stood silent between them. So, for once, did my mother.

'You could have arranged a marriage for her any time these past seven years.'

'And why have you not been busy about this affair?' Jonty was proving to be obstinately uncooperative. 'You are head of the family, after all.'

'I have spent every hour of every day since my father died in trying to raise money to bolster our law cases, intent on securing our Fastolf inheritance.' He rounded on me. 'In God's name, Margery, how could you drag our family into atrocious scandal? Have we not enough on our platter without this? The Duke of Norfolk is casting his avaricious eyes over Caister Castle, as we knew he would. It was only a matter of time before he showed his hand.' He slammed his own hand against the table with a dismissive gesture. 'You are enough of a Paston to know that Caister is liable to come under attack. Do we not have enough threats to our standing in this county, without your undertaking marriage with a man who has no higher recognition than a wood-louse?'

'Which is a false calumny!' I raised my chin. I would not be my aunt Elizabeth, browbeaten by those around her. 'I am twenty-one years old. I am free to wed where I wish. I thought that one of you might support me,' I added, turning to Jonty, since Sir John had already betrayed my confidence. Sadly, his frown was as dark as his brother's. On this occasion the two were much alike, Jonty's usual light-heartedness quite overlaid by disgust at the whole procedure, while Sir John had clearly stoked his anger since our meeting on the stairs. I was to be the target to deflect from his own lack of involvement in my future.

'Why would you think that? You know what is due to our family.' His anger exploded in vitriol. 'I will not have you selling candles and mustard in Framlingham.'

That was the crux of it.

'That is foolishness!' I remonstrated. 'Richard would never ask me to do that.'

'Who knows to what you might be reduced if we allowed this marriage to continue. Calle will have to find some means of making an income now that we have cast him off! Who will employ him now in Norwich?'

The questions were fired at me from left and right.

'How could you have acted in such secrecy?'

'Did he take advantage of you?'

'Were you so lacking in morality that you agreed to share his bed?'

'If you claim that you were ignorant and deceived – duped even – we might get somewhere towards denying it.'

'Duped?' I picked up on that particular point. 'I was not. How would Richard treat me with so little respect? I knew what I was doing. It is what I want. I knew that you would never consider our marriage, so we had to take it into our own hands. I love him and I swear that he loves me.' I looked at my two brothers. 'You have employed him and trusted him for so many years. You cannot now hack his character to pieces. He is a man who deserves respect, and I will not deny my love for him.'

'Love is not the prime consideration,' Jonty growled. A repetition of what my mother had said. 'He can bring nothing of value to this marriage.'

'He brings honesty and diligence and trustworthiness. You can find no fault with him. You have trusted him implicitly for years to handle all your affairs, Jonty. You have trusted him with your money and your land. He went to prison for you. Why can you not trust him with your sister's happiness?'

All to no avail, as I knew it must be. Despair silenced my words. Since my family could never be won round, we would be separated unless Richard could devise a plan. I had none, but if I was sent to the Duchess of Oxford, it might be possible for Richard to visit me in London. It was not a prospect that gave me any hope. We had taken the vows, blinded by love, without considering the future. Now here it was for me to face. And Richard had been cast out without a position or income or reputation.

'It is a misalliance. That is the end to it. It must go no further.' At last my mother joined in the condemnation of me.

'What do you intend to do?' Sir John asked, happy to put the burden on other capable shoulders.

Her answering regard was unbending. 'You are head of the

family. If you had taken action earlier, we would not have been in this situation. You will make the decisions now.'

Thus, with no place to hide, Sir John bent his frown on me, and his judgement was painfully cruel.

'You will remain here under our surveillance until this sham of a marriage can be brought to an end. Calle will not cross the threshold. You will not see him or receive letters from him. You will not meet with him, here or in the street or at Mass. He is no longer in our employ. I forbid you to write or contact him in any way. Do you understand?'

I knew enough of the law to make a claim. 'I understand what you wish to happen. I deny your power to separate a man and a woman joined together in the eyes of God.'

My refusal to accept the family dictates shocked all, thus ending any civilised conversation, brought to a final conclusion by my mother.

'The knot that has been tied so secretly with deceitful fingers can be sliced through with one bold stroke. The Pastons will wield the knife. And you, Sir John, will sharpen it.'

My situation proved not to resemble that of my Aunt Eliza. I was not beaten by my mother, nor was I locked in my chamber, but I was not free within our house or beyond our door. A close watch was kept on me by our servants, under direction from my mother. As for Father Gloys, his hostility could not be denied, nor could his undoubted influence in the household. My mother had known him since he was a young priest, before my birth, when she had rescued him from attack in the streets of Norwich, taking him to task for his arrogance. Now he seemed to have an overweening influence over her and took it upon himself to have priestly words with me. Although now spare of flesh and bent in old age, his face as lined as a sour prune, I did not think that his arrogance had waned one jot over the years. My mother was still prone to accept his advice, through habit more than any affection for him.

'Will you confess your sins, Mistress Margery?' he asked me, unctuously persuasive in his black garb.

'I confessed them at Mass which, as you are aware, I attended with my mother.' How I disliked him and his precious piety.

'And yet you have many sins.'

I bridled.

'It is a sin if you stand against the word of God, day after day,' he pronounced.

'Which word is that?'

'To honour your mother. To be obedient.'

'I do honour her. As for obedience, should I not be obedient to my husband?'

'It is a sham.'

'You do not know. You were not there.'

With my brothers departed, my mother occupied with her own concerns, a tense atmosphere prevailed. There was no one with whom I could speak, no one who would give me counsel. No letters. No possibility of my writing any. All I knew, from a snippet of gossip amongst the servants, was that Richard was in London, without employment or wage, trying to find work in the crowded streets and Inns of Court, where and when he might. Who would give him employment? Some guild or company that needed a capable man to oversee their finances or collect their rents. Perhaps, in the end, Richard would be forced to return to Framlingham to ask aid from his own family.

Although I was determined to hide it, misery increased within me in this silent, angry household. Whatever his promises that he would come and claim me, I truly believed that I might never see Richard again.

I did not even possess a marriage ring to remind me of my status as a wife.

My own lady and mistress, and indeed my true heart before God...

A letter. A letter written by Richard.

Did I ever worry that he had not written at all? That he had changed his mind and decided that a Paston wife was not worth the destruction of his livelihood? Oh, I did, in the dark of the night when all thoughts were of the blackest. When my mother was sharper than usual with none of the care I recalled from my earlier years.

'Why do you think that you will see him again?' my mother asked. 'He is in London. He will find work there. Why would he return to Norwich where there is nothing for him? The best you can do is deny that there is anything between you. We can all forget the past and look towards a future that will gild the Paston name. No one knows that you took a binding oath but you and Calle. If neither of you speak of it, it will be as if it never happened.'

Perhaps she was right. If we were kept apart long enough, my marriage would crumble to dust. How many letters had he written to me that had been intercepted and destroyed, gone astray into my mother's hands, consigned to the fire after she had read what he had dared to write to me? I would never know.

My mother and brothers were the keepers at the gate.

'He has forgotten you. The best you can do is forget about him, and give thanks that you did not carry a child from that unfortunate affair.'

But here was a letter in Richard's writing, begrimed and well used as it passed from hand to hand, yet still a letter and still sealed. Now that I held it in my hand, guilt swept over me, that I should have doubted him. He had not forgotten me. He would never forget me.

It had been delivered by someone who knew my daily routine, that I had been tasked with menial jobs to keep me and my thoughts occupied. Every morning I was sent with a basket to collect the eggs from the few chickens we kept here in Norwich for our household needs. It had no effect; I could worry and think about Richard when I sought beneath the feathery bodies for the eggs. Someone who knew I would be here with the chickens had placed the letter in one of the hen boxes, risking dismissal. Someone had compassion for me, for us. I called down a blessing on that unknown who would risk everything as I dusted the grime and droppings and stray feathers from the cover.

I could not open it. Not here. Not until I was assured of not

55

being interrupted. It burned a hole in my sleeve for the whole of that day. Then, at last, it was evening, after supper, and I was alone. I opened it slowly, then savoured the careful formation of his words, the tidy handwriting, trying to call his image into the room. How long now since we last met? More than a month and memory proved to be a duplicitous commodity.

I started to read.

My own lady and mistress, and indeed my true heart before God, I commend myself to you with a very sad heart as a man who cannot be cheerful and will not be so, until things stand otherwise with us than they do now. I can only hope that you feel the same.

There was no comfort here. Despondency was expanding to fill my whole body, and yet any anxieties I had that he had abandoned me were dispelled like hoar frost in sunshine. How could I have been so mistrusting? His own sadness pervaded the room, his own misgivings that my affections had not stood the test of time. I was not the only one to be suffering.

I acknowledge the great love that has been, and I trust still is, between us. We who ought to be most together are most apart. I would rather be with you than possess all the wealth in the world.

Richard was alone and must feel the distance as cruelly as I. It made me shiver for my own weakness and my own suspicions, so that I must set aside his writing lest it become smudged and so illegible. When I recovered, I read on. He could not tolerate what I was having to suffer for what we had done together, yet he felt quite justified that we had acted honourably in the face of our love. Here was some comfort that the solemn bond of matrimony did indeed exist between us. My family might deny it but here was the truth.

I sat and thought, the page open on my lap. I must not be selfish. I must not centre on my own fears, but rather on Richard's sacrifice for his love of me, knowing what he was risking. His employment, his friends, his standing. His income, his good name for loyalty and reliability. It was all there in his letter. I had never known him speak so openly, but here it was written. All the despair and resignation, the defiance and the hope.

Endure it as cheerfully as you have done so far, my dear wife, and be as stalwart as you can. One day God will allow us to live as we should according to His law. You have had much sorrow on my account. I wish that all the sorrow you have had might have fallen on me. I fear that I have drawn you into an abyss of suffering which you do not deserve.

I all but wept again.

It is a painful life we lead.

Hurt rose within me that we should both be so wantonly used by my family, but I would swear that our love would remain true. But for how long? Could we remain apart for ever? No. And no. Something must be done.

And then I read a line that horrified me.

It is my belief that they do not believe that we are contracted to each other, even though we spoke plain words. My courier was told that you have repented and shown my previous letters to your mother, begging her forgiveness for entering into a relationship that you now regret. Would you do that? I do not believe it, but it may be so.

Silence from you allows unworthy thoughts to intrude.

I ask your pardon if I have misjudged the depth of your commitment to me.

All thought of succumbing to useless tears vanished, replaced by a cold anger. I recognised this. They meant to divide us. Here was a plot to sow dissension between us, Richard all but accusing me of abandoning him, handing his letters over to my mother. I had received no letters, nor would I ever hold them open for public scrutiny. This was a device to separate us, to layer blame upon blame so that neither would trust the other.

At the end, the letter had been written with great difficulty.

Forgive me if I have been intemperate, but a recent bout of fever has worn me down. Never doubt that I love you, but it would be unwise of me to write again. All I can do is beg of you not to show this letter to anyone, but burn it once it is read.

Yes, he had been intemperate, but I understood why, and that he could not write again, would not out of pride. I had a suspicion that he had made light of an illness that had indeed attacked his spirits.

I knelt beside my bed and offered up prayers for Richard's health and for his strength to weather this tribulation. I prayed to the Blessed Virgin for succour. I prayed that he would never believe me guilty of betrayal, as I must never condemn him for neglecting me. Even in my prayers I could see no path ahead for us, no smooth highway for us to be reunited.

The thought slid into my mind. What would my father have done, when faced with such opposition? Gone to the highest power, of course, to demand justice – even to the King himself. Richard and I must arrange this for ourselves, for there was no help for us in the family, but I did not know anyone of influence who would even listen to me, and I feared that Richard might not either. Who would listen to a mere bailiff and uphold his case before the law? We were destined to be answerable to the power of my family and it did not bode well. How could we have ever thought that it would? Aunt Elizabeth, who might have been sympathetic to my plight, lived her own life far away in Southwark.

There were footsteps outside my door. I froze, still on my knees as, with a light knock, the door opened and there was my mother. I thought that she looked weary as she walked slowly to stand beside me, placing her candle on the nearby coffer.

'Father Gloys said that he heard you still moving. That you were not yet abed. I came to see if you were quite well. He said that he thought that you might have received bad news.'

Her voice was kindly and concerned, but I could not respond, knowing what had been done with her collusion.

'How could I receive bad news when I am forbidden all contact with those outside this house? It is a pity that Father Gloys has not better things to do than listen at my door and report back to you.'

'He has your best interests at heart, my child.'

'I would deny it. For a man of God, he seems inordinately cold-hearted.'

She hesitated, seemingly unwilling to stir more ill-feeling between us, yet I knew that my mother had not given up. All my life I had been a good daughter, obedient to her demands. She thought that she had merely to discover my weakness in this episode and use it so that I would relent. She came to sit on the edge of my bed. Aware that the letter still lay exposed under my hands, I calmly pulled the linen covers across to hide it.

'There must be an easier way than this for us to get on together, Margery.'

She seemed so unperturbed, as if her ultimate victory was assured.

'So I think also, Mother. If you allow Richard and I to live together as man and wife, all the anger in this household will be wiped away.'

'That cannot be.'

'I do not need you to tell me of his parentage again.'

Picking at the edge of my bed-cover, unfortunately loosening the threads, she struggled to appear amenable.

'If you continue to refuse to admit that this marriage is false, then the only way out of it is through an annulment.'

'How can it be annulled? It is the truth.'

'All things are possible. Sir John will arrange it.'

I think that in spite of all my efforts, my lip curled and I laughed. 'Are annulments not very costly?' I did not know, but I could hazard a guess that all such legal problems cost a bag or two of gold coin. 'Sir John will be loath to spend money on an annulment. He is always claiming penury and his battles over the

Fastolf inheritance bleed him dry, so he says.' I saw the truth of it in her face and so added, remembering a line from Richard's letter, 'I remain wed to Richard, and it is on your conscience if you keep us apart from vows we took before God.'

My mother's control was diffusing, her voice becoming as harsh as her eye. My heart was beating hard and my hands trembled.

'Has Richard ever written to me?' I asked boldly. 'Have any of his letters been intercepted? Has Father Gloys destroyed them?'

She shook her head, but I did not believe her.

'You should be asleep. The day will start early tomorrow. All seems difficult now, but it will change with time.' I felt her kiss against my hair, a soft benediction, before she rose to her feet, retrieved her candle and walked to the door. 'If you will but deny this marriage, all can be put right.'

'I cannot deny it. I will not.' And then on a thought: 'Do you know the power of love, Mother? Do you not know that it cannot be repulsed when it lives within you day after day?' And then, risking a rebuff, I asked, 'Did you ever love my father?'

My mother seemed taken aback that I should even ask but she replied readily enough. 'Love seems to me to be a wholly uncomfortable experience. Yes, I loved your father when I came to know him. But I was not besotted. I knew his faults far too well.' There was a deep sadness in her. 'I miss him every day since his untimely death. Now go to sleep, Margery. Perhaps tomorrow you will make the sensible choice, as do all women who are destined to support their family in a prestigious union. Richard Calle is not for you.'

Alone, I settled against the bolster with a determination to bring us both out of this maelstrom if I could find a way. The letter I would hide. I could not burn it, whatever Richard's advice. I needed it for my own reassurance. One day I would show our children the evidence of their father's love for me. One day.

I should write a reply, although how to get it to Richard was beyond my understanding. I must remember that Father Gloys was my enemy. No, we could not go on like this. I constructed it in my head, for I could not sleep.

To my dearest Richard,

I am in need of rescue. I have received but one letter, and for that I am grateful although full of remorse for your situation and your health. Always believe that I am your true love and as loyal as you could wish. I can live no longer in this despair. Send to me if there is ought I can do to open the door of the prison we have made for ourselves.

I weep for us both, but I will remain strong and your lawful wife for ever.

Your loving Margery.

It was a letter that was never written, never sent, because who would take it? I fell asleep full of compassion for my Aunt Elizabeth, who had fought against such monstrous difficulties in finding a husband whom she could love and who would fulfil the demands of the Paston family, only to lose him in battle. Were all Paston women, even if they discovered love, fated to experience loss and heartbreak?

I woke with an ever more fervent resolve to find some means of reaching Richard. I refused to accept that we had been parted for ever.

CHAPTER SEVEN

ELIZABETH PASTON POYNINGS

The Poynings' House in Southwark, May 1469

'Marry again,' my man of business had advised me after Sir Robert Poynings's death, leaving me a widow in severe difficulty. 'Take a new husband who will protect you and the Poynings estates against the raptors that are hovering.'

'Particularly the Percy carrion, picking over our entrails,' I added.

John Dane, my man of affairs, grown old in the service of the Poynings family, bowed his head with its shock of white hair in respectful agreement. If he were any other man he might have sworn viciously. The Percys had attempted to imprison him for some nefarious and totally fabricated crime, to rid me of his support and good advice. John Dane preserved his impeccable sangfroid.

'We must discover one who will be of use to you, as well as providing good company, of course.'

Excellent advice. How to achieve it?

I was Elizabeth Paston Poynings, a widow with a young son. I had suffered a perennial and dangerous attack on my husband's Poynings estates from the powerful Percy family. I was a Paston by birth, my young life blighted by a mother who lacked compassion and a cold policy of refusing any man as my husband whose income was not appropriate to Paston plans. Mistress Agnes's hands were as flint-like as her heart. Nor were my brothers thoughtful in their attempts to find me a husband. They were too busy, they claimed, even though a husband with connections would have been advantageous to the Paston ambitions to hold on to their manors.

It was a matter of general rejoicing when, sent away from the Paston household to board with Lady de la Pole in London, I met and wed Sir Robert Poynings, a brave, honest man with strong Yorkist principles. As his wife, I established my own household and bore a much-loved son. Was it a love match? No, but a strong affection developed between us and I laid claim to happiness at last. I was Dame Elizabeth Poynings and could not believe my good fortune.

Why were our estates in Kent and Surrey under attack? Because Robert had a niece, Eleanor Poynings, who had wed Henry Percy, the Earl of Northumberland and was now his widow. The Poynings estates were rich pickings for them. And the basis of the whole difficulty was the Kentish anomaly of gavelkind, by which an estate can be passed on to a female. Robert's niece Eleanor was claiming all the Poynings estates in Kent through her being her father's sole direct heir, even though Robert had inherited the bulk of them as the next male in line. Now, with the might of the Percy family behind her, Eleanor was claiming the whole of the Poynings inheritance, whether in Kent or elsewhere.

Sir Robert had successfully fended off the legal threats. Now I was alone to take on that impossible task. My happiness had lasted so little time, indeed barely three years, before Sir Robert died on the battlefield at St Albans, fighting for the House of York, leaving me as sole trustee in the name of my little son Edward. It was my role to safeguard his inheritance, a role in which I had singularly failed, for I soon discovered that I could do little to prevent our Poynings manors being nibbled at by a particularly malicious Percy rat.

My body no longer bore the bruises of my youth, but my mind had not lost them. I was alone and helpless. My Paston family was not quick in coming to my aid, nor did I expect it, given their violent clashes with the Duke of Norfolk over Caister Castle, so I lived in constant fear of attack and in lonely despair.

Thus: 'Take a new husband,' John Dane had advised.

But there were difficulties. I was not an attractive proposition.

A widow, probably nearing the end of her childbearing years, owning nothing but as trustee to a young son. My home here at Southwark was a substantial town house with a solid door that could be bolted but it would never survive a direct assault from a determined enemy. Who would want me with a coffer-full of problem estates? It had been difficult enough my attracting one husband when I had at least some youth left to me, much less a second. Where would I meet such a man, given my somewhat isolated lifestyle, for I did not frequent the Court. It was not necessary that I should love him. If we could find respect and even affection, it would be enough, but the chances seemed slim. John Dane was the only man with whom I exchanged more than the common-place.

Where would I find advice? My brother John was dead, my connections with my older nephews tenuous at best, the younger ones lacking experience. To my regret I had allowed my friendship with Margaret Paston to lapse.

How had I allowed this to come about? When my mother's hard hands and even harder heart had been used against me, Margaret had been the only one of the Paston household to show me any compassion. She had taken me under her wing, consoled me, given me sharp advice in her inimitable fashion so that my confidence had not been completely trampled underfoot. I think that she had loved me as she would a true sister. And yet with the passage of time and our physical distance we no longer communicated to any real degree. Why would Margaret have any interest in my concerns when holding on to Paston manors had filled her every waking hour since her husband John's death; when, if rumour ran true, she was faced with the terrible legal problem of her daughter's clandestine marriage to a man not of Margaret's choosing?

'I think that you should do it speedily, mistress, this search for a husband,' John Dane persisted with more than a hint of anxiety, for I had discovered that I had been frowning at him. 'The country is ill at ease with insurrection, so a man of authority in the house would be of value to all of us. The Percy family is not known for its tolerance or patience.'

Then Margaret it must be, to give me her counsel. I discovered that I was averse to inviting her brisk comments, but there was nothing else to be done. It had become necessary for me to withstand her admonishments, which I knew would be delivered with cruel honesty, but would still be of value to me. If I needed a husband of merit, to protect me from the mighty Percy family, Margaret Paston was without doubt the best source of guidance in entrapping such a man, if she could find the time to prise herself away from the trials of Caister Castle and the looming threat of family disgrace.

CHAPTER EIGHT

MARGARET MAUTBY PASTON

The Paston House in Norwich, June 1469

'What's afoot here?'

I raised my voice to make myself heard over the hubbub.

I might have expected to meet with a disapproving Father Gloys and an unrepentant and silent daughter, but not this. Returned to Norwich after a visit to my manor at Mautby, I could hardly find room to dismount in my own courtyard on Elm Hill. It was crammed with high-class horseflesh and a clutch of liveried servants, not such as we usually saw. Some of the livery was recognisable to any inhabitant of Norwich.

'Visitors, mistress.'

It was not helpful. Pushing my reins into the hand of someone's groom, I thrust through the throng with the help of the well-armed Paston servant who had accompanied me from Mautby, as travel was dangerous in these days. He lifted the latch and opened the door for me to pass through, there to find Father James Gloys, my chaplain, grim faced, awaiting me like a hovering raptor, ready to pounce as soon as I walked in.

'What's going on?' I asked again.

I could hear voices raised in the chamber leading off the hall where we usually dined. There was laughter and loud assertions. It sounded as if those within had partaken readily of my ale and wine.

'It's Master Paston, mistress.'

'Oh?' Of course it was. 'What's he doing here? I thought he was at Caister.'

I did not expect an answer; I would get it soon enough. I could read my chaplain's disfavour in the downward curve of his mouth, but then it was a frequent expression. Why did I put up with his constant disapproval? Out of habit, I supposed. We might not always see eye to eye, but he always had the Paston well-being at heart. I could tolerate his lack of compassion and harsh judgements since I knew that he would do nothing to harm my family.

The door to the chamber was opened, and out came a flamboyantly clad stream of men with words of farewell, one to the other. I was almost forced to flatten myself against the wall until they saw me and realised that I was not a servant. They bowed and murmured apologies, asking after my well-being, before going out to reclaim mounts and retinues, leaving my son Jonty to face me. His face was flushed, with wine or success I was unsure. Probably from both.

'I did not expect you today, Mother.'

'So I see.'

'I was entertaining.'

'I see that too.'

He grinned, entirely unabashed at making use of my property and my food supplies when he knew I would be absent. There he stood, brimming with confidence and enthusiasm, all Paston with the dark hair and straight nose, his clever features alive with mischief, his long fingers curved around the costly belt he had recently acquired.

'Since you are so sharp, Mother, you might have noticed which powerful magnates have had their aristocratic feet under our table.'

'Indeed. I am sharp enough to have taken account of the livery. I'll not comment on the extravagance of velvet and jewels. Let me sit down and you can explain why you have been making free with my food and wine.'

I followed Jonty into the now-empty chamber, where he helped me to remove my travelling cloak and hood and, while I straightened my veil, he ushered me to his own high-backed chair at the head of the table. From the debris he discovered an unused cup that he filled with our best ale. He waited until I had drunk a little and sat beside me.

'How was Mautby?' Jonty asked smoothly.

'You will not distract me,' I replied.

'I did not suppose for one moment that I could.'

I surveyed him, my son who least resembled my husband John, dead now for three years. Jonty had all the liveliness that John had lacked although he had the same long Paston nose and determined chin. For the briefest of moments, I felt the lack of John with his angular features and stern convictions at my side. No, I had not married him for love. As an heiress it was my obligation to marry at the dictates of my family. I had not questioned it, but it had been a joy to me when a strong fondness had grown between us. I still missed him, and not just because of the weight of responsibility that had fallen on my shoulders with John dead. There were days when I wished simply to talk to him, to exchange opinion and even local gossip. Some days there was only Father Gloys within my four walls. He was rarely an edifying experience when I needed a lightening of spirits.

I hoped that Jonty would achieve a marriage as satisfying as mine had been.

'Mother!' Jonty nudged me.

Blinking back into the present, still wishing that John was sitting at my side and dispensing advice, I surveyed the remnants before me. 'Quite a feast,' I observed. I pointed at a flat platter that bore the remnants of a large bird. 'Is that the remains of one of my swans?'

'Would you accuse me of so heinous a crime? I would not dare.'

'I am relieved to hear it. Now tell me why the Woodvilles were here.'

The men I had recognised from their Woodville livery, all bright with silver and gold and red: Lord Scales and Sir John Woodville, both influentially powerful courtiers since they were brothers to the Woodville Queen. I could accept them. I might even accept the need to impress them with roast swan to turn a simple meal into a banquet, but I needed to know what Jonty had in mind.

Jonty, with great insouciance, continued to explain the Woodvilles' presence. It was all very simple, to his mind.

'I decided that to entertain them and a good few members of the royal party would not come amiss, to win them to our side.'

'And did it work?' I gestured open-handedly to the remains of the feast. 'I would be interested to know how much this has cost me. Particularly if it was a worthless exercise.'

'Who's to know?' My son had suddenly acquired a lugubrious air. 'Yes, I spent generously. They enjoyed themselves and seemed well content. We'll only know when we ask for their support at Court against the Duke of Norfolk.'

The Duke of Norfolk, as everyone was well aware, was the most dominant of all the magnates with lands in Norwich, and bidding to take possession of Caister Castle from us. His legal claim was false but his influence was too strong to discount on a mere legal wrangle.

'What has the King said?' I asked hopefully.

'I haven't seen the King.'

'Why not? Since he's here on our doorstep, it would be the best chance that we would ever get. Why not get yourself an audience, rather than having to sidle up to the Woodvilles?' It was June and excellent weather for pilgrimages. King Edward himself, on his pilgrimage to the shrine at Walsingham, had passed through Norwich. 'Could King Edward not be persuaded to give us justice? Better to go to the King himself than to his hangers-on.'

It was bad news. I could read it in Jonty's face before he even opened his mouth. I pushed my cup away, but it did not pass my notice that Jonty chose to refill it, as if I would need the strength from a draught of ale.

'Tell me the worst.'

'Uncle William saw the King. Uncle William actually rode beside him as he passed through Hellesdon.'

William was my husband's younger brother, a man of clever legal skills and much ambition. His marriage to Lady Anne Beaufort had given him a foothold at Court, even though the Beauforts were out of favour with the House of York. I valued William's support but did not altogether trust him. He had made it clear that he had an eye to some of the Paston acres for himself.

'Hellesdon!' I repeated. Now there was a permanent thorn under the Paston flesh since Hellesdon had been a Paston manor, until it was wantonly destroyed by another of our aggressive neighbours, the Duke of Suffolk. 'And was the King compassionate to our loss of Hellesdon?'

'No.'

It was hard to believe.

The Duke of Suffolk, another of our perennial enemies, had sent in a small force to rob and steal and destroy, not only our manor house at Hellesdon but the church and the houses of our tenants. All had been laid waste and we had been unable to gain redress, even before my husband John's death. Now even King Edward was turning a deaf ear to our plight. How could a Paston, without powerful aid, succeed against the mighty Duke of Suffolk?

My irritation was building like water behind a dam. Reaching for the cup I took a hearty gulp.

'Did William actually take the King to see the worst damage in Hellesdon?'

'Yes.'

'Did the King not see the extent of the destruction done to our property? To the lives of our tenants?'

'Yes. He saw it. Uncle William made sure that he saw it.'

Jonty's grim assessment was punctuated by thuds of one of his fists against the table that made the bony remains of the bird shudder on its platter.

'And?' My irritation over-flowed. 'By the Virgin, Jonty. Are you ever to tell me?'

'I'll tell you, Mother. You won't like it. The King said that there was no need for his intervention. The buildings in the manor of Hellesdon might well have fallen down of their own accord through lack of care. There was no evidence of foul play. Thus he would not interfere to get restitution for us.'

'Was he blind?' I would not show disrespect to our King, but how could he not have seen? 'Did he not tally the wanton damage?'

70

'The King said – according to Uncle William – that if we had been wronged at Hellesdon, why had we not already sued for restitution from the Duke of Suffolk through the courts in Norwich? Why had we waited so long before voicing our complaints? The King thought that it was mere mischief-making on our part against the Duke of Suffolk, and the fault was all ours in poor estate management. He will do nothing.'

I stood, pushing back my chair so that it scraped on the tiles, unable to sit and listen and accept that our king could be so wilfully obtuse.

'Why have we not sued for restitution? Because we would not get justice in the courts in Norwich. How can we get justice here where the Duke of Suffolk's minions hold sway! Is the King a fool?' I found that I was still holding my cup. I put it down with a snap so that the ale slopped over the rim. I was never one to throw a good cup in a fit of rage and so damage it. 'I wish that I had been at Hellesdon to meet with the King. I would have told him a thing or two about living here, where the King's justice does not hold true!'

Jonty, too, was on his feet.

'Perhaps it is as well that you were not there.'

'Why not?' I walked towards the door, opened it and called for servants to come and clear the repast and mop up the ale. 'I would have given him a list of all the possessions that were stolen from us at Hellesdon. All my featherbeds, Margery's ivory comb, Sir John's books, not to mention the kitchenware. The Duke of Suffolk's creatures took the lot. Or did they all disappear when the houses fell down of their own volition? It was a terrible loss for us, and I'll not allow the King to argue an act of God.'

'And you would probably get us all clapped up for treason. But that is beside the point, Mother. The King said that he would not treat or speak for us. The law must take its course, without his aid. In other words, he won't raise even a royal finger in our direction.'

'So much for royal support for the families who have remained loyal to him through all the conflict with those who support Lancaster.'

I stepped aside to allow the servants to enter and begin the clearing of my best silver dishes. Jonty had certainly been out to impress.

'Will Lord Scales speak for us?' I asked Jonty, who had now come to stand with me by the door.

'I think that he will.'

Lord Scales, Sir Anthony Woodville, courtier and master of the tournament, owned vast estates in Norfolk since his marriage to the Scales heiress. It might just be in his interests to put a spoke in the wheel of such great lords as the Dukes of Norfolk and Suffolk, who snatched up any piece of land for their own profit. To help us might well strengthen his own influence in Norfolk. But the Duke of Suffolk was married to Elizabeth of York, the King's sister, which might persuade Lord Scales to turn his shoulder against us. In these uneasy times it was important for families to stick together. Scales would be a fool to antagonise his brother-in-law the King over a trivial matter of Hellesdon.

There was no more to be said about the matter, except to wait until we suffered our next attack. Then we would see where the Woodvilles stood in their allegiances. There was no point in repining, but I was aware of the perennial black cloud that hovered over my head and gave me a head-ache that no decoction of feverfew in warm red wine could cure.

I looked accusingly at my second son, unwilling to let him escape without further explanation. But suddenly I felt weary to the bone.

'Where is Margery?' I asked, a question that had lately become a habit.

'In her chamber, so I believe. She helped me to set out this repast.'

Which was to some extent solace to at least one of my troubles. She had not absconded with Calle in my brief absence. I would go to her later. I could not face yet another endless discussion about the inadvisability of her inappropriate marriage.

'And Sir John?'

'In London, so I believe.' Jonty smirked. 'In the company of his betrothed, Mistress Haute.'

'Then let us hope that this betrothal to the beloved lady rapidly becomes a marriage. It continues to hang over us without resolution, like a New Year's wreath in midsummer. Surely marriage with the cousin of the Queen would be of advantage to us. As Dame Anne Paston she could make a good case for our rights.' Why did my eldest son not see the value of pursuing this strange betrothal to its obvious conclusion? 'Far easier to get a wife to plead the Paston cause, than woo the Woodvilles with ale and fine meats!'

'My brother will do as he wishes, when he wishes,' Jonty answered with little enthusiasm. 'Even you told him to sort out his own affairs before taking Mistress Haute as his wife.' So I had. And he had made it clear that it was none of my affair.

'Is she a comely woman?' I asked since I had still to set eyes on the lady.

'I have not been introduced to her but have seen her.' Jonty grinned in open appreciation of his brother's betrothed. 'I would say that she is beautiful. My brother says her hair is the gold of corn at the summer harvest, her eyes as clear as sea-glass. I don't know why he does not announce the marriage to all and bring her home to flaunt her before the worthies of Norwich.'

I shrugged my similar incomprehension and, almost out of habit again, asked if Richard Calle was in the house and free to report on whether the malt had been sold, before I remembered that I must appoint a new bailiff. Old habits die hard. The problems seemed to be piling up around me, but I shook my head and straightened my shoulders. Those problems could wait for another day.

I drew a hand over my face. 'I have received a letter from your Aunt Elizabeth Poynings. She too is suffering assaults on her manors. At the hands of the Percy family.'

Jonty guffawed in inelegant style. 'I hope she is not expecting us to ride to her aid. We have enough problems of our own without taking on the Percy family as well.'

'No.' I sighed a little at my helplessness. 'Although she is in distress. She asked my advice on finding a husband with pre-eminence and a good sword arm.'

This time Jonty's inappropriate laughter echoed from the roof timbers. 'Our advice? It is not as if we are doing well in the matrimonial stakes. What did you say?'

'I have not yet replied.'

'Just don't commit us to any more legal entanglements.'

It seemed a harsh judgement but I knew it to be true. We were in no position to help Eliza. Perhaps Uncle William could aid her in finding a husband who could thwart the Percys. Jonty was no help and I would not ask Sir John.

'Do you stay here tonight?' I asked. 'Who is looking after Caister in your absence?'

'There is no need to worry. My sergeant at arms will keep a good watch and there is no sign of manoeuvring forces in the area with the King here. I'll return tomorrow.'

'Then I will see you at supper and we can talk about affairs that are not to do with attack and counter-attack.'

'Do they exist?'

I smiled at him and kissed his cheek, willing to accept his guilt. I retired to my chamber, removed my shoes and lay down on my bed, intending to rest. Instead, the memories of Hellesdon rushed in. The sacked church, the burnt manor, the distraught tenants who called to me for help that I could not give them when I had ridden through that ruined village. All at Suffolk's hand.

And then there was our castle at Caister, inherited with all the rest of the inheritance when my cousin, Sir John Fastolf, made his will. That will had been the making of us as a family. To own a castle was the making of a family that had risen from lowly peasant class to stand on the edge of the gentry. Owning a castle gave any family rank, a position to be respected. A voice to be heard, as well as a place of refuge when under attack. I remembered taking refuge at Caister after the Hellesdon attack because it was the one secure place we had within its moat and strong towers. But the will had been questioned and was still not settled. That will had made enemies for us, powerful men who accused my husband of malicious contrivance to rewrite Fastolf's original desires, to place the whole Fastolf estate into our hands. Now the Duke of Norfolk had an eye to that fine castle. In the balance of power, where there was no true balance, for how could there be, how could we prevent him from driving us out and taking occupation? He might have no legal right to do so, but power was the name of the game to my mind.

'I'll not hand over Caister Castle to any man! Nor will I hand over my swans!' I announced to the empty room, punching the bed-hanging with my fist.

Eventually, I fell asleep, thinking about the fate of my swans on the moat at Caister, but it was an uneasy rest, full of premonition of disaster. If the King was against us there was little hope for us.

Throughout the weeks of high summer of that year, I held to my hopes that aid would come to us despite the King's outright refusal. Jonty was always optimistic in these days, even when he had no grounds for it. He had been in service to the Duke of Norfolk for seven years, a member of the ducal household, even invited to attend the inauguration at Court when the young duke had stepped into his deceased father's shoes. Would not such long and loyal service give Jonty the right to approach the Duke and negotiate terms which would leave Caister in our hands? But this year, the young duke had failed to offer Jonty livery, thus discharging him from service. An ominous decision. We could no longer rely on the Duke's good offices.

'Perhaps the Duke's conscience troubled him, if he would employ you with one hand and rob you with the other,' I remarked to Jonty when he had come to Norwich to break the bad news to me.

'He has no conscience when it is in his interests to dispense with it. I expect he will make confession of it before his priest and earn forgiveness. All we can do is wait on events.'

'And keep your ear to the ground.'

'I'll do more than that.'

Jonty, always quick to see and seize an opportunity, rode off to visit the Dowager Duchess of Norfolk, claiming some acquaintance with the lady, in whose entourage he had travelled overseas to the marriage of the Lady Margaret, the King's sister, when she had wed the Duke of Burgundy. It did not take him long to return.

He shrugged and beat the dust from his felt cap, his habitual good cheer severely dented.

'She refuses to become involved, doubtless advised against it by her son the Duke. She was friendly enough and received me, but she would not speak of Caister. The Duke will go his own way, and I fear to our detriment.' He paused. 'She sent you her best wishes.'

I grimaced, recognising her dilemma. 'How flattering to be sent well-wishing by a Duchess! Clearly, she has no control over her son.' Thinking of Sir John still absent in London, I ignored Jonty's crack of laughter: 'She has my sympathies!'

By July the King, too, had his own difficulties, and serious ones at that. The Earl of Warwick, together with the Duke of Clarence, the King's younger brother, and now wed to Warwick's elder daughter Isabel, invaded England with treason in mind. After the disastrous battle of Edgecote Moor, King Edward was taken prisoner and sent to Warwick's castle at Middleham, where he was kept under restraint while Warwick attempted to rule the country.

I might have had compassion for King Edward's woes except that he had shown none to us. Besides, his woes impacted on us, too. The country was without a sovereign. The great magnates were now free to follow their own ambitions without fear of the King or royal justice. For us, affairs went from bad to worse.

'What is it?' I demanded as Jonty rode up Elm Hill at an inappropriate gallop and entered the house with such a thrust of the door that it slammed against the wall, shaking the whole. 'The Duke of Norfolk, I presume. What has he done now?'

'What you would expect. We knew it was only a matter of time. Only demanded that we give up Caister Castle on the grounds that he, the Duke, had legally purchased it from Judge Yelverton.'

Judge Yelverton, a name that was never spoken in this household. One of the original executors of Fastolf's will, who had become one of our most vocal enemies. On his death bed, with only John as witness, Fastolf had changed his will, John noting the changes. The executors were demoted en masse, the whole inheritance left to John. Of inestimable value to us, but such a bone of contention between those such as Yelverton who might have hoped for some pickings from the Fastolf estates.

'The will has still not been proved and lies in a cloud of dust before the courts with no present hope of a solution,' Jonty continued to rant, as dusty as the foresworn will, marching from one end of the hall to the other, rattling my new hangings with the speed of his movement. 'Thus the Duke makes his claim.'

'What have you said?'

'I said no.'

'Should you have discussed this with Sir John?' *Or even with me?*

'I did not need to. I refused to even consider that damned impertinent ducal demand. Would you have advised me otherwise?'

'No. I don't suppose that I would.' I might have worded my refusal a little more carefully, though, so as not to antagonise the Duke even more. 'Can we hold it?'

'I don't know. But I'll not give it up without a fight.'

There was nothing more to be said. I held on to the chance that all might be put right, listing for myself the advantages in our situation. Caister was a highly defensible site. Jonty had been training his handful of forces for many weeks now. Most pertinent of all: would the Duke of Norfolk risk a breach of the peace that might bring King Edward down on him?

Unfortunately, it could be argued that Edward was no longer King. Even I had to admit that he was no longer in a position to object to anything the Duke of Norfolk might do. The Woodvilles were also hampered with Warwick in control. There was no love lost between them.

Thus all the horrors of our situation came to pass, a development that almost drove my frustrations with Margery from my mind.

The twenty-first day of August in the year 1469 was a day engraved on my heart. A day in which all my worries came to a head.

An army of three thousand armed retainers belonging to the Duke of Norfolk laid siege to Caister. Our castle came under fire from guns and culverins as well as archers. We had all of twenty-seven defenders inside, including Jonty himself.

I sent off to Sir John a diamond clasp that he had requested, one of the Fastolf gems, knowing that it would be the last I would see of it. My son would undoubtedly sell it to raise money to buy support against this sudden aggression against our property. Unless he wasted it as a gift to Mistress Haute.

Despair took a cruel hold so that I could not separate one problem from the next. A siege on one side, a profligate son on the other, both overwhelmed by Margery's defiance and an impossible marriage. It was enough to drive me to my knees at my prie-dieu to beg the Blessed Virgin's tolerance for my ill temper. I was in desperate need of a guiding light through the morass of difficulties that trod on my heels at every venture.

CHAPTER NINE

MARGERY PASTON

The Paston House and the Bishop's Palace in Norwich,
August 1469

A man in the black clerical robes of a priest came to our door
and was admitted. Such was his demeanour, and so clear the livery
badge of the ecclesiastical power of the Bishop of Norwich on his
breast, that, although my mother was at Mautby, beleaguered by
the siege of Caister Castle on her threshold, Father Gloys ushered
the cleric into the parlour. I had been cutting a length of frieze
into tunics for Walter and Willem, my two youngest brothers,
both as mischievous and wilful as Jonty's new young hounds, and
growing as fast as the willows on the banks of the River Wensom.
My mother had devised multiple ways in which to keep my hands
busy.

'Thank you, Father Gloys,' the priest said, his severity making it
abundantly clear that this was to be a private conversation.

While he reluctantly closed the door, I curtsied to the visitor.

'I am Father Anselm,' he said. 'I have come to speak with
Mistress Margaret Paston, but I understand she is not here. You
must be Mistress Margery.'

Father Anselm, gauntly austere, regarded me with a bleak eye
which travelled from my head to my feet, then returned to the
shears that I still clutched, and to the wisps of wool that clung to
my skirts. It was not a friendly assessment.

'Yes, sir, I am Margery Paston.' I refused to be intimidated, or
even to look away.

'Then you are the one I actually seek, mistress. I am sent to carry a message to you from his Grace the Bishop of Norwich. He wishes to speak with you.'

My heart leapt with surprise, before swooping into the depths of anxiety. Why would the Bishop of Norwich wish to see me? I could think of only one reason, only one sin to my name that would demand the Bishop's intervention. My reply was less than courteous.

'Now? What would the Bishop have to say to me?'

'If you will come, mistress, I expect that his Grace will make all clear. I should warn you that he is not best pleased. I suggest that you bring your maidservant, who will escort you home after the interview. And perhaps you might change your gown ...'

Without hesitation I made ready, for to disobey the Bishop would merely make matters worse. Would this interview be for good or ill? I had few hopes of a favourable outcome, but to linger would not be to my advantage when summoned by a high cleric. I exchanged my wool-flecked skirts for a close-fitting long-sleeved gown in patterned wool, demure, plain, and most suitable to our position in Norwich. Instructing one of the maids to accompany me, I left information with Master Pecock, our steward, that I had gone to the Cathedral, and stepped out of our house. There was one thought in my mind: how had the Bishop come to hear of my situation?

'Why does the Bishop wish to speak with me, sir?' I asked again as I kept pace with Father Anselm through the crowded streets.

I had only ever seen the Bishop, all garbed in gold and embroidered robes, crowned with a mitre, crosier in hand, when we had attended some particular Mass on a Saint's Day. He made an impressive figure in a ceremonial procession. We usually attended the church of St Peter Hungate, closer to our home. Why would he wish to see me? I had a suspicion that my mother had a hand in this. Was he to pray over me and divert my earthly passions into those appropriate to an obedient daughter?

Father Anselm all but sniffed. 'I am not privy to his Grace's business, mistress, but I doubt it's anything to your advantage. His

Grace rarely summons young women of no account for an audience in his august presence.'

After that I kept my own counsel and my mouth shut.

The Bishop's Palace was as impressive as its owner. I was led in beneath the great tower gatehouse, across the Great Hall with its high vaulting – where I was chivvied to quicken my steps – and up a flight of shallow stairs, until Father Anselm abandoned me and I was kept waiting, seated on a wooden settle in an audience chamber hung with tapestries of biblical scenes. Those who wished to petition the august Bishop were not considered in need of comfort. Rather the fearsome depiction of souls in Hell would cast any petitioner into terror. Though I was now well used to the luxury of Caister Castle, for we had moved frequently between Caister and Norwich when matters of business had demanded my mother's presence, still I was overwhelmed by the gilding and carved finials, but my surroundings soon lost their interest for me. I sighed, shuffled a little, as the time went on, then rose to look out of the window, down into the courtyard below. The Bishop was in no hurry to see me after all. I wondered what my mother would say when she returned home and found me gone to the Bishop's Palace. Was this perhaps Sir John's doing, rather than my mother's, to force me into an annulment? If he had hoped to overawe me, he had succeeded. The black-frocked priests constantly coming and going, the heavy sense of righteousness and sin, the underlying scent of incense, all cowed me into a sense of my own shortcomings.

How long before anyone noticed my existence? I had barely returned to my settle when a heavily carved door opened to my left and a priest walked out. Father Anselm reappeared and beckoned, directing me in with a scowl of warning.

'His Grace is a busy man. Do not waste his time.'

Thus I was left in the hallowed presence of Walter Lyhert, Bishop of Norwich. My hands were clenched in the fine cloth of my skirts as I waited for whatever judgement would fall on me.

Rising from his chair, he proved to be a tall man, well-built but with some elegance, of middling years that had greyed his fair hair. I had expected him in cloth of gold, not the plain clerical garb, all in black except for the girdle with gold tassels around his waist. There was no mitre, just a neatly tonsured head. The heavy gold cross on his breast invested him with a weight of authority, yet the Bishop was not unwelcoming when I entered. He was more encouraging than his emissary, waving me forward as he stepped towards me.

I knelt and kissed the episcopal ring on his hand which was marked with age. Here was a man of experience as well as authority.

'Stand up, my child.' And, when I did, he continued, 'Mistress Margery Paston.' He almost smiled. 'Thank you for agreeing to come here today, although I fear it may be a waste of your time. All, sadly, will not fall out according to my plans.'

Which would have unnerved me, yet he set me at my ease, indicating for me a low stool at his side when he took his seat in his high-backed episcopal chair. He looked at me, considering me, as if he were waiting for inspiration. Why would his plans, whatever they might be, have fallen awry? I spoke up, encouraged by an unexpected gleam in his eye.

'I do not understand why I am here, sir. Did my brother Sir John ask you to speak with me? Or my mother? I am sorry that they should have engaged you in our family circumstances.'

'No, Mistress Paston. I have had no communication with your family.'

Which left me even more in the dark. The Bishop rose to his feet and went to look down into the courtyard, much as I had done, as if he were waiting for someone.

'Of course, you will be wondering. It was the Paston bailiff called Richard Calle who wrote to me.'

'Richard wrote to you?'

Richard's doing! Blessed Virgin be praised. I felt my cheeks flush with rich colour. Richard had done it. When I thought that he had abandoned me, he was working hard to reunite us. I should have had more faith. Of course he had known what must be done, seeking out a man of influence, a man of the Church. I had never believed that he would look as high as the Bishop of Norwich, who must now know every detail of my predicament. And yet I sensed no overt hostility in him.

'Master Calle says that the situation between you and your family is now so grave that it needs a man of my authority to set it right,' the Bishop continued, looking across the room to me. 'Do you think so?'

'Yes, I do. It is grave indeed.' I stood, since it seemed wrong that I should sit while the Bishop was standing.

'And will you agree to speak the truth to me, Mistress Margery?'

'Yes. I have never told a lie about myself and Master Calle.'

'We shall see.' He walked slowly back towards me, abandoning his vantage point. Whoever he was waiting for had not arrived. 'It is a most serious affair, to indulge in a marriage without a priest or your family's agreement. What persuaded you to do it?'

I could not meet his eyes, fearing condemnation, instead focusing on the gleaming cross that rose and fell gently on his chest.

'It is love that holds us in sway, sir. My family will not approve, but he is a man of integrity, much admired in the town, and I am of an age to make my own choice.'

'That is what we must determine. It was my proposal to speak with the two of you on the same day, but Master Calle is detained on his journey here. We must, it seems, wait another day. I think it is important that I see you and talk with you together.'

'Yes, your Grace.'

So Richard was on his way. I was suddenly aware of a lightening of spirit, just the faintest hint of joy. I would not be alone to face this.

'Then this is what we will do, my child...'

The Bishop paused, chin tilted. There was a noise beyond the door. Raised voices, female voices. The door was pushed open by Father Anselm.

'Forgive me, your Grace. There are two women here who say that the situation with Mistress Margery Paston is their business. They ask that they should speak with you. Indeed, they will not go away without speaking with you. This is highly irregular.'

My momentary lightness of spirit collapsed into dismay. Here was the opening of a quite different page in the tale of my woes.

On the threshold stood my mother, together with my grandmother, Mistress Agnes, who had travelled all the way from Oxnead because of the dire situation in the Paston household, whether it be the siege or a clandestine marriage. They must have arrived at the Paston house only shortly after my departure. Here they marched in, pausing to curtsey, for at least they were not lacking in respect. Then we stood facing the Bishop: a trio of Paston women. Three generations and not one pleased with the other. If my mother had her way, the Bishop would not listen to anything I might have to say. My grandmother would insist on speaking her piece as she had done throughout her life. Neither my mother nor my grandmother were in any manner as overawed as I had been.

The Bishop was not as welcoming as he had been to me. He addressed my mother.

'It seems that you think that you have business here, Mistress Paston? Perhaps you will explain it to me.'

My mother occupied the centre of the chamber as if it were her own, for in her own world she wielded as much authority as the Bishop did in his. Neat and well-groomed, her appearance was one of wealth and respectability, her hands encased in kid gloves, her hair hidden in her habitual soft roll of damask, her only jewellery a plain rosary. Mistress Agnes, my grandmother, was growing old and increasingly frail but not in spirit. Her thin figure, slight, black-clad and severe, spoke of her determined widowhood. She was never one to mince her words.

'I do have business here, your Grace,' my mother announced. 'Margery is my daughter. This is a family affair. I would ask your Grace to postpone any action you would take until my sons can be assembled. They should be here too. My sons should be party to any decision.' A glance slid in my direction. 'I do not understand why my daughter should be here alone in the first place.'

His Grace smiled slightly at the implied criticism of his actions. 'She is here because I sent for her, Mistress Paston.'

He looked from one to the other, as if wishing the Paston women, all three of us, anywhere but in his private audience chamber. I thought he would concur and postpone the whole issue, but I did not want my brothers here as well. What hope would there be for me with their combined voices raised against me, even if Richard had at last arrived?

'It is not right that she should pester you, your Grace.' My grandmother said, as crisp and dry as a last-year's corn stalk. 'We have come to take her home with us. We will deal with the situation behind our own doors.'

Which was the last thing I wanted. Here at least was a chance for a settlement.

'If it please you, your Grace—' I said in desperation.

He raised a hand to stop me. My heart plummeted. The Bishop once more addressed my mother.

'I have been asked by Master Calle to have conversation with Mistress Margery and make my judgement on this claim of their marriage. I have agreed. I think it would be remiss of me to either refuse or delay such a questioning.' Yes, he was severe, but not unkind. I allowed myself to breathe a little more easily. 'Master Calle was reasonable and dignified in his request. He deserves an answer from me.'

'But if it please you, your Grace, will you not wait?' my mother asked. 'Another week, or even two, when I can send for my sons to be here, would make no difference.'

'It is only right that Sir John, as the head of the family, should be given a voice in this,' Mistress Agnes added.

There was a pause as the Bishop, expression unreadable, looked from me to my mother.

'I have made my decision. I do not see that your sons will make any difference to this interview. I wish to see Mistress Margery here before me tomorrow morning after early Mass. After I have questioned her, I will talk with Master Calle, who I expect will also be here in Norwich tomorrow. Mistress Margery has agreed to this. There is nothing more to be said.'

I could see the bright anger in my mother, as if a candle had been lit in a horn lantern. My grandmother's mouth was as firmly closed as a rat-trap.

'I do not agree, your Grace.' Still my mother persisted. 'I am her mother and I have authority over her actions.'

How soft, how gentle was the Bishop's reply. 'But, Mistress Paston, I am a servant of God and I have authority over her soul.'

My mother was still not discouraged from pursuing her assault on my freedom to put my case to the Bishop.

'Then I will bring her, your Grace. I will stand beside her when she gives her testimony.'

I trembled for her, addressing the Bishop in such a fashion, but of course she would have her way. Would not the Bishop support a mother's control over her daughter?

'I would hate to remind you, Mistress Paston, that such disobedience to the dictate of a mitred Bishop could call down a punishment of excommunication.'

My throat dried at such a reprimand. For once my mother, stricken with outrage, could find no words.

'This is what will happen. I will send for this young woman by one of my household tomorrow morning, and she will come. There must be no attempts to stop her. Do you understand me?'

'But, your Grace, there were no witnesses to this travesty of a marriage.'

'It has to be said, Mistress Paston, that witnesses are not always necessary to prove legality. I have some compassion for your heartbreak,' Bishop Lyhert interrupted, his patience full-stretched. 'Your daughter's behaviour has not been of the best to keep amity in the house of Paston, but it seems that what is done is done. I will speak with her and I will ascertain what can be brought out of it. Perhaps the wound can be healed, but perhaps not. The decision will be mine after I have talked with her and Master Calle. That is all I have to say.'

The audience was over. We curtsied. I was to return for a formal interview in the morning, and Richard would be there. Meanwhile, we returned home in a simmering silence. Whether my mother approved or not, I was now firmly under the authority of the Bishop of Norwich.

CHAPTER TEN

MARGERY PASTON

The Bishop's Palace in Norwich, August 1469

True to his word, the Bishop sent for me next morning, early in the day after I had broken my fast, not that I had much appetite for more than a bite of bread and a mouthful of beer to sustain me through what I knew would be an ordeal. It was brought to my chamber by a silent maidservant, so that I and my sin would not have to blight the atmosphere with my mother and grandmother.

My mother stood at the door and watched me leave, her features engraved in stone.

'You must say the right thing,' Mistress Agnes all but hissed. 'Remember the debt you owe to your family.'

I curtsied in dutiful farewell but said nothing.

This morning my escort was clad in full clerical regalia as the Bishop's representative, intimidating my mother into silence by the gold embossing, and drawing attention as we walked through the streets, where many bowed in acknowledgement. We walked in silence, disapproving on his part, nervous on mine, and I took my place once more on the wooden settle in the antechamber, looked down on by the same suffering and gory souls who were tortured in Purgatory.

Was Richard here? Was he speaking with the Bishop at this moment? Although the room was cold, I felt the heat of alarm and wished it all over. My previous hopefulness had leached away.

'Bishop Lyhert asks that you will enter.'

A nameless priest summoned me. There was no sign of Richard.

Once again, I was invited to sit. The Bishop was in full regalia except for the mitre which rested on the coffer beside him, for this would be a formal interrogation and his decision would be beyond question, even by my mother. I wondered if he would have a clerk to write down all my answers, but we were alone, which afforded me some relief. Bishop Lyhert folded his hands, one on the other, on the table before him where there were documents and scrolls, their seals softly red in the light. His rings gleamed as did the crucifix. I gripped my hands tightly together in my lap.

'You remember, Mistress Margery, that yesterday you promised to be honest with me.'

'Yes, your Grace. And I will.'

'It is important that we have a record of our conversation.'

'Of course, your Grace.'

A clerk entered and stood at a lectern, his quill pen poised over the pot of ink. My dread increased at the thought of every word I said being on record, but I would not be deterred from speaking out. There was one fact that I would know before we began.

'If I might ask, is Master Calle here, your Grace?'

The faint smile acknowledged my concern. 'Yes. He arrived nigh on midnight. He knows how important this is to you, to both of you. And now we must start this investigation.'

The smile vanished and the Bishop began with a stern lecture, as if he were in the pulpit and I in the congregation. Family was very important to a young woman. And her friends were invaluable. Would it not be better if I were to be ruled and guided by them, for my own happiness? Would I not find my life much simpler if I accepted the advice of my mother and brothers, who would have my future happiness much at heart? If I remained obstinate in what I had said in the past, I would risk destroying all that good will from both friends and family. Was that what I wanted? I was still very young. I ought to welcome the care of those around me. To destroy that care would bring me no contentment.

The mitre gleamed with its weight of heavenly justice at his right hand.

But not once did he talk of what might be a sin on my part. It was all about what would be best for me within my family. I listened gravely, taking in every point. It was no different from any of the observations that had come from my mother over the past weeks.

'Do you understand me, Mistress Margery?'

'Yes, your Grace. I understand you very well. I know that you have my happiness within my family at heart.'

'Then it may be best for everyone, do you not agree, if you retract what you have claimed. Perhaps it was all a misunderstanding on your part, and that of Master Calle.'

I thought about this, but only for a moment, now meeting his eyes with bold certainty. 'I cannot do that, your Grace. I cannot retract what I have said.'

'But if you cannot, what rebuke and shame and loss it will be to you, my child.'

The endearment almost made me weep. 'I understand that, your Grace.'

Placing his hands flat on the table, he leaned forwards as if to do so would encourage me. 'Is your professed love for this man more important to you than the standing of your family? Is it more important than the goodwill and kinship with your family?'

How hard it was to answer such brutal questions. But I would do it. 'Yes, your Grace.' It was almost a whisper. 'My love for Richard Calle is paramount.'

'They do not approve of this man whom you say you have taken as your husband.'

I looked up. I met the Bishop's eyes again and spoke from the heart. 'My family approved of Richard Calle as their bailiff. None could be better. But not as my husband because he has no wealth, no land, no status other than that of an employed man from a family of shopkeepers. My mother and grandmother were both heiresses who wed beneath them. Have they ever told you that? They have fought all their lives to uphold and strengthen the Paston name. They will not tolerate Richard, no matter how good and kind and upright he is, no matter how loyal and hardworking. No matter how useful he has been to them in the past. They think he will drag them down if he weds me. They fear the gossip in the town.'

He looked surprised at my flow of words but I could be silent no longer. I was my mother's daughter, strong-willed enough to proclaim my innocence for all to hear.

'They used him in their battle to retain the Fastolf estates. They spoke of him as a friend. They trust him implicitly to collect the monies from our tenants. Yet they will stand in the way of my wedding him. So, we have done it in the only manner possible, and I think that it cannot be undone. I have known him since I was a child and my love for him is fervent. I also know that his love for me is sincere, even under the onslaught of dismissal from my family.'

The Bishop sat back, blinking in some surprise. Perhaps he did not meet so many young women who were voluble and assured. He did not know how hard my heart was beating, how tight my fingers were interlocked. The Bishop looked at his clerk, shaking his head to indicate that my explanation was not what needed to be written down, to the clerk's relief. Then he looked back at me.

'Then let us see where we stand, my child. Tell me what you said to Richard Calle that makes you think that this is a legal case of matrimony. My clerk will make careful note of this.'

I told him. I was certain. I had known what I must say and had practised so that I was word-perfect, recalling every word we had exchanged and what we had done together.

'Master Calle said to me: "On this day I take you as my wife, Margery Paston. May God bear witness to what I say in His presence." And I replied: "On this day I take you as my husband, Richard Calle. May God bear witness to what I reply in His presence."'

The Bishop frowned. 'Did you say these exact words?'

'I did, your Grace. We intended it to be a matrimonial bond, and we spoke plainly. We knew that it must be plain. Richard knows enough of the law to be certain that what we did had a legality about it.'

Bishop Lyhert sighed deeply. 'You do realise that if this is so, then your family will not receive you again?'

I could not believe that they would be so intolerant. At first, perhaps, but would they not be accepting when they saw that

Richard and I had made a good marriage? My mother would not so condemn me for ever. When Richard and I had children, she would surely welcome them, her grandchildren, back into the family. Did my brothers not have enough affection for me, that they would eventually forgive what they now regarded as a terrible mistake?

'I would hope that I could persuade them,' I replied. 'It will be an honest marriage, your Grace. A marriage with much affection, with true love, at its heart.'

'You have more faith in your powers of persuasion than I would have, when faced with Mistress Margaret Paston.' He steepled his fingers, to rest them against his lips.

I could think of no reply to this. Instead, I asked: 'Are my words binding, your Grace? I recall them most clearly.'

'Probably they are.'

'What do I do now?'

'I cannot persuade you to un-recall the binding words, I suppose.'

'No, your Grace, you cannot.'

He watched me carefully. 'Did you and Master Calle share a bed together?'

I would not deny it. 'Yes, your Grace.'

'Which complicates matters even more, although in truth it is the words spoken rather than the deeds done that will drive this case to its conclusion.' He stood, signalling to the clerk that his work was complete for now. 'I will talk with Master Calle. But privately. I think it will be better if you are not present.'

'May I not see him, your Grace?'

'Not yet. I will speak with him first.'

'And if our words are in agreement?'

'The impatience of youth.' He sighed a little sadly. 'I cannot be hasty, so neither must you. There may be other affairs to prevent this marriage, of which I yet know nothing. If you will wait in here –' he took my hand and led me to a small chamber, comfortably furnished, where I could sit at ease without the environs of sin and Hell – 'I will come and see you when I have spoken with Master Calle and tell you of my decision. You do realise, do you not, that to persist with this union will, of necessity, bring you nothing but pain?'

'I know it.'

But did I? I was not yet aware of the weakness of my experience. What did I fully understand about the path I had chosen to take? But take it I had, and there was no regret in me as I waited. Richard was here. I had not spoken with or seen him for so long, that now I could barely wait. The time slowly moved on while I fretted, trying to imagine what would be said between them.

At last the door was opened by the Bishop and I was invited in. There stood Richard, immediately turning to face me.

How the room brightened at the sight of him. My first thought was that he looked pale and drawn, with faint lines between nose and mouth, but then I knew that he had been ill. His regard, fixed on me, was clear and full of encouragement.

'I will leave you together, but only for a short time. Tell each other whatever it is that you have to say.' Such compassion from the Bishop, so much understanding when my mother had had none. 'I will come to you within a few minutes and tell you what I think you should do.'

He walked out, gesturing to his clerk to follow.

Ridiculously, I stood in silence, for I did not know what to say. This man was my husband but the distance between us seemed extreme. There was a formality demanded of us in the Bishop's chambers. I might wish to cast myself into his arms, offering my lips for his kisses, but I could not do it, and neither could he ask it of me.

'And all still hangs in the balance. Do we say our farewells, my dear one? The Bishop may well declare against us,' Richard said as the door closed, leaving us alone.

'I know not.'

So little time. I was as shy as if I did not know him, so long apart with all the weight of uncertainty and antagonism stirred up by my family between us. We had risked all, and still we did not know what fate had dictated for us. Where I had hoped for encouragement, Richard was harsh and uncertain, which left me floundering. And then, his expression lightening into sheer delight at our reunion, he awarded me a flamboyant bow, with a flourish of his hat and more than a glint of humour.

'Good day, Mistress Margery Calle.'

It took me aback. How could I not respond in similar vein? I awarded him a deep curtsey, as if to the Bishop himself.

'I have missed you so much, Master Calle. What wife does not miss her husband after so many weeks apart?'

'Will you then stand apart from me for ever?'

Abandoning shyness, when I walked across the Bishop's chamber at last Richard took me into his arms and held me close as if not even the Bishop could separate us. I could feel his heartbeat, steady and sure, while his lips were warm and marvellously possessive on mine.

'I am full of contrition that I have forced you to face all of this,' Richard said at last. 'There was no other way. The Bishop was our only hope for a future.'

'Your letters did not reach me. Except for one of them. You must never doubt my love for you.'

'I do not. We have taken this step. We will reach the end of this particular road together. We will not be parted.'

How confident he was. 'What will the Bishop do?'

'I know not. He warned me that I would lose any chance of employment here in Norwich.'

For us there was no going back. We knew the consequences and would accept them. It was as if Richard had read my mind.

'Knowing the truth of our marriage and facing the consequences are not one and the same, Margery. We must be formidable in our own defence.'

'As we will be.' A touch of impatience now. 'How long will it take his Grace to decide?'

As if he had heard, there came a courteous knock against the door as warning and the Bishop entered. Richard took my hand and I held on. The next few moments might determine the rest of my life, and his.

'I have made no decision as yet, Master Calle. I am sorry if that disappoints you but so it must be. I will continue to investigate your claim to matrimony. I will give my verdict in the week after the Feast of Michaelmas.'

Whereas I struggled to count the weeks, Richard knew exactly how long into the future that would be. I felt him exhale slowly.

'So long, your Grace.'

An errant beam of sunshine crept into the room to emblazon the Bishop's tonsured head, making of it a halo, although casting the rest of the room into deep shadow, as if at so bleak a decision.

'A few weeks only. What is a matter of weeks in a lifetime? Until the twenty-ninth day of September. If your love is as strong as you claim, if your commitment to each other is as steadfast, you will withstand the parting.'

Richard bowed, one hand on his heart. 'All we can ask is that you will be guided by the truth, your Grace.'

'I live my life by God's truth, my son,' the cleric replied dryly. 'Meanwhile, the two of you will remain apart until it is decided. You will go home to your mother, Mistress Margery. It may not be comfortable for you, but it will be for the best. I trust that you will strive for an equitable atmosphere. Meanwhile, I suggest that you return to London, Master Calle. I know that you must now seek employment. Or perhaps your own family in Framlingham will come to your aid.'

'My thanks that you have not cast out our plea without consideration.'

The Bishop's tone continued as dry as the scratching of his clerk who had returned with him to record the final judgement. 'I have to say that I would be pleased to deny this marriage. I dislike inconsistencies when the laws of matrimony are swept aside. Sadly, from what I know, I cannot deny it, but I will continue to make enquiries.'

My hopes disintegrated like a handful of blossom under a keen frost. The Bishop might be a kindly man but he would do all in his power to part us. Richard's smile was humourless although his reply was even enough.

'Then I must return to London. As you say, your Grace, I have a living to earn since the Pastons have made good their threat of casting me off.'

'You cannot blame them.'

'No, I do not. I knew the risk when I took this woman as my wife.'

'It was a great risk, my son. You must say your farewells to Mistress Margery. Whether you will meet again will depend on my interpretation of the letter of the law.'

We parted under the Bishop's eye with no more words spoken, only the pressure of Richard's hand on mine and his lips pressed against my fingers in farewell. Once again, in an aura of my impending disgrace, Father Anselm escorted me back to my home where I must survive the coming weeks with calm fortitude and mild words, leading me to the door. He knocked and it was opened quickly, as we were expected. I heard the ringing of the noon bell in the city. So much decided, or not, in so short a time. I resolved to live out the time as best I could until the decision was made.

I stepped around Father Anselm to step across the threshold.

There stood Father Gloys.

'Mistress Margery has returned home,' Father Anselm announced. 'If you will be pleased to give your mistress this message from his Grace the Bishop.' He held out the Bishop's written decision.

Father Gloys took it without a word while I waited to enter my home.

Father Gloys moved in front of me, to bar my way.

'If you please,' I said, not understanding. I thought that such a lack of good manners was a mere thoughtlessness on his part.

The priest did not move. 'Mistress Paston has decided that you will no longer reside here.'

The strain of the morning had rendered me unreceptive to such discourtesy. I could not quite take in the meaning of his words. Behind me I heard a hiss of breath, inhaled through his teeth, from Father Anselm. Had we both misheard?

'Allow me to enter,' I said.

'Mistress Paston has forbidden it,' came the reply.

'It is my home.' What species of holy malice was this, expressed in his calm delivery?

'I am to tell you that your behaviour is such that Mistress Paston will no longer receive you, here or in public. This is no longer your home.'

Still, I could not believe what I was hearing. The Bishop had said that I might be cast off. I had agreed, but had I truly believed it? My blood stilled, my thoughts awry. If I was cast out, where would I go? My grandmother would be as hard-hearted as my mother. Yet I could not believe that my mother would do this terrible thing. Was there not some vestige of love left in her heart for me, her elder daughter? My mother was argumentative, opinionated, wilful, but never cruel.

What would I do if I had no home? I looked at the man who stood in my way.

'Did you persuade her in this?' I accused Father Gloys.

He flushed, an unhealthy colour on his sallow complexion. 'Mistress Paston makes up her own mind.'

'I cannot believe this. This is my home.' It was all that I seemed to be able to say. 'My mother would never close her door to me in this manner.'

'You are no longer welcome here.'

I turned my head, looked at Father Anselm for aid. What would I do? He looked as astounded as I, as helpless as I. The Bishop had not expected this. Perhaps after his judgement, if it was made in my favour, my mother might act out of pique, but not now, not when all still hung in the balance.

Practicalities took hold. So did my authority as a grown daughter of the house.

'I insist on coming in to retrieve my possessions. If I am not allowed to stay here, at least I can take my clothes with me.'

I was still struggling for reality, under a storm-cloud of disbelief. Oh Richard! What should I do? Father Gloys was unmoved.

'You are not welcome. You no longer live here. You do not have permission to enter.'

'I wish to speak with my mother.'

'Mistress Margaret is not here.'

Did I believe him? When I put out my hand to the door jamb to steady myself, Father Anselm came to my rescue at last, seeing my distress.

'Come, mistress.' He took my arm in a gentle hold. 'There is naught you can do here. Let us return to the Bishop. He will decide.' His stare at Father Gloys was all censure. 'His Grace will not turn his back on you, even if your family will.'

Once more I was escorted back to the Bishop's Palace, where, once again, I was left to sit on the wooden settle. Homeless. Helpless. Heartbroken. I found myself praying that Richard had not yet left, but what could he do? There were no tears to be shed, only a terrible anger that shook me. Paston women did not weep; I had never known my mother to shed tears, even when my father died. Of what value were tears? But I was blind to the cost and magnificence of the tapestries around me. They meant nothing to me. I had been abandoned to fend for myself.

Reflective of the emergency, I soon was shown once more into the audience chamber of the Bishop where Richard was still there, in conversation with him, but it was the Bishop who took command, stepping to meet with me as I entered the room. He took my hand and drew me in.

'Come and sit, my child.'

'I have been barred from my home,' I stated.

'Yes. I have been told. You have been rejected. I did warn you.'

'And I did not believe that it would ever happen quite like this. Or so soon. I was not even allowed to collect my clothes...'

Richard remained aloof, yet I could not deny the latent fury in him. His face was ashen, his lips hard-pressed.

'You are not without friends, Mistress Margery,' the Bishop assured me. 'I will not allow you to suffer beyond what is acceptable.'

'What can I do? I have nowhere to go.' How young I sounded, how desolate. I was immediately ashamed, so that I took control of my emotions. 'If it please, your Grace, I need advice. I can survive this rejection but indeed I need somewhere to live.'

'I will find somewhere for you,' Richard announced. 'You will live under my protection.'

'Oh, Richard...'

All my dreams had been brought crashing around my feet. Both Richard and I would indeed suffer for this.

'That must not be,' the Bishop said, the least disturbed of the three of us. 'It will complicate an already difficult affair. Living together is not the answer, unless you wish to exist for ever under a pall of disparagement. It is important that you seek God's Grace in this. I understand your need to protect the lady, but indeed you must wait until I have given my judgement.'

'Would you not give it now?'

'No, it must not be uttered under duress, without consideration. That would be unthinkable. It would always leave a slur against your final wedded state, if that is what is to be.'

Richard's reply was barely polite, determined to resolve my predicament.

'Yet it might draw a line under the issue, your Grace. You have heard our witness to our vows. I would suggest that there is no more evidence to collect. To whom would you apply for further information? There was no one to either see or hear us. It must all rest on how honest you deem us as witnesses.'

'You must have patience, Master Calle. All things will come to us in their time.'

I was weary of such men's talk. It did not solve my problem at all.

'What do I do, your Grace? Where do I go?'

Not my brothers, that was clear. My Uncle William in London? My Aunt Elizabeth? I was incapable of making a decision, and was not even sure that any one of them would open their door to a wayward daughter who had demanded the right to marry where she chose. That was not how Pastons did things.

The Bishop was speaking.

'There is no need to be distraught. I will not have you living homeless in the gutter, my child. I have already sent Father Anselm to arrange for one of our most reputable Norwich families to give you shelter. I am almost certain that, at my behest, Master Roger Best and his wife will be willing give you bed and board in their house in Norwich.'

'I do not know them.'

'They are a merchant family. And most respectable. Kindly, too.'

I was not persuaded. 'Will they take me in?'

'Of course.'

'Even if my mother tells them that they must not?'

'Whatever your mother might say. I do have some influence, my child, even though it is sometimes not as much as I would like.' He took my hand again and held it strongly. 'They are sober, hardworking people, for whom I have absolute respect. They will do as I ask them. You will be comfortable there. When I have made my decision, we will meet again. Until then, I forbid you to meet with Master Calle, unless it is for a specific reason. And then you must seek my permission. Is all clear?'

That was all I could ask.

I was deluged in a storm of bitterness at what had transpired. My mother had truly cast me off, so that I must be taken in by a family I did not know, under the auspices of the Bishop. And until the Bishop decided otherwise, I could not speak with Richard again. All was even more uncertain than before the Bishop had involved himself in the matter of my marriage vows.

I curtsied my thanks to the Bishop, bowed in acknowledgement to Richard, and set out through the streets of Norwich with Father Anselm to meet Master Robert Best and his wife. I could not see my way forward, for it seemed that there was a vast chasm that had opened before my feet. In that moment I feared that whatever path was dictated to me, it would be without Richard. How could my mother have driven me from my home? Was the fate of Caister Castle and the honour of the Paston family more important to her than my present happiness? I feared that the answer was yes.

CHAPTER ELEVEN

MARGARET MAUTBY PASTON

Caister Castle in Norfolk, late August 1469

This was what disaster looked like in the flesh. This was the end of all our strivings. I had determined to see it for myself, whatever advice I had been given to stay away. This was the physical threat to our much-prized castle, for which John, my late husband, had lived and, with the strains of his later years, had died. It was a festering sore to my heart.

With a small escort for my protection, and for my self-esteem, I sat on my mare, looking across the expanse of wetland to where Caister Castle was shrouded in mist, until a strong ray of sunshine breaking through illuminated it: the strong walls, the barbican, the glint of the moat. The Paston colours flying over all. What I could also see was the surrounding force raised by our enemy, the Duke of Norfolk. I could make out tents and pavilions, the ant-like scurry of soldiers in clear definition of blue and red livery. There were banners, proclaiming Norfolk power. How could we have any hope of driving off this force? This was a siege that would surely grind us into the ground.

A distant explosion of gunpowder made me stiffen, while my mare tossed her head, but it was not aimed at us. The puff of smoke was from a cannon fired by our attackers at our walls.

'Do you suppose it hit?' I asked, of no one in particular.

'I know not, mistress.' William Pecock muttered. 'But there's a reply.'

Another shot, another cloud of smoke; a different noise, a different gun.

My second son, Jonty, was there, incarcerated within, directing the resistance. It would be impossible for him to hold out without a miracle. He had only twenty-six men to hold the siege at bay. Another crack of an explosion from one of the cannon reached us. I imagined the crash as the castle wall took the brunt of the shot, but could not see.

'I do not know why you are here, mistress. What good can it do? This is no place for a woman to be. This is men's work.'

Neither did I know. There were major issues at home to which I ought to bend my mind. An obstinate daughter and a hostile Bishop were problems permanently camped on my Norwich threshold, as well as a sharp-tongued mother-in-law, but here was a full-blown siege which I could not ignore. William Pecock, my doleful steward, was solicitous in his gloomy fashion, as the warm wind whipped into knots the veil that confined my hair, yet how I wished that the more abrasive but practical Richard Calle was with me. Richard Calle would never ride with me again.

'I am here because I would see for myself what the Duke of Norfolk has dared to do. And there is no need for you to shrug your shoulders in that fashion. You know I would not be able to stay at home.'

'It could be dangerous. You should go home.'

'I will, but not yet. I do not fear for my life.'

'But you should for your freedom, mistress. If you are taken prisoner for a ransom, what would Sir John say?'

'That I am a foolish old woman. But Sir John will not know. My experience tells me I need have no fear of that. Now stop shuffling and look. What do you see?'

I had travelled to Mautby and from there, exchanging a carriage for a mare, I had ridden to what might be called a hill in this flat part of the world, the higher land above the marshes to give me a distant view. The River Bure and marshland prohibited easy travel. With me was Thomas Stumps, William Pecock and three men at arms in case of trouble. It was some months since I had ridden so far and my forty-eight-year-old joints creaked. I would pay for this in aching limbs on the morrow.

'If you will bring your men in Paston livery, I'd say it's asking for trouble, mistress. You should have brought Master Edmund with you.'

I had not managed to silence Master Pecock, who pulled his felt hat down over his ears and shrugged his shoulders once more as if denying any involvement in my decisions. It was a frequent gesture of his but, on this occasion, I would not rise to the irritation.

'I will not sit here looking at my own property in disguise. And Master Edmund has other fish to fry.' Edmund, my third son, as competent as his father had been in law, had completed his education and was seeking some remunerative position in a noble household. Meanwhile, he was making himself useful in mine. Gaining experience of manorial difficulties, I informed him when he groaned at the dullness of it all. 'Now look over there and tell me what you see.'

'And you claim to be a sensible woman, mistress.'

Master Pecock was becoming quite as abrasive as Calle. Yet still he cast his eye over the scene as I had directed.

There we sat, looking out over the disaster that had unfolded with such speed. No, I was not sensible, but for once I allowed emotion to overrule good sense.

'I don't suppose the Duke himself will be here,' I said.

'He will have sent his chief commander,' Master Pecock growled.

'And I wonder who that might be! Anyone we know?'

The morning was brightening again, mist lifting, the view of my castle becoming clearer. I scanned the troops, then turned to Thomas Stumps, who sat his horse, low in the saddle.

'How many men did you tell me, Tom?'

Thomas Stumps had been one of the garrison at Caister. He had been sent by Jonty to warn me of the siege, escaping through the postern gate before Norfolk's troops had taken up their positions. He might lack fingers on both hands from some past disagreement with a sharp sword, and thus be of limited value as a soldier, but his loyalty to the Pastons was without question.

'Three thousand, mistress.'

'Well, I'm not counting every man at this distance, but I doubt it. Three hundred, more like. What do you think, Master Pecock?'

'About that. Still enough to endanger us.'

How true. There was no way in or out. 'You'll not get back in through any postern gate, Tom, so resign yourself to staying with me.'

He surveyed the scene through squinted eyes. 'I might try, mistress.'

'And lose more than your fingers? I forbid it.'

'One less to fight against the enemy, if I cannot get back in,' he grunted.

'And you have more fingers left to you than wit,' Master Pecock said in disgust that he should even try, given the circumstances.

I did not wish to hurt Tom Stumps's feelings, that without fingers his efforts would be marginal. Besides, my interest was elsewhere. Somewhere within those walls was Jonty. I doubted that he would see me and my entourage, distant figures merging with the fen. He would be concentrating on those closest to his gate, from where there sounded another distant explosion of gunpowder. I could imagine shards of shattered stone flying in all directions. How many hits would it take to breach the wall with a hole large enough for the enemy to enter? How long could they hold out until hunger and thirst weakened them and drove them to surrender? How many men would die because the Pastons wished to keep Caister Castle? If I allowed such thoughts to surface, I would weep, and what would be the value of that? I thrust all such emotions deep within me and turned to my steward.

'I remember, Master Pecock, that we have a number of guns stored in the cellars,' I said, hiding my anxieties with more poise than I had thought possible given the churning in my belly. I had seen about twenty of various types and usefulness. Some were so old that they looked as if they would explode on use.

'The Duke will probably be sending for more.' Pecock was particularly lugubrious. 'Sir John is in London trying to arrange legal action to stop the siege.'

'What good is that?' I snapped, knowing full well where Sir John was. 'What good is a legal case when cannon are being fired at our walls? They could be flattened before our plea for a legal judgement even comes before a justice, much less the King, wherever he is at the moment. Whichever King it is that now wears the crown.'

Two most reliable men of our household, John Pamping and John Daubeney, were in there with Jonty. My worries increased as another cannon shot was fired.

'I should be there,' Tom Stumps continued. 'I could fire a crossbow.'

'You're better off out of it.'

'Sir John sent four professional crossbow men to us,' he added.

'Much good that will do.'

'They're clever enough, but too keen on getting cup-shotten.' Tom grinned, showing a wreck of teeth.

'Then let us hope, for all our sakes, that Master Paston keeps the ale under lock and key.'

'They have been practising, I'll say that for them. They've broke three or four crossbows already.'

I could think of nothing to say. At that rate they would have no weapons to use. The cannon fire continued but the troops remained stationary. There was no attack planned to scale the walls this morning.

'He won't want to batter us into submission if he wants to own it himself,' I suggested. 'Why would the Duke destroy what he most wants to possess?' It was all I could cling to.

'Stopping food and supplies will be his best plan to starve us out,' Pecock agreed. 'The Duke will then offer terms. I hope they will be acceptable to Master Paston and Sir John. We might all come out of it alive.'

'I doubt it,' I said, knowing Jonty's dislike of having to back down, although Sir John might be more amenable to negotiation, simply to draw it all to an end. Despair was not far away as more cannon fire echoed across the fen. I knew what the terms would be. Give up the castle in return for peace and freedom. Would even Sir John be willing to give it up entirely? I thought not. I might as well return to Mautby now that I had assessed the worst that the Duke of Norfolk could do.

'You've been seen, mistress.' Thomas Stumps gestured with a

maimed hand over to our left where a small group of horsemen had begun to ride in our direction. Of course they had seen us. Did I think I would escape from this unscathed? Did I even wish to? I had come here to make a Paston presence, and make one I would. I had been doing it all my life.

'I think you should retreat, mistress,' Master Pecock advised, careful as ever. 'It's too dangerous to stay.'

But Master Pecock did not know that I had been carried bodily, shrieking and kicking, from my rented house in my usurped manor at Gresham, back in the days of my youth, when a villain named Lord Moleyns had decided to drive me out and take it for his own. I had made a scene. It came into my mind that I would make one again.

'What will they do? Take me prisoner?'

Pecock leaned to grab my rein, but I pulled away. 'Shake out the banner, Tom.'

Tom Stumps did as he was bid, holding the staff firmly between arm and body, so that it was clear to all that this was the gold and blue of a Paston surveillance. The little group of horsemen in Mowbray livery approached steadily, while we sat unmoving. They pulled to a halt before us, eyeing the banner. The Captain knew who I was, as I knew him. He was often seen in Norwich about his master's bidding.

'Go home, Mistress Paston.'

'That is my home.' I pointed towards Caister. 'That is my castle and you are attacking it and preventing my entry. You have no right to do so. Your lord has no legal claim against it. Take me to your Commander.'

The Captain inhaled visibly. He had not expected me to resist; he had not expected a challenge. He thought that I would ride off towards Mautby without a word, intimidated by the whole situation.

'You had best come with me, then, mistress,' he replied, and ushered us to ride in front of him and his escort. 'And I don't advise you to do anything foolish.'

'I have no intention of doing anything foolish.'

I rode straight-backed before him, assessing the weight of

soldiery, the effect of cannon fire on my walls. It was a tidy camp, well organised with good discipline. I could as yet see no holes in the walls, only abrasions where the cannon fire had hit its target. The Paston banner flew bravely from the keep. Mine, still clutched by Tom Stumps, answered. I wondered if Jonty was aware of what I was doing. If he was, he would curse me for my utter stupidity. I did not think that I was in any way worthy of such criticism.

The Commander was waiting outside his tent, tall and rangy, as thin as a heron, but just as watchful when a fish swam past; his hands were fisted on hips in what I thought was a typical attitude. I eyed him with some displeasure, and with lowering spirits, for this was a man whom I would never have called enemy. It drove home a blade in my heart that trust was in such short supply in these days of insurrection and warfare, but I would not allow it to weaken my resolve, or my response.

'I did not expect to see you here, sir.'

'Nor I you, Mistress Paston. You have decided to live dangerously, it seems.'

'I have decided to live honestly, sir. Which is more than you and your men are doing.'

With a laugh he swept me a clanking bow, in no way hindered by the plates of armour on shoulder and breast; he helped me to dismount, kissed my cheek, and indicated that I should sit. Stools had been brought out for me and for Master Pecock, although the Paston colours had been taken from Tom Stumps and placed out of sight. A servant appeared with cups of ale. I took one and sipped.

'Have you become the enemy?' I asked.

It was Sir John Heveningham, an old family friend, or so I had thought; his father had been a close associate of Sir John Fastolf, whose inheritance had brought us into all this trouble.

'I am no enemy of yours personally, Mistress Paston.' He was still smiling.

'Then what are you doing here? It seems that I can trust no one these days.'

'You can trust me enough not to do you any harm, mistress. The Duke of Norfolk has made me Commander in his siege of Caister while he goes off about other business.'

'I suppose it is worth your while financially.'

'Indeed it is. And to be recognised by the Duke, who is close to the King.' His smile had at last faded. 'You should go home, mistress.'

'So everyone keeps telling me. I would argue that *that* is my home!' I waved a hand towards the castle walls. 'You do not, then, intend to keep me prisoner.'

'No, as you very well know. Our war is not with you. Nor is a siege camp somewhere we would contain you.' His smile this time was a bold show of teeth. 'We simply want your castle.'

'And we intend to keep it.'

'Look around you, Mistress Paston.'

And I did. My heart fell even further than it had already. It might be only three hundred men but their demeanour and equipment made it clear to me that victory for Jonty would be impossible.

'There is no point in my arguing against the legality of your being here.'

'None at all, mistress. I am ordered here by his grace of Norfolk and here I will stay until he tells me to do otherwise. I do not consider legalities, merely the desires of my lord the Duke.'

Of course this had been a fruitless venture, serving only to polish my self-esteem.

'Will you offer terms?' I asked.

'Yes.'

'When?'

'When his grace tells me to do so. We will both – I and Master Paston, who hopes to repel us – wait on the Duke's good will, or otherwise. Now I suggest that if you have finished your ale, you go home to Mautby, an easy ride for you.'

There was nothing I could say or do in the face of such determined good humour.

'We will escort you onto the road to Mautby.' He grinned. 'Or I could leave you here at the gate and you could join your son in the siege. We would grant you free passage either way, of course.'

I shook my head as I put down the cup and pulled on my gloves. 'We both know that it would not be a good plan. To be within the walls would clip my wings. If I remain outside, I can work to defeat you.'

There was an unfortunate twinkle in his eye. 'Perhaps, then, I should insist on them opening the gate and pushing you in.'

'You are presuming that my son would want me.'

'If I were your son, I think I would not wish you to be looking constantly over my shoulder and issuing orders. But perhaps Master Paston has a stronger stomach than I have for female interference.'

In spite of everything, we smiled at each other. It was always good to deal with a man of honour, and he had been a friend of long standing. No, it was not his war. He was a soldier who would carry out instructions. He escorted me through the camp where his men were banking down the fires for the day after breaking their fast. The detritus of food was cleared away. Yes, it was a well-ordered camp.

He helped me into the saddle.

'Good day, Mistress Paston.' Even the Paston banner was restored to Tom Stumps's inexpert grip. 'Travel safely. You are in no danger from my men.'

I nodded in acknowledgement. 'I regret that war and greed make enemies of friends,' I remarked. 'But if I find any traces of my swans' feathers in your camp, I will go to the King. They are not for your eating.'

'Feel free to do so, mistress. When you have decided to which King you should appeal. I hear tell that roast swan makes an excellent dish.' And then he looked up at me in all seriousness. 'Hear me, Captainess. If your sons agree to let the Duke take Caister, he will be generous, I believe, and recompense you for all the wrongs against you. It would be worth considering. If you will not, then I fear that you will lose all.'

Which just about summed it all up. We were helpless – the Pastons and my swans.

I had never believed that this could happen. None of us had. Our ownership of Caister Castle was a mark of arrival into the ranks of the gentry. The Pastons might have once been mere peasantry, even if John had denied it, but a castle put a seal on our acceptability. We would never willingly give it up.

My final words, with a lift of my chin, because it was all too painful to consider the repercussions if we lost Caister, were defiant: 'Don't you dare to offer my swans to your cook. If you do, I will set Master Pecock here on to him with his gelding knife!'

It was worth the casual vulgarity just to watch them both flinch.

What to do? Sir John was still in London seeking a legal victory to force Norfolk's compliance, which I was beginning to consider a hopeless case. Jonty was sitting tight at Caister. I worried in Norwich. With no coming and going allowed from Caister, and no communication from the Duke of Norfolk, it was like stitching a tapestry in the pitch-dark. We were all working blindly.

Until news was brought to me one morning in the second week of the siege by Sir John Heveningham himself, clad in a soft tunic and felt cap with a conspicuous jewel on the brim, rather than the metal plates of our last crossing of paths. I met him in my Hall, offering refreshment, but he was in a hurry. For a long moment I thought that Caister had fallen.

'Why are you not at Caister?'

'I'm travelling with the Duke of Norfolk. There are other captains in control of the siege.' He must have read the fear in my face. 'Your son is still safe behind his walls. But it may be of interest to you that the Duke is here in Norwich, Mistress Paston. In his town house.'

The fear fled, my attention immediately arrested. 'Is he now? How long does he stay?'

'I know not.'

'Then there is no time to be lost. Will he offer terms?'

'I think that he will be willing. The problem will be, do you accept them?'

'We won't know until we see the details.'

I was already calling for my cloak and hood, sending my maid scurrying.

'Do you go without an invitation, mistress?'

'I most certainly do. I may not receive one.' I was already halfway up the staircase. 'I'll not chance it. And you can escort me.'

I turned to my maid, who handed over my outer garments. 'Tell Margery...'

I shook my head, my mouth closing on my command.

Tell Margery to make ready and she will accompany me.

But Margery no longer lived here. Margery would never be my daughter again to learn the ways of the Pastons. Would I ever grow used to her loss? There was a space in my mind and my heart that she should have occupied. How had I allowed her estrangement to go this far? Duty and love were uncomfortable bed-fellows and I had not dealt with it well.

Pushing aside my inner torment, and my guilt, I was on the ducal doorstep within the half-hour, Sir John Heveningham beside me, demanding admittance. I shook out my skirts. Perhaps I should have taken more care with my appearance and donned my finest velvet gown, but I doubted that the Duke of Norfolk would even notice if I wore rags.

CHAPTER TWELVE

MARGARET MAUTBY PASTON

The Town House of the Duke of Norfolk in Norwich,
late August 1469

Although the Norfolk town house was a fine dwelling, as fine as any in Norwich, I was determined not to be impressed. I was here for a matter of business, not to be cushioned in luxury, wrapped in Italianate hangings or soothed into compliance by the light glinting red and blue through stained glass high in the windows. I was ushered into a room where there were books and writing implements, more tapestries on every wall and a popinjay on a perch beside the window. And the Duke himself. I had thought, while I waited, that he would fob me off with his bailiff, but he had more courtesy than that, I was forced to admit. I recognised him but, unlike Jonty, I could claim no real acquaintance.

He was a young man of some twenty-five years who had succeeded his father in title and power eight years before. Becoming hereditary Earl Marshal had given him a superior air, but he was not unfriendly when I was announced. The Duke rose from his chair, carefully placing his pen, and bowed. I curtsied. We might be enemies on this occasion but who knew where fate might lead us? This young man had been Jonty's patron. He might well become so again if things fell out at the royal Court. And might there not be some lasting loyalty between this young magnate and my second son? If we could ignore the fact that, young as he was, he had been raised in a spirit of greedy acquisitiveness. It would be difficult to have faith in any promise he uttered, particularly when he saw Paston manors as his for the picking in these troubled times.

'Mistress Paston.'

'My lord.'

'We will not pretend that we do not know the reason for your visit here.'

His voice was light and youthful, completely assured, although perhaps not one for shouting commands on a battlefield, but then he did not need to, with capable captains in his employ. And what a comely young man he was when he smiled, but I would not be won over. Nor would I admire his fashionable dark velvet doublet, its long sleeves brushing against his thighs. His carefully curled hair, longer than any man of my household might wear, proclaimed that he had an overweening love of appearance, but I would not allow my disdain of such extravagance to colour my visit here. I had one purpose, and one only.

'We will not so pretend, my lord. The future of Caister Castle must be settled.'

He regarded me, chin tilted, before speaking. 'I could simply wait until the siege runs its course and your son and his garrison are starved out so that they must stagger from the gate or die of lack of sustenance. Thus a fait accompli. And all to my benefit.'

There was no arguing against it.

'How long will that take?' I asked as if discussing the weaving of a length of cloth.

'Not long. I have knowledge that there is no means by which your men might acquire supplies. Hunger will drive them to open their gates to me.'

'You are sure of your success, my lord.'

I was fast marshalling my arguments. I had not expected him to be so direct. I should have known, of course. The Dukes of Norfolk had never been slow in proclaiming their pre-eminence above us lesser folk.

'We both know that I will win, Mistress Paston. Do you wish to risk the deaths of those who hold the castle in the Paston name? Either from starvation or injury, when finally I give the order to take the castle by force. Your walls will not last for ever.'

It was a chilling query. My reply was equally direct.

'Of course not. Nor do I believe that you will batter down the walls of a castle that you covet. What would be the sense in that?'

'Do you offer surrender?'

'Never.'

He smiled. 'So you wish for terms.'

'I wish to discuss terms with you. There is a difference.'

It would all depend on what he was prepared to offer. Unfortunately, he was in a position of power, I in a slough of weakness.

'Do you speak for your sons, mistress?'

'Yes.' There would be no weakness for him to attack in that quarter.

'But will you accept the only terms I am prepared to offer?'

It was like negotiating with a crafty civet cat, elusive but much sought after for its musky tones to enhance perfumery. Would that Jonty had learned this skill.

'I might, if I know what they are. I know not how much it costs to operate a siege, my lord, not being in the business of warfare. If the siege continues, it will cost you heavily to keep your forces in military array. I agree that you hold the whip-hand, but would it not be in your interest also to bring this debacle to a halt?'

'It might.' He tilted his chin again, as if he had discovered an adversary worthy of his time and interest. He held my gaze. And then: 'Sit, Mistress Paston, and I will make all clear for you.'

I did so. So did he, pen once more in hand. He began writing. I waited, the scratch of the pen a continuous background, occasionally accompanied by soft noises from the popinjay as it pulled its quills through its beak. All I could think was that the Paston King was under threat from all sides in this Norfolk chess game; I doubted that we could ever prevent the Duke from declaring checkmate. At that moment I felt a surge of hatred for the supremely self-possessed Duke of Norfolk who was young enough to be my son. I would like to have taken him by his elegantly clad shoulders and shaken some generosity into him.

And then he spoke: 'Here is my offer. Do I read it to you?'

'I can read it for myself.'

'Forgive me. I did not mean to imply that you could not. I should know that Mistress Paston is well able to deal with all matters of business herself. And yet I will. This is my offer.'

He read it out in a gentle voice, as if it were a much-desired gift. If we allowed the Duke to occupy the castle without any further opposition or bloodshed, the Duke was prepared to recompense us for all wrongs done to our men and equipment. Much as Sir John Heveningham had suggested. It was not what I wanted, but if we would lose the castle anyway, better to surrender with some hope of remuneration.

But the Duke had not finished. He read on, making it more than clear that remuneration would only be paid if the courts found in our favour, that Caister was legally ours, thus he would in effect right a wrong. If Sir John's legal battle failed and the courts rejected the legality of our claim, the Duke would pay us not one groat.

I sat, silent and resentful, determined not to show it. How dare he think that we should be so taken in. If the courts found in our favour, then the castle should have remained ours. But how would the courts do that, with the Duke of Norfolk and his liveried retinue breathing down their collective necks? There was no place for negotiation here. There was no deal to be made. I stood, while the Duke applied his seal and handed the document over.

'Thank you, my lord. I will give this offer to my son, Sir John Paston.'

Sir John would not agree. We would be handing over our castle with no recompense at all. I must send it hotfoot to London. Jonty would have to remain in ignorance of our present failure to release him and our men.

Sir John Heveningham, lurking by the door as I departed, raised his brows so that they all but disappeared beneath the brim of his felt cap.

I shook my head. There was nothing to say.

My brother-in-law William Paston was forced to listen to my complaint since my two elder sons were not available. We sat at ease together in the little garden to the rear of the Norwich house, comfortable in our years of long acquaintance despite my suspicions that William would snatch up a handful of Paston acres for himself as soon as my back was turned. I poured ale, enjoying the scents of the herbs in the hot sun, but here was no time to share gossip of family or past reminiscences. Instead, I launched into my tirade against our adversaries.

'We are in jeopardy, William. All I hear is desperate news from Caister. We lack food. Two of our men are dead, so I hear by some rumour-monger, but who they might be I know not. The Duke of Norfolk is collecting more men and armaments to make a great assault. We cannot withstand such an attack. Perhaps his intention is merely to frighten us into surrender.'

William thought about this, rubbing his forefinger along the length of his nose as John used to do, giving me a sharp memory of my husband. William had become stout with age and good living although his thickening waist was masked by the swathing of a long gown in green and black damask, his thinning black hair disguised beneath a matching velvet chaperon. William had always had an eye to his appearance, but his judgement was solemnly given. He had clearly given the problem much thought.

'But would his arrogant lordship risk wholesale damage to a fortress that he wanted for himself?'

'No. And so I told him. Better to starve them out and threaten their lives if they do not surrender fast. It's what I would do.'

William thought again. 'You have to decide, Margaret. Which do you value most? The lives of your men, or the castle itself? It is a hard choice but it has to be made. How valuable is the castle to you?'

I scowled at him, even though he had come to the same conclusion as I had reached on the previous day. It did not help to have the bad news confirmed. In the end I sighed and nodded.

'I am not so hard-hearted, William. I know that we will have to give it up. But we need a safe conduct.'

'And who will give it? Where is the King? Who is the King? It seems to me that Norfolk is free to do just as he likes.'

'You are no help to me, William!'

'At least I am realistic! What does Sir John say? If that is of any value to anything?'

William did not always have a high opinion of my son. The old dispute over the will of William's father, Sir John's grandfather, continued to rankle between the two of them, since William was always keen to claim that he had not been given his fair share of the Paston inheritance, all of it passing to my husband John, the heir.

William went on his way – surprisingly, to visit his mother who had returned to Oxnead, which should have alerted my suspicions, if I had given them more than a second thought, but I had no time to dwell on them, while I wrote again to Sir John, listing all the problems I had heaped on William's shoulders, as well as giving some advice.

I have heard nothing from you.

I advise you to appeal to the King Edward's brother, the Duke of Clarence, since he seems to have the power in the realm. Also you might appeal to his Neville uncle, the Archbishop of York. Anyone who will listen, in fact. Our garrison at Caister is in severe trouble. We cannot hold out.

Have you yet been in communication with the Duke of Norfolk?

And then, because I thought that I must, or Sir John would be liable to raise money in the easiest way:

I advise you not to sell or mortgage any Paston estates. It will only weaken us further. Although in truth, I would rather we lost a good manor than have more lives on our conscience.

Written in haste.

M. PASTON

'You have a reply from Sir John, mistress,' Pecock announced.

At least my waspish letter had achieved its desired effect. Not that I enjoyed its content, since it was disheartening and highly critical of me, saying in effect that I did not know what was happening in Caister or in London, so that it would be good if I stopped meddling and kept my tongue between my teeth. He would deal with any problem that emerged. It was a shame that I had seen the need to present myself, without invitation, on the Duke of Norfolk's doorstep.

I tapped the letter against my palm, recalling the days when husband John had written to me in ire. It seemed that Sir John was under pressure and not enjoying it.

I read on to the paragraph where his reply became specific and biting:

Our men are not dead. No one has been killed at Caister, whatever rumour, or Jonty, says. I cannot appeal to Clarence or the Archbishop since neither is in London. Nor will I think it to be any use. Rescuing our garrison will cost money. All I need is to raise a goodly sum and pay for more troops. I have written to the King with the hope of assistance.

Well, there was no hope there. The King was not in control of his own life, much less ours, since to my knowledge he was still incarcerated under Warwick's dominion in Middleham Castle. I read on.

I will always do my duty to my name and those dependent on me. I did not need you to write such a heavy letter to stir me to action.

It gave me pause for thought. I should perhaps regret my taking him to task. No full-grown son, and a knight at that, would appreciate criticism from his mother, even if we were in a cleft stick of Norfolk's making. I might have been stirred to compassion, except that he finished with:

I beseech you, send me money for, by my troth, I have but ten shillings. I know nowhere to get more.

My compassion evaporated.

Nor in truth did I know where I might find the money that he needed.

★

The days passed in summer heat. The situation at Caister grew no better. Sir John did not come to Norfolk and continued to be the usual bad correspondent, no doubt smarting from my pen. The Duke of Norfolk continued to refuse to negotiate further. He would have the castle one way or the other. Clarence and Archbishop Neville, according to William, were still trying to govern the country in the name of the King, who remained imprisoned under Warwick's authority. Jonty and his brave men continued to starve in Caister Castle.

By now I was at my wits' end so that my household avoided me when at all possible. No one could tell me of the state of Caister or of how Jonty fared. How would Sir John in London know who had lived or died? It was a worrying time.

Fear was my constant companion.

But when I fell asleep, it was not Caister that troubled me. It was Margery who haunted my dreams. Whether I wished it or not, the fate of the Paston family was in my hands. Had I done wrong by her, to bar her from her home, when I should have been forgiving? How could a mother condemn a beloved child to face her future alone? It was done and I feared that it could not be undone.

CHAPTER THIRTEEN

ELIZABETH PASTON POYNINGS

The Poynings House in Southwark, August 1469

I must mend the distance that had grown between Margaret and myself, by letter if not in person. And at the end of a long family rambling, I came to the crux of the matter:

> *I need a husband, Meg. A man who will fight for my legal rights.*
> *I need advice.*

Margaret's reply was fast and bleak, as if she had dictated it to her clerk between one emergency and the next – which, apparently, she had, although the signature was recognisably her own.

> *I have no time to consider your marital adventures, Eliza. I have*
> *enough troubles in my basket with Caister, a daughter who has*
> *wed against my wishes and another who is challenging every*
> *aspect of family duty that I have instilled in her. Not that I am*
> *unsympathetic to your needs. Go to your brother William. He is*
> *your best hope of resolution. Why did you not think of him?*
> *You have my compassion in your fight for your son's inheritance.*
> *Of course you do. I will pray for you. Go to William and stir him*
> *up on your behalf. It is time he did something useful for the family.*

My brother William Paston.

Why had I not thought of him before? He was a man of sufficient reputation and importance at Court to help me fight off my enemies, a man who had excellent standing since his marriage to Lady Anne Beaufort, despite the unfortunate treason of her family when the Beauforts had fought for Lancaster. With a good name in the legal fraternity and at Court, William would give better advice than most of my family. Living as I was in the Poynings house in Southwark, it would be no great distance to Warwick Inn across the river where William had taken up residence.

I dressed with an unusual exhibition of wealth, my bodice and skirts enhanced with fur and rich embroidery, all protected by the fall of a damask cloak lined with silk, to impress a man who had risen so high, and not least his high-blooded wife. Ordering a small escort, I set off with some hope now that I was actually taking action to determine my future. Surely William would know a man who could converse sensibly, fight doggedly, and not see marriage to a no-longer-youthful widow of almost forty years as a detriment to his political career.

The streets on the south bank of the Thames were still quiet as it was early in the morning when I made my way to take a small wherry across the river.

And then not so quiet.

Barely half a mile from my gate we were surrounded by a group of well-horsed men without livery or insignia. My heart began to beat faster. Here was no gutter riffraff who would rob an honest woman of her possessions. They had no intention of robbery. This was an abduction, for when I tried to push through, the new escort tightened its closeness around us. My own men began to draw their weapons, which prompted an instant reaction. Around me a scuffle broke out, weapons brandished, the early morning sun glinting along the length of swords wielded with intent. Before fear could grip me, I drew the dagger that I kept in my sleeve when travelling in these days of unrest.

Even as any clear thought was blanketed in this immediate fight for my freedom, I knew who to blame. This was the work of the Dowager Countess of Northumberland, niece of my late husband. She might have lost her Percy lord at the Battle of Towton, but she was not deterred, still intent on pursuing what she saw as her claim on the Poynings lands. She would abduct me and hold me to ransom until she got her hands on all the Poynings estates, with or without legality.

An unexpected blast of fury erupted within me. She would not take me prisoner. I would not go quietly. I owed that to my son. I would not give up my house in Southwark or my Poynings acres. I saw the Percy plan. To drive me out through fear of physical violence. Or to hold me until I signed over the documents of possession. Powerful lords took their ambitions into their own hands. I had not seen Eleanor since, newly widowed and grief-stricken, and with shattering boldness, I had forbidden her the right to enter my house. Margaret would certainly resist, and so would I. I would not go easily into captivity.

My escort was no match for our attackers, one of whom grabbed my bridle to drag me away, who knew where? I lunged with my knife, slicing through the skin of his hand, but, with oaths, he held on even tighter. My mare resisted, twisted to escape, reared, and I, not the best of horsewomen, fell off into the dust.

I crouched, covered my head, fearful of the worst either from the milling hooves or the men sent to waylay me. The short hennin covering my hair rolled in the dust beside me, the veil detached from its wires, my hair loosed from its careful plaiting. The knife was still in my hand, but I feared for my escort; I feared for myself. All I could think of was the relief that I had not brought my young son Edward with me. I was too winded to cry out.

The voices around me changed. More horsemen were there with shouts and running, the clatter of hooves, while I remained with my arms covering my head until a hand took my arm and lifted me to a sitting position, even when I resisted. A man was kneeling by my side.

I raised the knife, planning to use it if I had to.

'Careful, mistress. It would not look well for you to stab your rescuer.'

'How do I know that you are not my enemy?'

'You don't, of course. But I swear that I am not. Are you hurt?'

I considered the question, making a mental tally of my limbs. 'No, only to my pride.' My breathing was returning to normality.

I looked around. My attackers seemed to have vanished, replaced by a smart entourage in bright livery.

Was this a trick?

'They have gone,' my rescuer assured me. 'Not the common thieves you might expect hereabouts. Did you recognise them?'

'I did not. They had no intention of being recognised, and I was more intent on keeping my life intact.' I looked around again. 'Are my servants safe?'

'A few cuts and bruises and a broken arm, I think. Perhaps you would care to give me that dagger, which might be a danger to both of us.'

A striking face with eyes that were neither grey nor green but could take on either hue in the light. His hair curling beneath a smart low-crowned affair of beaver fur was the rich gleam of polished mahogany.

He smiled, but not without compassion for my dishevelled plight.

'Can you stand? I must restore you home to your husband. He might be anxious for your safety. But what he is doing letting you ride alone in the streets, I know not. Your escort was not satisfactory, neither in number nor in skill.'

He lifted me, brushed the dust from my skirts, and offered me a square of linen to wipe my face. My cloak, stained with the detritus of the gutter, was beyond re-wearing, as was the hennin. I sighed at the sad sight of them.

'You may restore me home with pleasure, sir, but I have no husband waiting there to welcome me.'

'That accounts for it. Come, then. Do you live close by? Can you ride? I have an old shoulder wound that would prevent me from carrying you. I could try, of course, as would any chivalrous man, but I might drop you in the dust again.'

Which made me laugh a little. 'There will be no such necessity, but thank you. I will not risk a second ignominy so early in the morning. I am no longer fit to be seen, so home is my only choice.'

After a word with one of his men, he acquired a stalwart cloak, wrapped it around me and drew the hood over my hair so that my dishevelment should attract no interest from passers-by who were beginning to fill the streets on their way to market. Despite the old wound, he lifted me with ease back onto my mare, which had been recovered, and escorted me home. I had stopped trembling by the time we had turned into my courtyard, where my steward Perching emerged to help me down and steady me as he guided me solicitously through the door into the shadowy hall.

'I said that you should not go with so few men to escort you, mistress.'

'So you did. And you were right, and so may feel virtuous.' I squeezed his arm in acknowledgement. 'This gentleman rescued us.' I looked up at him where he still sat at ease on his horse. 'Will you come in, sir? The least I can offer you is a cup of ale.'

'And I'll gladly take it. You should take care that your mistress does not ride out into danger. If I had not happened upon them, she might not be here to tell the tale.'

'It was not my steward's fault.'

'But you seem to have important enemies, mistress.'

'Yes. I believe I have. And more determined than I had realised. If you will enter, I will tell you. You deserve an explanation for your troubles.' It was the least I could do since he had put his own security at risk. I smiled reassuringly at my steward that all was now well. 'Show this gentleman into the front chamber, if you please, and bring ale.' And then to my rescuer. 'I will return immediately.'

My hands and face washed, hair once more neat under a plain linen coif, I made the acquaintance of my rescuer who was sitting, cup in hand, in conversation with my young son. A large man of solid proportions, he looked quite unperturbed after his morning's adventure as he immediately rose to his feet. I did not feel the same.

'I do not even know your name, sir.'

'George Browne, of various estates in Surrey that I am unable to claim as my own.' He bowed, hand on heart. An interesting reply that caught my notice.

'It was my fortune that you were present.'

'And you, mistress?'

'Dame Elizabeth Poynings, sir. Widow of Sir Robert Poynings. Killed for York at St Albans. I too have difficulties with my estates. The Poynings estates, that is.'

So now he knew my political connections. If he was for Lancaster, then he could make his exit hastily. He did not. There was no coolness in his reply.

'So many good men lost in the maelstrom. My father, Sir Thomas Browne, was executed for treason after the battle of Northampton.'

A Yorkist victory. So his father had indeed fought for Lancaster. I expected him to tell me more, but he did not. There was time for me to discover, if I decided that I wished to know more of my rescuer.

'And this is my son, Edward Poynings,' I said, as courtesy demanded, drawing my son to my side. 'I hope that he has not wearied you. He has the ability to chatter like a jackdaw.'

'Not at all. We have been discussing the merits of horsemanship. Your son was disappointed that his mother should fall off her mare into the gutter.'

'So was I.'

'I have told him that the fault was that of the mare who became distressed with a sword waved in her face.'

'Thank you. That is some sop to my dignity. It was not a pleasant experience, and I fear that some of the fault was mine.' I propelled Edward towards the door with a hand on his back. 'Now go and tell Perching to bring a platter of sweetmeats, if you will.'

'May I return with him?' Edward's eyes were alight with interest at this confident visitor.

I nodded, then on his departure, I posed another question to my rescuer in the light of his previous reply.

'Were your estates attainted? You were clearly pardoned, if your father fought for Lancaster. You said that you had a wound. Was it in a battle?'

'Yes, my estates were attainted, and remain an issue through a family complication. I was wounded in a skirmish to reclaim one of the most important of my estates in West Betchworth. I am happy to say that I am now back to full agility, but I did not recover the manor. I was regarded as a trespasser so there was not much sympathy for my cause.' He circled his shoulder where a wound obviously still pained him, whatever his claims.

'And do you still lean towards Lancaster?'

He frowned a little. 'I think that my present loyalties are towards York.' And that was that. Clearly George Browne had no desire to expand on his choice of York over Lancaster. It seemed that he would be as reticent as had been Sir Robert. Perhaps all men were so. Except the Pastons, who were outspoken to a man.

'You must miss your husband,' he observed.

'I do miss him.'

'At least you have a son to inherit.'

Yes. But, as you see, he is still very young. Far too young to take up the sword. I regret that St Albans robbed him of his father before he barely knew him. Do you have sons?'

'I am as yet unwed. Which is perhaps fortunate given my present landless circumstances.'

By this time we had taken seats, Perching had brought more ale and sweetmeats, Edward had returned, and George Browne poured me a cup even though I was the hostess. His assurance was a pleasing quality to watch.

'Your estates seem to be in dire trouble, sir.'

He laughed softly without humour, a frown marring his attractive features.

'They are in the hands of my stepfather, Sir Thomas Vaughan. He wed my mother when she was left a widow, and laid claim to the Browne estates. He has no legal right to them but is determined to keep them out of my hands. Unfortunately, he has the ear of the Yorkist King Edward. It is not an enviable situation.' And then: 'Enough of my problems.' His frown was quickly smoothed over. 'Tell me who attacked you, mistress. Did you recognise them?'

'I did not. They were carefully devoid of livery, as you will have noticed. But I know who it was.'

I cast a glance at Edward, but he was occupied, having picked up my dagger, which he was busy polishing on his sleeve. A young hound, a new addition to the household, curled at his feet.

'A personage of influence.'

I gave a brief explanation of my problems with gavelkind and those of Percy allegiance.

'All I can do is hold on to what we have until my son is old enough to fight for his inheritance. And take care to engage a larger escort next time I travel into the city.' I looked at the ravages to my gown, regretting the damage to my costly formality. 'Next time I visit William Paston, I will go prepared.'

'Paston?' His ears almost pricked as those of Edward's hound might.

'William Paston is my brother. I am a Paston by birth.'

'I know of them. I am acquainted with Sir John Paston. And his brother...'

'They are my nephews. I regret to say that I do not keep closely in touch with them.'

'Could they not help you in your struggle for legal justice?'

'They could, of course, but their time and efforts are taken up elsewhere. Pastons are, if nothing else, self-centred.'

If I had intended to quench my bitterness, I had failed. There was nothing more to be said, beyond my repeated thanks for my rescue.

Yet as he was leaving, George Browne asked: 'May I call to-morrow, to see that you suffered no hurt?'

'But I have not, as you see.'

There was a decided twinkle in his eye. 'It would be gracious to accept the concern of your rescuer.'

It might have been a criticism of my lack of grace, but I knew instinctively that it was not. I flushed, discovering that I wished it above all things.

'Then it will be my pleasure.'

Thus it was that I met George Browne, a man with whom I would be happy to further an acquaintance. I had almost fallen into his arms, and he had proved not averse to picking me up. His problems with his estates were almost worse than mine. I suspected that he might be a man whose company I might enjoy, as I discovered on his second visit, when he proved to be vivacious, loquacious, a man of great charm. In the coming weeks, George Browne became a frequent visitor, with or without an excuse that he happened to be riding past my gate. I began to look forward to his appearance with far too much pleasure. I enjoyed the easy discourse, the light flattery.

Until the day when he informed me that he must needs travel into Sussex where his stepfather, Sir Thomas Vaughan, had issued an enfeoffment whereby the whole of the Browne property would be tipped into his hands, thus leaving George permanently landless with no hope of redress.

It was difficult to know what to say. Compassion would bring him no remedy. All I could do as he took my hand was to wish him farewell, hoping to hear better news. He saluted my fingers with great aplomb.

'Come and tell me of the outcome of your visit when you return.'

'Indeed, you will be the first to know.'

'God speed, sir.'

He tilted his chin, considering a reply.

'Would you consider marriage, Dame Elizabeth?'

'I would consider it, sir.'

'I do not mean in a generality.'

I could not help but smile. 'Are you proposing marriage to me?'

'Yes, I am.'

'Why on earth would you wish to wed me?' I was astonished. And not a little pleased. But there was an issue that I must clarify. 'I am some years older than you are, sir.'

'Does that matter, Dame Elizabeth?'

'It may do so to you.'

'Then I assure you that it does not. Would you consider marriage to a youthful supplicant such as myself?'

'Why would you wish to wed me?' I repeated. Would he not desire a younger bride?

'I like you,' he said.

Which made me laugh. 'It would double your problems, sir.'

'And treble my pleasures. Marriages have been made on worse propositions.'

How honeyed his words, but could I trust them?

'I think you should reconsider,' I suggested, reluctantly.

He was silent, for the blink of an eye. 'There, I have reconsid-ered. Do wed me, Dame Elizabeth.'

Well, why not? 'I might, if you would agree to call me Eliza.'

His lips on mine were even more persuasive.

In what seemed an astonishingly short time, in a fashion that my legalistic Paston family would have found horrifying, although all agreements and contracts were duly signed and witnessed by a relieved John Dane, George Browne and I were wed.

I had forgotten that such happiness existed.

CHAPTER FOURTEEN

MARGERY PASTON

The Best Household in Norwich, September 1469

It was a time of strange placidity, I with my new household, Richard in London. It was a time of loneliness, too. We had lost so much: Richard, his livelihood and I, my family. It was also a time of self-seeking, of searching my conscience. Had I made a terrible mistake? If so, I had done much harm to both Richard and myself. I begged forgiveness on my knees for my waywardness, my disobedience to those put in authority over me, as the Bishop said that I should. I truly regretted my sins. But I could not regret the place that Richard Calle had created in my heart. I hoped that the Blessed Virgin would understand and have mercy.

Meanwhile, the Bishop continued, I supposed, with his own enquiries, although he found no need to speak with me again. Equally, my mother and grandmother found no opportunity to visit me and I had not the courage to stand again on the threshold of the Paston House, only to be turned away by Father Gloys.

Nor did I receive any communication from Richard. The Bishop had ordained that we remain apart. There would be no case to be found against our honesty, but who knew what the Bishop might consider to be useful to deny our vows.

I grew into a harsh maturity in those days. I was no longer the same young woman who had acted so imprudently as to defy her family in the name of love. In the Best household I was all prudence, cautious in my conversations, living on charity, clad severely in the few shifts and gowns, as well as a pair of shoes, sent on to me in compassion by some kindly soul from the Paston house.

There were some days when, in the depths of that despair, I sat with Mistress Best. They were good people, kindly enough, but I noticed that they were unwilling to allow me to remain alone with their own three children, as if what I had done might spread like the pestilence, to contaminate them. Nor were they slow to point out my transgressions. Would it not be wise for me to repent?

'Thank you for your hospitality,' I said on more than one occasion, for I was well aware that they might not have chosen me as their guest. I helped Mistress Best stitch garments for her coming child. Her belly was large and she was becoming increasingly indolent. At least I could be of use to her, although she had enough servants to overlook the running of the household. My stitching was neat and precise and she was soon willing to turn over some of the more delicate cloth for my attention. She was a comfortable woman who left the work of business to her husband, so unlike my mother. Mistress Best did not interfere, she did not keep the account books. I could not imagine her dealing with land and rent disputes. Not that she needed to. Master Best was, as so many in Norwich, engaged in the cloth trade, in the buying and selling of wool rather than the chivvying of tenants.

'I would not have chosen to invite you into my home,' Mistress Best admitted, confirming my fear with the painful honesty that I was coming to accept from those around me. 'I would not wish my own daughter to behave as you have. But the Bishop wanted it and so it must be. My husband is keen to keep the good offices of the Bishop.'

'I hope that his Grace paid you well.'

'Yes. He has been most generous.'

Which told me clearly why I had been taken in.

'I am afraid that I am a burden to you.'

'Yes. It was not my choice.'

'I hope that you are paid sufficient to make it worth your discomfort.'

Mistress Best glanced at me through her lashes, deciding to ask the question that intrigued her, although perhaps it should not. She lowered her voice as if the walls might have ears and make note of her interest in salacious gossip.

'What made you do it? I swear you were raised well by Mistress Paston. You lacked for nothing. They would have negotiated a good marriage for you. Why would you defy your family in this manner?'

I was candid in my reply since I could do nothing more. 'I fell in love.'

'But why did you allow it, with such a man? You should have turned away from him. A woman cannot choose whether she will love her husband or not.'

Which explained much about the Best marriage.

I was even more honest than she.

'I was given no choice, mistress. How could I deny an emotion that invaded my soul? I have known Master Calle for so many years. Love swept over me, or crept up on me, I know not which, and I wanted nothing more than to be wed to him.'

'He is so unsuitable.'

'He is a fine man.' I heard the instant edge to my voice and softened it. 'He is well received in many households. I swear that he will make a name for himself, and for me as his wife.'

'If the Bishop agrees, of course. My husband says that his Grace hopes that he finds enough evidence to deny your claim. He is asking your neighbours what they know of your taking vows with your bailiff.'

I heard the scorn in her voice, read it in the flush of her cheeks. Such scandal. She would not support it in her own household, as my mother had not in ours.

'What are they saying about me in the town?' I asked when a little silence fell between us, broken only by a sigh as Mistress Best unpicked some of her stitching.

Mistress Best sighed a little more. 'You do not want to know.'

'But I do. It will be no secret. I would rather not be in ignorance, and there is no one else to tell me.'

'Then this is what is being said and it will be no comfort to you. Even if the Bishop denies your marriage and orders you to return home, I would not think that your mother will welcome you back. Equally, if he accepts the marriage as a true one, Mistress Paston most certainly will not. You will never again have a bed in any Paston house.'

I dropped my sewing into my lap. It was not the shock that it might have been but it still hurt me. I could think of no response.

'Where will you go, if your marriage is denied?' Mistress Best asked, more inquisitive than caring.

'I will go to Richard, whatever the decision.' But I did not know. All my thoughts were awry. 'Perhaps to my Aunt Elizabeth. She might take me in, although there is little communication between us.'

'And if the Bishop does agree to your marriage, where will you live with Master Calle?'

'I do not know that either.'

She leaned forward as if her words might leave an impression on my skin. 'Master Calle will have no income. Neither will you. No dowry, no jointure.' Her whole demeanour was anxious although she owed me nothing. 'Are you certain that what you have set in motion is worth the doing? Is love so important? How many women marry without love but find a comfortable existence? Some women find love after the vows are taken. Will you not take my advice, Margery? Why not return home and allow your family to find you a husband whom they can support and take into their household with enthusiasm? I swear it will never happen with Master Calle, no matter what the Bishop ultimately says.'

I wondered what she had heard.

'What does my mother say of me? I am sure that you hear the gossip.'

She looked away towards the window where the light was failing as we eased into evening. 'It will not give your heart rest.'

'My heart has no rest. My family have closed the door against me. I need to know what my mother says.'

'Then if you will have it plain. Mistress Paston says that you are a worthless person. You are no loss to the family. Even if Richard Calle were dead, she would not take you to her heart again.'

'She would not say that!' Horror struck hard, that she had spoken so viciously. 'Have you heard her say those words?'

'No, in truth I have not. But it is commonly spoken of.'

Unable to believe that my mother would condemn me as worthless and even anticipate Richard's death, I could no longer contain my emotions, against all my inclinations shedding bitter tears, until Mistress Best touched my hand to give me a square of cloth, probably so that my tears would not stain the garment I was stitching.

'You could still deny all and be reconciled.'

I sniffed and blotted my tears, borne up by a resolve that shocked me. 'I cannot. We will live with the truth. Richard's lot will be worse than mine. He has lost his livelihood because of the love he bears for me. How can I abandon him? And why would I? All I want in life is to be his wife.' Despair almost shook me again into tears. 'What is happening about Caister?' I asked, when clear speaking was possible.

'It is not good news either.' Cynicism gripped Mistress Best. 'The siege continues apace and there seems to be no remedy for it.'

'Are my brothers safe? I know nothing of them.'

Despite my own woes, I had been aware of a constant throb of worry that a siege could bring death to those closely involved.

'I hear of no harm to them, although I think Master Jonty has the siege in hand. Sir John is in London. The younger ones are here with your mother in Norwich.' Mistress Best looked up from her endless stitching of garments for the coming babe, with a wry glance in my direction. 'I think that your family might regret losing Master Calle's talents at this moment. They might regret losing him more than losing you!'

The Bishop was leaning towards generosity, it seemed. I was allowed to meet with Richard, newly come from London, suitably chaperoned by Mistress Best, who stitched and pretended not to listen. Richard, looking well-recovered from his afflictions earlier in the year, stretched and touched my hand across the table, despite Mistress Best's sidelong glance and mild frown. Such a fleeting contact, but so much desired. He looked confident and prosperous; his fair hair, longer than I recalled, gleamed when he removed his fashionable chaperon and bowed to our reluctant companion. I presumed that he was able to make a living of sorts, and was thankful. Or had he been driven to borrow the money to pay for the dark blue wool of his cotehardie and the fine-quality Holland linen visible at his throat? He would not wish to appear a beggar before past friends and acquaintances in Norwich.

'Mistress Best tells me that you are in good spirits,' Richard said.

'I try hard to remain sanguine. Where are you living?'

'I lodge with a friend in London, until we hear from the Bishop. I swear it will not be long now.'

'Have you had any contact with my family?'

'Very little, until the Bishop forwarded a letter from your mother in Father Gloys's hand. She speaks for her sons, of course. That is the reason I am here in Norwich with the Bishop's blessing.'

Was this a sign of hope? That my mother would resurrect communication with Richard?

'What do they want with you?' I asked.

'Nothing advantageous for me, I fear. Were you hoping that they might find a need for me since they are beleaguered with Caister? Not so. They want the return of all the valuable estate documents that are still in my keeping from my days of employment when I was a trusted man.' His mouth twisted momentarily in sharp acknowledgment. 'What more could I have expected? Mistress Margaret has taken their return in hand because Jonty is so angry and will not write to me or meet me, even if he could. The siege is a terrible drain financially, but he says he would rather be hanged than have me remain bound to the Pastons. He refuses to make contact with me, and Sir John is otherwise engaged in London. Thus I discover my worth.' He laughed, a harsh sound in the quiet room. 'It is mostly property deeds and financial accounts. All are in my keeping, as they have been for years.'

'What will you do?'

'Simply deliver the documents and let your family deal with them. It will be like trying to untangle a spider's web, unless you know the habits of the particular spider, as I do, and I wish them well of it. So many tenants are refusing to pay their rents for fear of Paston enemies landing on their doorstep to punish them. Those who might have lent money to your family in the past are now retreating until they see the outcome at Caister. Your family are in true difficulties. All the Paston servants are in arrears of pay. As I know, since I usually arranged the payments.'

I frowned. 'Have you still not been paid?'

'Not for the last year. Now that I have been dismissed, I have no hope of it.'

A thought came into my mind. 'Where will you take them, to hand the documents over?'

'It has been agreed on a neutral place. I will go to the Shire Hall tomorrow at noon.'

My decision was made in the blink of an eye. 'I will come with you.'

'Would that be wise?'

'No. But still I will do so. The longer I remain alienated from my mother, the worse it will become. Perhaps, if my mother sets eyes on me, she will at least speak of me with kinder words. Better to attempt a reconciliation than to sit here and repine the vast distance that has opened between us. I will not have her describe me as a worthless daughter without trying to remedy it.'

Mistress Best was no longer pretending not to listen. 'You cannot do that, Mistress Margery. The Bishop would forbid it.'

'I can do it and I will. Perhaps you will lend me one of your maidservants to escort me there and back?'

'Well...'

'I have no intention of absconding. Where would I go? Nor will Richard and I be alone together at any time.'

She looked between me and Richard.

'On my honour,' he said, 'I will return her safely. Would you deny her the chance of making amends with her mother? Besides, the Bishop did not forbid her to communicate with Mistress Paston.'

Still she hesitated.

'I would not be so disobliging to you after your kindness, Mistress Best, but indeed I am not your prisoner,' I reminded her gently. 'Did the Bishop say that I must not set foot beyond your door? I will not tell him, and nor need you.'

Mistress Best lent me her maid.

It was the strangest of meetings at the Shire Hall, a new addition to the town in recent years, of which we were suitably proud. By far the largest building of its kind in all England, except for those in London, the glass in the windows kept out the draughts to the comfort of all. There was much coming and going, but we took up a position in a quiet corner beneath the tapestried walls of one of the smaller chambers on the ground floor with the maid and two servants borrowed from Master Best. My mother approached, walking directly towards us as if this was a meeting that she did not relish but must be tolerated. She overlooked my presence as if I were not there and greeted Richard with a curt nod of her head.

'You have the documents, Master Calle?'

'I have, Mistress Paston. Everything appertaining to your property is here.' He hefted the leather satchels that he and the Best servants had carried, then placed them at her feet. My mother beckoned to two of the Paston servants who had accompanied her to come and take them away.

'Are you certain that there is no Paston material still in your possession?'

'I am certain of it, Mistress Paston.'

She would have immediately turned away, the business of the day complete. If there was any heartbreak within her, any sorrow at what had occurred, I did not see it.

'I think that the affairs of this meeting are not complete,' I said.

She looked back over her shoulder, an element of surprise in her expression, while I summoned all my courage to right a palpable wrong.

'Richard will not ask you. He is too proud. But I will. You have not paid him for his services to you for over a year. It would not be good business to sever his employment, leaving him in arrears.'

I felt Richard's fingers around my wrist but I had not finished. I would not beg for myself, but I would for him. 'The business community would be appalled to know that you had taken his labour without due recompense. Will you see to it? Will you put all such matters right?'

Might we be overheard? There was no one close by. Would my mother refuse, or, a woman who had always fought for justice, would she concur? Still she hesitated.

All I received was a brusque nod of acknowledgement. 'It will be done.'

'Do you promise? Since we have no document to sign to make the pact. I know that legal proof means everything to you and to my brothers.'

I could not believe my bold query, but at least she looked at me. I held her gaze with mine.

'I have given you my word.'

Before she had taken two steps away, this time it was Richard who stopped her.

'Mistress Paston. If you ever have need of me, I will willingly offer my services again, when matters have eased between us.' I looked at him in amazement. His face was still, controlled, and I knew what it cost him to make this offer. 'I think that Caister will continue to burden you. I can help with that since I have know-ledge of the Paston estates. I will look elsewhere for employment, as I must, but I will be willing to offer you my talents, at least at keeping accounts. Indeed, I will not take a new master until Sir John has formally refused my service.'

My mother regarded him with no softening in her, although I thought that, just for a moment, her mind was taken up with some thought that disturbed her. And just for that moment I hoped that a reconciliation might be possible. Gathering all my courage, risking a rebuff, hoping that all might be mended and once more I might be accepted back with affection and forgiveness, I held out my hand.

'Mother, will you not remember that I am your loving daughter? I may not regret what I have done, but I will still ask your forgive-ness for the manner of its doing.'

But no retreat here. My hand was ignored and my mother replied to Richard instead. It was a brutal rejection, without a word being spoken to me.

'Why would Sir John re-employ you? I can see no future when we would reconsider your re-employment. You have helped my daughter along the path to destroying herself.'

I could not remain silent against this unjust accusation, or the fact that she had forced Richard to abandon his pride in his search for restitution. I knew why he had done it. He must earn a living to keep a wife. Thus he would cast this pride beneath the soles of my mother's unforgiving feet. If I had not admired him before, I did so now, threefold.

'There is no fault in Master Calle,' I said. 'It was my wish, too.'

She regarded me again, but briefly, already turning away. 'You were persuaded by a man who should know the ways of the world better.'

'What will you do if the Bishop rules in our favour?' I asked.

'Nothing. You have made your bed; you must lie in it for ever.'

'I did not think that you would be so very harsh.'

'I did not think that you would do your utmost to bring our family down to the level of a shopkeeper. God make of you a good woman. I see none before me now.'

Michaelmas came and went. Still no word from the Bishop. Still no Paston reconciliation. I thought I was becoming an increasing irritant on Mistress Best, who was near her time. I, with no experience of childbirth, was unable to offer her advice when her back ached and sleep failed her. I was finding it nigh on impossible to remain hopeful. What had the Bishop discovered that would make his decision so tardy? Richard, returned to London, did not visit again, nor did he write to me. We knew it would not be wise. Besides, what could be said that had not already passed between us?

Master Best began to consider the need for more space in his house when the new child was born. There was an obvious solution for him. Could I not find new accommodation?

I could not. To my mind, the Bishop had placed me here until his decision was made, and here I would stay until he decided otherwise. Worry began to keep me from sleep. I considered writing to Richard, but what would I ask him if I did?

Then, at last, Richard and I were summoned.

We stood before the Bishop who remained seated, turning various documents in his hands before spreading them out before him. He looked up, encompassing all of us, Richard and I on one side, my mother and grandmother on the other. It was a relief that not one of my brothers had come to witness the outcome. The silence was disturbing, not even broken by the scratch of a clerk's pen, for there was no need for an account of this meeting. Soon it would all be over, one way or another. His garments, plain and dark, all unadorned, matching the severity of his face, Richard caught my gaze with a little smile that barely lifted the corners of his mouth. Today we would know our future. My mother and grandmother stood together, their whole attention on the Bishop, as if we were not there.

His Grace nodded, lips pursed. He had made his decision.

'I have assessed all the evidence in this unfortunate case.'

I was holding my breath, my hands clasped together, when he inclined his head in my direction, and then towards Richard.

'There is no wrongdoing here. The vows of Master Richard Calle and Mistress Margery Paston stand in my considered opinion as a legal undertaking. Whether we approve or not,' his regard moved to my mother and grandmother, 'they entered into a matrimonial bond. I dislike the notion of it, without priest or witness, yet still their words are clear and binding in the eyes of the Church. To release them from such a vow would require a papal dispensation.' He regarded my mother. 'I advise you, Mistress Paston, not to consider it. The cost would be prohibitive and might not be successful.'

Now I breathed out, long and slow. I still could not believe what I had heard, but there was still no relief, rather an emptiness. Should I not have been rejoicing? The Bishop had declared that Richard and I were truly wed. Ridiculously, I dare not even look at Richard to see his reaction.

'All I say is this,' Bishop Lyhert continued, raising a hand to prevent any intervention by my mother. 'That this man and this woman must of necessity regularise their union in a church before a priest. Then no one will question it. Their children will be born in wedlock, beyond any doubt, without any taint of illegitimacy. That is my final decision on the matter. I have discovered no evidence to point to a different outcome.'

He rustled all the documents together and folded his hands on top of them as if that were indeed the end of it, and awaited the outcry that he must have known would ensue.

'My grandson, Sir John Paston, will ask for an annulment,' my grandmother said.

This was not a surprise to me.

'Not if you do not wish a long-drawn-out case.' The Bishop's response was blighting. 'One that will splash your name throughout Norfolk and, as I said, cost a deal of money. I advise you to accept my judgement and draw a line under this sad case. There is nothing more to be gained by pursuing an illegality when it does not exist. I will not support you in it. Nor will the law.'

The Bishop stood to announce his ultimate decision to the little gathering. 'These two young people who sought my advice are free to go.'

At last it began to sink in. 'May we be together, your Grace?'

It was Richard who answered for the Bishop. 'No. Not until we are formally wed. We will observe all legalities, Margery. Then we will live as man and wife.'

'An excellent decision.' The Bishop promptly ushered Richard and Mistress Agnes from the room so that I was left alone with my mother. He looked back before closing the door. 'I advise you, in my role as carer for your immortal souls, to try for a reconciliation, in the circumstances.'

We were alone, yet standing apart, my mother and I.

'It is decided,' I said.

'Yes.'

'Will you forgive me? Will you receive me again as your daughter, when I am wed?'

I thought that she would. I hoped that she would. What would she gain by continuing to refuse to recognise me? Surely now that the path to legality had been made smooth, and all cause of gossip swept aside by the Bishop, she would relent. How could Richard and I drag down my family with the Bishop speaking for us?

'No, I will not forgive.'

Her voice was even, unemotional. This was my worst fear, but I had developed a new strong fortitude in recent weeks.

'Is this what you wish, Mother? Or is this Father Gloys speaking?'

I would never have dared to ask such a question, but now I had nothing to lose. Was Father Gloys the one persuading my mother that forgiveness and compassion were not acceptable when a sin had been committed? It took a long moment before she replied.

'Father Gloys is a man of God. He gives me advice, but I act on my own judgements.'

'Have you neither compassion nor understanding?'

'As much as you had for your family when you embarked on this. You have made your decision. You must make what you can of your new life. Do not come to me for aid if all falls awry.'

I still could not believe it, that she would throw away all we had had as I grew into adulthood. I made a final attempt.

'Not even when Richard and I have children, who will be of your own flesh and blood? Your own grandchildren?'

'I will not recognise them.'

'Mother! I am your daughter!'

'I know. And I have loved you well. Your choice today has put a stain on the Paston name. You must now live with that choice.'

Her voice, her face, were as flat and unresponsive as the surface of a new dish of whey.

Once again, as I had done at the Shire Hall, I stretched out my hand to her, palm up in supplication, but she had already turned away, straight-backed, striding towards the door. I watched her go, accepting that there was nothing more that I could say or do. What was in her mind I could not imagine. Perhaps here was the proof that for my mother the disaster unfolding at Caister Castle took precedence over the problems of an obstinate daughter. The depths of my grief at this separation could not be fathomed; life in the Paston family would continue on its ever-turning wheel without me.

After two disastrous attempts, I vowed never to hold out my hand in offered reconciliation again.

CHAPTER FIFTEEN

MARGARET MAUTBY PASTON

The Manor of Mautby in Norfolk, September 1469

I moved my household to Mautby, three miles from Caister Castle, far enough away for safety from Norfolk's forces but close enough that I could feel involved in what was developing day by day. In Norwich, I felt too distant. Besides, Mautby was a manor in which I felt most comfortable, my own inheritance, although much improved due to my husband's rebuilding. I enjoyed the comfort of higher ceilings and wide fireplaces, and not least the floors tiled with flowers and singing birds that John had delighted in giving me. I had also purloined some of the finer tapestries from Caister to hang on my walls. Mautby suited me very well. And I had a plan. It was not a good one, but better than prowling my rooms, without hope, waiting for a response from Sir John. It might just work. It might, with a little good fortune and careful investigation of the local area. The siege had been underway for all of three weeks and I could not sit behind closed doors and do nothing.

I summoned my steward, Master William Pecock, who shifted from foot to foot, suspicious of what it was that I might ask him to do.

'Do we employ any wildfowlers hereabouts, Will?'

'Yes, mistress.'

'I wish to speak with them. Find me the best. Men of some years and experience.'

'Aye, mistress.' He looked askance. 'If it's birds for the table you need—'

'No. I need information.'

He probably thought that I had lost my wits. How I wished that Richard Calle was still here. I must not think it. I must not think of Margery.

Two of the local men were brought into the chamber where I habitually conducted affairs of business, both inhabitants of Mautby, introduced as Tom Luddon and Geoffrey Grimston, both stocky men of middle years with the weather-reddened faces of those who spent much time outdoors in the fen. A pungent aroma of mud and rank water entered with them. They were families known to me, tenants of many years. There would be a fine line between poaching and wild-fowling in their households, I imagined. They would doubtless make free with the geese and duck that frequented the marsh with the onset of spring weather. They stood before me, looking uneasy.

'You have committed no crime,' I assured them. 'At least not to my knowledge.' Culpability hung heavily over them. 'How well do you know the environs to Caister Castle?'

I had been considering the lack of my own knowledge with some frustration. I had lived there. I had enjoyed the pleasure of its spacious rooms, treading the wall walks, sitting in the well-planned garden when I had a moment's leisure to do so. I knew where the postern gate was situated, to the south, opening into the area of the fish ponds. But beyond that all I could recall was marsh grass and reeds, their seed-heads heavy with hoar-frost in winter, a-twitter with small birds in summer. If my plan was to work at all, I needed better knowledge.

'How well do you know the area to the south of the castle?'

They looked at each other, perhaps expecting a trap.

'Well enough, mistress,' Luddon ventured. 'We shoot duck in that area. It's not forbidden.'

'And geese, when they fly here in winter,' Grimston added with a slide of eye towards his fellow tenant. 'We send them to your table when your bailiff demands them.'

But not often, I thought. They caught more than I ever ordered. They made a good living out of my birds.

144

'I am sure that you do,' I said with a softening curve of lips to encourage them. I needed their help. 'Can you tell me this? How was the moat first constructed, back in the day when Sir John Fastolf first had the castle built?'

They looked at each other again, unsure of what crime they might now be accused, in spite of my assurance.

'It was dug out, mistress, then lined with—'

'Of course,' I interrupted. 'I know that. Tell me how it was filled with water.'

A simple question that caused no distress.

'From the River Bure, mistress.'

'Is that not some distance away?'

'Well, it's like this.' Grimston, the more loquacious of the two, waved his hands to indicate place and distance. 'A ditch was dug from the river to the moat. Connecting the two, if you see my meaning.'

'Yes, yes.' Simple enough. 'So the water flowed from the River Bure along the ditch and filled the moat.'

'Yes, mistress. My father helped to dig the ditch, and so did his. It was a mighty task but we was well supplied with bread and ale. At first, the water in the river was dammed back, then the dam removed and the water flowed down the ditch and filled the moat.'

Which was to me all excellent news. But here was the crux of it.

'Does the ditch still exist?'

Luddon shrugged slightly. 'Aye, mistress. I suppose it does.'

'Is it overgrown? Or silted up?'

If it was, my plan could be undermined before it had got off the ground.

'No, mistress.'

'When did you last use it? Or when was it used for any purpose? Is it navigable?'

Grimston thought, wrinkling his brow. 'In spring, I reckon, mistress. It can be navigated by a small barge or a punt. Sir John Fastolf used it to bring supplies sent from Yarmouth along the River Bure. It ends at a storage hut next to the wall, where the postern gate is. It may be a bit overgrown after the summer heat, but it will not be silted. Any reeds or grass can be chopped out. If it wasn't for Norfolk's troops, of course. They've put a stop to our duck-shoots, that's for sure.'

Never mind the ducks. 'So there is access to the castle by water.'

'Aye mistress. Just about.'

'Do you suppose the besiegers will know of it?'

'I would expect so. Any clever commander will have searched out any weak spots in his position. He'll know about the postern and the ditch.'

So he would. And yet here was a chance, perhaps the only chance.

'Can you work a punt for me?'

'Not so well, mistress; the damp gets to my knees,' Luddon admitted. 'But my sons can.'

That was one problem solved.

'Can you find out for me if Norfolk's troops are camped near the ditch, without damage to yourselves?'

'Expect we can, mistress.'

'How quickly?'

'By tomorrow, maybe? Do we bring back a duck or two, mistress?'

'If you wish, but I need the information more.'

They were gone, well supplied with ale and bread and cheese.

The following morning, they returned.

'What news?' I asked.

'The ditch is reeded up, mistress. The entry from the River Bure is hard to see, but still usable by a punt, if the waterman knows the way.'

'Could your sons do it?'

'They might.'

I knew that it would cost me but it would be worth it.

'Tell me about the troops.'

'They are not camped close to the ditch because the ground is waterlogged. Nor close to the postern because of the fish ponds that have been allowed to flood. Norfolk's men have kept clear, except for when they are taking the carp for their own cooking pots, of course.'

It might be worth a try.

'Would it be possible, Master Grimston, for a punt to make its way along the ditch to the postern without being seen? At night?'

'It might well. It might be best if there was a moon. But then Norfolk's troops would see us. A lantern would be too risky, but it could be done by a brave lad or two.'

They were hardly enthusiastic. I was not to be put off.

'Would you do it for me?'

They looked at each other.

'For a remuneration, mistress.'

It was a word that I thought he might use frequently.

An agreement was made. Tom Stumps would go too. He might just return to his castle through the postern.

On the banks of the River Bure that night, two punts were well loaded with supplies, all that I could lay my hands on. Gunpowder, crossbows, two elderly fowling guns. And then from our own stores at Mautby, dried food, smoked meats and fish, bread, cheese and a tun of ale. All to keep the garrison fed for at least another month until perhaps Sir John could gain a ruling in the courts. It would give us a tiny breathing space. I had considered using punts to help the Paston men to escape, but that would be of no value. They must stay and hold the castle against the siege. Feed them and supply their dwindling armaments was the best I could do.

A moonless night. A shuttered lantern or two. Expert punting. Norfolk's troops camped at some distance. All we needed was good fortune to make landfall near the postern. Furthermore, it had been a day of heavy rain so that the wetlands would be even more sodden. I prayed that it would keep the besieging troops around their camp fires or in their tents. How to alert Jonty of his delivery I knew not but Tom Stumps might have an idea. The wildfowlers must find a way. Surely Jonty would have the postern guarded and be alert to any unusual occurrence.

Then I waited, wishing that I could have been there with them, but I would have been nothing but a hindrance. There was little sleep for me that night, or for Master Pecock who kept me company.

Dawn came with no news. Perhaps on this occasion no news would prove to be good news, and Jonty would be the recipient of enough to keep his men in good health. If our attempt was successful once, it could become a regular delivery when the weather proved co-operative.

All we had to do was evade any suspicions from Norfolk's troops.

Hours passed and my heart began to lift. We had done it.

'Visitors, mistress.'

It was William Pecock, looking even more glum than usual.

'Well?'

'Not good news, mistress.'

I went out to the courtyard where Sir John Heveningham himself awaited me.

'Mistress Paston.'

He gestured to those who followed him. Guarded by two of his soldiers, roped together with a cord from wrist to wrist, were Tom Stumps, my two wildfowlers and three young men whom I presumed were the sons who had manoeuvred the punts.

'Good morning, Mistress Paston. I think that this group of reprobates might belong to you.'

'Master Stumps is one of my household,' I admitted.

'And the rest in your employ?'

There was nothing I could say that would not be futile.

'A crafty ruse, but unsuccessful,' he continued. 'I am returning your property. I doubt you will deny that you had a hand in it.'

What use in denying it?

'At least you did not kill them.'

'No. They are damp and uncomfortable with a bruise or two for their sins, but I am not in the market for killing those under instruction to deliver food.'

I scowled at the dishevelled group.

'I don't suppose you could return the supplies as well. Or make recompense.'

He grinned. 'Your plea touches my heart, Mistress Paston, but no. We will make good use of them. Fresh food is hard to come by, and we always need gunpowder.' The grin disappeared. 'I advise you not to risk another rescue. I may not be so compassionate a second time.'

He bowed and remounted, handing the rope end to Pecock.

'How were they discovered?' I asked before he could ride out. What a pity that he was such a likeable individual.

'Easy enough. Would we leave a postern unprotected at night? Perhaps in the day, but at night it is an obvious place for a sortie. Besides, there were a surprising number of ducks awake and quacking after dark. Enough to wake the dead, as well as your son within the walls. Not the most subtle of ruses to pass the information that a delivery was approaching.'

No. Not subtle at all.

'Thank you.'

The Commander rode away and I dispatched my sheepish plotters.

'It was a good try.' Master Pecock sniffed his disdain, but whether at my planning or the foolhardy plot to scale the defences I could not determine. Sir John would condemn me for my interference, but it was difficult to leave a son to starve. Not difficult, I thought, as I sat at my table with a pen between my fingers and let distressing thoughts run through my head, but impossible. I had failed, leaving Jonty at the mercy of the Duke of Norfolk's highly efficient siege. Fear took a grip of me. At this rate my son might either be starved to death, killed by a stray arrow from the besiegers, or taken prisoner. I knew that Jonty would put himself in harm's way without a thought for his own life if there was a chance of his breaking the siege. Fear grew into a state of terror that made my head ache. I could not just leave him there.

What to do next?

CHAPTER SIXTEEN

MARGARET MAUTBY PASTON

The Manor of Mautby in Norfolk, 26 September 1469

'It never rains but it pours, mistress.'

'I see no rain clouds, Master Pecock.'

It was very early, one of those bright crisp autumnal days which should raise the spirits, but on this occasion failed to do so. I had barely sat down to break my fast and, to be honest, I resented the intrusion. What was Pecock thinking of? These days he seemed to be nothing but a harbinger of doom.

'A matter of speech, Mistress Paston. There's troubles at the mill pond. Miller Martyn says you should come.'

I pushed aside my platter of bread and cured meat and sent Pecock to fetch my cloak. If there was disagreement amongst my tenants, I must not ignore it. It did not surprise me that law and order had become an uneven debate when the lord of the manor was engaged in a siege. I was tempted to call down curses on the head of the supremely confident Duke of Norfolk. The sooner I sorted out the matter, the better.

By the time I had arrived at the scene of the dispute at my mill pond in Mautby village, it had become physical. Miller Martyn was standing over Thomas Amyson, one of my tenants, who lay on the ground with a bloody nose. Beside them, flapping weakly to death was a large pike.

'Mistress Paston!' The miller hailed me. 'This good-for-nothing has been poaching again. I caught him at dawn, dragging this fine fish from the mill pond. He denied it but here's the evidence before your eyes.'

There was much bad blood between the pair, as I knew, Amyson accusing the miller of giving short weight of flour for his grain, the miller accusing Amyson of grinding his own grain at home. It was a long-running dispute, into which I stepped.

'Did you catch this fine pike, Thomas Amyson?'

'Well, mistress...'

'Don't tell me that it was lying on the bank, waiting for you when you came to deliver your grain?' I looked at the miller. 'Has he delivered grain this morning?'

'No, mistress. He has no excuse for being here other than to take what he could.'

I turned back to the culprit. 'Did you catch it?'

'Yes, mistress.'

'You thought I would not miss it.'

By now he was on his feet, wiping the blood on his sleeve. He would not meet my eye.

'If I hadn't taken it, he would've,' he growled, eyeing the miller. 'He's been boasting about it all week at the inn.'

Which was probably true. The miller was not beyond helping himself to the inmates of the mill pond when dusk hid his actions from any who might be interested and report back to me.

'They are my fish and you will not catch them! Do you under-stand?'

'Yes, mistress.'

'What is the penalty for poaching the lord of the manor's fish?'

'Mistress Paston.' Master Pecock, standing behind me, was tugging on my cloak.

'Later—'

'I think it must be now, mistress.'

'One minute until this pike matter is settled will not hurt.'

'It's Master Jonty, mistress,' Miller Martyn added with conspicu-ous sympathy.

All thought of the illegal fishing was pushed aside. My breath caught, my thoughts whipped into disarray.

Jonty!

Here was the news at last, and all of it bad.

Approaching on horseback was Jonty with John Pamping and two retainers. I knew what that must mean. My heart that had thumped in relief that he, and our servants, were unhurt and alive, now sank into abject dismay. There was only one reason why my son would not still be holed up in Caister. He dismounted. I resisted touching him even though my instinct was to fold him into my arms. Jonty would not enjoy maternal commiserations in so public a place, however much I might wish to experience his restoration to me.

'Go into the mill house, mistress. You can have some privacy there.'

Of course. Everyone would know what must have happened. Pamping and the two soldiers remained at the door, but we were in no danger. It was all over. The Duke of Norfolk had won the battle and Caister Castle was his.

Inside the mill, the great mill wheel was turning, the air full of the harsh grind of the mill stone and thick with dust. The September sun was golden through the windows, lighting every-thing within in a soft bloom, but my son looked grey with fatigue. He walked beside me with a heavy tread. His clothes were clean and well presented, but beneath the attempt at making a good appearance they were worn and stained, and I noticed that they hung loosely on him. His life might not have been in danger but the siege had been a long strain on his vigilance. I wondered how much sleep he managed when an army was camping beyond his door. There were dark prints beneath his eyes.

All this I took in as I waited for him to speak. I did not rush him.

'It's gone.'

His first words.

'I am so sorry.'

I said no more. I did not need more to clarify the inevitable.

Now he was so close to me that I could see the lines gouged deep beside his mouth and between his brows. His face, indeed his whole body, looked high-strung and hungry. My young, carefree son was no more.

He walked away from me and took up a stance beside the mill stone, his face turned away as if in shame at what he would see as his failure.

'Write this into the history of the Paston family,' he said. The bitterness was overwhelming although he told the tale as smoothly as one of the Bishop of Norwich's minstrels who entertained with slick composure at every notable feast. 'On the twenty-sixth day of September in this year of 1469, I, Jonty Paston, surrendered the garrison at Caister Castle to Sir John Heveningham, military commander of the Duke of Norfolk. The castle, duly inherited by the will of Sir John Fastolf and so legally ours, is lost to us by force of arms. Our loyal friend and servant Daubeney is dead. Any legal claim we have to the castle is destroyed, for who will challenge the powerful Duke of Norfolk in the courts? Whatever Sir John Paston might say, it is a lost cause. The Duke of Norfolk's troops are in occupation and cannot be dislodged by a Paston. The King will not support us, so our failure is writ large across the acres of Norfolk. Write all of that into our history and I will be condemned for my negligence.'

So that was the end of it. After ten years of struggle, all that my husband John had striven for, had clung to, had spent months in the Fleet prison for. I smothered my despair, for there was more here than stone and mortar. Here was Jonty's failure and his despair, although in truth there had been little hope of his success in holding on to the castle. I followed him and placed a hand on my son's arm.

'You did all you could.'

'Did I? Many will remember and say that it was my fault.'

'But I know that it was not. Better men than you have been starved out.'

He turned to look at me. 'At this moment it does not seem to be an argument that holds weight. We should have been able to hold out longer. It seemed shameful to us to take the safe conduct.'

'Not when food runs out, Jonty.' I would not allow him to wallow in self-recrimination. We must be practical above all things. 'Do you allow your men to starve to death?'

He shrugged, unaccepting of what he would see as an excuse.

'What is my brother doing?'

'He's in London bending the ear of the Duke of Clarence.'

'Why Clarence?'

'He seems to be the one who wields the power of the sword at present. Sir John is appealing to him and any other magnate he comes across to exert their influence on Norfolk. When he is not speaking with them, he is writing to them.'

'Without much success.'

The silence between us was heavy. What else was there to say? No, nothing would mitigate our failure. But there were practical matters to attend to. It would turn Jonty's mind from loss and humiliation to the need to care for our people.

'We must speak with Daubeney's family, Jonty. How did he die?'

'By a crossbow bolt in the chest. There was no saving him. I regret his death.'

'We must give thanks that there were no more,' I continued, keeping my tone even. 'What has happened to the garrison?'

'Safe conduct, thank God.'

'So Norfolk kept his word.'

'Perhaps my brother's many letters, particularly to Clarence, had an effect after all. The Duke of Norfolk allowed them to march out unharmed.'

Did he know that I had been to see Norfolk a second time? That I had asked the Duke if we could trust him to allow safe conduct for our men if it came to a surrender? Now was not the time to tell him. If he thought it Sir John's doing, then all well and good. There was a strong bond between them and it would be good to keep it intact. Loss of Caister must not be allowed to fester and come between my two sometimes combative sons.

Jonty sank into silence, his gaze far beyond the trappings of the workings of the mill. Our fortunes had struck rock bottom, and his part in it had hurt him sorely, not least his pride. Leaving him sunk in his morose mood, I walked to the door and dispatched a somewhat gaunt John Pamping with kind words to the manor where he would find food and solace in the kitchens.

'My thanks for all you have done for the Paston family, John

Pamping. This is not the first time that you have worked hard for us, or risked your life when imprisoned for our sake.'

His exhausted face broke into a smile and he pushed his matted dark hair from his brow, reminding me of his youth. Perhaps it was time that we promoted him within the household. And even discovered for him a good wife in Norwich.

'It is always my pleasure, Mistress Paston. It is good to be free at last. Be sure that I will see to the needs of the rest of the Paston retainers.'

He bowed incongruously in his filthy garments, while I returned and stood beside my son.

He was frowning. 'What are you doing here at the mill?'

'Just a dispute over fish. Of no importance.' How could it compare with Jonty's experiences? I drew him to sit on one of the grain sacks while I sat on another. 'Tell me about it.'

'I don't think I can.'

'But you will. It might help.'

And thus he told me, in all the terrible detail of it, his words at first hesitant and unsure, then becoming more fluent and detailed as he relived those final days. I could see it. It was as if I had been there with him. His gaze was fixed on the distance as if he were still there.

'We were running short of food, with no way of getting more through a long siege. Flour had all but gone, so had the meat. Fish were beyond our reach in the fish ponds. Our gunpowder was in short supply. And then used up entirely. My garrison's heart was no longer in it when it was clear there would be no rescue. Twenty-seven men against three hundred? With more arriving each day to plant their banners in plain sight. What could we hope for? I could not leave them to die slowly. Even the postern was well guarded. No supplies could be ferried in. We tried shooting birds as they flew over but it would not save us from starvation. Ale and wine long ended, even though I rationed it. Some were growing weaker by the day, for we had not been prepared for a long siege in the first place. Which was my fault, of course. I should have known that Norfolk would use the obvious method to get us out. I could not fault the loyalty of our men, but there was no hope, you see. No one would come to our rescue.'

And my efforts had failed miserably.

'So you took the safe conduct.'

'I took the safe conduct.' He glanced sideways. 'Do you blame me?'

'No.'

'Sir John might. Uncle William, too, would be all for holding out until the bitter end. The worthies of Norwich who take every opportunity to pick and poke at us.'

'Your brother was not there to see. Nor was William. I would not support any scheme that would put our men's lives in more danger.'

'We were allowed to ride out with all our personal bags and baggage and our horses, unharmed, but leaving behind all our armaments.' He looked across at me, this time turning his head, then his whole body on the grain sack. 'You should also know that the contents of the castle are lost to us. The furnishings, the clothing stored there, Sir John Fastolf's books and all our private possessions that we could not carry. If there was anything of value to you, Mother, it is gone from you.'

There it was. Gresham and Hellesdon all over again, but this time so much worse. I would not press him for more details. They would come later.

I stood, leaned over him and kissed his cheek, and he did not pull away.

'Is the castle still in good repair?'

'Yes. A bit battered in places but the walls were not breached. Norfolk wanted it in good shape when he took it for his own.'

'So, if we can get it back through the courts...'

'I doubt we will ever do that. We don't have the money to bribe those with influence.'

'If we can get it back through the courts,' I said again, 'it will be defensible.'

'Yes. Will the courts ever be amenable?'

I abandoned that pathway. But there was another that must be dealt with.

'Our garrison and men of the household. Can we keep the men in service or must they look elsewhere?' I asked. 'Do we have the money for it? I have none. Nor has Sir John.'

'He never has!'

Jonty shook his head, pushing himself to his feet, dusting the flour from his tunic. Yes, he had lost condition around his face and neck, that had added years to his appearance. 'I know not what will be possible. I gave the sum of forty shillings to each member of the garrison for all they had done for us. It was all I could do. It was all I had. You behold before you a penniless son.' He managed a wry smile.

'I will see what can be done,' I promised. 'They will not lose by their valuable support for us. I will see that they have some recompense.'

But where I would find it, I could not fathom. Perhaps some of Fastolf's treasure must be sold after all. I had some of my own silver plate. Perhaps this was the time to make more use of it than merely a platter for a grilled pike overlaid with red wine and rosemary, a dish that I had little liking for because of the plenitude of bones. My mind incongruously swerved to the dying pike, the present source of antagonism between my miller and Thomas Amyson.

Jonty brought my mind back to the present disaster.

'Daubeney's will must be carried out, as he would wish it. His debts must be settled with all honour. His wife and children must be cared for.'

Jonty was all business-like and yet his bleak expression roused an immediate suspicion that all was not well with my son.

'What about you?'

'What about me?'

'You marched out with your life and freedom as the Duke agreed. Is that the sum total of the affair?'

His smile was sardonic. 'I am pleased to see that you remain as cynical as ever. No, it is not the end of the affair for me. I am threatened with arrest for disorderly conduct, for ordering our men to resist the Duke of Norfolk.'

Much as I had thought. One more fear to keep me company in the dark of the night.

'Can he do that?'

'Who can stop him?'

I dispatched Jonty to the house where the servants would welcome him and make him comfortable, while I returned to the dispute, so different from a siege, but still the source of much local irritation. Some judgement must be given. I dragged my thoughts back to the clash of wills.

There was Thomas Amyson, still waiting my return, Miller Martyn glaring with hands on hips. The pike lay dead on the grass, where I considered its glassy eye, already growing dim. I should take the fish and fine the fisherman. I did not have the heart. I turned my gaze upon him.

'Go back to your wife and children and take the fish with you. You will eat well tonight.'

He blinked in disbelief.

'In return you owe me two days' work on my land.'

'But, Mistress Paston. It's harvest and—'

'Your sons can harvest your grain for two days. You will work for me. It's that or a fine, and I take the pike.'

'Yes, mistress.'

'And you will ensure that all your grain is delivered to Miller Martyn for milling. Do I make myself clear?'

'Yes, mistress.'

He knew it could have been worse.

'Is the matter settled?'

They both nodded.

'And stay away from the mill pond. Both of you. The fish are mine and you do not catch them.'

I addressed it to both of them, then turned and headed home to face the repercussions of a lost siege and a castle we no longer owned. I had solved the problem of a filched pike but I had lost a castle. Nor could I solve the worrying issue of Sir John Paston, who continued to be absent whenever a dispute erupted, as well as escaping the highly valuable bands of matrimony with a royal cousin.

CHAPTER SEVENTEEN

MISTRESS ANNE HAUTE

The Royal Court in the Palace of Westminster, October 1469

'Are we wed, or are we not wed, Sir John?'

Sir John Paston, clad in Court finery, not least his shoes with their extravagant toes in the finest red leather, regarded me with his usual insouciance.

'We are, Mistress Haute, and yet we are not.'

His smile held that particular charm that had encouraged me to give my heart to him in the first place, even though I knew full well that he possessed a lascivious eye. Rumour, which did not lie in this instance, laid claim to the existence of a certain lady named Constance Reynforth, the mother of Sir John's illegitimate daughter. That knowledge did not hinder my falling in love. It might have hurt my heart that Sir John had had such an intimate relationship with another lady, but it was before we had made our pact, and clearly he had not wished to take Mistress Constance Reynforth for his wife. He would take me if I had anything to say in the matter. Both in law and in the eyes of the world.

It seemed that I did not.

'That is no answer to an honourable woman! Am I your wife or am I not?' I persisted.

'I was under that impression, dear heart. Did we not make a vow to be man and wife, from that very day forward?' he asked.

'We did. In the middle of a carole dance in Calais.'

Sir John tilted his chin, eyes glinting as if he recognised my deception.

'Or was it perhaps at a Court celebration after the churching of the Queen?'

So he did remember. He remembered perfectly when and where we had pledged ourselves in matrimony, in words of commitment even without a priest. I pressed on.

'Whichever it was, are we truly wed? We seem to have taken no further steps forward. To all who know me I am still a woman seeking a husband.'

'It was a vow, dear Anne.'

'And was our vow binding? Am I Dame Anne Paston or still Mistress Haute? I would prefer that a priest had had a hand in it, to enclose us in holy rites and sprinkled holy water.'

'I will arrange it,' he said promptly. 'When I have the time. And the money.'

How often had I heard the same refrain? Sir John lacked money like a summer-moulting falcon lacked the ability to fly. Yet a falcon recovered after a season of discomfort. Sir John apparently did not.

'When do you suppose that we will express our love in physical union, in either your bed or mine? Do you not yearn to show me the depth of your regard for me?'

'When I have a bed and an hour worthy of your presence,' he replied promptly.

'And when do you suppose that will be? I live in anticipation.'

This might have sounded flirtatious. I kept the light-heartedness as well as I was able. In truth I was exasperated.

'You know the pressures on me, Anne.'

'I do know. You tell me of them daily when we are in each other's company. They are prodigious.'

In August, Sir John's prize castle at Caister had come under siege from the forces of the Duke of Norfolk. By September, the siege had been successful and Caister was no longer Paston property. Sir John was beleaguered in his attempts to discover sufficient coin to buy influential patrons in this unstable royal Court. Yet I would not be put off in this manner. Sir John might have money troubles for the rest of his life. Did that mean that my hopes of matrimony were already moribund to the point of death?

'Or perhaps you have discovered a young woman who takes your interest more than I have been able to do,' I suggested, refusing to be drawn once more into dire discussions of Caister and rents. 'One with a substantial dowry.'

As a younger daughter, even though now so very well connected at Court, l lacked a dowry large enough to attract a man in need.

'How could you accuse me of so infamous a deed? Do you not know that my heart is yours?'

'I do not know who owns your heart,' I said. 'Tell me again.'

He drew me into a private space in an alcove behind a rich arras depicting heroic Greek warriors, an arm confidentially around my waist.

'My brother Jonty tells me that I am the best chooser of a gentlewoman with whom to keep company than any man of his acquaintance. My brother knows me very well and has a high regard for an attractive woman. He says that I am fastidious in my choice. How could I not choose you?'

'I suspect that your brother knows you better than I!'

He sighed as if accepting his limitations.

'One day, as my wife in the eyes of the world, you will know all there is to know about me, within this shallow shell.'

Oh, he had a way with words. I knew better than to think him lacking in self-regard. Sir John took my hands and kissed them, then drew me closer and kissed my lips.

'I love you dearly, Mistress Haute.'

'I am honoured, Sir John.'

'The honour is mine.'

I could never shake from my thoughts that he loved my cousinly connection with the Queen and her powerful brother Lord Scales more.

'But do you love me?' he asked.

'I love you as much as you love your beautiful new doublet.'

'Which I love extravagantly!'

It was of the newest fashion, short and close fitting, padded and stitched, all in costly emerald-patterned velvet.

'Then there is your answer.'

He drew my hand through his arm so that I could stroke the nap of the fine cloth as I walked with him from the alcove into the lively mass of courtiers gathered under the aegis of the Earl of Warwick and the Duke of Clarence. The blast and thump of shawm and tabor assaulted our ears on all sides.

And how perfectly Sir John Paston fit into this milieu. What a damnably attractive man he was who could dance and sing and participate in the tourney in equal measure. I was the object of envy for all unmarried women. Yet I could not pursue the next step with any degree of success. He was clever with words and with legal detail, avoiding any challenge I might make.

When would I be Dame Anne Paston?

He had never taken me to meet his family. I had not even met the inestimable brother who was so flattering of Sir John's ability to pick out the most beautiful woman in the room, and assuredly, apart from my cousin the Queen, I was probably the most comely woman present. I might lack the perfect oval of her face and the bright gold of her hair, but I had a perfection of skin and a sparkle of eye that, given the recent travails of the Queen, had faded from the woman who had ensnared the King.

'I have never once met a single member of your family,' I complained.

'Then come with me. Jonty is here.'

'Why did you not tell me?'

'Because you were too taken up with upbraiding me for my lack of interest in you. But come and meet him.'

I was introduced to a young man of square build and dark hair, the striking Paston features of straight nose and decided chin very evident. He bowed. He did not have quite the elegance of his brother but he was well-versed in Court manners, as he would be since he had been for some time in the household of the Duke of Norfolk.

'Mistress Haute.' He saluted my fingers lightly. 'I have heard much of you.'

'And all to the good, I hope. Sir John tells me that you converse frequently and at length.' He looked wary. 'What does he say to you?'

Young John, known to all the family as Jonty, laughed, perhaps relieved that I did not produce some sin that he had confessed to Sir John.

'He gives me advice on how to seek a wife.'

'And will you tell me how he suggests that you go about it? Perhaps Sir John has something to learn from his own advice.'

'First I must approach the lady's mother in a spirit of humiliation.'

'My mother is dead,' I observed, slanting a glance at Sir John.

'My regrets, lady. Then I am told that I should appear humble to the lady in question, pursuing her with all speed, but willing to accept that I might fail and fall at the final hurdle. And it must not matter too much if I do fail. It will merely mean that the lady in question is not for me. That fate intends another lady to be my wife.'

I was disturbed at the cynicism in this advice offered in all seriousness by Sir John to his brother. I turned my head to regard my husband by law. He had moved away, treading easily between groups of people, conversing as he went. I noticed that when he was not governing his features there was a shadow cast over them. His loss of Caister Castle had hit him hard.

'Did he indeed say that?'

'Indeed... Perhaps I should not have told you.'

'I am fascinated to hear Sir John's methods of entrapping a wife.'

Jonty's smile became a trifle cunning. 'I think that you might have entrapped him, Mistress Anne. You would certainly entrap me.'

I laughed. He was as charming as his brother. And perhaps more trustworthy. I was pleased to meet him.

There was one other person of influence in Sir John's family I had never met. His mother, Mistress Margaret, was a ruling entity in the Paston household. I knew that he had informed her of our exchange of vows. She had not remonstrated with him, as I thought that she might since he had gone about this event in what some would say was a sly fashion, but she warned him that he should get his affairs in order before he fully committed himself to marriage. He should make his claim to Caister Castle a secure one before fully promising himself to me.

I had actually read her advice, sent to Sir John.

I want you not to be too hasty to be married until you are more sure of your livelihood. Be surer of your land before you are married.

Now Caister Castle was lost to him after the siege and Sir John's claim to it in turmoil. If he was to be sure of his land before he wed me, then I might be in my dotage before I knelt before the priest. Yet to my imperfect knowledge Sir John, with all his legal training, must know that he was already committed. A solemn vow of intent in the company of a vast number of courtiers, even if they were ignorant of what we did, was to my mind a commitment. Was the whole family taken up with the need for money? It seemed that this was so, and I was a bride with no vast dowry to hurry the matter along.

As if picking up my train of thought, Sir John smiled at me across the room, the shadow again banished under a layer of courtly pleasure. Feeling my blood warm at his distant appraisal, I wished that we had physically celebrated our union. Perhaps that was the next step for me. I knew all about his sister Margery and her unfortunate entanglement with the family bailiff. Sir John had not spoken of it after breaking the news with vicious comment on the disloyalty of Paston servants, but it was clear enough that consummation had made their marriage vows a valid entity which required the attention of the Bishop of Norwich if it was to be broken.

I did not think that Sir John would be unwilling to take me to his bed if I offered the invitation.

'Do not warm his sheets, or allow him to warm yours,' the Queen my cousin had warned with lamentable inattention, too preoccupied with her own troubles to be concerned with those who might be wallowing in their own miseries. 'Or not until this irregular marriage is recognised before the world.'

There seemed to be little chance of it coming to pass. Sir John was quick to make protestations of loyalty but reluctant to put them into practice. Time was passing, the years imprinting themselves on my face; age was not beneficial to any man or woman. Did he not need an heir? An illegitimate daughter was not the answer to the Paston inheritance problems. I was filled with restless impatience. Yet the more impatient I became, the more absent Sir John Paston seemed to be from my life. I was beginning to see only hopelessness.

While I sought to ensnare Sir John Paston into the rigours of a formal marriage, the royal Court continued on its uneasy path. Treason rustled in the wind on every corner. King Edward was still languishing as a prisoner of the Earl of Warwick and the King's brother the Duke of Clarence, still incarcerated in Middleham Castle far to the north.

'Now there's an unholy alliance,' complained the Queen, plucking at her sleeves in abject anxiety. 'Edward never did trust his brother of Clarence, and here it is proved by a treacherous revolt, hand in glove with their cousin of Warwick. They will assuredly take the crown, set it on Clarence's worthless head, and Warwick will pull the puppet's strings.' She stalked away from me when I tried to still her fingers that were ruining the miniver edging. 'What can I do to help Edward?'

Nothing,' I replied brusquely, following her, for what point was there in raising false hopes? There were plenty at Court who would but as her cousin it behoved me to be honest. At least it had given me more to think about than Sir John's dealings with me.

'So we allow Edward to remain incarcerated? Have you no advice, Cousin Anne? What would Sir John Paston say?'

'I have no idea. I have not asked him. I would say that all we can do is wait and pray.'

Which we did, for although the Queen showed her teeth in a furious grimace, she and her children were quick to take refuge in the holy sanctuary of Westminster Abbey, and I with her. There we remained in a state of constant fear that we too might be placed under restraint, until our fears were proved false. Warwick's failure to keep the country at peace destroyed all his political scheming. It necessitated the King's release and restoration to his Court and his Queen.

'I watched Edward riding into London,' Sir John informed me when I emerged briefly from our royal sanctuary to meet with him and gain some knowledge of the past days, tracking him down to the mews where he was inspecting a newly purchased goshawk. 'There he was in an aura of confident splendour with his brother the Duke of Gloucester and Lord Hastings riding beside him. It was an event of such celebration and without doubt London welcomed him home. Warwick and Clarence must perforce watch their joint steps. Our King might hand out pardons as freely as a royal fool offering sweetmeats, but I foresee a reckoning to come.'

'The Queen says that Edward does not trust his brother of Clarence.' Although it had become my habit to look over my shoulder when making such a dangerous comment in the present climate of the Court, there was no one in the mews but the two of us and its usual rustling inmates.

'Does anyone? If I gave my allegiance to Clarence, it would be like putting my head into a noose.' Sir John thought for a moment, stroking the breast of the hawk which was just growing its new feathers. 'Do you suppose that the King will now sponsor me in my conflict with the Duke of Norfolk over the ownership of Caister?' Without waiting for an answer, he continued, 'Once I would have thought that there was little hope of it, but now he might need every friend he can get until the loyalties of Warwick and Clarence are settled. Even a Paston might be worthy of royal cultivation.'

I sighed. I had hoped for a more amorous reunion but I could not compete with Caister Castle for Sir John's attentions, even when it was no longer his to claim. Nor could I envisage matching the victory of Margery Paston and her low-born lover. Unlike Sir John's sister, I seemed destined to a cold and lonely future unless either Sir John fulfilled his promises, or mayhap another suitor would appear to offer me his hand in marriage. I had not been overpowered by their multitude.

Even the moulting goshawk achieved a more affectionate caress than I.

CHAPTER EIGHTEEN

MARGERY PASTON

The Bishop's Palace in Norwich, October 1469

'Where do we go?' I asked, reunited with Richard in the Bishop's antechamber, empty now of all Pastons except for myself. A burst of autumn sunlight coated the chamber with gold, as if in heavenly blessing. The tapestries came alive, the hounds and hawks bounding through the ever-blossoming trees. Everything was new and possible. The Bishop had spoken, and it seemed that I could, at last, breathe freely again.

For a few moments we had merely stood, absorbing what had been done in so short a passage of time in the Bishop's chamber. I still could not quite believe it. Yet here was Richard, holding my hands, then drawing me into his arms, my forehead pressed against his shoulder. Relief was a softness beneath my heart. But then the sun moved behind a bank of cloud which doused our surroundings into sombre shadow, the creatures withdrawing into their stitched undergrowth. How pertinent it seemed to me. The Bishop might have pronounced on the legalities but nothing was yet clear.

It was time to face the immediate future with all its uncertainty. Where would we live until our bond was officially tied before a priest? The reading of banns was required, as was the arrangement of a ceremony. I still had nowhere to go, and Richard was still without regular employment. Even he seemed stunned at the final suddenness of it all, with no immediate vision of our future.

'What do we do?' I asked under the weight of an awful

helplessness. 'It is as if we are standing on a ledge. One step and we will fall into an abyss. I should be rejoicing but I cannot see further than this room and the house of Master Best.'

'I have no idea,' Richard admitted as we stood beside a tapestry of five fish ponds where carp swam. 'And I a man of legal affairs!' He smiled at the incongruity of it. 'I suppose that I thought that the Bishop would declare against us. I have made no preparation for what we should do when we walked out of that room.'

He was as shocked as I. We had both feared the worst.

'I think that I need further discussion with his Grace. Wait here for me.'

Once more I sat on that unforgiving wooden settle until he returned, where I set myself to a task of incongruous uselessness, of counting the silver and gold carp. I had barely reached a score when he returned. It had not taken long, which might mean good news or bad.

'Do I return to the Best family?' I asked. 'I think I might have outstayed my welcome there.'

I did not wish it, but I supposed that it would be no real hardship if that was the only door to open for me. It would not be for too long.

'No. You may say farewell to Master and Mistress Best, with grateful thanks. The Bishop has other ideas. I would not have thought of this, but it might work well for us both.'

'What will you do for employment?' I asked.

Richard took my hand and led me down the stairs and out into the courtyard which was once more warmed by the unpredictable sun.

'My employment has still to be decided on, but is not for you to worry over,' he stated, perhaps with more confidence than such a statement deserved in the circumstances. 'I will earn enough to keep you in shoes. Come, my wife. We are not to be parted again. Let us face our future together.'

Blackborough Priory in Norfolk

The Bishop, in his kindness, lent us a pair of horses and a mule to carry our belongings, a maid to give me some respectability and a man at arms in episcopal livery to offer us protection. We rode slowly, savouring the strange freedom, drawing no attention to ourselves, staying at inns where the Bishop had told us that we would find a quiet welcome. We spoke gently, intimately, enjoying for the first time in our lives the thought that we were together and would remain so, no longer under duress. Just to ride side by side without interference, with few travellers on the roads, was a blessing. Those we saw nodded in greeting or hailed us as we passed. We had no reason to give for our journey, no excuses to make. To them we must have appeared as a married couple travelling on private business.

Richard was solicitous, caring of my comfort.

It was three days before we came to a halt before the great west door of Blackborough Priory, a Benedictine foundation built in red stone, far to the north-west of Norwich, near to King's Lynn; a mere handful of months since that day when we had plighted our troth at Elm Hill in Norwich, and yet a span of time of parting and anguish that had seemed endless. It was a cold day, the coldest we had suffered, with no sun to warm the russet hue. Birds, winter visitors, were congregating in the bushes to feast off the autumnal berries. All was quiet except for the creak of our harness and the hungry twittering of the birds on the hillside above the low marshy land in the valley bottom where the River Nar ran sluggishly. I thought it would be unhealthy in a wet winter with mists and lying water but now it was a refuge.

A bell rang in the far distance, calling the inhabitants to prayer.

'What was the Bishop's motive in sending me here?' I asked Richard.

It was a small establishment, once housing monks and nuns but now the habitation of nuns only, and only nineteen of them at that, who had dedicated their lives to the Blessed Virgin and

St Catherine. I surveyed the walls that kept visitors out and the nuns within.

'Did his Grace think I might be tempted to take the veil to escape all the scandal? If so, why not leave me in the nunnery at Carrow, outside the walls of Norwich, rather than have me make this journey?' I considered the possible duplicitous mind of the Bishop. 'If I took the veil and rejected you – and all men – it would relieve him of having made a judgement that at heart he regretted.'

'I don't suspect him of that,' Richard said. 'It is secluded here, away from the bustle of any town. Perhaps Bishop Lyhert thought the isolation would be most suitable for our situation, before our scandal could be put right before the eyes of our families and neighbours. As well as offering us the opportunity for reflection and penance, of course.' He turned in his saddle to look at me, his eyes bright. 'You weren't considering taking the veil, were you?'

'No.'

I stretched across the divide between us and took his hand, until our horses pulled apart and we were once more separate entities. In those days of travel we had strengthened the bonds between us with talk and laughter despite all the unease of what would be our lot. We had travelled chastely, sleeping apart – I, as a woman and her servant. We would not share a bed again until the Church blessed our union. We did not speak of it, but it was in both our minds.

'Let us go in and accept the hospitality offered,' Richard said.

'Mistress Paston. Master Calle. Our Bishop warned us of your arrival. He has explained all.'

The Prioress in her black Benedictine habit, noticeably thread-bare and as aged as the Prioress herself, met us on the steps. There was little income in this establishment, unlike Carrow with its closeness to the town and the generosity of the townspeople. Blackborough would receive few visitors and even fewer endowments to give the nuns comfort.

'Good day, my lady,' Richard replied, saluting her hand. 'We are grateful for your hospitality.'

'Warned' was a strange word for the Prioress to use, yet we were made welcome and I was given a cell rather than a bed in one of the dormitories. It was cold and sparsely furnished, but I relished the privacy within its close stone walls, from where I was free to join the nuns in their daily life or sit in the cloister. They provided me with a missal for my prayers, and linen to stitch into shifts. It was good to feel occupied, to keep from dwelling on what I might be doing at my mother's behest in Norwich or Oxnead. I shared the nuns' silent meal when we listened to the *Rule of St Benedict*, read for our encouragement.

Some were very pertinent.

The first degree of humility is obedience without delay. This is becoming to those who value nothing as more dear to them than Christ, on account of the holy servitude they have professed, whether through fear of hell or on account of the glory of life eternal.

There was no attempt to draw me further into the religious community than I wished to go. It was a strange life for me of enforced leisure and strict observance amongst such a small, ageing community, for none of the nuns were youthful vocations. The services gave me peace, a grounding, that I had lacked since I was turned from my home.

'You must make peace with your mother.'

The Prioress, sitting by my side in a patch of sunlight as if her old bones might soak up the comfort of warmth, had been informed of those past difficult weeks.

'My mother will not forgive.'

'That does not mean that you cannot pray for her. Or that you should shun her when your marriage is at last solemnised. Take my advice, my child. Families matter and it would be wrong of you to wield the knife that cleaves your own family in two. I will pray for you.'

And I felt the weight of tears within me.

'I would be grateful, Mother. It grieves me that we are apart in mind as well as in body.'

'I will pray for your husband-to-be also. I think that he will need our prayers.'

Richard had been given accommodation in the guest house just beyond the abbey walls. There were no other visitors thus he had no need to explain his presence. Food was delivered to him but otherwise I understood that he was left in isolation, free to travel to neighbouring villages where he might find a demand for his talents, although with what success I did not know. At first it was frowned upon that Richard and I should meet and converse, and then it appeared that we were to be allowed to do so.

'Master Calle is waiting in the herbarium, if you wish to talk with him,' an elderly nun informed me, shoulders bent from prayer and tending the herbs, her gnarled fingers encrusted with soil. 'I will chaperone you, of course. We have taken pity on him. He misses you.'

I went immediately to where Richard met me with a smile and kissed my hands.

'You look like a nun.'

I had borrowed a habit and linen coif since my own clothes were showing much wear, and it was seemly that I should honour the sisters in this manner.

'I think that it would dishonour a nun to kiss her on her mouth,' he continued.

'And yet you will, if she is your wife.'

He did so.

'By the Virgin, Margery, I have missed you. How long is it since we shared any intimacy? If you have become a nun, then I am assuredly a monk and it does not suit me.'

Yet for form's sake and respect for where we were, he released me and drew me to walk between the herb beds. Our black-clad chaperone smiled and nodded towards us.

There was mischief in Richard's eye.

'Why have the sisters become so friendly?' I asked, suddenly wary. 'Why are we allowed to meet?'

He drew me to the centre of the garden where a few bees were making desultory sorties on the last of the sage blossoms before winter set in.

173

'They have discovered that they have a use for me.'

I picked a sprig of rosemary, shredding the leaves, releasing the sharp perfume.

'The sisters have found that I can be of value to them, to over-look their accounts and their books, to visit tenants who owe them money. A man on a difficult tenant's threshold, threatening legal redress, has a stronger effect than an elderly sister who promises to pray over his inability to find the rent by next month. Their income is much improved. I have won my way into their hearts, and thus, being a man of honour as well as ability, I am entrusted to meet with you. As long as it is not within too holy a patch of ground. This herbarium under the surveillance of the watchful sister must seem to them a perfect compromise.'

'Do they pay you well?'

'No. They feed me, but they have no means to pay. It does excellently well for my reputation.'

It pleased me that he had found work.

Thus we met daily for a brief half-hour as the herbs lost their fragrance in the approaching autumn chill and we waited until the banns had been called, with no fear that any man would step forward and prevent our union.

'Look,' urged the Prioress one night after Compline, when the sky was dark and we made our way to bed, lingering in the cloister. 'A shooting star.'

'What does it foretell?' I asked.

'God's blessing.' I could not see her smile but I heard it in her voice. 'Soon the banns will be read and all will be well.'

The shooting star had augured falsely. All was not well.

'Your family is not content with the Bishop's decision, Mistress Margery. I am informed that your brother Sir John and Mistress Paston have been in discussion with his grace the Bishop again.'

I had been summoned by the Prioress after a rare courier had brought letters to Blackborough. So was Richard also summoned. We stood together before her, under the soaring arches of the Chapter House, after the daily office.

'And what is the outcome of this discussion?' Richard asked, calmly enough.

'Sir John is anxious that you do not wed in haste.'

'We are already wed.'

The Prioress clicked her tongue in mild disapprobation.

'Be that as it may, Master Calle, Sir John is anxious to know how you propose to care for Mistress Margery and where you will dwell. Will you have sufficient employment, sufficient income to give her a good home? He is suggesting that if you are unable to do so, then this marriage should be postponed until better times.'

'Sir John could remedy the situation immediately by giving his sister a dowry, as is her right. He could also discover such salient facts for himself, if he were willing to speak with me. It is his choice that he will not. I have made it clear that it is not my intention to steal Margery away from the family. There is no rift here of my making.'

'Except that you took Mistress Margery in marriage without her family's consent.'

'Only because they would never give it.'

I heard the edge of temper and intervened. 'What is it that my brother wishes the Bishop to do, Holy Mother?'

'To delay the wedding until at least Christmas. Your mother is, of course, in agreement with this.'

Richard replied with what was in my mind. 'And then it will be Lent and we will still be unwed.'

The Prioress bowed in acknowledgement of what must be clear to all.

'That is what they might hope, of course. The longer you remain without God's blessing, the more likely it might be that your marriage fails.'

'Yet I doubt that I will ever be welcomed back across the Paston threshold, whatever the outcome,' I said.

I thought that I read some compassion in the Prioress's eye.

'I think you will not make a good sister here, Mistress Margery. You do not have the patience.' She awarded us a bleak smile. 'The Bishop says that he will not concur, but I thought that you should be warned. Despite all his best efforts, the Bishop could find no fault with your marriage except for some impetuosity. He tried very hard.' She paused on this note of optimism. 'But then, bishops, as we know, have a habit of changing their minds. My advice, Mistress Margery, is not to count your chickens until the eggs have hatched and a priest pronounces his blessing on you and Master Calle at the church door.'

The warning sent my spirits plummeting once more, even though I should have been used to the precariousness of our position.

My nights were full of bleak misgivings. They drove me to prayer, but I had little faith. My vows taken with Richard in Norwich receded further away into a shadowy distance. Richard, absent on a visit to King's Lynn, sent me a few sprigs of St John's Wort to preserve my spirits, but as they crumbled, so did my convictions that all would be well.

On a bleak October day, when the sun did not even once break through the clouds, Richard and I stood together at the church door in Middleton, the nearest settlement to the Priory, where the church was overshadowed by the bulk of a newly built castle. My hand was cold in Richard's. I would not admit to nervousness that at the last someone would step forward and declare against our marriage, but their shades hovered on the edge of my sight. In some fantastical image I saw Father Anselm ride up, in full canonical vestments, brandishing an episcopal cross and documents with the Bishop's seal, to forbid the marriage after all until at least Christmas. Or even Father Gloys, with mischievous intent. Or Sir John and Jonty, riding as if in a battle charge, coming to forbid us. I was trembling with cold and fear. Richard's grip was firm as he turned his head to look at me, his expression unexpectedly severe.

'No one will stop this. No one will ride up and snatch you away. We will exchange these vows before a priest and there will never again be any question of our status together.'

How could I believe it?

And then, with no shattering disturbance other than a noisy conflict of crows squabbling on the church roof, it was done.

It was a simple taking of vows in the presence of an unsmiling priest and two witnesses whom we did not know, no more holy in our eyes than that exchange in my chamber in Norwich which had caused all the upheaval for us. There were no guests, no bride gifts, no well-wishing, but we were wed at last and no man could part us. The nuns, my only present family, were forbidden to come. My own family had not come, even if they knew that my marriage was taking place. Nothing would part us now, only death, and I prayed that it would be far into the future. We would find a home, we would raise a family, Richard would find work and make a name for himself.

At the end, Richard pushed a thin gold ring onto my finger as a symbol of our union.

Where now? We stood hand in hand, a little lost, the priest rapidly taking refuge from the cold after the chilly ceremony.

'Do you wish to start back to Norwich today?' Richard asked me.

I thought. Then: 'Let us at least mark this day with an element of celebration.'

'And where would we do that?'

'I know a place.'

He was amused at the prospect.

We returned to the Priory where the sisters allowed Richard into the refectory, since we were now respectably wed. They broached a small tun of ale and we toasted our future with surprising joy. For the first time for many months, I felt happiness steal into my heart. Tonight, I could be with Richard as his wife, in the eyes of God and Man. We were beyond censure.

'I am the first of this generation of Paston children to wed,' I proclaimed with more than a hint of self-satisfaction as the nuns left us to attend Compline in the chapel.

'Not through want of trying by Mistress Haute,' Richard replied wryly. 'Sir John is proving a hard fish to land.'

I wished the distant lady well. Surely her path could not be as fraught with difficulties as mine had been.

★

In their goodness, in their tolerance of life outside the convent where love drove men and women to improper actions, the nuns had provided a room for Richard and I to spend the first night of our wedded state in the visitors' accommodation. There was no comfort other than the narrow bed, a stool, a crucifix on the wall, but to us it was a sanctuary, a refuge, a shelter from the storms to come. The covers were well laundered even if threadbare. The bell calling the sisters to prayer was an assurance that all was well with the world outside our four walls. What more did we need? I remembered, fleetingly, because it was no longer important, the only time when Richard and I had plighted our troth in physical union, when I had been nervous, virginal, shivering, while he had been considerably gentle. Our knowledge of each other then had been a tiny mark on the vast universe. On that distant afternoon with the golden dust motes showering us with the only blessing we received, we had become man and wife. Now our union was confirmed in this holy place when the moon-rays crept through the high window and granted me shadows to hide my lack of experience.

It was all that I recalled, and more. An experience of warm breath on skin. A touch, a halting sigh. A possession. A delight in learning what it might be that gave Richard pleasure. A haven where we pretended that all would be well. Now no man could separate us. Only death could do that.

My last thoughts, before I slept: Where would we go? What would our life be now?

It was as if Richard read my mind, as he often did.

'We must return to the real world, Margery,' he murmured against my hair as he cradled me in his arms. 'We must return to the world of the Pastons and Calles and make a new life there for ourselves. We can be dependent on no one but our own ingenuity and will. And I will hold you. I will not let you fall.'

'But what will you do?'

I did not hear his reply.

The decision was made for us, almost immediately, and some of the answers offered.

'Now you must leave,' the Prioress advised on the following

morning. 'We do not have enough work for a man of your abilities, Master Calle. You need to use a wider net to catch your fish. We will pray for you. The Priory of St Leonard's in Norwich is one of our foundations as well as the Cathedral Priory of the Holy Trinity and the convent at Carrow. We will recommend you to them for your good work. We will miss you with your heavy hand against those who do not pay their rents, but it will be best for you if you go.'

'You are most gracious.' Richard saluted her hand with grace and, as I was aware, with gratitude. 'I will accept your recommendations with a glad heart.'

'Can you accept returning to Norwich?' Richard asked before we parted.

'I can.' I had thought about this. Life was easy enough in a distant place where we were unknown, where we would not be the subject of surveillance or discussion, but it would not be good for Richard. 'It would be the best plan. If my mother sees us established in society there, she may relent. And if she does not, then at least we have tried to mend the rifts. The Prioress was most anxious that I should try. And now you have the promise of employment there.'

We turned our faces to Norwich, full of joy in each other's company, and much silent trepidation in my heart as to what would become of us. Neither of us was willing to burden the other with our fears.

CHAPTER NINETEEN

MISTRESS ANNE HAUTE

The Royal Court in the Palace of Westminster, October 1470

A note found its way to me by one of the royal pages, brief, as Sir John's notes usually were. And infrequent. I had not seen him for some weeks.

> *I have excellent news, my dearest love. Meet with me at the hunt.*

I was not of a mind to rush to do so, except that to refuse would not be to my advantage. I borrowed a spritely mare from the Queen, together with a heavy velvet cloak, and set off, not surprised to find that he was already waiting for me, full of spirit, his eyes smiling even though his face remained solemn. It was as if he had won a notable clash of arms in the tournament, except that there had been no tournaments in these difficult times. I had not been the cause of his elation, but knowing him full well, it must be Caister.

I addressed him as I drew my mount to a halt.

'You look like a cat that has lapped the last milk from the cook's bowl, or raided the palace fish ponds. Beware retribution, Sir John!'

When I had dismounted to talk more comfortably with him, he seized my hands, stripping off my riding gloves and dropping kiss after kiss on my knuckles. The Queen was not riding today, the birth of another child being imminent, so there were no demands on my time other than my own pleasure.

'No retribution this time, dear heart. Not quite so satisfying as a dish of cream, perhaps, but I see the sun rising on my horizon. I am come from a meeting with Waynflete.'

I must have shown my ignorance.

'Bishop of Winchester. Once Lord Chancellor before politics got in the way and he lost the post to George Neville, the Archbishop of York. Our friendly Bishop of Winchester is portly and avaricious but can sometimes be very useful.'

Which did little to assuage my incomprehension of Sir John's air of achievement. 'What I still do not know is why a meeting with this Bishop would put you in such good heart.'

'Waynflete has been a good friend to the Pastons in the past when we have needed negotiation, and so he has proved again. I think we have reached a compromise.'

Of course, it was Caister. No query as to my own health and situation. Had I expected more?

'I am so pleased to hear this,' I said in dulcet tones which might have indicated my irritation if Sir John was listening. 'But does not the Duke of Norfolk at present hold Caister?'

Sir John remained oblivious. 'Yes, but we have discovered a way out of this mess.'

We strolled in the palace gardens, leading our horses, allowing the hunt to leave without us. I recalled strolling through the gardens at Calais when his whole interest had been in wooing me. Not so now.

'It is not all good news for me, but the best we can achieve. Shall I tell you?' He had kept hold of my hands and now led me to a bench drenched in sunlight against the wall, and proceeded to tell me whether I wished it or not, and in considerable detail. After five minutes of legal details, I wished that I had joined the hunt.

'A compromise, as I said. It does not satisfy me completely, but I can see no better outcome. Waynflete has agreed to support me if I will reward him. It is a high price but I think I must pay it. Are all bishops greedy to fill their own purses? I expect that they are.'

'Then tell me what you have agreed.'

'Simply this. I will keep possession of the Fastolf manors of Caister, Hellesdon and Drayton, and some other properties. The castle will be mine.' Thus the gleam in his eye. 'In return for his help in the courts, Bishop Waynflete will take the rest of the lands.' A slight frown marred his brow but it was brief enough to show that he had come to terms with at least one issue. 'Waynflete will not do anything for nothing. My father, God rest his soul, would not approve. Nor, I think, my mother. But I will keep Caister. My mother finds it draughty and cold and would rather live at Mautby, but I see the value of owning a castle. How best to be noticed than as an owner of a superb fortress such as Caister?'

I had never yet been to Caister, so I could not say. Perhaps one day he would take me there. Sir John was on his feet, tightening the girth of his horse as if he intended to follow the hunt after all. I could see a problem here. Surely he could too. It made no sense to see this as a scheme that could be achieved.

'But can this be done?' I asked, from where I remained seated.

He looked around over his shoulder, brows raised. If he saw the problem, he would not admit it without my needling him.

'If Caister is still in the hands of the Duke of Norfolk, what hope is there of your regaining it?' I enquired. 'How can the useful Bishop support you in taking ownership of a castle which is not available for you and he to discuss? I doubt the Duke will listen to fair words from the Bishop to hand it over to you. The Duke will rather have the castle than the Bishop's blessing. And since we have King Edward returned to us, the Duke will feel that he has no enemies, thus he will have a free hand to do as he wishes.' I frowned at Sir John. 'To make such an agreement with Waynflete is like making a fruit pie when the cherries are not yet in season to provide the filling. And even if they were, the blackbirds would squander them before you could get your hands on them.'

Sir John walked back towards me. 'All that you say is true. But one day I have to think that the wheel of fortune will turn in my favour, without a great outlay of money from me.'

'But you will lose some presumably valuable manors to Bishop Waynflete!'

'I will have my castle back!'

There was no arguing with him, and perhaps Sir John's plans would be fulfilled in this changeable Court. I stood, kissed his cheek and tucked my hand in the crook of his arm. Clouds had approached to cover the sun and a little wind got up to shiver the leaves that remained on the trees.

'Then let us leave this draughty place, abandon the hunt that will probably be drenched within a half-hour, find a cup of wine or two and drink to your success.'

He was not reluctant, directing his page to take the horses back to the stables while I pulled on my gloves once more. I still did not understand how this compromise would possibly come about unless the Duke of Norfolk had a complete change of heart.

Would this bloodless victory, if it could be achieved, facilitate my marriage?

'You know a way to a man's heart, dearest Anne,' Sir John remarked as we hurried our steps towards shelter. 'I know that you will always give me good counsel. As well as the sweetest of kisses.'

In spite of all my doubts, my hopes were ridiculously rekindled.

For many of the days that followed, Sir John Paston and the fate of Caister Castle were not high priorities in my mind. Not even my own marriage – or lack of. Danger and fear concentrated the mind on the immediate situation.

The mighty Earl of Warwick, the treacherous Earl of Warwick, was once more doing all he could to overthrow King Edward and strengthen his own powers. With one Neville daughter wed to the royal Duke of Clarence and the other to Prince Edward, son of the ousted King Henry VI, Warwick's position was supreme. To the astonishment of all, a deal was struck in France between Warwick and Queen Margaret of Anjou, two old enemies willing to come together under the aegis of the King of France to remove King Edward. Warwick was on his return across the Channel to rouse his tenants and all the disenchanted magnates against Edward.

Cousin Elizabeth, heavily pregnant beneath the folds of her velvet gown, was wringing her royal hands in distress.

'What do we believe?' she asked in a swirl of foreboding. 'We hear tell of violent uprisings supporting Warwick and Clarence, spreading through the north. We must suppose that they are true.'

'Since the King has taken his forces north, then we must accept that battle is imminent,' I agreed. 'Be calm, Elizabeth. You cannot worry about this child and the King. You will wear yourself out.'

Elizabeth was not the only woman to whom this would be bad news. If Edward raised his standard and faced Warwick in battle, would Sir John Paston fight at his side?

'What do we do?' Elizabeth demanded as she had so many times before, as if any of the women of her household would know the answer. Elizabeth, usually so calm and confident, was feeling the pressure of an absent husband, exacerbated by the imminent arrival of her child.

'We wait,' I said, compassionate to her state. There was nothing else that we could do until we could see which way the wind would blow when Edward faced his disloyal subjects.

'I hope that this child can wait,' Elizabeth complained as cramps beset her, enough to make her groan. 'I would like it to see its father when Warwick has been dealt with. I pray daily for Warwick's defeat and ultimate death.' It did not seem that Warwick's defeat was a certainty, but I would not tell Elizabeth of such a depressing state of affairs as news of his forces marching north swirled round Westminster. Since the Battle of Edgecote Moor in July of the previous year, Elizabeth had been driven by dreams of a vicious revenge against the Earl.

'I pray for the day when Warwick lies dead on a battlefield!' she had raged on hearing the news, and on numerous occasions since, refusing to be pacified.

I did not need to ask why, but she told me anyway.

'It was Warwick's doing that my father, Earl Rivers, and my brother, John Woodville, were taken prisoner. It was Warwick's doing that they were both beheaded at Kenilworth Castle. They deserved better justice. I will never forgive him.'

I could not blame her.

I continued to hear nothing from Sir John Paston. Was he with the King? I had no idea but thought not. Jonty, my other source of Paston information, was also absent from Court. Cousin Andrew Woodville, Lord Scales, now Earl Rivers after his father's death, was no source of information for me either. At least I knew that he was with the King.

The tension at Westminster tightened. And then became agonising beyond tolerance.

'The King has fled,' a courier announced urgently in the Queen's chamber in Westminster, falling to his knees before the Queen. 'King Edward has fled to take refuge across the sea.'

Elizabeth's face became ashen as she questioned the courier. Faced with a country apparently united in support of the Earl of Warwick, Edward had chosen not to face his enemy on the battlefield but had fled the realm, taking ship from King's Lynn for Flanders.

Elizabeth had, to all intents and purposes, been abandoned.

'I am alone,' she stated with praiseworthy regality, despite the tears that stained her cheeks. She thought for a moment. 'Queen Margaret, King Henry the Sixth's wife, led her own army down from the north, to keep the crown from falling into Yorkist hands. Her troops defeated the Yorkists at Wakefield. Could I not do the same, lead an army, to keep the crown safe for Edward?'

I regarded my cousin, as if to give some semblance of weight to her suggestion. Margaret of Anjou had proved to be a belligerent woman, quite capable of leading her army. My cousin Elizabeth, beautiful and elegant in her distress, was not of the same calibre. She might be capable of political machinations, but she was not one to take to the battlefield to personally direct her forces. How to tell her without making her feel even more helpless?

'No, you cannot do that. Not in the physical state that you are in now,' I reassured her, leading her to a cushioned stool. 'It would be difficult to lift you into a saddle, much less fasten you into battle armour. The seams of your robe are straining over your belly as it is.'

'I would risk it to bring Warwick to his knees.'

Which was mere foolishness, brought on by fears that troubled her dreams.

'It would be a risk too great. This child could be Edward's male heir. The baby needs to be nurtured and cared for at the time of its birth.'

Which did the trick. Elizabeth straightened her shoulders and took the only possible action open to her. She and her household, her three small daughters and this imminent child, took sanctuary once again behind the walls of Westminster Abbey. They would remain there as they had once before in safety and in isolation until the future became clearer.

'We will not trust ourselves to Warwick's tender mercies.'

A sentiment with which I agreed. So, as the Queen, my cousin, settled to a life of prayer and solitude, and of security – for no one would break the sanctuary in fear of God's wrath – I watched the playing out of bloody politics.

And I worried. Not about my cousin, who would be safe from all harm in the sanctuary of the Abbey, but about Sir John Paston.

Jonty had paid a rapid visit to Westminster as we were making our chaotic way, with all the necessities for a long sojourn, to take up residence in the Archbishop's accommodations in the Abbey. I halted, allowing the Queen and her children and entourage to go on ahead. Jonty was lacking all his habitual exuberance.

'If it's bad news, don't tell me,' I warned after a morning of suffering Elizabeth's indecision. 'We have enough of it here.'

'It's bad enough,' he announced.

'What is it?' I asked with a terrible moment of foresight. The only reason he would come to see me was if his brother had sent him or was in some danger. Was he with the army after all? I gripped Jonty's arm, pulling him closer. 'Are you going to tell me?' I shook him impatiently, a world of anxiety opening at my feet.

Jonty's statement was a bald warning. 'It's Sir John. He is ill and, so he claims, close to death. He thought that you should know.'

'Death?' I whispered, my voice caught in my throat, my eyes on his, compelling him to tell me the truth. 'He is dying?' My mind could not quite grasp the enormity of this news. There was always pestilence rife in London. If that was his affliction, he would surely die. I was distraught. 'Tell me!'

Jonty had the grace to drop his gaze. Had he deliberately intended to frighten me? 'Well, perhaps not quite death. My brother exaggerates.'

I breathed out slowly and punched his arm for so frightening me.

'And you are wickedly malevolent, Jonty Paston. You should be ashamed. Do I visit him?' I asked.

'Better not.' He grinned at my accusation. 'No need to worry too much. He is dosing himself on some nostrum and complaining of its vileness.' I must have expressed the horror that I felt. 'It is not the pestilence, mistress, I assure you.'

'Then what is it?'

'A fever.'

'Do I fear for his survival?'

'I expect him to recover soon enough. You might offer up a prayer.'

'You seem remarkably sanguine about the situation.'

'I have no fear that he will die, Mistress Haute.' A sly gleam of humour appeared in his face. 'Although if he did, it would solve your marriage problem in a most emphatic manner.'

A reply that shook me, as was intended, for the second time.

'And you are impertinent, Jonty Paston.'

He bowed in impudent farewell.

Leaving me to realise, as I followed the Queen, that in spite of all Sir John's failings, I would not have his death and my release happen for the world. As my heart resumed its normal steady beat, the idea touched my mind that an ailment that took him to his bed might have provided an excellent excuse for not joining his King on the battlefield. A useful political device indeed. But perhaps I was doing him a disservice. He would not be so disloyal.

But there was definitely a mischievous streak in Jonty Paston that would bear watching. Was it to teach me a lesson? Did I care for Sir John? It seemed that I did, for in that instant when death had been present, my heart had been wrung with loss.

Sir John Paston recovered without either my presence or my tender care, and perhaps even my prayers had been superfluous if his sufferings had been of a political nature, so that now I stood with the two Paston brothers to watch this astonishing event that was unfolding before us. The Earl of Warwick had released the old King Henry from his imprisonment in the Tower of London and had arranged his Readeption which on this day entailed a victory procession through the streets. Henry, looking old and ill, far more aged than his forty-nine years, wore the crown once more, a symbol of the restoration of the House of Lancaster and the fall of the House of York.

He did not wear it well, rather as a bauble in which he had no interest. His smile for the crowd was weak and without understanding of the importance of his place in the centre of this upheaval. If this was a victory, he had no sense of it. I took note that he was hardly arrayed as a prince, nor was his garment, a long full-skirted gown, as clean as any King might wish for. The ermine at sleeve and hem was decidedly moth-eaten.

I watched with some interest, marvelling at the audacity of the Earl of Warwick to put on this display of loyalty to the man whom he had taken prisoner at the Battle of Northampton, but my mind was sadly elsewhere.

The man who stood beside me was a shadow of the man with whom I had exchanged vows. My suspicions had been ill-founded after all. His skin grey and sallow, his shoulders were bowed, until he remembered to straighten them. Even his clothing was restrained, the discreet lawyer in grey and black rather than the extravagant courtier. He looked as if he had only recently risen from his sick bed.

'Should you be here?' I asked.

'Probably not.'

He blotted perspiration from his face with a kerchief. Jonty was without compassion.

'He could hardly hold up his head two days ago. He needed a staff to support him to descend the stair in his lodging, looking more like a ghost than a man in his prime.' He grinned at his unreceptive brother. 'More as if he had risen out of the earth than out of a fair lady's bed.'

Upon which Sir John roused himself enough to punch Jonty on the shoulder.

'Forgive me, Mistress Haute,' Jonty said. 'I meant no disrespect. My brother's loyalty to you is beyond question, as you will know.' And then to Sir John: 'Mother will send you any number of remedies, if you tell her.'

'Then don't tell her. I'll do well enough without her physicking.'

'She travelled to London herself when our father took sick in the days before he died. To soothe his fevered brow.'

'And obviously to little effect. Don't tell her.' Sir John's brow creased in thought. 'You do realise, Jonty, that the return of the Earl of Oxford from exile in the company of Warwick will present us with some difficulties.'

'What difficulties?'

'Those of loyalty and implicit treason. We may have to make a difficult choice. Do we support York or Lancaster in the future?'

I knew not the reference, although I was acquainted with the Earl of Oxford, a capable soldier from a strongly Lancastrian family, as well as being brother-in-law to the Earl of Warwick. I shuffled the Earl aside, as of no immediate account. I had been struggling with worry about Sir John yet here was Jonty tossing in the accusation that he was sharing his bed with another Court lady. Nor did I entirely believe his denial.

All I could do was hope that it was mere mischief making and that Sir John had been far too ill to look for comfort elsewhere. They began to talk business appertaining to the Earl of Oxford's allegiance and I left them to it with a brisk farewell. The shade of a certain lady named Constance Reynforth, the mother of Sir John's illegitimate daughter, had risen to make of us a quartet which did nothing for my peace of mind.

I returned into sanctuary with the Queen and left Sir John to his own devices, although, in spite of his preoccupations, he had the grace to capture my wrist and press his lips to where my heart beat there, in a thoroughly romantic gesture as we parted that did little to ease my concerns. Would I ever discover a supporting voice in the Paston household? It was unlikely that Mistress Paston would even consider my situation when Caister continued to hover on her particular horizon. It was not a subject I felt that I could raise with my betrothed.

CHAPTER TWENTY

MARGARET MAUTBY PASTON

The Paston House in Norwich, October 1470

Pushing aside the problems of poaching and deceitful millers, we kept a close eye on the tense situation between King Edward and the Earl of Warwick, not that either could be wagered on to come to Paston aid, but in this month the Paston family changed its allegiance. Loyalty was a thing of the past. It became of interest to us to exchange the white rose for the red, and with that change our spirits were lifted from the mire of desperation to the ranks of the angelic angels. There was hope for us at last.

How did this complete reversal in Paston loyalties come about?

All because we had seen the red rose of Lancaster restored to power when Warwick and Clarence returned from exile in France and re-crowned King Henry VI. King Edward himself was now in exile, his wife the Queen in sanctuary in Westminster Abbey, so that the white rose of York was of no value to the Pastons, who were in dire need of a patron at Court. When Warwick set his victorious foot once more on English soil, with him came John de Vere, Earl of Oxford, which proved to be excellent news for the Pastons. The Earl of Oxford had offered patronage to Sir John. How valuable would that be to us, with Oxford at the centre of the newly restored Lancastrian Court and with the Earl of Warwick held close in solid friendship? Caister would once more be ours.

'Tell me why the mighty Earl of Oxford is interested in becoming patron of such a minor family as ours?' I had asked Sir John when first told of this development. 'Is it wise for us to be dragged into any of Oxford's Court ambitions? And is he not very young?'

Sir John was typically short-tempered. 'Of course it is wise. Who is the most powerful magnate in East Anglia after the Dukes of Norfolk and Suffolk? The Earl of Oxford, of course. He might have lived less than thirty years, but he is a man who has earned an honourable name for himself. He sees us as another stone in building up his defences against his rivals. What will we get in return? A powerful sword arm when we come under attack from our greedy neighbours.'

Which was a clear enough reply. After some casual gossip in Norwich, I liked what I heard of the Earl, a clever young man with a reputation as a commander in the field. His father and elder brother had both been executed for treason by Yorkist King Edward, meaning that his only hope of political power was to side with Lancaster. All good for us in the present circumstances, if he would stand by us, yet while I was now in a position to hope for better times, I was still living in straitened circumstances. And still my husband's much-neglected grave was no further towards completion, despite all promises to remedy it by his eldest son and heir. The gravestone bearing John's name and escutcheon at Bromholm Priory had never been completed. Sir John had sent a fine-enough cloth to cover the bare slab, probably to keep me from what he saw as shrewish scolding, but it was a superficial remedy; with the years passing, the cloth was now much worn and tattered round the edge, and still no impressively carved tomb. What a terrible indictment of the Paston family and of Sir John's negligence! I set my teeth and got on with the immediate problems.

I decided it was time to part with some of my Mautby possessions. My sons were desperate for money in London, but with the excellent news that the Duke and Duchess of Norfolk had agreed with the Earl of Oxford to look kindly on our demand that Caister be returned, I would willingly send them what I could. Two silver platters, six dishes and six saucers, all to the value of twenty pounds or more. I warned Sir John to take care with the spending of it. Our revenues were down, expenses up, creditors rubbing their hands and pressing hard. Out of it all I found the money to keep our Caister men in meat and drink until Hallowmas at least, the first day of November. I could do no less. It would dishonour us simply to turn them off without sustenance. I did not tell either of my elder sons that my own circumstances were so parlous that I was considering breaking up my household. My penury was becoming the subject of sly gossip in Norwich.

But matters grew worse. In spite of all my advice to the contrary, Sir John mortgaged our newly recovered manor of East Beckham to a Norfolk lawyer and moneylender for a hundred marks. And if that were not bad enough, Jonty came with more worries. The Duke of Norfolk, malice akimbo, no matter what he had promised to the Earl of Oxford, had decided to take on the cases of two widows against us. Their husbands had been killed at Caister and they would sue against Jonty for their loss.

'And can we guess why he is doing this?' I asked.

'We can indeed. He threatened to sue me, to stop Sir John from suing him for the recovery of Caister.' Jonty, on an unexpected visit to Norwich, regarded me sternly, as if I were a dependant rather than his mother. 'Have you patched up your quarrel with my brother?'

'I have instigated no quarrel with your brother.'

'You know well what I mean.'

'If you mean have I apologised for castigating him for lack of effort on our behalf, no, I have not. Have I apologised for warning him not to mortgage any of our manors, then I have not done that either. Nor have I remained silent when he went against my advice.' I took a breath. 'But the tone of our last letters was at least on a friendly level.'

'Thank God for that. I don't think that Sir John has ever stood up to you in his life.'

'No. The last time I took him severely to task, in the days when his father was hounding him, Sir John fled the house and informed me by letter he was gone. I remember it well.'

Indeed, I was pleased that Sir John was more communicative. I did not need any further rift in our family. I could just about forgive him that he had not had the money to leave London and come home to Norfolk. This situation had urged me to dispatch bolts of cloth to him, sufficient for two shirts. It was the least I could do.

Thus I was pleased to see Jonty with enough ready coin to return to Norwich, even if it was only to meet up with the Earl of Oxford. I thought that he looked dismal but he hid it well enough when in my company. Since he was here within my orbit, and since it was impossible to get Sir John to attend to what I might say, I sat him down with a cup of ale and faced him.

'What now?' he asked.

'Will you take some advice?' I suggested, ignoring the lack of respect in his sharp question.

'I will listen.' He was wary.

'How many men will you take with you when you see the Earl of Oxford?'

'A goodly number.'

'Excellent.'

'Why?'

'So that Oxford does not think that you speak for yourself only. He needs to see you as a man of influence. I consider that the Earl is no fool, and so needs to be convinced that we are worthy of his efforts on our behalf.'

'Sir John has already told me that,' he replied. But at least he was listening.

'And I would advise you to leave your sword at home.'

He bridled. 'Why would I be so unwise?'

'To prove that you are not a riotous person, out to cause a disturbance, but rather a man of substance. The Duke of Norfolk has already threatened to have you arrested for disturbing the peace at Caister.'

He thought about this for a moment. 'Excellent advice.'

Why did I believe there was something that he was not telling me?

'I am surprised that Sir John is not here with you,' I ventured.

'He has been ill.'

I sat up, a sudden unease shivering over my flesh. 'Why did no one tell me?'

'He did not wish to worry you.'

'So that discovering it later would make me worry less?'

Discovering no pertinent reply Jonty took himself off to clothe himself as befitted a peace-loving gentleman of Norfolk society, leaving me to recall my husband falling ill in London. I would not think of his death. Sir John, who did not wish me to fuss over him, was young and hale and would doubtless recover left to his own devices and, presumably, those of Mistress Haute. Fleetingly it crossed my mind: would I ever know if Margery fell ill, even if she died? Would Calle come here to tell me? I brushed the thought away for I had no answer, only the uncomfortable thoughts of making beds and lying on them.

CHAPTER TWENTY-ONE

MARGERY PASTON CALLE

The Calle House in Norwich, Summer 1470

We rented a house from the nuns at Carrow at a most amenable rate in return for Richard's attention to their accounts and rent rolls. It was a small two-storied dwelling in one of the narrow streets off Tombland, the market square to the south of the cathedral, a home for us constructed with stone foundations and much lath and plaster. No great distance from the Paston house on Elm Hill, it was a world away in comfort and social standing for those who might dwell there. The walls were damp, the windows small, the rooms cramped and difficult to heat, but it was a house that we could call our own.

Richard began to attract work with craftsmen who found a need for an able man to survey some financial irregularity or a collection of rents, small enough employment, but sufficient to keep us from starvation. We slept in our own bed in our own chamber. In the dark winter mornings before the sun rose, I lay in his arms, thinking about our life here. What would I do in so small a household? There would be more demands on my time when I quickened with a child. Until then I took up my old skills of spinning and weaving when my time was not demanded by the needs of any household, to purchase food and prepare a good table, such as I could. We would not be ill-dressed, nor would we be ill-fed.

At first, I was reluctant to go about in the town, anticipating the lack of welcome that I might receive. I feared mostly my path crossing that of my mother. I could not imagine what we might say to each other.

'You will say what is in your heart,' Richard said when I poured out my anxiety. 'You are Mistress Calle with some dignity and the blessing of the Bishop. It would be a brave man – or woman – who would now condemn you. Are we not put right in the eyes of God? The Pastons cannot claim superiority. Now come and kiss me and I will go to a meeting at the tannery where a delivery of hides appears to have gone astray. And it's not the first time.'

'Could it be lucrative?'

'It may be so. It is a good business. They make vellum for the use of the religious houses, so there is always a need.' He wrinkled his nose. 'It is the stench of the tannery that is the worst of it, but if it pays well, I will accept returning home reeking as if I have spent my day in a midden.'

'Then the Blessed Virgin go with you! I will promise to scrub you clean when you return.'

There was one uneasy image that continued to play in my mind. For my own peace of mind I must remedy it.

One morning, before Richard left to deal with the accounts of one of the leather-workers, I pulled on a cloak and hood, and a pair of gloves decorated with cat-fur, a grateful gift from the tannery for Richard's work there. They had been less generous with coin, but I appropriated the gloves for my own use.

'Is this an early visit to the market?' Richard asked.

'No. Not that.' I asked one boon: 'Will you walk with me to Elm Hill?'

He turned to look so searchingly at me that I thought he would refuse. 'Why?'

'I wish to walk past my old house.'

'Are you sure?'

'Yes.'

'I see no advantage in that. Only heartbreak.'

'I would just like to do it. A whim, if you wish.'

I had lived in many Paston houses during my life, at Paston, Mautby and Oxnead. I had stayed for a time in Caister Castle. But this house in Norwich was the one that I loved the best. I would probably see it from the outside many times over the years but now, on my wedded return, I wished to walk along the length of Elm Hill and envisage my past there.

'But why?'

'I think that it is a test of my mature emotions. Just to see if I have recovered from knowing that the door will never open to me again.'

Richard surveyed me, then nodded in acceptance.

'Then I cannot refuse. I don't like the pain it will cause, but I will walk with you. You will know that you are not alone.'

We walked along Elm Hill with its two rows of respectable residences, past the house where I had lived, but on the opposite side of the street. To me it looked exactly the same, even though it was quiet and there was no one abroad. The roof line, the gables, the shutters to keep out the winds from the east, the stalwart lath-and-plaster walls. The carved wooden door through which I had so often entered. A substantial house of a reputable family, all part of my life that I had accepted without thought. Had I hoped to see my mother? Perhaps not. Then what had I hoped for? I did not know that either. I felt strangely empty of all feeling, but at least I felt no return of the old grief. I had a new life now, and a new child was growing beneath my girdle.

Then I turned my face away.

There was no welcome there.

'These walls do not make a home,' Richard said, the edge in his voice making me look up at him, surprised at the cold anger on my behalf. Seeing the concern in my eyes, he forced his expression and his voice to soften. 'Let us go home, my dearest Margery. There is no longer anything for you here. A small rented dwelling is enough for us for now. We will make our own life there and be happy in it. Our life will never again be dependent on the whims of Mistress Margaret Paston.'

It was difficult to accept but I seized the thought. My mother would no longer hold dominance in my household, for was I not Mistress Calle, capable of proving that marriage had not robbed me of a Paston determination? Even so, after all the hostilities, I hoped for a reconciliation. Was it hopeless? If my mother could achieve a good marriage for my sister Anne, it might draw the sting. One satisfactory marriage might just cancel out an unacceptable one, and gain me access to the Paston House again.

'I hope that Anne is satisfied with the husband my mother finds for her,' I said later, breaking the silence as Richard and I lay together on a very lumpy, newly-purchased, wool-stuffed mattress.

'Let us hope that he can provide her with a better bed!' Richard, shuffling to find a comfortable spot, was duly cynical. 'I doubt that your mother will risk another debacle. Anne will be tied up into some local family of standing before the year is out.'

I felt a brush of guilt, that my scandal might well be the cause of a hasty marriage for Anne who, to my knowledge, was still boarding with the Calthorp family. Perhaps they would discover a young man of good temper and wealth for her; I could not worry about what I could not influence.

'Let us not waste time on marriages other than our own,' Richard advised after more shuffling. 'Come and kiss me since I am not of a mind to sleep.'

I was more than willing to comply. The discomfort of the new mattress lost its importance.

CHAPTER TWENTY-TWO

MARGARET MAUTBY PASTON

The Paston House in Norwich, October 1470

I needed no more troubles. They made my head ache. But here on my threshold was what might become one. A new one.

I was distracted and short-tempered so that any interruption to my day was resented. Margery's return to live in Norwich was a burr against my skin. Caister was still securely in the hands of Norfolk. But there on my doorstep stood a young woman with a maidservant at her side. The horses were just being led off to the stables.

'Anne!'

It took me a moment to collect my wits, even though I had been expecting her, ever since that unsettling letter had reached me. My first thought was that she had grown in height and some elegance since I had last seen her, although her face was pale and her mouth set in stern disapproval. She was all but a grown woman rather than the young girl I had sent to live with my cousin. A curl of her hair escaping from her lace-trimmed coif was the same deep russet of a ripe chestnut, inherited from some distant Mautby, an attractive tint that I had always much envied in my daughter, for I was mouse-brown. I should have drawn her into my arms in a maternal embrace. I should have smiled and shown pleasure. I knew that I should have done both. Instead, perhaps due to the ache in my head, I said:

'I hate to think why this has come about, Anne. What have you done?'

From the frown between my daughter's brows, it was not what she had hoped for. A sharp wound of regret now made me take hold of her hand and draw her into the hall, nodding to her maid to follow.

'What has happened?'

At last it struck me that Anne had yet to speak a word. To make amends for my lack of welcome, I drew her to the fire that did little to dispel the cold of the hall and pushed her to sit down, leaving the maid to find her own way towards the servants' quarters. I sat beside my daughter on the settle, lifting her chin to the light, until she gently pushed my hand aside and turned her face away as she unfastened the clasp of her cloak. I saw that she wore a kerchief of fine cremil around her shoulders, one that I had sent to her since she had so little finery of her own in my cousin's household.

'Is there a problem?' I repeated, unable to quell a frown. 'I hope you have not been sent home in disgrace. Nothing was clear in my cousin's letter.'

My daughter made her thoughts clear in a voice that was low and well controlled, devoid of any emotion.

'No, Mother. I am not in disgrace. The demeanour of at least some of our family is impeccable.'

A short answer that made me bite my tongue.

This was my younger daughter, boarded out with my cousins, the Calthorp family. Sir William Calthorp, of Cockthorpe in Norfolk, a relative of mine through my Mautby family. He was a man with an excellent reputation and local standing, as well as a growing family; he had, for a financial consideration, been pleased to allow Anne to live with them and to be useful in the household, and to provide her with an education in a gentry family. It had been my intention that she remain with the Calthorps until a husband could be found for her and the storm of Margery and Richard Calle had blown over.

She was six years younger than Margery.

'What has happened, daughter?' I softened my tone.

'I am sent home, as you see.'

'I was of the understanding that you were well settled there.

Why would Sir William ask me to remove you? I did not like the tone of his letter. It had an air of superiority about it. Have you done ought to displease him?'

Not only superiority had weighed down that missive. Sir William had demanded that I make immediate arrangements for the removal of my daughter from his house. Had he caught her out in some wrong-doing? I regarded her young face, the clear naïvety of her eyes, the sweetness of her softly curving mouth – when she was not as cross as a wasps' nest – and warm brown hair which escaped at the temples from beneath her neat turban. She was perhaps the prettiest of the Pastons, despite the straight Paston nose, and the most amenable with, as I recalled from when she was a child, an even temper. How could she have displeased my cousin? She had only just reached her sixteenth birthday.

'I have done nothing of which I am ashamed, Mother,' Anne announced. 'It hurts me that you would so accuse me.' Her expressive mouth twisted in bitter acceptance. 'Of course, in the circumstances, I know why you presume that I might.'

In the circumstances, although I thought I could have been forgiven for my suspicions of the actions of any of my children, there was resentment in Anne's response, and perhaps she was right.

'I accuse you of nothing. Tell me what has occurred.'

'It is quite simple. Sir William has decided to reduce his household,' she explained bleakly. 'And I am sorry for it. I was happy there.'

'Why would he do that?'

'The birth of yet another addition to the family, a daughter.'

I nodded, doing a quick count. 'Their fourth child. It will be a busy household. I would suppose that you would be useful to him.' And then the obvious answer. 'Is he short of money?'

'So he says. His tenants are slow in paying their rents. I was the one who could be dispensed with, despite my usefulness in dealing with growing infants, and the financial incentive of my boarding, of course. They will no longer have to feed me.'

'I doubt you would take much from his pocket,' I remarked, eyeing her still unformed figure. Like most of the Pastons, she would not be a tall woman nor large of bone. 'It seems a specious argument to me.'

'Sir William says that I am now full grown and that you must find me a husband.'

'Yes. He told me as much in his letter.'

Was this indeed a reflection of what he had heard about Margery, for assuredly the gossip would have spread to the Calthorps. Perhaps Sir William feared that her youthful grace and fair features would cause problems with his servants. But he had daughters of his own. Could he not order his household in such a way that there were no difficulties between servants and family?

I sighed a little. How could I accuse anyone of careless handling of a household? I had not managed it well. I could hardly blame my cousin Calthorp for something at which I had signally failed. Margery should never have been allowed to fall in love with Richard Calle.

Anne raised her eyes to mine, her expression uncommonly stern for such a young girl, as if she had decided to say what might not be the most diplomatic answer. 'Perhaps it is the scandal in the Paston household. Perhaps Sir William wished to be rid of me – and it – from under his roof.'

So there it was, as I had suspected.

'There is no scandal here,' I said. 'Not any more, at least.'

'Perhaps Sir William thinks that there is. Or at least the lingering taint of it.'

Her eyes fell but she made no further comment. I did not know whether she was happy to be home or if she would rather be at Dame Elizabeth Calthorp's beck and call, but decided not to pursue Anne's judgement.

'Well, you are here, and I am pleased to welcome you home.' I really must make more of an effort. Here was the only daughter left to me after Margery's debacle. Yet still I found myself asking:

'I trust you have made no inappropriate friendships while you were at Cockthorpe.'

'None, Mother.'

'You must not waste your time now that you are home. There is no time for reading or day-dreaming here.'

'I did not waste my time at the Calthorps,' she said.

'Then you will have been instructed into good habits.'

I stood, and she stood with me.

'Where is Margery?' Anne asked as we climbed the stairs to her chamber, which had been made ready for her. She held my stare as I turned round. 'They never speak of her at Cockthorpe so I do not know.'

I was tight-lipped and continued to climb the stair. 'Margery no longer lives here.'

'Was that your choice?'

I thought it was an impertinent question from a daughter but turned to look at her once more. And I answered. 'It was Margery's choice. She put her relationship with Calle before her duty to the family.'

'Is Master Calle still employed in the household?'

It was quite a catechism. Anne had learned to speak up for herself at Cockthorpe. It struck me uncomfortably that she had developed a strong resemblance to myself in my young days.

'No.'

'I am sorry.'

'It would be impossible.'

'Is Father Gloys still a member of the household?'

'Of course. Why would he not be? He has served the Pastons since long before you were born.'

I tried to ignore the curl of her lip. How could it fail to come to my notice that although I valued Father Gloys's advice, not one of my children had any liking for him. Why did I keep such an abrasive and confrontational priest with me in my household, for indeed his character had not mellowed with age? Perhaps because he had remained faithful to the Pastons for the whole of my marriage, through good times and bad. He had come to me with the Paston household I inherited on my marriage. Mistress Agnes had managed to put up with him and so must I. Husband John would cry foul from his grave, and so would Mistress Agnes, loud and shrill in life, if I cast him off now, even though sometimes I felt that his decisions were less than godly. Old loyalties truly died hard.

★

I left Anne in her room while I returned to discuss matters of flooding with one of my tenants whose home was being inundated. My heart was not in it. Did he think I was preoccupied? It was true enough almost to the point of discourtesy as he left, business complete.

Margery had broken my heart. It was not my intention to make the rift between us permanent. I would not have banished her from my door. Father Gloys had taken it on his own head, but then all had spun out of my control. The Bishop, the marriage, the decision for Margery to live in the Best household. I tried not to remember my harsh condemnation of her. How could I have been driven to speak such bitter recriminations, words that might never be forgiven? Yet Father Gloys had persuaded me that it must be for the best, to cut all connections. Margery must know how tenuous was our footing in the ranks of the gentry. Marriage to Richard Calle had the offensive stench of being of the lower classes, even if he was an excellent bailiff.

Margery's fateful affair was for me a terrible anguish. I had lost her. In my confession I acknowledged that I should have been more willing to compromise, but why could she not see the consequences of what she had done? We were clinging to the first step of being a gentry family. Any misstep would cast us down again. I could not bear that, for John and all he fought for.

And yet was it not my fault that I had banished Margery? Of course it was. I could put the blame on no one else's shoulders. I had thought it would bring her to heel; Father Gloys had advised me that it would. I did not know that he had told her that I would never see her cross my threshold again. And that was my fault too, to allow Father Gloys such a loud voice in my household.

Sometimes I was too tired to care.

And yet I wished there was some way to mend the cruel wounds. I could not see it and my sons were not willing to begin a reconciliation. What would happen when Margery and Calle had their own children? Would I ever see them? It was a weight on my heart. Mother and daughter, both made from the same clay, both unwilling to compromise. I now knew that they had been wed, legitimately, before a priest, and were renting a house from Carrow Priory.

Should I visit and make a gesture of reconciliation?

I could not. My pride was too great.

But the alternative was to accept that we were estranged for ever.

God would surely hold me to account on the day of my death.

I knew that I must not make the same mistake with Anne. Just as she must not be allowed to make the same mistake as Margery had done. But that was foolishness. There would be no opportunities for lightning to strike twice in the same household.

All would be well. Perhaps one day I would be reunited with Margery, while Anne was proving to be the most inestimable of daughters. And then there were my sons; Walter and Willem, still young but driven with the ambition of all Pastons, continued to pursue their education while Edmund was still under my roof, looking for a position with some man of substantial means. I could rely on Edmund to make a well-reasoned choice. Father Gloys continued to give me advice as well as God's blessing.

Which did not stop me from writing to Sir John to find Anne a husband who would do us all credit. I could see no difficulty in this. She had the makings of an excellent wife.

'When did you arrive?' I asked.

'A half-hour ago.'

It seemed that my family was returned to Norfolk. Following the sound of the loudest voices, it was to discover Jonty, sitting in the kitchen, a platter of food before him, but with little interest in it. Elbows propped on the table, his fingers were dug into his forehead, the picture of indecision, even though Anne, sliding to sit beside him on the settle, pestered him with questions about what he had been doing.

I could hear another voice elsewhere in the house.

'So Sir John is with you.'

'Yes.'

Even when I came to sit opposite him, waving the servants away, Jonty barely looked up. He was twenty-six years old, with all his life in front of him, the patronage of the Earl of Oxford assured, but I was becoming concerned for him. The loss of Caister had been a blow to his pride and to his livelihood. What was there for him to do with his time? For obvious reasons he no longer had any hope of an attachment to the household of the Duke of Norfolk; it was impossible to trade blows in a siege on one day and sit at dinner together on the next. Mautby was no place for him to be, with Caister a bare three miles across the fields. Mistress Agnes would not want him, restless and unoccupied at Oxnead. Affairs might change as the crown passed back and forth, but Jonty was without direction, without employment, which would give him an income and a sense of purpose.

Unless I could put some ideas into his head.

'What am I going to do with you?' I asked. 'Since you seem to be at a loose end.'

'My ends are very loose,' he growled. 'You could send me off to visit some Paston manor where the rents are in arrears, I suppose. I may as well do that as sit here and look at this platter of eel fritters for which I have no appetite.'

Enthusiasm was definitely not noticeable. For perhaps the first time I saw a strong likeness between him and Sir John who never enjoyed the daily grind of land ownership. The strains of Caister's loss had smoothed out a little; not the disappointment, nor the determination to take it back, but at least the day-to-day threat of facing Norfolk's army and the fear of failure had seeped away. It was in my mind that Jonty had enjoyed the siege. It had given him excitement and a purpose.

'May I go with him?' Anne asked.

I shook my head. I had one idea in mind for Jonty. I had had it for some time now.

'Which manor needs me most?' Jonty asked. 'Of course Anne can come. Or perhaps it's time that we sought out and interviewed a new bailiff who can replace—'

That was not a direction which I wanted our conversation to take.

'Talk to me about marriage, Jonty,' I interrupted him.

'Marriage! Do we not have enough problems with marriage

without my taking a step into that dangerous pond?' He bared his teeth in a grimace as he pushed his platter aside, the food now congealed in its savoury sauce. 'If you wish to talk to me, let us talk of other matters. Have you heard the latest from my brother's endlessly intriguing life of love and infatuation at the Court?'

'No. And I have little interest in it. He will do as he pleases without any help from me.'

I knew well to what Jonty referred. Sir John still seemed to be caught up in a betrothal which could neither be broken nor advanced into a marriage. Much his own doing, I suspected. He had seen the opportunity for an alliance with a woman who had royal connections, but was not prepared to spend the time to complete the deed. I feared it would never happen, and indeed my advice, which he might or might not take, was to smooth his own estate problems before taking a bride. And now with the loss of Caister, would he ever put his mind to establishing Mistress Haute in her own household? Margery was irrevocably lost to me. Now a husband must be found for Anne. And here before me was Jonty, regaling me with Court gossip, enjoying my disapproval.

'Never mind the affairs of the King and the Earl of Warwick. Talk to me about your proposed marriage,' I interrupted. 'What happened to the Boleyn girl? You have said no more about her.'

'Because Alice Boleyn and I came to nothing.'

Some three years before, Jonty had been in pursuit of Lady Boleyn's daughter, but there had been no great eagerness for it, even though, for a Paston, it would have been a good match.

'So you are not overly disappointed.'

'Not I!' He grinned, life returning to his face. For me it was unsettling. Rumours abounded over Jonty's successes and failures with the fair women of Norfolk and beyond. It was time that he settled into marriage and produced Paston sons of his own.

'Was she pretty?' Anne asked.

Jonty drew his hands down his cheeks. 'In truth, it's hard to remember.'

Sir John walked in to hear our last comment, so that suddenly the kitchen was full of energy. Not the place to discuss family affairs, but the servants had wisely withdrawn about their own work.

'Sir John.'

He planted a kiss on my cheek, hugged Anne, and dropped onto the settle beside me. He had recovered from whatever ailment had afflicted him, without my worrying over him.

'Ask my little brother about a certain Mistress Katherine Dudley,' he advised with a sly nudge of his elbow. 'A lady known for her fine neck and elegant shoulders.'

I raised my brows at Jonty, whose features had become suffused with high colour. 'Well? Who is she? Would she be a worthy bride?'

Sir John's laughter filled the room. 'He's not likely to find out. She won't have him.'

'You lie, brother, you lie,' Jonty responded, but without animosity. 'Truth to tell, we were much taken with each other but the lady claims to have many who admire her who might please her just as much as I do. Mistress Dudley says that she has no intention of becoming a bride for another two years. I tried to negotiate but it seemed to me that the lady is happy with her life as it is.'

I watched his expression. It was difficult to tell whether he was disappointed or relieved that the lukewarm Mistress Dudley had turned her much-admired shoulder against him.

'She does not know what she is missing,' Sir John said. 'I wouldn't wait so long. Nor would I want a reluctant bride, of course.'

'You already have a bride, if you would but make it legal,' Jonty retaliated.

'We shall see.'

Once again, I had the impression that Sir John would slide out of this unfortunate commitment with Mistress Haute. With Sir John's marriage in abeyance, we needed more male Paston heirs. Surely Jonty had thought of that. I would not ask him now with his brother here, but I would when I got Jonty alone again.

'I will continue searching,' he was saying. Then looked up at his brother, his face suddenly serious. 'Pray get me a wife somewhere! You will see all the women of beauty and high connection at Court. Put in a good word for your little brother.'

Sir John filled four cups of ale, pushing one towards Jonty, raising his own in fraternal mockery of a toast.

'Am I to woo them for you?'

'Jonty can do all the wooing,' I said, taking my own cup. 'Simply discover a good name or two with Court connections. You may as well earn your keep while you otherwise waste your time there.'

He accepted my low blow.

'I will do what I can. Perhaps Mistress Haute will have some suggestions.'

'I would rather Mistress Haute had suggestions about how to get your betrothal to one fulfilment or another.' I frowned. 'Perhaps you should look elsewhere after all. If the Woodvilles are out of favour, what value to you in taking a Woodville wife?'

In all seriousness, he bowed gravely.

'It is something I have considered.'

We parted, nothing settled, while I took Anne off to occupy her with some useful task rather than listening to the Court chatter of her brothers. I had little confidence in Sir John's efforts. Besides, would it not be of better value to make a connection with a local family of note? I mistrusted the raw ambitions of the Court. I must discover some local girl of good family, or perhaps there was nothing amiss in looking at wealthy London merchants. They had money and might be pleased to be connected with a gentry family, even an impoverished one as we were. What an unending confliction it was becoming.

'Why is marriage all we ever talk about?' Anne grumbled, preferring to remain with her brothers.

'Because a good marriage is the foundation of every successful family. The Pastons have excelled at it. And with God's help, will continue to do so.'

'Then we should pray that my brother legalises his union with Mistress Haute. If he does not, we are faced with yet another blot on the page of Paston honour.'

It was an astute observation, and one that I chose to ignore.

CHAPTER TWENTY-THREE

MISTRESS ANNE HAUTE

The Royal Court in the Palace of Westminster, December 1470

I met with Sir John Paston in Westminster Hall when the cold rose through my soft shoes and permeated the layers of shift, overskirts and gown. Even the fur cloak I had borrowed from the Queen was not sufficient; my ears were cold despite the turban of beaver fur I had also borrowed. I was not in the best of moods after the weeks of isolation. There was no celebration today for the newly crowned King Henry. Edward was still in exile, the Queen still in sanctuary. The only change in their circumstances was the birth of a royal son and heir in the previous month, named Edward for his absent father. A father he might never see alive. It was a worrying time for us all and the Queen was fractious.

As for my own state of mind, Sir John's absence fostered a tiny nugget of concern. Even though, knowing him as I did, I should have expected it.

What did Sir John Paston want with me now?

My first thought was that he was much restored to health. Whatever had stricken him had been healed. Eyes bright, skin clear, hair shining, he was full of vigour, apparently oblivious to the cold, although he too was wrapped around in fur and heavy damask.

'What is it?'

I was not inclined to be friendly, but Sir John absorbed none of my ill favour as he invariably failed to do when preoccupied. He broke his news to me without even a semblance of a greeting as might be expected between lovers.

'Caister Castle.'

I sighed. 'What of it?'

'It is mine again.'

Considering the dread fate of the House of York, and the terrible chill, I was unmoved.

'I thought that you were here to ask about my well-being.'

'Of course.' His eyes shone, picking up the light from a nearby branch of candles that did little to lift the gloom of the Great Hall. 'But I knew that you were safe in holy protection.'

'I thought you might even come to ask after the Queen's health.'

'She is safe, too.'

'We have a royal son and heir. A new Yorkist heir for the crown that has been stolen from us. And all you are interested in is the fate of a single castle.'

Perhaps I was unfair but I was not in a mood for fairness. I was suffering from chilblains for which the mixture of egg and wine and pounded fennel root produced no cure, despite the recommendation in Bald's *Leechbook* which was owned by Cousin Elizabeth as a remedy for all ailments. The heating was poor in the Archbishop's chambers.

'That single castle, as you put it, is of vital importance to me.'

'What's more, you have only achieved it because of Warwick's victory.'

'But it is still a magnificent achievement.'

Sir John's hopes for the Fastolf inheritance, and mine, were realised, but through no victory of his. It was the one bright star in the heavens, and for most men at Court it would have gone unrecognised.

'It paid off, dearest Anne, my courting the Earl of Oxford as my patron.'

'Ah...'

Now I understood, for Warwick had rewarded the Earl of Oxford for his support. Oxford had been created Constable of England under the new power. How well this patronage had come to Sir John's aid.

'With Oxford as Constable, the Duke of Norfolk is forced into the surrender of Caister. The castle is once again a Paston possession. We have needed a patron to offset the power of the Duke of Norfolk for so many years. Oxford has proved to be an excellent sponsor for Paston interests. I could not have given my support to a better man.'

'I congratulate you.'

Sir John ignored my sardonic reply.

'With Oxford behind us, we will regain all of the Fastolf manors. My situation in the county of Norfolk will be impregnable. It is my plan to go there immediately.'

'Your mother will be much pleased.'

'Of course.'

I achieved a seemingly-mellow smile worthy of a weary mummer in a Court masque.

'Will Mistress Paston, do you suppose, now that your inheritance is settled, advise you to regularise our marriage? Will our marriage now be recognised for all to see? Even your mother cannot complain that you have put pleasure before business. Will you discover a priest who will sanctify our union, do you think?'

I was of a mind to think that my question surprised him, causing him the slightest pause for thought.

'It is my wish, Anne, as much as it is yours. But you must first come out of sanctuary.'

'How will the Queen do that, with Warwick holding the reins of power? I would not wish the royal children to fall into his hands.'

'There is no reason for you to remain with the Queen.'

So I would play traitor to my cousin. Sometimes my betrothed was thoughtless beyond measure.

'Of course,' I agreed, just to see what he would say. 'I could leave today and you could take me to Caister. There is nothing to keep either of us here.'

Yet I thought that he was not enthusiastic. I waited to hear if he would make an excuse for me to remain where I was. Even so his reply was genuine enough and he took hold of my hand, glove against glove.

'I would like nothing better than that you should come and rejoice with me.'

My smile became a little more genuine. Was this not the opportunity that I had been seeking, that I would be foolish to reject?

'Then let us rejoice indeed,' I said, lowering my eyes in faux modesty. 'Let us make our union complete beyond question. Do you not desire me for more than my name, Sir John? Take me to your home and make me your wife.'

His eyes gleamed in a sudden shaft of sunlight, as if some vibrant need had taken root, with the return of the exuberance of early days. The regaining of Caister had relit a flame that had not seemed of late to burn for me, but was now mine to tend. His whole regard was focused on me.

'Let us indeed, for how could a man not desire so beautiful a woman? Why wait to go to Caister, which will take far too long for my ardour to withstand. Surely it is not beyond our ability to discover an unused chamber in this place?'

Was he suggesting that we consummate this marriage at last, here at Westminster? I could not believe it. My first reaction was to offer a maidenly refusal. How foolish that would be. Was this not exactly what I wanted?

He stripped the glove from my right hand and kissed my palm.

'Dearest Anne. Have pity on me. I have been abstinent for far too long. Now all is mine, my land, my fair inheritance, and I would make you mine, too, the one lady who holds my heart and my loyalty between her hands.'

His lips on mine in the cold were warm and encouraging.

The frost within me was beginning to melt.

'Discover a room for us,' he murmured when I returned his kiss with equal heat.

It was not difficult to find a bedchamber suitably furnished, if chilly, but unoccupied. We had no interest in the furnishings, only in the width of the bed and the softness of the mattress.

Although many at Court would have disbelieved me, since I was skilled in the art of flirtation, I was virginal. Sir John was not, but with me his experience was layered in careful and gentle usage. Was I disappointed? Never. He worshipped me with his body while I drowned in delight. When he lit flames along my skin, I burned with desire. His mouth was a promise and a demand; his hands aroused a passion of which I had no perception. All my doubts were erased. All my hopes of a true marriage came together in that one breathless deed in a disused chamber in the Palace of Westminster when the King was in exile and the Court in turmoil.

Afterwards he wrapped us both in the fur cloak and wound his fingers into my unpinned hair, kissing his way along the edge of my jaw which made me laugh. I experienced a moment of true happiness without even looking towards the unknown future.

'Where do you go now?' I asked eventually, too cold to be drowsy for long.

'To Caister, to lay claim. I will walk in and put my seal on it.'

'What of me? Do I come with you?'

Why did it not surprise me that he put me off?

'Go back to the Queen until all is legally clear, then I will come and announce to all that you are my wife. You will come to Caister and I will welcome you with a priest. We will celebrate and my family will be there to make it an event of superb triumph. The Pastons will be restored to greatness.'

In that moment, much like the clang of a warning bell to drive out my happiness, it seemed that we were no further forward, except that Sir John Paston had claimed my maidenhead.

'Will it be long?'

'No. I believe not. A matter of weeks to set all to rights. There is nothing for you to be concerned about. The sun shines on the Pastons today.'

'Not in here it doesn't!'

I shivered. All I could see was further justification for denying that one final step.

We dressed, Sir John turning his deft fingers from searching legal documents to making some semblance of order to my clasps and laces, and as we did so, now that our passions were satisfied, as so often, our thoughts turned to the state of the realm.

'Have you heard the rumours?' I asked as I tried to make suitable restitution to my hair, finally giving up. My hood would have to cover it. 'We hear, even in sanctuary, that the Duke of Burgundy is supplying Edward with ships and money to aid his return. What if Edward comes home with a force and unpicks all that Warwick has done? What happens to Caister then, when you have so firmly set your foot in the Lancaster camp with the Earl of Oxford?'

Had he not thought of that? I could not believe that he would be so naïve as to deny the possibility.

Sir John, never naïve, always calculating, shook his head. 'I hear the rumours, too. I know the dangers of my position. I will think about my future and that of Caister, if and when Edward's return comes about, for I do not have the power to influence it in any way. For now, the castle is mine.'

'I wish you well.' I leaned against him, my palms flat against his chest. 'Your victory is excellent news.' But his thoughts were already far away from me, and my irritation returned four-fold. 'I hope that you will remember me, your wife, when you are celebrating your success with your family in your castle.'

'How could I not?'

'I fear that you could easily not.'

Sir John pulled on his doublet and buckled his belt, looking up at me with some puzzlement. 'I would that you have more faith in me.'

'You must earn my faith, my dear. Taking me to your bed was very pleasant but a marriage demands more.'

'I will give you more. I am now able to do so. I will kneel at your feet in adoration in my hall at Caister.'

'I await it keenly. I will look for your courier to bring my invitation to travel to Caister. Do I arrange my own priest and bring him with me?'

'There is no need. I will put all in hand.'

I looked back at the room that had witnessed our consummation while Sir John bowed and, with a brush of his lips against my cheek, departed. Not the most affectionate of partings considering the disturbance of the bedcovers. I returned to straighten the embroidered coverlet before going back to support a frantic Queen. Sir John had departed, I presumed, to gloat over his prize, which was not me.

★

'You look aglow, cousin. And not just with the cold air.'

'I think I am, my lady.'

Cousin Elizabeth was eagle-eyed despite her burden of fear.

'And I suspect that your hair is tumbled beneath that hood. Is that my cloak, by the by? Should I object?'

'Yes, and yes, my lady.' I curtsied as required. 'I thought, since you would not be wearing it, I might borrow it for an hour or two.'

The Queen's eyes narrowed at my disarray.

'Sir John Paston?'

'Yes. We have talked of the future.'

'And done more than talk, if my eyes are sharp enough.' She surveyed the buttons at the tight-fitting wrist of my gown that I had not fastened completely. 'Is this marriage consummated at last?'

I could not suppress my glorious sense of achievement.

'Yes, my lady. We took advantage of an unused bedchamber. And he has Caister Castle returned to him.'

'Much good will it do him – or you.'

'I think it will.'

'And when my lord returns? When Edward takes his rightful place? What then?'

Queen Elizabeth was sour and not in the mood to rejoice with me. But I did. I rejoiced indeed. Sir John had at last committed himself to me bodily as well as legally.

But that one thought continued to intrude, as Elizabeth had so pertinently expressed it.

What if – when – King Edward returned?

Elizabeth's joy would be my dismay. If the Yorkists could retake the crown, Sir John Paston in the Earl of Oxford's retinue would become a traitor overnight, his life and estates forfeit. Caister Castle might just slip out of his hand once more, like a trout evading capture in a fast-flowing stream of political instability.

The news smuggled into us over the next weeks was true enough. The year turned and with it came King Edward, landing at Ravenspur with a group of fervent supporters but dependent on the country rousing itself to his support. Elizabeth was alight with the news as personal letters arrived, scrawled by the King himself. We followed his footsteps as he made his way south. His entry into London, the thanksgiving in St Paul's, his journey to Lambeth Palace to take possession of old King Henry and return him to imprisonment. Then there were more thanks offered up in Westminster Abbey before the shrine of King Edward the Confessor.

Only then did King Edward come to rescue his wife, even though she had been stranded here in isolation for six months of intense anxiety. I thought that he might have come sooner but should have known better. Were all men so dilatory in the care of their women? Sir John was as bad, if not worse. But here was Edward at last with Elizabeth weeping on his shoulder, presenting him with his heir, who fretted through the meeting while I wondered what the fate of my betrothed might now be.

Elizabeth and Edward spent the night of their reuniting at Baynards Castle on the banks of the Thames. There was no reuniting for me.

As was to be expected, Sir John was not seen at Court. No letters, no courier to summon me to Caister now that our sanctuary was over. How could he expect to be a Court favourite when he had shown no hesitation in hopping into bed with Warwick, and what had become the Lancastrian cause? He was now Oxford's man. Men who turned their coats so swiftly could not expect to be made welcome, and everyone knew that there was a battle in the offing. The alarm bells were sounding. Would Sir John fight? I knew not.

Selfishness took a tight grip of me when my cousin rejoiced in her happy situation. I presumed that Caister Castle would become once more an issue, as would my wifely insecurity. My happiness had been swept asunder by Edward's return. How easy it would have been to blame Sir John for giving his allegiance to the Earl of Oxford in the first place, yet, familiar as I was with Court machinations, I knew better. Patrons were not there to be unearthed from every Westminster stone. It was just a terrible mischance that Sir John had ended up on the losing side.

'Don't give up hope,' the Queen said, her eyes shining with joy.

She did not mean it. In her rejoicing, my cousin had no real compassion for me.

'How can I not?' I retorted with bleak reality.

How indeed. I had had little enough to begin with. Perhaps I should not have allied my star so readily with that of the Paston heir. Instead of rising to illuminate the heavens, it was likely to plummet both my lover and my hopes of everlasting delight into the mire of treason. It was a wound to my heart, but better that than a fatal end to Sir John from a random sword blow on some distant battlefield.

CHAPTER TWENTY-FOUR

MARGARET MAUTBY PASTON

The Paston House in Norwich, Spring 1471

John Pamping. John Pamping! Of all the men who could have laid claim to Anne's affections. It was enough to wake in me a fury so great that I deliberately dropped my favourite slip-ware platter, smashing it to pieces on the tiles in the kitchen.

As if the state of power in England was not enough to unsettle me.

The country was in deep discussion over the return of King Edward from exile and what would be the outcome between him and the Earl of Warwick. Would there be a battle? There seemed to be no way to avoid it. And if it resulted in a Yorkist victory, what would become of the Lancastrian King Henry, his wife and son? Anxious as I might be for the old King's wellbeing, it was our own circumstances that should have troubled me most since were we not now tied to the patronage of the Earl of Oxford, who was unquestionably a staunch ally of Warwick. Did Sir John not realise that we would be taking a stand against the restored King Edward? And what would that do for our standing in Norfolk, for our hold on our manors? It was all becoming far too complicated and threatening for me to consider with a quiet mind. Yet with such looming events that might shatter our family, as well as the peace of the realm, the only name in my head was that of John Pamping, a servant in my household.

Who would have believed that John Pamping, loyal servant to my dead husband, as well as to my sons, would be the cause of so much renewed misery for me? A matter of months after my daughter Anne's return to live again under my roof, all my fears concerning both my daughters had returned and, in furious but restrained mood, I was writing a letter to Jonty.

I would be grateful if you would find employment in London for our servant John Pamping. I would not wish to turn him from our door but he is not using his time well in Norfolk. He would be better employed by you away from Norwich. If you cannot, then perhaps Sir John can oblige me. I believe that it is becoming urgent. I will leave it in your hands and will explain when I see you, but not here in writing.
    I wish you to achieve this position for him immediately.

The letter dispatched, I sat and fought against despair as well as anger. I resisted the need to bury my face in my hands. Instead, I took myself to my private chamber where I could implement my fury by beating the dust from my bed-hangings, a task I usually gave to one of the servants.

John Pamping!

How I castigated myself as I filled the air around me with dust particles, enough to make me cough. I should have learned my lesson. I should have realised that a young woman of sixteen years without the immediate prospect of a husband would look close to home for friendship. Even love, or some semblance of it. At least, a despised flirtation, more fitting for a scullery maid. Had I not learned my lesson from Margery? I had seen her attraction to Richard Calle and thought it a matter of little moment. A fleeting flowering like a spring bloom that would soon wilt and die, the petals falling when the reality of life and marriage took hold. At least, in her favour, Margery had known Richard Calle all her life. Anne's knowledge of Pamping was of little depth. Had she even set eyes on him before her return to Norwich?

How could I have been so blind at what was happening under my very nose? Now that Caister was returned to us, I should not have been preoccupied with what was going on outside our four walls. I should have seen it. Here was a young man, of good stature and fair features, who crossed her path every day, while my daughter was as comely as he. Why would they not find an attraction in each other? But this was not what I wanted. No Paston would want this terrible repetition of past allure between daughter and retainer.

John Pamping, the servant I had trusted beyond all others after the disaster of Richard Calle. The man who had waited on my husband John during those dreadful days when he was locked in the Fleet Prison, keeping him in good spirits and good health, purchasing clothes, making sure that he ate enough. I would have trusted him with my life, as I had trusted him with John's. But Anne had been lured into exchanging kisses with John Pamping. What other inappropriate conduct had taken place between them I could not guess at. Was this what she had been taught by my cousin Calthorp? It made me even angrier. To his detriment, my husband John had always blamed others for his problems, loath to accept his own culpability. I would not be guilty of that. I should have been the one to keep Anne under my eye. And Sir John should have found her a husband. A betrothal, a date set for a marriage, would surely have prevented this happening.

This could not be!

Oh, John Pamping was a good man, a good servant who had been in our household for more than a decade since he had arrived as a young boy. He had served the Pastons well, he had even been arrested and imprisoned for loyally supporting our cause against tenants who would rather pay their rents to the Duke of Norfolk. Had he not stood by Jonty throughout the siege, to defend Caister against Norfolk's forces? Loyal and capable, yes, but marriage? The taint of Calle and Margery still soured my relations with my neighbours.

John Pamping was nothing more than a servant, not even of the position of bailiff. At least Calle had some acknowledgement in Norwich as a capable man of business. I knew nothing of Pamping's family. If Richard Calle had nothing to recommend him as a Paston husband, John Pamping as a mere employee had even less. Not another Paston daughter to be wasted on the servant class. Had Anne learned no better with the Calthorps, who were as careful of their lineage as were we? Here was a man of inferior breeding encouraging my daughter into an inappropriate liaison.

Thus the anger that had gradually died a little since the legalisation of Margery's marriage was reborn. Were both my daughters incapable of discrimination? There would be no clandestine marriage this time. I would not be put in that position again. I would not subject the Pastons to renewed whispering in corners.

I watched him as he went about his daily tasks. What did she see in him to attract her youthful eye? It was not difficult to work it out, and my daughter had all the charm and beauty of a young girl just grown into womanhood, lovely to anyone's gaze. I considered the young man. Confident, easy in his manners, attractive enough with grey eyes beneath well-marked brows and a shock of dark hair. A man of worldly experience, even of elegance in his dark clothes, a man who would draw the attention of a young girl who had seen so little of the world.

When I had caught them in an unfortunate proximity, he was kissing her fingers, then her palm, holding her hands clasped between his own. What's more, Anne was encouraging him, whispering in his ear as he bent his head. If I had not arrived at that moment, I swear he would have kissed her on the lips. This did not look like an impromptu meeting but one that had been arranged in the shadowed alcove between scullery and stables. In the cold of early spring it would take a level of hot passion to lure them out of doors. The only reason I had stepped out of the house was a complaint from my cook that town curs had found their way into our herb garden and were wreaking havoc.

Pamping released my daughter's hands immediately, Anne stepping back, turning her face away so that I could not see the hot flush of embarrassment. Pamping, left to face my dismayed silence, was calm enough, although not exactly apologetic.

'It was not Mistress Anne's fault. There is no blame on her, Mistress Paston. She did not encourage me.'

I was not inclined to be forgiving. 'I see you needed no encouragement.'

'I should not have—'

'No, you should not. You presume on my valuing your loyalty

above your present behaviour.' I turned to my daughter. 'Go to your chamber.'

But Anne moved to stand beside him. 'I have done no wrong.'

Her defiance astonished me, but I kept my tone even as if in a negotiation over the price of grain.

'Perhaps not. Nor will you again. I will not give you the opportunity. Go now. Such behaviour in a Paston daughter is unbecoming.'

'Is that what you said to Margery?'

Yes, oh yes. The memories flooded back, but I must not allow it; I could not believe such insolence from Anne.

'Go to your chamber. Before I forget that I am your mother and decide to chastise you.'

Anne fled, leaving me to regret such harsh usage. Oh, how domestic disaster could drive us to unforgiveable words.

'I will speak with you later,' I said to Pamping.

I followed my daughter who was standing at her chamber window, looking down to where Pamping had just stalked from courtyard to house. This was going to be difficult. Unless I had a care, I might either lose another daughter to a disgraceful union, or drive her into wilful disobedience. I kept my voice low and calm, unthreatening, even as I blighted this blossoming of first love.

'I will not allow this, Anne. You must see that it is impossible.'

'All I see, Mother, is that I enjoy his company. And you will prevent it.'

'How far has this gone? Has he declared love for you?'

She remained standing as she had been when I entered the room, her figure highlighted with the sun, refusing to show me anything but her stiff shoulders and rigid back. Oh, she would be defiant.

'No, he has not. But I think he will.'

So it was not yet as disastrous as it might be.

'You will dissuade him. Do you hear me?'

'I do hear you, Mother. But why should I dissuade him? He is a man who knows his own mind. Why should he not love me?'

'Are you so naïve? Did not the Calthorps make it clear that a Paston marriage must be with a man of rank?'

How I sounded like Mistress Agnes, who refused to choose a man for Elizabeth because his estates were entailed or his income insufficient. Elizabeth had suffered dreadfully. Did I wish my daughter to be the same, left a spinster until she was almost thirty years old? I did not, but Pamping was unacceptable.

'Yes, Mother. So I was instructed.'

'Has he given you any promises of the future?'

'No, he has not.'

'Has he given you any gift as a sign of his intentions towards you?'

'No. How could he? His wages have been insufficient to buy any token of love, even the most trivial. Our servants have barely been paid.'

'And that's at the heart of it. Our servants. By the Virgin, Anne! He is a servant!'

'It does not make him less admirable in my eyes. I believe him to be a man of integrity and impeccable honesty.'

How long had this been going on? Only since her return from the Calthorps, I would swear. There was still time to nip it in the bud and I could not be gentle about it. I did not know what Sir John or Jonty would have to say, but I could imagine that it would not be flattering to my care of their sister. I addressed my daughter so that she should be left in no doubt.

'You will not spend time with him. You will not be alone with him in any place in this house. You will not make assignations with him outside. Do you understand me?'

'Yes, Mother.'

'Look at me and make your promise.'

Slowly she turned, her face pale but her gaze still defiant. 'I will not make assignations.'

The dutiful daughter. I was not sure that I could trust her, but surely Anne would not defy her whole family in this matter.

'It seems that you have not enough to fill your time and thoughts, Mistress Anne Paston. I will soon remedy that.'

I dispatched her to Master Pecock with orders that she be given occupation in the laundry. At least, this time, I had warning. I would not be faced with an announcement that a marriage had already happened, with or without a priest. Unable to put off this conversation I sent for John Pamping, with whom, standing face to face in the centre of my hall, I wasted no words.

'I value your work for us. There can be no questioning the loyalty that you have given to my sons or to my late husband. There will, however, be no consideration of you as a husband for my daughter Anne. Am I clear?'

'Yes, Mistress Paston.'

His eyes were steady on mine, but the ready smile was absent today.

'You will not seek her company.'

'No, Mistress Paston.'

'Then that is all that needs to be said on the matter. It will not be discussed again in this household.'

I thought that it would indeed be the end of it, but John Pamping held his ground.

'There is one question I would ask, mistress.'

'Then ask it.'

'If Mistress Anne and I love each other, would you condemn us to live apart for the rest of our lives?'

'Yes. And you know the reason why.'

'Because you fear the censure of your neighbours.'

Uncomfortably honest, but true. We would not again become the subject of gossip, of innuendo, of social isolation.

'I would. And there's an end to it. Besides, I doubt the lasting quality of what you might term love. My daughter is young. She will recover, and you will find another young woman who will be suitable as a wife.'

He bowed as if in agreement, but I was dismayed at how quickly I had moved from trust to wariness. I would hate to lose his service, but young people were not always reliable when they believed their emotions to be engaged.

I watched my daughter like a hawk overlooking her chick. There was no repetition to their intimacy as far as I knew and yet the suspicion remained, a burr beneath my sleeve to irritate my skin. Sometimes Anne was, without reason, bright eyed. Sometimes there was an innocence about John Pamping's demeanour. Anne might be noticed wearing a sprig of blackthorn blossom from the garden which she would have claimed that she had picked for herself if I had demeaned myself to ask her. There were so many opportunities for them to meet and prolong this new pleasure discovered in each other's company. Although I could understand Anne's infatuation with these first steps into love, I could not live with the possibility of her following in the footsteps of her sister. One daughter wedded to a servant was too much. Two daughters so doing would reduce us not merely to an object of gossip but to a laughing stock.

Thus, this one morning, when the whole country was concentrating on the return of our exiled King and the political ramifications, found me writing to Jonty. The only way to stop this possible debacle was to separate them for good. I had failed to do that with Margery and Calle; I would not fail this time.

But then the worrisome matter of my daughter and John Pamping was cast into the abyss, as was the hovering uncertainty of Mistress Haute, and all for me was awry. What did marriage matter when I was faced with life or death? My two eldest sons had made a decision, without even consulting me, one that I had refused to consider, and one that now engulfed me in terrible fear. War appeared, fully armed on my threshold.

CHAPTER TWENTY-FIVE

MISTRESS ANNE HAUTE

The Royal Court in the Palace of Westminster, April 1471

I received an invitation to visit Warwick Inn. I was curious at the direction until I recalled that Sir John's uncle William Paston now resided there with his Beaufort wife and family.

What would Sir John want of me now?

> *You will understand my difficulties, my dearest Anne, in presenting myself at Court since I am now recognised as being firmly on the side of the enemy. I understand your irritation over my absence after our tender uniting, and with my preoccupation with my inheritance. I hope that you can find it in your heart to come to Warwick Inn where I will explain all.*

I would go, although it had to be said that I no longer anticipated meetings with him with my previous joy. Now it was with a lowering dismay as I imagined the forthcoming conversation. Sir John would no doubt list all the reasons for us not to be together. I anticipated plentiful excuses, most of which I could devise for myself. In the cold light of day, as I left Westminster to travel to Warwick Inn, I was forced to admit that my betrothed, whether through carelessness or deliberate intent, was gnawing away at my trust in him. There were distinct holes in the span of my faith in our future together.

William Paston lived in some style, his connections with the Court clearly lucrative. It crossed my mind that I might not be received warmly by his wife, Lady Anne, who would not appreciate my connection with the House of York that had decimated her own family to such a terrible degree. As for William, his allegiance was given wherever it would best fulfil his own ambitions: at present with King Edward, now reinstated at Westminster, he was a staunch Yorkist. Even so, it was a relief that there was no sign of William or his wife as the door was opened to me.

Now to discover what it was that Sir John had to tell me.

I did not expect his first words when I was shown into the chamber in William Paston's home where he awaited me, idly turning the pages of a book, clearly without reading any one of the words set down there. Abandoning it, he strode across the room to take my hands in his, as if we had not been parted for four months.

'I needed to see you, Anne.'

'And here I am.' I was not willing to be too accommodating in spite of journeying across London to see him. 'What is it?'

'There will be a battle.'

It was no surprise to me, but I had not expected Sir John to be on the battlefield. The Pastons were not known for their military prowess. Was Sir John so involved in the struggle for power? I did not think so. And yet my heart gave a strong beat of anxiety at the thought that he might don armour and risk his life. My heart was more engaged than I was sometimes prepared to acknowledge.

'I expected as much,' I agreed. 'The King can hardly allow Warwick to continue to ride freely through the country, wreaking havoc.' I frowned. 'Will you fight? I had not thought it.'

'I am no coward!' His brows snapped together.

'I know well that you are not.'

He kissed my hand and then my cheek in a somewhat perfunctory manner since his thoughts had been driven elsewhere by my question.

'I must fight, it seems. The Earl of Oxford has sent out a summons to all who owe him service, to come and fight for him in the name of King Henry. Who is probably King no more, but it still gives power to the demand. My father always managed to make excuses not to be present on the battlefield through pressure of work, but I owe the Earl too much to refuse him. Patronage exerts a high cost, as I am about to find out. I cannot refuse, so I am about to bloody my sword for the first time on a battlefield as a Lancastrian.'

'Will your brother fight, too?'

'Yes, Jonty is also summoned.'

Now a cold finger of fear stroked lightly against my heart. There really was no way out of this battle for him. With the Earl of Oxford as his patron, Sir John had been forced to side with those who had lost in the recent reversal of power. All very well when Edward was in exile and Warwick controlled the strings of King Henry VI. The Earl of Oxford could be comfortable in his position as Warwick's ally, and so could Sir John. But now King Edward was restored with Burgundian money behind him and Warwick as the enemy who must be removed at all costs. Of course there would be a battle for control of the crown.

All was to play for. My own concerns over marriage and my future paled into insignificance beside the threat posed by the Earl of Warwick to the security of King Edward's crown. The royal brother Clarence had come to heel at King Edward's command, but Warwick had an army that the King must defeat, and Sir John, for good or ill, at Oxford's proprietorial demand, would be fighting alongside him.

So many reasons for me to be fearful. It built within me as I mentally tallied what might lie in wait for this man who was still holding my hands. The thoughts leapt and bounded through my mind that Sir John might die on the battlefield. Even if he survived the expected onslaught, if King Edward emerged victorious, then those who fought with Warwick would pay the penalty of defeat. Sir John would be declared traitor and his lands and head forfeit. Sir John might worry about Caister Castle, but I worried about his life.

Sir John's words brought me back to the present.

'There is no need to be afraid. It has not happened yet.' The wryest of smiles accompanied his assurance. 'If I should die, you should know that I have loved you with all my heart.'

There was nothing I could find to say. My fingers curled round his to make a tight bond.

'Will it be soon? Edward is still at Westminster with Elizabeth.'

'I fear so. As you said, he cannot afford to allow Warwick too much slack rein.'

'God keep you safe.'

'I pray that He will. I thought that I should tell you.'

I read what he did not say. This might be the last time that we saw each other. I might become a widow before I had even truly become a wife. With that thought I clung to his hands.

'Come back to me.'

'I assuredly will.'

But, of course, how could he know? It was a tender parting. Returned to Westminster, all I could do was wait. I seemed to have been waiting all my life for Sir John Paston, one way or another. Meanwhile, I must remain at Court to make my peace with Cousin Elizabeth who, quite rightly, might object to her cousin being espoused to a traitor who was intent on raising his sword against her husband.

King Edward marched out of London on Holy Saturday, dragging an unresponsive King Henry along with him as a symbol of Edward's restored power, leaving his newly born heir and his daughters with cousin Elizabeth once more safely installed in Westminster. Warwick, he had been informed, was marching in a line of direct confrontation towards the royal army. With the treacherous Earl marched the Earl of Oxford, Sir John Paston, and his brother Jonty.

On Easter Sunday, we waited for the news of battle. Edward's courier, sent hot foot, said that it would be at a place called Barnet, despite the ground being covered with thick mist.

'It will still be better than the snowstorm at Towton,' Elizabeth fretted. I did not know much about Towton but knelt at her side as Elizabeth fell to her knees in her chapel and prayed fervently. We should have been rejoicing at the Resurrection of Christ to New Life but our thoughts were elsewhere through the prayers and canticles, our ears strained for news of blood and death.

'For whom do you pray?' Elizabeth asked bitterly when the prayers had been said and Easter Day celebrated in strangely muted terms by a nervous priest. By the end of the day the Earl of Warwick might once more be in the ascendant and we back in sanctuary for good. But if that were so, then Sir John Paston would be once more secure in his estates in Norfolk.

'For whom do you pray, Cousin Anne?' she repeated when I gazed blankly at her.

'For Sir John Paston.'

'A man who will fight against my lord. Do you not pray for Edward, too? Is it possible to pray for both?'

'Yes, cousin, it is possible. There is much conflict in my prayers. Such is the lot of women when men go to war. I fear that the Blessed Virgin must be bemused by the requests for succour for one side or the other, but I must trust in Her mercy.'

I had tried to be conciliatory but the Queen was beyond conciliation.

'What a pity that the Pastons could not remain loyal to their King.'

'What a pity that the King could not support the Pastons against the greed of the Duke of Norfolk,' I retaliated without thought that this was the Queen of England to whom I spoke. 'Then they would have remained loyal.'

We looked at each other in mutual irritation. And then in despair.

'Let us pray that both come out unscathed,' I offered.

Elizabeth accepted my platitude. 'Forgive me. I am in fear.'

I touched her arm in compassion. She knew what death was in battle, or in the dread aftermath, losing her first husband, her father and one of her brothers in the carnage between the great magnates.

We both suffered a sleepless night waiting for a courier. We both knew that it would be a battle to the death. King Edward would never again hold out the hand of mercy and negotiation to the Earl of Warwick. Silently we were both preparing to return to sanctuary in the Abbey if things went amiss.

★

'Where? When?' Elizabeth demanded.

The courier fell to his knees and kept none of us waiting as he gasped out the news.

'A battle at Barnet. The King is victorious.'

Bright colour suffused Cousin Elizabeth's pallid cheeks as she clasped her new son to her bosom.

'Thank God. Stand up, man.'

He struggled to his feet, grey with fatigue, his livery almost obliterated in mud and dust. Handing the child to me, Elizabeth grasped his arm with one hand as if to prevent his escape before he had delivered her all the pertinent information.

'The Earl of Warwick is slain, my lady,' he said. 'And his brother.'

'And the King?'

'Untouched and in good heart. He sends you his love and affection and thanks you for your prayers. He will soon return to you and assure you of his good health.'

'What of the King's brothers? Clarence and Gloucester?'

His breathing was settling now, allowing him to give more detail.

'Both alive. Gloucester suffered a minor wound but nothing to trouble you. Both are in good spirits.'

'Blessed Virgin, keep them all safe.'

She released him, her face alight with joy, taking the child from me to hold closely.

My emotion knew no such release from cold dread. The Queen had seen no need to ask after Sir John Paston and his brother, nor was it likely that the courier would know. The Pastons might even now be lying dead on the battlefield at Barnet beside the Earl of Warwick. When Elizabeth departed to offer thanks on her knees, I kept the courier back, despite his impatience to discover food and drink.

'Did many die?'

'Aye, mistress. It was a bloody affair, with all the mist of early morning. The enemy fled. We cut them down from behind.'

It did not sound good.

'What of the Earl of Oxford?'

'His forces fled, too, but he was able to regroup and bring them back to the battlefield. It didn't go well for them.' He settled into telling me the terrible result, for a moment distracted from a need to slake his thirst. 'They mistook friend from foe in the mist when it was impossible to recognise the liveries with any accuracy. Oxford's banner of the Enrayed Star looked much like King Edward's Sun in Splendour. It made for mistakes on both sides.'

'You will know none of the names of those killed.'

'Hardly, mistress. It was a bloodbath, as I said, with bodies strewn across the field. Oxford got away but I know nothing of his men, only that they were subject to a shower of arrows, perhaps from their own side.'

Which gave me no comfort at all.

While the Queen rejoiced, I mourned, but now she could afford to be generous. Her smiles had returned, her waspish tongue laid to rest.

'All is not lost, Anne,' she urged me. 'With Warwick dead the country can return to peace under Edward's hands.'

'And I am grateful,' I assured her. 'But I see no gains for me. Sir John is either dead or a traitor. Unless he is alive and the King is of a mind to be open-handed to his enemies.'

'Why should he be? They would have happily cut my lord down on the battlefield.'

'I know. I have no argument to make for Sir John. Or his brother.' I slanted a glance. 'Except that every man must answer the call of his liege lord.'

Elizabeth regarded me.

'Do you think my lord should offer a pardon?'

'I might like him to consider it. Sir John only fought because the Earl of Oxford demanded that he should.'

She smiled. 'I may speak with the King for you.'

Emotion threatened to overwhelm me, surprising me by its intensity. I covered my face with my hands, muffling my words.

'Of what use would that be if Sir John is already dead?'

The dread of it anchored itself in my flesh, in my soul, like an apothecary's leech, keeping me company through the hours of day and night.

CHAPTER TWENTY-SIX

MARGARET MAUTBY PASTON

The Paston House in Norwich, April 1471

War came to the Pastons, and I lived in mortal fear.

My husband, with considerable cunning and self-preservation, had managed to excuse himself, one way or another, from any suggestion that he appear on a battlefield. Not once did he don armour and sharpen his sword. No such good fortune for my sons. When their retained lord the Earl of Oxford called them to fight for him, there was no good reason for them to resist. If we were going to succeed in our struggle against the Duke of Norfolk to preserve our hold on Caister Castle, then we must be noted for our loyalty to the Earl of Oxford. Denying his right to call on our military support would not be politic.

Thus, when spring was full of life, Sir John and Jonty turned their thoughts to a possible death and became Lancastrians on the battlefield. I could only be relieved that my younger sons were not called upon to take up the sword. Whoever won, my sons could be dead in a fatal conflict. Or branded traitor and all our possessions forfeit.

I became fractious and uneven-tempered throughout the Easter celebrations.

Any tears I might have shed, even if I denied them, dried up in a desert of trepidation.

There was a battle, near the small town of Barnet to the north of London. Couriers brought the news to Norwich that King Edward had been the victor and had taken back his crown. The

Earl of Warwick and his brother the Marquess of Montagu were dead on the field.

But what about the Pastons?

On the losing side, my sons were either dead or traitors with their lives and property forfeit to the King.

I slept little on those nights for there was no way for me to discover more. The Earl of Oxford had fled for his life, which was no consolation to me. In the privacy of my chamber, I cursed him that he should have taken my sons into such danger.

'You must sit, mistress.'

Pecock dispatched a maid for a cup of wine, took my arm, and urged me to a narrow settle in my hall. The letter, in Sir John's hand, had drawn all sensation from me, such that I felt faint with relief, my legs suddenly shamefully weak. I shrugged off Pecock's grip but remembered to smile my thanks for his kindness. We would all be experiencing the same reassurance. If Sir John could write to me, he was not dead. But what of Jonty?

'Read it to me,' I ordered. 'Where is he?'

'In the Fleet Street lodgings, mistress. Sir John is well and unharmed, although must wait to see if the King – King Edward, that is – will extract revenge.'

He had not mentioned Jonty. I feared the worst. 'And Jonty?' I asked, because I must, my voice a dry croak.

Pecock skimmed down the page, turning it over, then back.

'In the name of God, William Pecock, tell me the worst,' I demanded unable to withstand the uncertainty.

'Alive!' Pecock announced at last.

'Blessed Virgin!' Some of my fear began to drain away.

'But wounded.'

'How bad?'

The fear returned in full flow.

'Nothing serious, mistress. You must not be distraught.' The maid returning, Pecock pressed the cup into my hand, and I drank, grateful for the warmth of it in my belly.

'Then why could you not have told me this straightaway?' I complained, even though neither son was dead.

'I ask pardon. This letter was written in haste and is not everywhere legible. Master Jonty was hit by an arrow in his right arm beneath the elbow. A surgeon has seen it and dressed the wound. Sir John says that he believes that Master Jonty will soon be whole again, in a short time.'

I took a deep breath, ordering my heart to still its frantic beat.

'Write and tell Sir John. Tell him this. Send my son home. Send him home to me at once.'

I could not accept that he would die in London under the hands of some false dabbler in herbs and dubious knowledge. He would come home to me and I would heal him, as I was unable to heal his father.

Jonty did not come home. Neither did Sir John.

'And what do you suppose I will discover here?' I asked, opening a letter two weeks later, written by a clerk for the incapacitated Jonty and the obviously preoccupied Sir John. I was weary of listening for the sound of their arrival. This letter would confirm my worst concerns, that Jonty was too ill to travel. I was already mentally packing my coffers to go to London to see for myself.

My son Edmund, who had intercepted the letter and had already made himself cognisant of the contents, grinned. 'Nothing to fear here, Mother. Jonty's demanding, in the politest of terms, of course, money to pay for his care from the London leech.'

'How true.' I was now reading it for myself. 'And for the curing of his horse, which has suffered a wound and he fears will die without expert care, and become horsemeat for the King's hawks. Neither he nor Sir John have any immediate plans to come home.'

I should have expected no less. Sons could be a grave disappointment, even when they had survived a battle. An arrow in the arm had not brought Jonty to his deathbed.

I handed the letter back to Edmund. 'What do you think? Do I pay up as requested?' I asked him, suspecting that he might have had his own personal communications with his brothers, and I would assuredly get an honest reply.

'I think that you should,' Edmund replied with a firm stare from his superior height; he was the tallest of my sons but still with the recognisable Paston nose and dark hair. 'It will show your confidence in him, and your concern, which would be good policy, I think. It would not cost more than the sale of one silver platter which we never use. I can arrange it, if you wish.'

Well, that was a thoroughly reasoned comment. I pursed my lips, considering the advice and the giver of it. Edmund would go far in the legal world if only I could find him a position to allow him to take the next step on the legal ladder. I could well imagine him fearlessly arguing his case with solemnity and conviction.

'Very well,' I said. 'And I'll let you deal with the rest since you are so keen to be of use to me.'

For Jonty had listed the clothing from his coffers that he wished to be sent on to him in London: gowns, doublets, a jacket and hat, as well as various writings that we were instructed not to read. I had no confidence that Edmund would resist a squint at them.

'Mother—'

'Yes?' I was already on my way out of the room. Paston affairs had been sadly neglected while I was immersed in fright.

'Jonty says that he is well and expects to be cured of all his ills by next week,' Edmund's voice followed me.

'I know. I read it.'

I walked from the room for I would not allow Edmund to read the worries that continued to gnaw at my mind. I thanked God that Jonty was on the road to recovery and set my mind to discovering a source of money to send to him. I might even have to sell all my woods, which would not be good policy, for there were many wood sales in Norwich, resulting in little demand and low prices. I sighed. Far better to keep them. My sons would receive a much higher income from them after my death.

As long as they lived long enough to inherit. What Sir John and Jonty needed above all was a pardon to keep their necks free of the axe, a delicate matter which was outside my encompassment. We must all wait helplessly on the decision of King Edward. I had no wish for either of my sons to predecease me. As for Mistress Haute, she might well lose her stubborn husband to the axe before she succeeded in dragging him to acknowledge their vows before a priest.

CHAPTER TWENTY-SEVEN

MISTRESS ANNE HAUTE

The Royal Court in the Palace of Westminster, April 1471

Sir John Paston was alive. Master Jonty Paston was alive. Here they were at Court. I drew in a breath, suppressing any inward relief beneath a calm exterior since it would not do to show support for the men summoned to meet with their newly restored King Edward. My mouth was dry, my throat tight with the tension in the room. The first I knew of this living proof of their survival· was this moment when I stood at the Queen's side as witness to a formal audience in the King's private chamber.

A severe voice whispered in my ear: *They might both be alive but treason could have nasty and bloody repercussions.*

Across the room Sir John Paston, dressed with plain but impeccable neatness and sobriety before the highest power in the land, straightened from his obeisance and his eyes met and held mine. I could read nothing there, no message, no sign to be acknowledged. I was not the only one here to be holding all feelings in check.

The Queen had been as good as her word, and Edward of a mind to consider the traitors in his midst; thus this small gathering, all faces I knew, and amongst whom were both Paston brothers. Their Uncle William Paston, too, was present with them. Although he had not taken up arms, he was tainted by his wife's Lancastrian connections. It was well known, of course, that her father and three of her brothers, all with royal if once illegitimate Beaufort blood, now legitimised, had lost their lives fighting against the House of York. Uncle William was also a feoffee of the treacherous

Countess of Oxford. The Earl had fled abroad for his life, but those associated with him must answer for their actions.

There was no guarantee that the King would treat any of them with mercy. He might condemn them all. I knew the King, my cousin by marriage, to be a man of humour, of honour, of fairness in his dealings with his subjects, even if his indolence, his flirtatious manner was a besetting sin. That is until those subjects raised arms against him and drove him into temporary flight. The expression on his fair face was now anything but one of humour, and nor could I blame him for it, since Warwick and his allies had sought his death. Treason might just be dealt with in a bloody fashion; within a half-hour his judgement might condemn me to a state of widowhood.

King Edward sat in regal splendour, apparently little harmed by his exile and subsequent battles, unless it was a hardening of the lines of experience of his face. At his side, Queen Elizabeth who had chosen to wear formal robes. I too was in full Court dress as a lady in waiting, butterfly veiling aflutter. Before us the ranks of those who had raised arms against their king, where William Paston looked resigned and Jonty pale and favouring an arm that was strapped to his chest. He had been wounded by an arrow, painful but not a threat to his life. Sir John's features were clouded, probably in acceptance of what was to follow.

Edward had said that he would hear them, listen to their excuses, but would he listen with mercy? At a sign from him they knelt, heads bowed, to hear the terms of the royal retribution. There would be fear in many hearts. There was in mine. My relief at seeing Sir John was short-lived so that I shivered with an excess of anxiety.

'I will listen to your treacherous reasoning,' Edward announced, pitching his voice so that it filled the small room. He wore a gold and jewelled coronet despite the early hour and his robe, trimmed with ermine, was enhanced by a jewelled collar. There was no doubting who was King here. King Henry and the now dead Earl of Warwick had been banished to the past. 'If it is good enough reasoning - which I would doubt - I might relent, but to plot against the King is treason. Why would you raise your swords against your King? Were you so shackled to Warwick's desire to oust me?'

They made their excuses. They were all predictable and did not excuse treachery if the King wished to push his case. He turned to the little Paston grouping.

'Stand up, man,' he said to Jonty whose discomfort was palpable. 'All of you. What a problem the Pastons have proved to be for me.'

The three stood.

'Well, Sir John Paston?'

Sir John's reply was clear and even, without inflection.

'I regret raising my sword against you. It was not my choice, my lord.'

'I should have thought not. Have we not been a good friend to you?'

Would he be honest? It could be detrimental to the outcome if he chose to be so.

'I could have hoped for more support over Caister, my lord. The Duke of Norfolk saw fit to take it from me, without legal right. I had hoped for a royal judgement in my favour.'

I trembled for him.

'So you fight against me, because I did not support you over the ownership of one small castle?'

I found myself praying for a diplomatic answer from Sir John.

'No, my lord. I had need of a patron who would support me against my lord of Norfolk. The Earl of Oxford was gracious to give me that patronage when no one else would. He fought for Warwick and this commanded my military support and that of my brother. I had no choice when he called on the service of my sword.'

'And your answer is the same, I suppose.' The King scowled in Jonty's direction.

'Yes, my lord. We were not in a position to disobey. The Earl of Oxford claimed our loyalty. Because of his support, in your... in your absence, my lord, Caister Castle was restored to us.'

Another dangerous allusion. With King Edward in exile, the Pastons under Oxford's protection had benefited.

'Perhaps you regret the outcome of the Battle of Barnet.'

King Edward's gaze returned to Sir John.

'Not so, my lord.'

What more could he say without condemning himself further? Fear began to tighten its grip on my breathing.

'Will you continue to support the House of Lancaster if I grant you your life?'

'No, my lord. I will not.'

'I am not convinced. Your brother deserves his wounds. A shame that you came out of it unscathed.'

All going from bad to worse. If Elizabeth had spoken up for Sir John it seemed to have had little effect on the outcome of this meeting.

'And you, Master William Paston. Have you nothing to say for yourself?'

William Paston bowed, hand on heart.

'I am wed into a family notable for its Lancastrian support, my lord. That is as far as my allegiance goes. I would not take up weapons on a battlefield against you. As for my wife, she cannot answer for the actions of her father and brothers.'

'And yet the Beauforts have proved amazingly untrustworthy over the years.' King Edward now showed his admirable teeth in a snarl, until the Queen placed a hand lightly on his arm and it became instead a smile of sorts. 'I will consider the matter. I am in no hurry to pardon traitors. You will please me by removing yourselves from my sight.'

The sharp blade of the axe had been covered, yet remained hanging over the Paston necks.

I was not yet a widow and yet I might very well soon become one.

I took stock of my situation. It was not difficult to do; it was not encouraging. My spirits had never been as low, Sir John remaining with his future hanging on a thread and no pardon forthcoming from the King.

'I cannot speak again for you and your wayward betrothed,' Queen Elizabeth announced before I had actually asked her to do so. She read my mind with the clarity of her image in her looking glass. 'My lord will do as he pleases.'

And so he did. The Duke of Norfolk with predictable pride returned to pre-eminence with Edward's victory, promoted to Earl Marshal for his valiant service to the Yorkist cause. As was to be expected, he snatched back Caister Castle. With Oxford still in exile, there was no patron to further the Paston cause. Sir John had once more lost his Queen in the ever-present game of chess. The pawns of the rest of the Fastolf manors were also under threat.

And yet for some there was progress. Edward pardoned William Paston, probably deciding that the Beauforts were no longer a threat to him and that William's financial skills were worth fostering. So William could breathe easily and sleep well of a night. Jonty too received his pardon because an old acquaintance, Sir Thomas Wingfield, who was a member of the Duke of Norfolk's council, spoke up for him.

No one spoke up for Sir John. He had no friend to speak for him.

My cousin Anthony Woodville, now Earl Rivers, had been wounded at Barnet, not sufficient to the risk of his life, but he had withdrawn from Court. I had petitioned him in the past to support Sir John; he could be of no use to me now until he was restored to health. My heart fell like a rock tossed in a carp pond, sunk to the bottom in the mud, with no way out. The Queen, so far tolerant of my misery, did not mince her words.

'End it, Anne. By the blessed Virgin, retreat from a conflict in which you can never achieve victory. Sir John is still a traitor. You'll not see him at your door, flattering you with his smiles and promises.'

I feared that she was right.

'Does love have no meaning?' I asked, even unsure that I felt any love for him.

'Not when it leads nowhere.'

'I cannot see any path. His absence from Court, and from me, is wearing.'

'This is no good for either of you.' The Queen, in her satisfaction that Edward had returned unharmed to her, became even more astringent. 'And I would question whether you ever truly loved him. Or that he loved you. I have never met two such self-interested people. It was in your interests to make a vow. Now it is not. Break your association with him and look elsewhere.'

That might be easier said than done.

'I cannot do that.'

'Why not?'

'Because I do not know that I wish to be parted from him.' I abandoned the Queen to her victory with a final ridiculously selfish but heart-felt complaint. 'You managed to wed the man you loved. Why should not I?'

I accepted that I must be certain of what I wanted before we met again. I took the little be-gemmed castle from my jewel casket, a symbol of our earlier love, so long ago in Calais when it had been so easy to consider making those vows. Had I indeed loved him then? Did I still love him? Yes, if being subject to love meant that I despaired at the thought of life without him. Sir John Paston might be self-interested, and so might I, but it seemed to me that there had been a meeting of souls which, in spite of our vicissitudes, had never been destroyed. He touched my heart and my mind. Not a day went past when I did not think of him, wish him here with me.

I put the little golden castle back again and closed the lid. This was a decision I must make on my own without soft reminiscences. We could not go on like this.

Sir John Paston did not come near me. I needed a sleight of hand. Were all the men in the Paston household so difficult to pin down to a decision?

CHAPTER TWENTY-EIGHT

ELIZABETH PASTON BROWNE

The Poynings House in Southwark, May 1471

'God be with you, my husband. May the Blessed Virgin smile upon you and keep you safe from all dangers and wounding. Do not take any unnecessary risks.' I drew a breath. 'And write to me when you can or I will assuredly grow anxious.'

Thus a request from a letter-writing family. How could he possibly write from a battlefield? I swallowed hard against the fearsome prospect.

I was standing in the courtyard of the Poynings House in Southwark as I acknowledged George Browne riding off to war. My heart was as heavy in my breast as one of the stone corbels on the roof above my head. I had done exactly this before, and my husband had not returned to me. Horror crept up on silent feet to grip me as the memories flooded back. My two elder nephews might have survived the battle at Barnet in April, but now here we were in May, another conflict was looming, and who was to say that George would survive the onslaught?

But this was a different time, a different man. George Browne, not Robert Poynings. I must not encumber him with my inner terrors.

Within a year of our meeting we had been wed, to our great mutual enjoyment. I had forgotten the pleasure of physical intimacy, which I enjoyed relearning in George Browne's bed. Or indeed in my own, since we established ourselves at Southwark until the Browne manorial affairs could be settled and we could move to

Betchworth Castle as was George's right. Nor was I beyond the age of proving fertile. In the days of our happiness, when there were no clouds on our particular horizon, we were to be blessed with a fine son, Matthew, and within two years, a daughter, Mary.

How could I ever have dreamed that I would find happiness again with a man whose thoughts ran in accord with mine, who stirred my blood to a forgotten heat? How would I ever have dreamed that I would soon be stitching my husband a pair of new leather and kid gauntlets and sending him off to war? A good husband was a blessing, but also the source of much anxiety. I walked forward and took a firm hold of his reins, ignoring his entourage that was ready and eager to depart. His horse tossed its head but I held on. It was in my heart to persuade him not to go, but that was not my way. He would follow his lord and patron, the Duke of Clarence, newly restored to the King's side after a time of insurrection and disloyalty. The Duke had called him to fight, so fight he must if he wished to win royal support in a battle that would not take place on a battlefield.

George leaned down and pressed a fleeting kiss to my coif. We had already said our farewells. Then he summoned my eldest son to come closer.

'Take care of your mother. Do not open the gates to any man you do not know. Try not to do any damage to yourself if you cannot resist borrowing my weapons. I hope to find you in one piece when I return.'

My son Edward's hands and arms bore witness to inept prac-tising with sword and shield. He grinned.

'I could come with you.'

'You could not. I'll not risk your death on my hands. What would your mother say?'

'She would say that I could come with you.'

'She would say no such thing!' I interrupted.

'Next time, perhaps,' George agreed.

If only there was a next time, although I would not wish a second battle on anyone. As long as George came home safe. As for Edward, my Poynings son was twelve years old, growing more like his father by the day with long features and masterful nose, although his hair was a denser brown and inclined to curl around his ears. He was also acquiring the Poynings stare when affairs did not suit him, as of this minute. I did not wish to think about his riding to war as well. Fortunately, my children with George were too young to be involved with such dangers. I lifted Matthew up into my arms so that he could make his own farewell to his father, silently thanking God that at barely two years he would have no understanding of war. Mary, a babe in arms, born that very year, was still in her cradle, watched over by a doting maid.

'Farewell, Eliza. You will remain my strength and stay and I will value your prayers. I will return.'

He clasped my hand in his as if swearing a binding oath. Pray God that it was.

I stepped back, he raised his hand and they rode out.

Edward and I stood and watched, Edward far more impressed with the banners and livery than I. Soon we could see them no more, only the cloud of dust as they passed.

The last time that I watched my husband ride to war he had not come home, only his squire leading his lame horse, carrying his sword and gauntlets. Sir Robert Poynings lay dead on the field after the battle of St Albans. Sir Robert Poynings, my first husband. His son Edward, only two years old at the time, who was now itching to go to war as well, had no memories of his father.

I tried to remain calm. I must believe that George Browne would return riding his horse, wearing his sword. I could not withstand another abandonment by someone for whom I cared deeply. Edward ran off about his own pursuits that meant escaping from his tutor who would teach him Latin, while I walked into the house, calling for Perching, with Matthew's hand still clutched tight in mine. I would continue with the usual round of demands on my time as if nothing were amiss. If I wept in my chamber, there was no one to see, and I would deny it.

The guard at our gate in Southwark – there were always guards at our gate in these days of insurrection – sent word by Perching that a man demanded entrance. Would I wish him to be admitted?

A woman alone could not be too careful. The Earl of Warwick

might be dead at Barnet, King Edward restored to his family and his crown, but there was no peace. Queen Margaret and her son, Edward of Lancaster, who also claimed the English throne, had landed in the West Country at Weymouth with a substantial force and had immediately found allies in the Beauforts, who welcomed them back and swore their allegiance. Thus the prospect of more upheavals. I wished George were here, but I had not heard from him. Of course he had not written. I had not expected it.

'He says his name is Paston, mistress.'

Well, now!

'Which one?' I asked.

'I know not, mistress. Do you wish me to allow him to enter?'

Oh, yes, I would wish it. When did one of my family last set foot across my threshold, while I was either a Poynings widow or a Browne wife? A situation that gave me much grief and irritation in equal measure.

Into my house strode a young man of mature years, a nephew of mine, whom I had last seen as little more than a child. He smiled at me with what I decided was practised ease, and swept me a bow full of Court finesse. His hat was enhanced by a feather and a jewelled clasp. His features were all Paston. This must be Sir John, my sister-in-law Margaret's eldest son.

'Aunt Eliza.'

'Sir John.'

He walked forward, placed his hands on my shoulders, and kissed my cheeks.

'We are family, after all.'

'No one could have guessed it.'

I could not prevent my dry reply, but was it not true? Since Robert's death at St Albans, when my battle with the Percys had become a battle I could not win, my family had been far distant, apart from the odd letter offering me advice. The Pastons rarely put themselves out for any but themselves, and since my troubles had no bearing on their own campaign to save Caister Castle, both before and during the siege, I had little importance for them. My connection had lapsed, even with Margaret, apart from her one piece of advice to consult William. The last time she had travelled to London had been when John was in the Fleet prison, while I had not attended John's funeral.

Should I have gone to Norwich? To Bromholm, where my brother was buried? I acknowledged a soft brush of regret as I assessed this elegant young man who was John's son. Perhaps I should, but my memories of my young life there had been too painful to make me enthusiastic. I had sworn never to go to Norwich again. Besides, what would we say to each other after so many years? And what should I say to this swaggering gentleman, my nephew Sir John Paston, now head of the Paston family, standing in my hall?

That did not mean that I had not kept my ear to the ground through my man of business, John Dane. I knew about the siege of Caister, that Sir John had lost the castle, then regained it, thanks to his patron the Earl of Oxford, only to lose it again after Barnet. I knew about his need for a pardon after fighting against the King at Barnet. I wondered what had brought him to my gates at Southwark.

'You keep a tight house here, aunt. I had to fight my way across the threshold.'

'It is necessary.'

'So I understand. The Countess of Northumberland has seized some of your estates.'

'She has. The intricacies of gavelkind have not been good to us. And the force of the Percys has been a stronger argument than those used by lawyers.' I gestured that my nephew should come into one of the intimate chambers where I received guests. 'I have seen little of you or any Pastons. Especially when I had need of them. But come in and take a glass of wine with me. I am not so poverty stricken that I cannot entertain you.'

He cast a glance around. 'I see that you are living in comfort.'

'I do what I can.'

'You should have fought to keep your estates.'

'And how would I do that without influence at Court?' I asked sharply. 'I hear that you have lost Caister Castle, with little hope of getting it back, even with your lawyerly skills.'

He had the grace to flush a little.

'Is this property safe?' he asked, regarding the chamber with interest, probably assessing the value of the tapestries and the fine glassware into which I poured red wine, handing it to him when he sat on a cushioned chair, stretching out his legs and crossing his ankles. His confidence impressed me and the ease with which he made an impression in my little chamber.

'I do not expect the Countess to turn me out onto the streets. The scandal might come home and bite her. Besides, her husband, the Earl, was killed at Towton, which has clipped her wings a little. You are quite safe. And in spite of my barbed words, you are very welcome.' Although I would wait no longer. 'What are you doing here?'

'I thought that I should visit. Is your husband at home?'

'No. He was called on to join the Duke Clarence's entourage. He rode out at the beginning of the month. You were not enticed into donning your own armour again?'

'No. Jonty and I had enough at Barnet last month.' He grimaced.

'So you found yourself on the losing side.'

'Yes. The result is that Jonty was wounded in the arm and we were both in need of pardons for fighting for Lancaster.'

'And will the King give them?'

'Jonty is pardoned, and so is your brother William, but the King does not yet seem amenable to removing the axe from my neck.'

'Why have you come here, Sir John?'

'Because I need a safe haven.'

I laughed aloud at his honesty. How ingenuous he was. How transparent. I could imagine his reluctance to be at Court, his shortage of money, his refusal to live on Margaret's charity. If he was anything like his father, his problems would be placed firmly at the feet of others rather than his own.

'Are you inviting yourself to stay here, my dear nephew?'

'If you will have me. For a little time.'

I laughed again at his naïve reply. 'Is this a bolt hole? Are you perhaps escaping from your mother?'

His eyes crinkled, in no manner put out by my suspicions. 'It seemed a good idea. And not just my mother.'

Ah ha! Deeper and deeper. 'Would your betrothed not expect

to see you at Court?' I asked in dulcet enquiry. I had heard of Sir John's strange predicament. A marriage that almost existed but not quite. 'Can the lady not help you to gain your pardon?'

'I expect that she would put a word in for me. I think that she already has. But that's not it.'

'Then are you short of money?'

'I am always short of money, God help me.'

'Have you asked your mother?'

'She is reluctant and warns me against mortgaging any property.'

I could well believe it. Margaret would be horrified at any such suggestion.

'Nor will she sell her woods. She says that it would be a poor deal, so I must make the best of it.' He shrugged a shoulder clad in green and black damask with a fur edging. There was no obvious poverty here. 'I expect that she is right.'

I disliked being imposed upon, to get my nephew out of an uncomfortable situation. Once I might have turned him from my door, but I owed him a debt, a great debt, on behalf of George in the first days after our marriage, when he had been accused of trespass by his greedy father-in-law, Sir Thomas Vaughan. Both Sir John and Jonty had given pledges for George's good behaviour in the dispute, with the result that the case between Vaughan and Browne had collapsed. George had been most grateful, so who was I to turn Sir John Paston from my door after a mere cup of wine and a platter of sweetmeats?

'You are welcome to stay. You can celebrate with us when George returns home.' I tried to ignore the dolorous thud of my heart. 'And now come and meet my children.'

Edward was polishing armour with rigour as if it was still his plan to follow George. Matthew stood with him, more of a hindrance than a help, but a keen participant. I gently removed his fingers from the sharp edge of a blade.

'Edward, come and meet my nephew, Sir John. This is Edward Poynings, heir to the Poynings estates.'

Edward, still clutching the polishing cloth, bowed, full of dignity after such an introduction. 'Are you a Paston, sir?'

'I am indeed.'

'You are the first one I have ever met.'

Which hit me hard, just how isolated I had become. Perhaps I had done ill by my children to keep them distant from my family. It also struck me, uncomfortably, that Edward was grown almost as tall as Sir John.

'Then it is our loss.'

'Are we cousins?'

'Near enough. My father was your mother's brother.'

'Do you live at Court?'

'Often.'

'Where do you live when you are not at Court?'

'As a lawyer, at the Inns of Court.'

'Do you take part in the tournaments?'

I admired the close questioning. Perhaps Edward had the makings of a lawyer too. Matthew, too young to participate, hung back but watched and listened, his eyes on his brother rather than this newcomer.

'I do,' Sir John said, 'when I am not fighting in battles. There are few tournaments at Court these days.'

'I would wish to fight in a battle. But my mother will not permit it.'

'Quite right, too. One day you will, when you have grown into your armour.'

Sir John indicated the abandoned pieces of metal that belonged to George, clearly too big for Edward.

'Do you know Earl Rivers?' Edward pursued.

'I do.'

'Have you fought with him?'

'Indeed. He is a notable jouster. Far better than I am, or will ever be.'

Which was all that Edward needed. They talked tournaments and battles and what Sir John had seen and done at Barnet, although I suspected that he omitted the most vicious elements of it.

'Will you stay?' I asked when, all unbeknown to him, Sir John had wormed his way into my admiration, not least by admitting that Earl Rivers could match him on a tournament field any day.

I did not need winsome conversation, only an encouragement of my son.

'I think that would be an excellent idea if you are willing to house and feed me.'

And that is what he did. To our great enjoyment, as the days passed into weeks and there was no news for me of George's fate. Sir John's presence was invigorating, even if it was only because his money coffers contained more moths than coins.

He taught Edward to dance.

'You will need it when you attend Court. It is essential if you wish to attract a wealthy and beautiful wife.'

Edward scowled as he tripped over his feet; I accompanied them on my lute, not with any distinction, which caused my nephew to comment on the lack of skill of both his aunt and his cousin. I refused to rise to the Paston bait of a good argument.

'It is not important for me to learn the steps of a dance,' complained Edward, 'if I wish to make my name on the battlefield.'

'It is possible for a man to do both. Any well-born lady would expect you to be skilled in all manner of accomplishments. Can you sing?'

'No!'

I, although a doting mother, was quick to respond and Edward laughed. Edward croaked like a crow on the stable roof so it was decided that it would not be pursued. I enjoyed Sir John's company and so did Edward. They fought, they rode together. Edward talked much of George while I sat and worried about his absence without news. My nephew at least managed to divert my thoughts away from battlefields, even though he and Edward were so often seen with swords in their hands. Matthew, too, lost his initial shyness, listening to Sir John, even if he understood not two words out of every three, admiring the glint of light from the heavy jewelled rings he wore. Occasionally Sir John allowed Matthew to push one onto his small fingers, and laughed with him when it fell off.

I would miss Sir John when he left, which of course he must do.

'Where are you going now?' I asked when he announced his departure one morning as we broke our fast. I would not attempt to guess whether it be the Court or Norwich, where Margaret might demand his presence. I knew that letters had come to him.

'I return to Court. There are matters of some importance to be faced. My mother has provided me with a list of legal errands and how I must deal with them. I am remiss in my efforts to take back Caister, using the power of the law and the voices of important men.'

I smiled. 'It sounds a dull life.'

'It would be if I did nothing but fulfil my mother's demands. It is a relief when she stops speaking to me and communicates through Jonty. But there are advantages in being at Court.' His smile was pure Paston, a man seeing an advantage that he would snap up. 'Then I am invited to celebrate Twelfth Night with Archbishop Neville. He is well known for the good table that he keeps and the celebrations he provides. He is a man who enjoys making an impression on friend and enemy alike.'

Was not Sir John dabbling in dangerous waters here, furthering an alliance with the enemy? I could not resist a comment as he prepared to depart.

'So you are indeed mixing with the great and the good. But perhaps it would be wise for a Paston not to do so, in the circumstances. The name Neville might be one to avoid.'

'The archbishop has been pardoned.'

'Will the King continue to forgive him for his treasons of the past?'

'I will take my chances.'

'Don't risk your life, Sir John. Your mother would be too distressed.' He mounted his horse. 'Thank you for your company. Edward was royally entertained. Matthew, too. You have given him a love of rings that I think he will not lose.'

'It was my pleasure. But I think that it did not take your mind from the impending clash between the King and Queen Margaret.'

That he had been thoughtful about my anxieties warmed my heart towards him, in spite of his obvious self-interest.

'Nothing could do that,' I admitted.

And with the reminder, the fear returned threefold. Would the

Blessed Virgin abandon me to losing a second husband in the terrible havoc of a battlefield?

'I expect that your lord will return.'

'How would you know?' I was ungracious, perhaps the result of sleepless nights. I did not want platitudes. And then I was sorry. Sir John had done his best and he had taken the time to visit, even if he had ulterior motives.

'Come and stay with us for Christmas, before you go off to the heady delights of the Neville Archbishop's hospitality,' I invited. 'George will be home by then.' Of course he would be. 'Will you bring your betrothed to visit?'

Did I detect a pause?

'I will come.'

Which was an ambiguous answer.

'Then bring Mistress Haute to join in the celebrations, if there are any. Depending on who might win the coming conflict.'

'Thank you, I will.'

Before he left, I made a decision and clutched at his sleeve, forced to abjure my dignity but seeing an intense need that I could not deny.

'I made a mistake, nephew. I should have asked for help from my family when Robert died and I was first faced with the Percy attacks on my manors. It was pride that stopped me because no Paston willingly came to my aid throughout my life. I should have buried my pride and come to you for help. Now I am asking, for myself and for my Poynings son. No more excuses. Use your influence; I beg you to keep the Percys at bay. Get your Uncle William on your side. My son needs to feel secure in his future.'

'Have I not promised?'

'I think that you and promises are strangers, Sir John.'

He left me with a catalogue of concerns. Somehow, I did not think that I would see my nephew again in the near future. As ever, Caister Castle would take pre-eminence. He might come to my rescue, but only if he saw an advantage to his own pursuits. It was also in my mind that even if we saw him at Christmas, he would not bring Mistress Haute, for I doubted that she would ever be his wife. How unfortunate that a man of such grace and charm was so lacking in endurance in bringing what would seem to be an excellent match to fulfilment.

Most urgent of all in my never-ending string of worries was when would I receive news of George? Did he still live?

How many women in England lived with that same fear? It did not give me any consolation.

I had taken a wherry across the Thames to see John Dane at the Inns of Court rather than have him travel to see me. I returned without satisfaction, but the day was fine and the crossing easy, the tide only just on the turn. The house being quiet without Sir John, I had enjoyed the bustle of the City. There had been a battle, the news on everyone's lips of a Yorkist victory, but that did nothing to ease my worries. There were dead on both sides.

I took Edward and Matthew with me for experience of the dry legal world and they were keen to come. Perching accompanied us to keep control, for travelling with energetic Matthew was still a dangerous experience.

A breeze began to pick up on our return, turning the smooth water into choppy wavelets that splashed inward, dampening our shoes and my hems. The traffic on the river was considerable so that our oarsman growled when we were impeded by larger craft supplying the Court, their wash tossing us about. I tucked my veil securely within the neck of my cloak and held tight.

It had been a melancholy business, dealing with the estates of the dead, and the absence of a man who might become another mortality. It embarrassed me that, despite the bright weather and the company of my two sons, my spirits were as low as if fallen into a well. Perhaps I was just weary of it all, but indeed I could not afford to be. I braced my shoulders and focused on the busy scene.

'Look!'

Edward, surveying the array of craft, suddenly turned his whole body round on the thwarts.

'Do sit still, Ned. I have no desire to swim across.'

The boatman grimaced, intent on a good price for the journey.

'I'll not tip you over the side, lady. I'll earn my fare right well.'

'You might not capsize us, but my son just might.'

Edward was waving. Matthew, still ignorant of dangers in a small boat, jumped to his feet, the little craft rocking madly while Perching clung to his arm.

'Sit down, Master Edward! Both of you!'

'Father!' Matthew's young voice rose an octave.

'Of course it is not!'

'It is, mistress,' Perching said quietly in my ear and pointed. There in a wherry coming towards us sat George Browne, smilingly in glorious health, waving with both arms above his head to attract our attention. My moribund spirits leapt in joyful astonishment.

'George!'

I stood up to the danger of all of us, until Perching pulled me down with a less than respectful hand to my cloak.

'Might I suggest, mistress, that you wait until we get you all ashore?' Our wherryman was less than amused.

I laughed, a watery affair, at my foolishness, my heart beating like a military drum.

'Yes, it is your father,' I said to the boys because it needed saying, even though it was an irrelevance. I needed to say it for my own belief in this miracle. Then George's wherry had pulled alongside and the boys were full of questions. But George's eyes were on mine. When we had managed to arrive safely at the wharf, I could not wait before he took me in his arms, lifted me onto my toes and kissed me. When he put me down, my first words were not welcoming.

'Could you not even write?'

'Not on a battlefield. It is difficult.'

'Could you not tell me that you were alive?'

'I am not a Paston who writes of every event under the sun!'

I kissed him again in delight. Solid and strong, his darkly russet hair longer than was his preference, he had suffered no ills in the campaign. My worries had all been for nothing, yet I touched his face with my hands, pressing them against his lean cheeks, a reassurance that he was real and had come home.

'How indecorous of you, my lady. And you a married woman,' he observed.

'How demanding of you, sir, when you know that I await my husband's homecoming from the wars. What were you doing on the river?'

'Coming to meet you, of course. I could not sit at home and wait.'

'You look as if you have slept in those clothes.'

'As indeed I have.'

I felt the heat of him through his jerkin, the strength in his shoulders as he held me tight. He was alive. He was living and breathing. I should never have had any doubts.

'Are you weeping?' he asked. 'You are very damp.'

'No. Why would I weep? It's the river that is wet.' And yet I wept from sheer blessed relief. 'I knew that you would return.'

'She did not. She's been in a constant bad humour ever since you left,' Edward observed with less respect than I might have hoped for.

'If you might just pay your fare, mistress, I can be about my business...' our wherryman suggested.

The unbearable tension was over. Money exchanged hands.

'Are you certain that you are not wounded?'

'Only my fair share of cuts and bruises. And behold,' George announced. 'Here you see a brave soldier knighted by the King himself on the battlefield.'

What could I say? 'Sir George Browne. I cannot express my pleasure.'

And nor could I, for the boys demanded detail after detail of the campaign as we walked slowly home, Edward carrying his sword, Matthew his gloves. It had indeed been a major victory for the House of York at Tewkesbury. The Lancaster prince was dead and his mother, Margaret of Anjou, our previous Queen, taken prisoner.

Our reunion was private and most satisfactory after some rigorous cleaning with much scrubbing and scented oils.

'Well, Dame Eliza?' Sir George asked at the end, perfumed ridiculously with violets and roses but undoubtedly clean. His hair fell in a shining wave until I found the time and inclination to trim it back into neatness.

'Welcome home, Sir George.'

My whole world became centred on that place, in that room. Events beyond held no meaning for me as we celebrated our re-union in fine style.

CHAPTER TWENTY-NINE

MISTRESS ANNE HAUTE

The Royal Court in the Palace of Westminster, February 1472

Edward had relented, for what reason I could not divine, resulting in Sir John Paston being summoned to Westminster and granted his pardon in so inappropriate a place as the royal mews, where Edward was inspecting a new pair of moulting hawks, all shivering with the cold. I was not present at so unofficial an event but I was waiting outside, shivering equally and sheltering from the light rain under the overhang.

'Sir John.' I curtsied.

'Mistress Haute.' He bowed.

I did not think that he looked overjoyed to see me. If I had to guess I would have said that the pardon had given him no respite after all.

'You are quite as lovely as I recall, Mistress Anne.'

It sounded like a rehearsed speech by a Court gallant.

'And you are as preoccupied, Sir John.'

'Until an hour ago I lived in fear of my life.' It was a sardonic reply. Then he managed a smile. 'All I can do is ask your forgiveness. You know my difficulties.'

'Yes. The Court is well aware. A castle is a terrible loss to a man.'

'I am well aware that I have neglected you. It comes close to the bone when my brother is bawled at in the streets of Norwich for being a traitor, despite the pardon. Let us walk.'

He was reluctant to talk with me but I seized the moment. I had had many hours to think of this and to come to a decision.

With the Queen's advice echoing in my mind, I knew that I must push him into action, one way or another. There was no reason now to hold back. The passion of our short occupation of the bedchamber had not been repeated, our meetings reduced to a brief acknowledgement and salute to my hand, if I was fortunate. This was a marriage that perhaps should never have been, and must now be brought to an honest and decent end to free us both.

'Walking will get us nowhere, Sir John,' I announced so that my voice would carry.

He took a few steps as if he had not heard me.

'Sir John!'

He turned his head but did not stop.

'Do we end it, Sir John?'

Now he halted. His gaze came back to my face, sharp, keen as a new-hammered knife-blade.

'End it?'

Had he expected me to accept this strange state of non-marriage for ever? I did not think that he had given it a single thought during these months of uncertainty when I had not occupied his interest to any degree.

'Yes. End it,' I said. 'This travesty of a life for both of us. This betrothal that is no betrothal. This marriage that is no marriage. I cannot believe that it is satisfactory for you. Should you not get yourself a regular union and heir? Would it not be better for all if we stepped away from each other? We cannot go on like this, neither one thing nor the other. Neither fish nor fowl. You need to wed and get an heir. I need a husband.'

He considered my request, his eyes searching my face, as if trying to determine if I actually meant it. It seemed that he failed.

'Is that your wish? That we break our vow?'

'I wish for something tangible. Perhaps your affections are given elsewhere.'

He shook his head. 'My affections, as ever, are yours to accept or deny.'

Could I believe him? Absence did not necessarily make the heart warmer. Mine had been cooling with each passing month.

'Perhaps it is you who have discovered a courtier who can offer you more than I can,' Sir John suggested.

Frustration and a frisson of anger at his accusation made me sharper than I intended, and certainly more outspoken on matters that had come to my attention. Indeed, they needed airing between us.

'No, I have not. I understand the difficulties you have suffered, but I think that you do not care. If you did, why have you not even written to me in past months? Did you see no need to reassure me? There is no point in pursuing the hare that is already dead. I know of your mistress Constance Reynforth, and your daughter with the lady. Perhaps you would rather regularise your union with her. Or is there another lady who might give you more influence or wealth than I? I hear tell of a Mistress Cecily Dawne with whom you have spent time. Is she a lady who attracts your interest as a wife?' I was aware of bitterness welling up inside me, applying an edge to my voice. 'If she is wealthy, then my advice is to take her. By the Virgin, I have no dowry to speak of.'

First, I saw reciprocal anger in Sir John that I should have retaliated in this brazen fashion. Then his gaze lowered from mine and, in that moment, I thought that he was in agreement with me. I braced myself for his rejection. I would not repine. I would not weep. I would think myself fortunate that this terrible indecision was at an end. When he stepped back to my side, I felt my spine straighten and lifted my chin, pushing back my hood despite the now-persistent rain. I would accept this abandonment with all the dignity I could summon.

'I think, Mistress Anne, that the marriage should go ahead. My regard for you has not altered one jot. I like to think that you still care for me in the same manner. Have we not shared a bed with mutual enjoyment? Do we not enjoy each other's company in spite of all the troubles of the past?'

'What of your mistress,' I pursued, 'is she just a trouble from the past? It is hardly complimentary to her. And Mistress Dawne too?'

He was all contrition, his brow creased attractively in penitence. 'Mistress Reynforth was one for whom I had an affection many years ago, but all is now over, and in truth I never discovered the passion that you stir within me, my delightful beloved. I ask pardon for the sins of my past, when you had not yet stepped into my life with your smile, your wit, your irresistible charm. As for Mistress Dawne, anything you have heard is mere rumour. She means nothing to me.'

'Do I believe you?'

'Of course.'

All confidence, Sir John seized my hand, untangling it from my cloak, pressing his lips to my damp palm, before pulling me close into his arms to proclaim his remorse with a kiss, lips to lips, of such heat that I trembled. Regardless of the beating rain, although it had been my intention to rebuff him, I responded with similar desire. When he released me, we were both breathless.

'We have made the vows,' Sir John murmured against my throat while I threaded my fingers through his drenched hair, tightening my hold as if I would never let him go. 'Let us live with them and continue to experience the physical pleasure that marriage brings.'

Freed from his kisses, astonishment gripped me. This was not what I expected. Did I want this? As so often in the past Sir John Paston had sidestepped my plans and taken me by surprise. Surely he was a man born with an ambiguity written clear in his character.

'You look astounded, Mistress Anne.'

His smile was easy, affectionate, yet still with that edge of long-ing that had made me shiver. All the earlier tension in him had drained away.

'I am. Indeed I am.'

'Do you agree? Do we pursue this hare that is very far from dead?'

I thought about this, but only briefly. 'Very well.'

Before I knew what I was saying, I was in agreement, casting the Queen's warning and Sir John's ambiguities to the winds.

'I will meet with you again and I promise that all will be well between us.'

'When?'

'Next week.'

'Why not now?'

'I have important business.'

Still I could not resist, still uncertain, still unsure.

'More important than our marriage?'

'Give me time, Anne, and I will put all to rights. If you trust me, we will come through this. Do you accept?'

The sudden urgency in him persuaded me, although perhaps it should not have.

'Yes. I think that I must.'

There was nothing I could say or do but wait for that meeting.

'Is all settled between you and Sir John?' Cousin Elizabeth asked.

'All will be settled, my lady.'

'I will await the outcome with suitable eagerness.'

If she could see the renewal of hope in my eyes she made no comment on it. She might consider me a lost cause. I was thinking that myself. I was far from convinced that I had made the right decision. I could see no future for us despite the muted passion of Sir John's lips on mine in farewell.

I paid a visit to my Cousin Anthony Woodville, Earl Rivers, who was well on the road to recovery from his wounds although not in the best frame of mind. As all men that I knew, he did not suffer ailments well. He sat by the window in his chamber at Westminster, a book open on his lap, his foot resting on a stool, his eyes on the scene over the river. The book was not taking his interest, nor, I suspected, the colourful craft ferrying to and fro. His glance towards me as I entered was cursory. Then sharpened with interest.

'What do you want, Anne? I can do nothing for you, as you can see.' He appraised my garments. 'Would there be a reason why there are feathers attaching themselves to your hem? Are you in moult?'

'I am delighted to see that you are recovering,' I replied, sinking to a stool beside him. 'And to know that you are pleased to see me. Shall I go away? The feathers belong to the royal raptors.'

He had the grace to grin. 'Do stay, Cousin Anne. I am bored with my own company and have no visitors.' He pushed the book onto the floor at his side; I clicked my tongue as its fall could well have damaged the gilded spine.

'I am not surprised if you welcome them in such a fashion. I need some information.'

In the past Anthony had been most useful in applying his influence to put Sir John in a good position with either his enemies or the King. He still stood well in the King's graces.

'Then ask it.' He shrugged off his ill-temper. 'I can at least give you the benefit of my erudition. As long as you do not need me to actually do anything. As you see, my leg still pains me. I presume it is once more the issue of your absent betrothed.'

I grimaced. 'Yes. When is it ever not? You may not know the answer to this but you are the best source that I can think of. I would like it to remain between the two of us.'

'Certainly.'

'How difficult is it to acquire an annulment?'

'Oho!' His eyes brightened. His fair brows rose. 'Are there differences of opinion in the Paston dovecote?'

'There are always differences in the Paston dovecote, Anthony. How difficult?'

'It is always difficult to get the Pope to listen and give judgement unless you have a purse-full of gold.'

'Then how much does it cost to arrange the annulment of a marriage?'

'It has never been in my experience to annul one.'

'This is a serious question, Anthony.'

'Then my answer is this. More money than you will have, Cousin Anne. And probably more than Sir John can lay his hands on with his present situation.'

'Yet tell me.'

He did.

It was a vast amount. Not that I was considering an annulment. At least not quite yet. But I just might need the information. Dusting it first, I replaced the book back on his lap, kissed his brow, and left Anthony to his reading.

CHAPTER THIRTY

ELIZABETH PASTON BROWNE

The Poynings House in Southwark, Summer 1472

'Do we all settle down now to live in peace and tranquillity?' I asked as we broke our fast, the table spread with bread and various roast meats which I would not have ordered, but to which George was partial. How quickly our household had returned to normality with his return.

'Only if I can get my estates back. But now I shine brightly in the eyes of the King. Now is the time to make a petition, for when parliament next meets.'

'Do you remain loyal to York? Or is it Lancaster?'

I recalled the days when he had flirted with support for Warwick and the Readeption when King Henry VI was re-crowned. Had he only appeared on the field at Tewkesbury for the Yorkists because of Clarence's patronage, fortunately one of the victors? How familiar it all sounded when my nephew had done the same, but had ended on the losing side at Barnet. But what now?

'I know where my best interests lie,' George replied, stretching his arms so that his joints cracked. 'There is nothing to be gained by my supporting Lancaster. I support the man who wears the crown. And that's York.' He looked at me. 'Do you agree?'

'It is exactly what my Paston family would do. And I know just the man who can help you in drawing up your petition. I refused to ask my family in the past when I was in desperate need. Now I will ask, and loudly.'

'Your nephews were useful to me once before.'

'And Sir John will be again. I housed and fed him for a good two weeks. He can earn his keep with some legal expertise. I have invited him and his betrothed to spend Christmas with us.'

'The value of the Queen's cousin, even if your nephew is still under a royal cloud. Are you hoping for the Poynings estates?'

'No. I think that is a lost cause.'

'I will petition for them when I am full grown,' stated Edward, who might still be working his way through a platter of beef but with ears keen on the conversation. 'I'll not rest until they are mine again.' He glanced at me with just a hint of censure. 'I will not see them as a lost cause.'

'And nor should you,' I agreed penitently. 'You must forgive the weak heart of a woman.'

My son grinned. Silently I prayed to God that it would not take a battle to achieve his ambition.

True to his word, Sir George Browne presented his petition to the King in parliament, that all illegal claims on his estates should be cancelled in light of his support for the House of York on the battlefield at Tewkesbury. His father's downfall had been deliberately brought about by Sir Thomas Vaughan for his own personal aggrandisement and inheritance. The estates should be returned to the rightful heir.

How successful was our petition before parliament?

King Edward was intent on keeping his friends close and his enemies closer. George received a pardon for all previous sins against the House of York. All judgements against George's father were declared utterly void. The Browne estates were put firmly into George's hands. He was now Sir George Browne of West Betchworth and was appointed commissioner of array for Surrey and Kent. He was elected to parliament and appointed Justice of the Peace.

To have the Duke of Clarence as our patron had been most valuable. To have the petition drawn up by Sir John Paston had also been of more merit than we would ever have hoped for. My gratitude to my Paston nephew was beyond reckoning.

Aglow with our success we took up residence in Tonford

Manor where George's father had gained permission to crenellate, adding four towers and a Great Hall, rebuilding the old stonework in impressive brick. There we lived in some style, when not at Tonford at Betchworth Castle, more a fortified manor than a true castle, but with walls and gatehouse to repel any aggressors and an impressive Great Hall where we held banquets for men of similar Yorkist persuasions and employed a body of minstrels. Yes, it was a time of peace and prosperity. A contentment. I could not believe that it would last for so long; my children grew, Sir George gained recognition and a reputation for fair justice. If this was happiness, then I had achieved it at last.

Sir John visited us for Christmas, he sang and he danced with verve, but he did not bring Mistress Haute with him.

I considered informing Margaret that now I too had a castle to call my home, but decided that it would be too cruel when Caister remained a thorn in her flesh. I doubted that she would see the humour in the reversal of our fortunes.

CHAPTER THIRTY-ONE

MARGARET MAUTBY PASTON

The Paston House in Norwich, Summer 1472

'Lady Elizabeth Bourchier,' Sir John announced. 'Widow of Sir Humphrey Bourchier, who was killed at Barnet. She will be the perfect bride for Jonty.'

This was Sir John's answer to the problem of Jonty's unwed state after much hounding from me. The presence of my sons on the battlefield at Barnet, not least Jonty's wounding, had the effect of concentrating my mind once again on the empty prospect of Jonty's marriage. We still had no new generation of Pastons to take on the inheritance. Sir John remained impossible to pin down on the problem of his own marriage but here at last he had produced the name of a lady who might be suitable for Jonty.

Our own involvement in that battle had put an urgency into any marriage proposals and the Bourchiers had some influence, Sir John informed me. It was a family with impeccable royal connections; had not Sir Humphrey been buried in Westminster Abbey? This could be invaluable to a family who had inadvertently ended up on the wrong side.

But there was a problem.

'Is the widow of such a great man willing to look at a Paston second son with a treasonous past?' I asked, not entirely convinced.

'It would seem so.'

'Even though we were fighting for the enemy that killed Sir Humphrey?'

'It may not be a problem.'

I was not hopeful. My sons might have achieved their pardon for their part in the battle but some might still see them as men to be avoided. So might the King, in spite of finally being magnanimous with his gesture of reconciliation.

'She is an attractive woman,' Sir John assured me, 'and would bring prestige to the family.'

'Then you must tell Jonty. It might lift his spirits.'

It was a good thought, and I presumed that there was a successful conversation between my sons until Jonty, having been summoned to present himself at Court to meet the lady, returned to Norwich looking less than cheerful. I stood in the doorway as he dismounted and watched him, all thoughts of his marriage obliterated by the worry that continued to present me with bloody images on a battlefield. He could so easily have been lost to us if the archer had had a better shot at him.

'Lady Elizabeth?' I asked when he had drunk a cup of ale and complained long about the itch that still afflicted his healing wound, even so long after the event. 'What do you think? Do I arrange to meet with her?'

A prospective betrothal might indeed restore his good humour. It did not.

'She will not have me.' Jonty's reply was curt.

'Does she dislike you?'

'So it seems.'

'Have you actually met the lady?'

'Yes.' A smile crept into his eyes at some memory. 'I attempted to woo her, although softly for a first meeting.'

'Is she youthful enough to bear children?'

'Yes, but there will be no Paston issue there. Sir John says that I was too enthusiastic. The ardour of my language was too extreme. How could I not be extreme if I wished her to know how much I admired her and wished her for my bride? She has an ample dowry, and a figure to match. I surmised that she would enjoy a young husband in her bed.'

'What did you actually say to her?'

'I said—' He paused. 'I think that I should not tell you.'

'I presume that it might shock me.'

'It might.' He had the grace to look away, discomfited by my questions.

'Jonty! Then I am not surprised that she went into full retreat. Your father would never have wooed me with such lack of sensitivity.'

'I cannot imagine my father wooing you at all!'

I refused to retaliate. No, he had not. There had been no wooing. It had all been arranged for us.

'You lack your brother's finesse,' I observed.

'I lack my brother's title and wealth!'

'Perhaps you need to take lessons from him.'

'I think I will not.'

I tended to agree with him. I thought Jonty would do quite well on his own, without Sir John's provocative manner, if only we could find a young woman with a family who would agree to an alliance. Perhaps we had looked too high with Lady Elizabeth Bourchier.

'I have given up on her,' he announced. 'I will look elsewhere. Now that I have received my pardon, I can frequent the Court where I am certain to meet a lady who will match my expectations.'

There was no need to ask about the amount of a dowry. I could scratch the name of Elizabeth Bourchier from our list of possible wives. I hoped that Jonty was not too optimistic as he rode off to seek his fortune in London.

My final words to Jonty as he mounted his horse had been, 'Tell me about Sir John and Mistress Haute! Will this marriage ever be formalised? Your brother is still being uncommonly reticent about the whole affair.'

Jonty merely shrugged with a lift of his expressive eyebrows, leaving me as ignorant as ever. Yes, I had initially warned him against this union when his own affairs were in such serious disorder. Now it seemed to me that it was a marriage to be pursued, and with some speed. It would be cruel to leave the lady in a constant state of uncertainty. Besides, we needed a new generation of Paston heirs.

★

Meanwhile, there was another irritation for me to bring to an end. John Pamping, whose future had been in abeyance with the horror of Barnet striking at us, left Norfolk to serve Sir John in London.

Together, we watched him leave, Anne and I. I had given him no time to express farewells, merely informing him that he was needed in London immediately, that he must pack his possessions and leave that morning. He did not demur. To do so would risk dismissal and he would not so risk it, although his face was set in displeasure. Hard-hearted? Yes, I was, but a quick separation would be less painful for Anne than a lengthy tear-drenched farewell. Nor did I wish to risk an elopement, with Anne fleeing my door across his saddle, to live with him in some flea-ridden hovel. It would be too painful for everyone concerned, and I wanted no repetition of my estrangement from Margery.

'Where is he going?' Anne asked, since I had not discussed my decision with anyone in the household.

'To London. Sir John is in need of a trustworthy servant, and Pamping is the best.'

I felt her stiffen beside me. 'Are there none that can be found in the whole of that city?'

'Perhaps there are. But we know John Pamping. We know his loyalty.'

I turned away from the disappearing figure and walked inside, but her question followed me.

'When will he be home again?'

I pretended not to hear.

That morning we spent harmoniously enough in setting up the loom to weave a new batch of wool that had been sent from Mautby, until Anne dropped the hank that she was combing and turned to me.

'He will not come home, will he? Not ever. You have sent him away. I will never see him again.'

I frowned at her excess of emotion, but I would not lie to her.

'No, he will not return,' I said, picking up the spun wool and attaching it to the shuttle. 'As long as Sir John is based in London, then Pamping will remain with him.'

I kept my voice calm, my hands busy, my eyes on my task. It had no effect on my daughter.

'You knew he was going for good and you arranged it. You did not tell me. You should have told me. We had no time to say goodbye.'

Once again it struck me that she had learned to be outspoken with Cousin Calthorp, but I did not take her to task for it. Indeed, as a mother, I grieved for her sore heart but she was very young and would recover from it. Thus I was bracing.

'No, I did not tell you. There was no need. You have no influence over my decisions, Anne.'

How harsh that sounded. Predictably, Anne wept over the wool. I sighed and went to her, placing my hands on her shoulders, as I had once tried to draw Margery to me, away from her fatal liaison with Calle.

'Tears will do you no good. You knew nothing would come of it.'

'Because you were determined to separate us.'

I fought against compassion. I had had no such experience of loss as a young girl, only in my later years when John was dead and there was no hope of our ever reuniting. Had I wept like this, a storm of emotion? Only, if I were prepared to admit it, in the privacy of my chamber before I took up the reins of the life he had left me.

Anne had not finished, resentment building in her. I could feel the tension in her shoulders as she resisted my attempt to give comfort.

'You are determined that I will not find happiness in a marriage. Will you lock the door against me, like Margery? Do I have to follow John Pamping to London and ask him to wed me?'

My hands tightened in despair. Would she attempt such an outrageous venture?

'That is all foolishness. You will do no such thing. Your brother intends to sail for Calais in the company of Lord Hastings and Pamping will accompany him.'

'Calais! So he could die in some foreign conflict and I would not know.'

'Unlikely, I would say. You are being irrational, Anne.'

'You do not wish me to be happy. I will live out my days a bitter spinster.'

'You will do no such thing. You will be wed soon enough.'

'A man of your choosing. Will you beat me, as Mistress Agnes beat Elizabeth?'

I raised my hands from her shoulders, stepping back. 'Have I ever raised a hand against you?' I asked sternly.

'No.'

'No. And I will not start now.'

She continued to weep until I took her into my arms and let her finish her sobs on my breast. At last it was a mere hiccup and snuffle.

'You must forget him, my dear child.'

'I will never forget him.'

'You know how it is.' I stroked her hair. 'You have always known. For us marriage is a matter of business, not one of sentiment or romance. We make marriages that will bring us connection, sponsorship, estates. Love and kisses do not play a role in the practical terms of our family. Or in many families that I know of. If you find contentment you will be fortunate. If you do discover love with your husband, it will indeed be a blessing. But marriage to John Pamping is not possible. You need a man of status and wealth, hopefully with a good reputation hereabouts and some land to his name. If he is young and comely, and able to give you a life of some luxury, then so much the better.'

'Not like Master Scrope.'

All my children had heard the sad tale of their Aunt Elizabeth and Master Scrope. Not from my lips, but the servants enjoyed the horror of that proposed marriage for Elizabeth to a man who was an elderly widower, terribly scarred, and lame. Mistress Agnes had been a keen supporter of Master Scrope, beating Elizabeth unmercifully when she refused him. Until Mistress Agnes discovered that the prospective groom's financial affairs were far from straight-forward and not good enough for a Paston alliance.

'Not like Master Scrope,' I said. 'Poor Eliza. She suffered such fears of being left unwed or joined with a man she could not tolerate. But eventually she met and wed a man of distinction whom she grew to love. And now that she has a new husband, she will find contentment with him, too, I expect, and with her new children. Why should that not be your experience? You are still young. You will be desired as a bride by an important family. Sir John will arrange it.'

I prayed silently that he would.

'Sir John is too busy trying to bring his own marriage to fulfilment,' Anne muttered but at least her sobs had ended. 'Did you wish to wed my father?' she asked.

'I barely knew him. It was arranged by my mother and your grandmother. And your grandfather was one of my trustees, so he was keen to make the settlement.'

'So it was money. And connections.'

'Yes. It was thought to be an excellent marriage for the Pastons because I was an heiress. Just as Mistress Agnes was when she wed Justice William.'

'There was no romance.'

'No. Not at first.'

'Would you have been allowed to say no?'

'I don't think so. But I did not say no. I was an obedient daughter, as you will be.'

She thought about this, sitting up and wiping her eyes on her sleeve until I tutted and handed her a square of linen. She blew her nose vigorously.

'Have you ever been in love?' she asked.

'I grew to love your father.'

'That's not what I mean.'

'I know what you mean.' I smiled, pleased when I saw that she returned it, if a little hesitantly. 'Some hot passion, swept off my feet by a knightly hero, so that I would think the world well lost for love.'

'Something like that.'

'I wonder what Cousin Calthorp has been allowing you to read?'

Her blood rose beneath her pale skin, from temple to chin. 'Margery knows what it is like to risk all for love.'

I sent her off to fetch more wool from the hall where it was awaiting our attentions. There was no use in allowing her to dwell on Margery's sins, or on the passion of her love for a mere bailiff. Anne's heart was not truly broken. All we needed to find was a young man who could make her forget.

I turned my thoughts to different undertakings as I began to apply the shuttle, issues that my eldest son had not completed. Sir John had still not arranged the gravestone for his father's grave at Bromholm, six years after his death. I detected gossip about the lack in the market place. He must do something about it or we would all be shamed. I determined to write to him. And would order four sugar loaves and four pounds of dates at the same time. Sir John in London might as well be of use to the family. And then there was a keg of wine for which I owed payment to Sir John.

Abruptly I sat down on a low stool, my hands motionless in my lap. Sometimes there was so much to do, and I lacked the energy to do it. I would not think of Caister, which seemed to be lost to us for ever despite all Sir John's legal efforts in the courts. Without pressure from higher places, such as the King, the Duke of Norfolk had no intention of handing it back. Why would he? And now with our patron the Earl of Oxford taking refuge in exile, we had no strong voice at Court. We had heard that he was attempting a return to take back his own lands, but if he ever dared to do so he would find himself imprisoned for his sins by a furious King Edward. There was no help for us there. The only outcome from the battle of Barnet to give me some brief joy was that my sons had survived the bloodshed and been pardoned. It cast my worries over the fate of my beloved swans into insignificance. When Anne returned to the chamber my hands were busy again and the length of cloth had begun to grow. There was no place for idleness in this house. Nor for regrets, although my guilt over my rejection of Margery remained a living entity.

CHAPTER THIRTY-TWO

MARGERY PASTON CALLE

The Calle House in Norwich, Summer 1472

'Where will you be this morning?'

'At Carrow after Matins. The nuns wish me to overlook their accounts at this time in the year, halfway to Michaelmas. And then a meeting with the shoe-makers' guild, followed by the possibility of some employment with the candle-makers' guild that is meeting at the Carmelites.'

This was how most of our days began.

The securing of regular employment occupied Richard's mind to the exclusion of all else when we were settled in Norwich, where we lived a plain but not uncomfortable lifestyle. He was not without work, supported by the recommendation of the Prioress at Blackborough, but he wanted more. He was as ambitious as he had always been. He gained a reputation for the collection of rents, the careful keeping of accounts, the solving of tenant squabbles, but all on a small scale in households and businesses that could not afford to employ a bailiff or man of affairs.

I was proud of him, and of the life he had made for us. He had a name for honesty and loyalty. I regretted, for his sake, that he would never be invited to be a member of the prestigious Guild of St George as my father and grandfather had been. Despite all his hard work I knew what was in his mind, and resented the humiliation it would cause him if he were to be refused. Had he not already indicated that he would accept employment from the Pastons if they changed their mind? I had hated that he had had to do so; they had not sought him out. I hoped that we would never be so lacking in income that he would ever find a need to go to them uninvited.

But I knew that he would. Was he not conversant with every aspect of their landholding and tenantry, every devious means of squirming out of paying what was due by Paston tenants? It was like an itch under his skin, a constant irritant that he should be barred from employ so perfect for his skills, while I made a home for us and carried a son.

We called him John at my request. I felt it obligatory in a family of Pastons, yet I promised that the second, for I was soon carrying another child, would be Richard.

'If you are thinking to win over your mother, I think that you set your sights too high,' Richard warned one morning when he had time on his hands. 'If you do not speak with her, how will she know of the honour you have done the family through the naming of our child?'

'She will know. She has a sharp nose. And ears worthy of a bat.'

'Go and tell her, Margery. Or even write to her.'

'No. I will not. And I dislike you having to abandon your pride and hope one day to bend the knee before my brothers to be re-employed.' Oh, I was sharp and regretted it, handing the baby to him, admiring the manner in which he tucked his son into his arms, holding him firmly as if he were a small bale of wool. 'I think we both know that neither Sir John nor my mother have employed a new bailiff in your stead.'

'I know that. And why should I not be willing to make fresh approach to your family? A little humiliation now, a good income tomorrow.'

'That's as may be, but I will not beg for you.'

'And I have not asked you to,' Richard replied gently enough.

It coated me in shame and I knew that I deserved it. Was it not the role of a good wife to further the prospects of her husband? I should be standing at the door of the Paston house even now, urging my mother to reconsider.

I could not do it.

And then one morning, well before Matins, Richard was already collecting his cap and gloves, smoothing down the fine wool of his new doublet.

'You look every inch a prosperous man of law and business,' I remarked.

His smile held more than a hint of satisfaction. 'The Pelterers' Guild has paid handsomely for my services.' He donned his cap, pulled on his gloves. 'And now I have a meeting.'

I raised my brows suddenly suspicious. 'With whom?'

'I will tell you when I return home. It may work for the best.'

I stared at him, challenging him to keep so momentous a meeting secret from me.

'I forbid you to leave this house without telling me. If you do not, I swear that I will follow you.'

Knowing that I would, Richard relented. 'How like your mother you are. I have a meeting today with Mistress Paston.'

I knew that I was scowling. After almost three years, could he truly believe that there would be a reconciliation? And he had not told me.

'You did not tell me.'

'But now you know and, if you are of a mind, you can smile at me and wish me well.'

'Make sure that you drive a hard bargain,' was all I would say, retrieving my newly walking son and holding him back from following his father through the door.

'I promise. As hard as when you are buying fish in the market.'

I was good at bargaining. We did not have money to waste on frivolity.

I kissed him on the doorstep, where indeed I smiled. 'Good fortune.'

'Do I give your mother your best wishes?'

'Only if you wish me to appear as big a hypocrite as my brothers who took all from you and gave nothing!'

Throughout the main task of the morning in dipping tallow candles for autumn, Richard remained high in my thoughts. However much I might dislike it, I prayed for his success.

★

Richard returned before dinner was even set out in the chamber. I could read nothing in his expression after a visit that may not have lasted more than an hour, but here was joy in his return. He flung back the door with a courtly gesture.

'I have a visitor for you, my love.'

I stood and stared at the young woman who accompanied him. Anne. My sister Anne. How long had it been since I had seen her? Not since she had been sent to live with the Calthorp family. I hesitated, such a slight lack of movement, to see if she would react to me with sisterly pleasure, regretting the wariness that had become so much a part of my life. But if she was tainted with the Paston condemnations, why had she come with Richard? Of course she wished to see me. I took a step and then another, until she fell into my arms. To my surprise she returned my embrace fiercely and with some emotion. Whatever had or had not been said by my mother, it had failed to turn my sister away from me.

I released her and looked at her, searching her face.

'Anne. I cannot tell you how pleased I am. Does our mother know that you are here?'

'No. She would disapprove heartily, but Richard offered to escort me.'

'Did you tell him that you would follow him home if he did not?'

'Yes.' There was the gleam of the mischief I recalled from when she was a little girl. Once we had been close, before she was sent to board with the Calthorps, enjoying the secrets and dreams of young girls. How could we have guessed that our hopes of being wed would bring us such anguish and heartache? And for me, such undreamed-of happiness.

'I could not refuse,' Richard announced. 'I will leave you to enjoy each other's company. When you have said all that needs to be said, I will escort you home, Mistress Anne.'

'Of course.' She looked at me as Richard departed, studying my face with a newly acquired maturity when I drew her to sit beside me on the settle. 'In spite of all I have heard, you look happy. There is a contentment about you.'

'I am content. And happy. Richard and I have what we fought so hard to achieve. And we have a son.'

Her smile was just a wry twist of her lips. 'Then you are not mired in sin.'

'No. Nor dragged down into the depths of society. We have friends in Norwich. We have a good life here.' As the light fell fully on her face, I thought that Anne looked strained, as if troubled with bad nights and disturbing dreams. There were six years between us, and I wished that we had been closer through those years of our growing up. 'Come and sit and tell me all I have missed,' I said, discovering a need to be close to my family.

'Would you wish to know?' she asked.

My son came into the room, pushing quietly around the door that had been left ajar. With a crow of delight, Anne took him onto her lap and hugged him.

'Good day to you, nephew.'

He squirmed to be released, upon which he sat at our feet with a roughly fashioned toy rabbit which he made to hop noisily across the floorboards while Anne launched into the quarrels that assailed the Paston household. There was much friction. My mother continued to hold all together, but bad blood was beginning to develop between Jonty and Edmund on one side and my mother on the other, chiefly caused by lack of fulfilling employment for either of my brothers. There was thus much falling out and arguing. With Caister snatched from our hands there was nothing to take Jonty away from home, and Edmund had still failed to find a place to use his lawyerly talents. Sir John stayed out of it all in London, another source of my mother's aggravations. And at the centre was Father Gloys, now promoted to be Rector of Stokesby near Mautby, who always took our mother's part and seemed to have more influence over her than was desirable.

'It was Father Gloys who refused to let me cross our threshold,' I recalled.

Anne had become remarkably astute. 'Was it his idea or that of our mother?'

'Our mother did not make any offer of reconciliation.' But I did not want to retrace the old pain. 'What about you? What does our mother plan for you now that you are returned home?' I tweaked a fold of her finely woven wool skirt. 'You are so well dressed for a morning visit that you should have no difficulty in attracting a family of substance.'

Anne's face closed, as a light cloud filtering the sun, and she looked away. 'I have nothing to say on that matter.'

'I do not believe that. I see unhappiness in your eyes.'

I took her hands in mine and turned her to face me.

'More like anger,' she said.

'Ah. Have they already found you a husband? The Paston family is not good at choosing husbands for its daughters.' I could not, after all, hide my own bitter memories.

'I have no dowry, nor a prospect of one. Sir John cries poverty.'

'I had no dowry.'

'You did not need one. Richard wanted you anyway, with or without a dowry. You married for love.'

There was the faintest glint of tears in her eyes, but she did not allow them to fall, releasing her hands from mine and wiping any suspicion of moisture with her sleeve. I thought there was more to trouble her than Sir John's habitual tardiness.

'Tell me. It will be in confidence, of course. Is there anyone you love?'

'No. No one to run off with.' She sniffed with an attempt at a smile. 'I am paying the penalty for your bad behaviour. They will wed me before I can find someone unsuitable.'

'I am so sorry. Was there someone unsuitable?'

Anne shook her head, her lips firmly closed. If there had been someone to claim her heart, he was lost to her. I pushed no further since she was unwilling to confide.

'I don't blame you,' Anne said, suddenly looking older than her years. 'I envy you. I would risk my family's displeasure if there was someone I loved enough, and who loved me to risk all.' And then she added, as if she had made up her mind that I could be trusted with knowledge of her grief: 'There was someone. I will not tell you his name, because it would be indiscreet. All I will tell you is that I loved him, and believed that he loved me. Now it is all over. My heart is so sore.'

I presumed that she had been abandoned. We sat in silence for a little while, her hands again enclosed in mine.

'I cannot help you,' I said eventually when the silence had become uncomfortable. 'I can give you no advice, nor would it be of any advantage for me to speak with our mother. Yours will probably be the lot of so many women who are given in marriage to men with whom they share no affection. Pray to the Blessed Virgin that you marry soon with a man who will give you a home and a child, and there you may find happiness.'

'How do you know if you love a man?' Anne asked. 'Truly love him?'

It was a question that surprised me. Perhaps she had not loved the unknown young man after all, or was at least uncertain of it. If the whole affair had been handled by my family with more care, Anne might not have been as unhappy as she was now.

'When you love someone, truly love him,' I replied, 'you will know. Your heart will tell you. Every breath you take will remind you that there is one man in your life, a man who will remain there until death parts you.'

Anne nodded and leaned over to ruffle the hair of my son who was resting against her leg, testing his new teeth on the ears of the unfortunate rabbit, until I scooped him up onto my knee. He bounced and patted at my face with his hands.

'I would like a child of my own,' Anne admitted.

'I pray that you will have one. Children bring a basket-full of worry but also great happiness.'

There was no more I could say that would comfort my sister when she would not speak of the real problem. Meanwhile, Richard arrived at the door to escort her home.

'Will you come again? I cannot visit you.'

'You could try.'

We both knew that I would not. 'Come here if you need me,' I urged.

'If I can. I would not wish to be parted from you.'

Our farewell kisses were tender ones, but we both accepted that we had exchanged empty promises. Sometimes, as we both knew, words were only to comfort and reassure rather than to heal the true wounds. Furthermore, Anne left me with an uncomfortably sharp sense of guilt, one that I had previously abandoned, that my determination to wed Richard had left my sister in such a parlous situation. Now that she was back in the Paston household she would never be allowed to marry any man who did not fulfil the Paston ideals, even if he turned out to be the love of her life.

Richard saw my sister safely home, then returned. I was waiting for him to learn more than Anne could give me about the situation in the Paston household.

'Your sister enjoyed the visit,' he said.

'Yes, now come and sit with me and tell me all. Were you made welcome? It did not take long. Was Father Gloys there or is he more often at Stokesby now? Have they offered you employment in return for past loyalties? If they do, it is because there is no one as good as you, and they are desperate.'

'Which question would you like me to answer first?' Richard sat down at the table and began to help himself to bread and cold meat while I poured cups of ale. He would not admit it but it must have been a morning of much tension, as well as the indignity of having to beg for work where he had previously been dismissed, but Richard was a man of stalwart principle with a firm belief in his own abilities, and I loved him for it. 'Not what I would call a welcome, but yes, they are in need of help. And perhaps there was a hint of desperation, but your mother hides it admirably.'

'My mother hides many things admirably. And so?'

'It is the loss of Caister again that is encouraging tenants to be reluctant to pay what they owe. After King Edward's victory at Barnet, Warwick's death and Oxford's flight, the Pastons were left in some jeopardy. The Duke of Norfolk emerged in the ascendant and took back Caister, with detrimental effects on the obedience of Paston tenants, and as it happened, good fortune for me. I am to be re-employed.'

'Who decided? My mother? Or was it Father Gloys?'

'I was relieved that Gloys was absent, and so were your brothers. It was your mother's decision, but with the consent of your brothers, as she was quick to tell me, although I suspect that was a falsehood. I doubt your brothers would agree, but Mistress Paston sees the need for my talents and so will arrange it on her own authority. Your brother Edmund was there in the house, but not in the meeting with your mother. She had obviously ordered him elsewhere. Your mother and I are to work together in secrecy. She will communicate by letter when there is a need.'

I thought about this. It was exactly what my mother would do.

'Did you agree?'

'How could I not?'

'Did she manage to smile?'

'No. Not once. I had the sense that there was much on her mind.'

'You are not to be bailiff once more.'

I could see the disappointment in the flattening of his brows.

'No, I could not expect that, could I? My work is far more temporary, but it will be a good solid income, and it is a job I can do well. Who knows how long it will last? Who knows what it may lead to in the future?'

He was more optimistic than I, but the affair of Caister might just push them over the edge of resentment into permanently employing the best bailiff they could possibly have.

'Your mother has much to deal with,' Richard finished his tale of Paston negotiations. 'It is not entirely her fault that she tends to be so combative. I imagine that some days she would simply enjoy retiring to her chamber to sip a cup of wine, leaving all the affairs of business to her sons. At present that cannot be.'

It astonished me that he could be so forbearing after all the pain that she had created for us. Richard's tolerance was a thing of wonder.

'Did she talk of me at all?' I asked finally.

'No, my dear love. She did not mention you.'

As we rose from the table he folded me into his arms and gave me much comfort until we were disturbed by our son, escaping the eye of our newly acquired kitchen maid, come to find his father. My life, within my new family, was once more full of happiness and I would not dwell on the space that should have been filled by my mother enjoying her grandchild.

CHAPTER THIRTY-THREE

MARGARET MAUTBY PASTON

The Paston House in Norwich, Spring 1473

When I recalled the letters that I had intercepted between Calle and Margery, it was clear to me that I must not relax my vigilance. Margery had thought that Calle had never written to her, but of course he had. Only one had escaped my careful net, and that one dangerous enough. The rest were swept up and burnt by me. I did not read them. I thought that they would be too painful.

Sure enough, the letters came from Pamping to Anne, brought into the house by various means which I could never determine. Most I intercepted. Did I read any of them? I wished I had not, but this one I did:

> *I will return to you when I have made a name for myself.*
> *If you are of the same mind, I will not rest until I have wed you.*
> *I will not let your family stand in my way. We know this can be done.*
> *Know that you will always hold my heart in your fair hands.*

I burnt this one with fear in my own heart, determined to prevent Anne from absconding to London to join him. Pamping did not encourage her to do so yet, but if Margery could show such a streak of wilful independence, then Anne could do the same. Where had they gained such tenacity? From me, I feared. Back in my young days I had ridden into our beleaguered manor at Cotton with the smallest of escorts and, facing a strong force of soldiers, demanded the return of the estate to me. All it took was courage and a sense of rightness. When no one else was there to help me, then I would help myself.

I was horribly aware that Anne might do the same.

Some of the notes worked their way through my vigilance, how I knew not. When Anne appeared lighter of spirit, I suspected that Pamping had more to do with it than the warmth of the sun or the friendly visit of a neighbour to bring gossip. There was nothing that I could do but keep them physically apart. I wrote to Jonty, thinking that he would be a more reliable correspondent than Sir John.

> *It is necessary that you find a husband for Anne immediately. Still nothing has been done about this. Tell Sir John when you next see him. I think that he is avoiding me. My propositioning Sir John to find Anne a husband seems to die a death every time I express the urgency of the matter. If he is too slow in coming to a decision, we may be faced with a scandal as great as that of Margery and Master Calle.*

I threw down my pen, suddenly torn with such sorrow. Such reckless love, to strike both Margery and Anne. I had no experience of it. For a blink of an eye, I wished that I had.

My letter to Jonty precipitated a visit from Sir John himself.

'What is the problem?' I asked when I had ascertained that he was in good health and needed no maternal fussing from me.

'The problem seems to be my sister Anne,' he growled as his father used to do when things did not go his way. 'Our finances are precarious. Where do I find the sum to offer a dowry for her that will tempt a man of means?' And then, when I might have taken him to task, he grinned, casting himself into a chair. 'It will please you to know, Mother, that at least one of your troubles is over. Pamping has left my employ.'

A little hope grew in my heart. Until I thought further about this. This might not be good news: if Pamping was no longer in our employ, there was no one to watch his actions or take note of his whereabouts. He would have more freedom to contact Anne, as Richard Calle had done when he had taken himself to London and from there had intrigued with the Bishop. This was not good news at all.

'Where has he gone?' I asked, showing none of my dismay.

'Would you believe? Gone to work for the Duchess of Norfolk.'

So Master Pamping indeed had ambitions. It was a good move for him. An excellent move, in fact.

'But that is not good for us,' I said. 'If he improves his repute with the Mowbray family as his sponsor, he might consider himself more than a suitable husband for Anne. And if he beckons, I fear that she will pack her coffers and follow him.'

'Surely not.'

'How well do you know your sister?'

Very little was the truth of it. Sir John had never taken the time to get to know the young woman who had returned from the Calthorps. I still lived in fear that she would thwart us all despite her obedient demeanour.

'There is no need for you to be anxious, Mother,' Sir John announced with a nonchalant gesture that did little to quench my suspicions that he had done nothing at all to discover a husband for Anne. 'Despite the problem of a dowry, I have plans. I have a suitor for her.'

I did not believe him. Sir John would say what came easily to his mind and deflect any criticism from me. I would not be deflected.

'Who?' I asked. 'Will I approve?'

'Probably not,' he said, 'but it will be a good match and heal some old quarrels in Norfolk society. Jonty agrees with me.'

'Who is this paragon?' I demanded when Sir John continued in this sly game of cat and mouse.

'It is William Yelverton. I have spoken with his family.'

I was aghast. Sir John knew that I would not give this match my blessing. Of all the young men Sir John could have chosen, he must fix his eye on young William Yelverton. To my astonishment, Sir John was already negotiating a settlement and expected me to praise him for it. All I could do was remember our dangerous dealings with Justice Yelverton in the past.

'I like it not,' I stated bluntly.

'Why would you not like it?'

The family was well known to me, as it was to most inhabitants of Norfolk. William Yelverton, the prospective husband, was grandson of Justice Yelverton, our one-time bitter enemy over Fastolf's will. Justice William Yelverton, now risen to Sir William, had been one of the original trustees for Fastolf's will who were all displaced when my husband John had claimed that Fastolf had dictated a new will on his deathbed. Justice Yelverton had questioned the whole episode, the bad blood erupting as early as Fastolf's funeral. I recalled my husband and Justice William Yelverton exchanging hard words in the church, for all to hear, as soon as the obsequies had been observed. Since then there had been no healing between our families since Justice Yelverton and John had crossed swords at every opportunity. We barely acknowledged each other in the street in Norwich. Justice Yelverton was now a knight and in close harmony with the Duke of Norfolk. The Yelvertons were members of the legal community, ambitious and ruthless in their search for power and land.

'Are you sure about this?' I asked.

'It seems a perfect solution to me.' Sir John was adamant, as was his wont when put under pressure, particularly by his mother, but he was no longer a youth, rather a man with opinions of his own, so that I could no longer sway him when his mind was made up. 'What better way to cover over the disputes of the past?'

'As long as the young man has not been brought up to think that all Pastons are bad Pastons. Justice William actually accused your father of illegalities, of falsifying Fastolf's will to get all the land for himself. I would not wish to negotiate Anne into a marriage where she cannot be comfortable.'

'No such thing.'

I was not so sure. I had no high opinion of the temper of the Yelverton family.

Sir John left as fast as he had arrived, claiming urgent business, leaving me to inform Anne of her future. Which I did with none of my own misgivings. She must embark on this marriage in a spirit of hopefulness.

'William Yelverton?' There was no recognition in her face.

'Yes. A young man of much your own age but with a strong family of excellent standing behind him. It will be a good marriage.'

'I have not met him.'

'It will be arranged.'

I did not tell her of the family feuds. She was too young to remember much of it and there was nothing to be gained by planting seeds of disaffection before the young couple had actually set eyes on each other. I hoped that the Yelvertons were abiding by the same strictures. As for Anne's response to the plan for her future:

'I must look forward to meeting with William Yelverton.'

So little emotion. Such lack of energy. I could only imagine that Pamping had cut his ties with her, realising that there was no hope. It would make Anne's marriage to the Yelverton boy so much easier when she had recovered from her disappointment.

Negotiations between Sir John and Justice Yelverton for her dowry went ahead. I began to feel some optimism that all would be smoothly achieved. Until, with typical flamboyance, Sir John decided to hold an official pledging between the pair at Mautby, within shouting distance of Caister.

'Why there?' I asked.

'To show them that I have not given up my claim on it.'

'It will be expensive,' I protested, knowing my son's liking for ostentatious display.

'It will impress the Yelvertons,' Sir John replied, tight-lipped. 'Money and land will always win over a Yelverton.'

'Better to spend the money on Anne's dowry,' I suggested.

'We'll spend well on both! Look to your money coffers, Mother!'

Jonty was unimpressed. 'He always does have grandiose schemes, even when we don't have the rents coming in. At this rate we will have to employ Calle again. At least he could be trusted as a bailiff, even if not to keep his ambitions away from our sister.'

'Do you mean that?' I asked, in my mind's eye seeing the still-meagre tally of rents and the empty rent coffers. They were in a desperate state, although of late they had improved.

'Why not? He'll probably do better than anything that we are achieving.'

'You refused to have anything to do with him ever again!'

'I will consider it. It is permissible for me to change my mind.'

I hid a smile. What Jonty did not know was that I was already employing Master Calle, without drawing attention to it, and would use him more if my sons were not averse to it. It had not mended my alienation from my daughter, nor would it unless either of us was willing to make that first step toward reconciliation, but it had established a hint of closeness that eased my mind a little. One day, perhaps, Margery and I would meet and make amends for the past.

For the moment, what Jonty did not know would not worry him.

Sir John, intent on impressing everyone within a distance of twenty miles, arranged a gathering at Mautby of the gentry and wealthy merchants of Norfolk, producing the best wine that we had and employing a group of itinerant minstrels who might mask any silences in the conversations. The Yelverton family was there in force, full of gracious courtesy for the sake of harmony. Such smiles, such greetings; they set my teeth on edge.

'We are pleased to be received here, Mistress Paston.' Old Justice William Yelverton, now Sir William, superbly clad in a long Burgundian gown of leaf-green velvet, the man who had called my husband a thief and a treacherous lawyer, beamed with untrustworthy pleasure on his bold-featured face. 'I never expected it in my lifetime.'

'Neither did I, Sir William.' I managed a close-lipped smile. 'Times change and we must change with them. It is for the younger generations to make their mark on society.'

'I trust the marks will be true ones and without hypocrisy.'

'If hypocrisy were present, I am sure that you would recognise it, Sir William. You have lived with it for many a year.'

We had each other's measure.

What did I make of the prospective husband for my daughter? The boy was well groomed and polite, clad in the expensively flattering garments so much loved by King Edward; a silk jerkin, padded and short to just below the waist to draw attention, with his sleek fitting hose, to his excellent figure. He could rival Sir John for length of the toes of his shoes, bright with gilding on the leather. A peacock feather adorned the low-crowned hat which sat jauntily on his gilt hair, cut longer than was usually acceptable in Norfolk but was the rage, so Jonty informed me, at Court. A young man of style, of extravagance, of worldly ambition, I decided. He shone as brightly as one of my ever-dwindling silver platters, and was probably just as costly in his habits. It could have been worse, but I had my suspicions and thought it a matter of still waters. Would he be a young man of discernment in his wooing of my daughter? Who knew what he was thinking behind that fair smiling face? At least he had been well raised with good manners and he could shine in company when called upon to do so. When Anne was introduced to him, he bowed, then took her hand and saluted her fingers most royally to the admiration of all present.

The quartet of minstrels proved that they could at least produce a tune and the young people danced. On the surface, all in all, it was a happy event and when the betrothed pair were toasted in good red Bordeaux, I truly believed that Anne would be well wed, contentedly if not happily, by the end of the year. On that night I was proud of my daughter who, clad in celestial blue damask and pale fur, showed herself to be the perfect well-bred Paston daughter.

'That went off to acclaim by all,' Jonty declared as the guests departed.

'Young Yelverton seems a good choice.' Sir John preened at the success of his business dealings, for that is what they had been. 'He has the confidence to do well in local affairs.'

Too much confidence perhaps, although I was reluctant to blame a young man for that, even though young Yelverton had become noisier and less discreet as the evening progressed, as did the quantity of the wine and ale imbibed. I made no comment.

Anne was quiet, her face drained of colour, so much so that I was concerned for her health when she made her apologies and went to her chamber. Later, when the house had been closed down for the night, I followed her. I would not truly wish unhappiness on her. She was sitting in bed, a psalter in her hands, open but I suspected unread. I doubted there would be any comfort for her there. I sat beside her.

'What did you think?' I asked.

Not that it would have any bearing on the marriage taking place, but I wanted to know. Her eyes touched on mine, and then away. They were too bright, although I did not think that she had been weeping. Her voice was flat with acceptance.

'He was good to look at and had fine garments. He was very gracious in kissing my hand.'

'Is that all?'

'As my brothers said, it will be a good match. The family is wealthy and has a formidable reputation. Better than ours. My betrothed informed me of it. I did not argue the point. He seemed amiable enough to be a good husband.'

'But you do not think so.' When I saw her about to deny it: 'Tell me the truth.'

'I heard him. I heard him say what he thought and I wish that I had not.'

Abandoning the book, she covered her face with her hands.

'What did he say?'

'He does not want me.'

'Surely he did not say that. Perhaps you misheard.'

'Misheard?' Her hands fell away. 'He was braying with laughter. His voice echoed off the walls. He said that he would have me if my dowry was forthcoming, and good enough for him to give a passing glance, otherwise he did not want me. He could do better than a Paston who had lost all they had ever gained and had no money in their coffers to buy him off. He said that I did not have even a vestige of beauty in my face to compensate him for the lack of coin.' I realised that her eyes were bright with fury. 'I heard every word of it. Did he know that I would hear him? I do not think that he cared. I know that arranged marriages are to be accepted, but I would not want a husband who hates me before he takes me across his threshold.'

Now she slapped the unread pages of the psalter together, disturbing the candle flames so that strange shadows rose and fell.

'I am to be the sacrificial lamb to heal the past wounds with the Yelvertons.'

There was no point in my saying that she had imagined it. Of course she had not. How many marriages began with such a cloud hanging over them? I wished young Yelverton had had the courtesy not to say it under our roof where he might be overheard, but as she had said, he did not care. He was as much in the control of his family as Anne was in hers. I took her hands in mine, but she pulled them away.

'He does not want me, and I do not want him.'

'But it will come about, Anne. You must set your mind to it. At least he is young and comely.' I recalled Elizabeth and her suitor with the scars and limp. 'They are reputable people. You will live in comfort and rule your own household. You will have your own children and enjoy the raising of them. Surely that would appeal.'

'It must. As you say, I have no choice. Margery said the same thing to me.'

Suddenly my confidence was under attack. 'Margery? When have you spoken with her?'

'Since I have returned to Norwich. We do not all ostracise her.'

Clearly, she would not say more. It troubled me but there was no advantage for me in pursuing this.

'Sleep now, and I will pray for you.'

'How can I sleep?'

What a dispiriting end to an evening that had held out at least the possibility of a marriage that would not bring Anne grief. I doubted that Anne would sleep, and neither did I as I cursed William Yelverton for his deplorable insensitivity. I cursed all the Yelvertons in the same breath.

And now here was Jonty, whose extravagant hopes, followed by indecision, also robbed me of words. After two years with no success, it might be best to lower our sights in finding a wife for

Jonty. In despair I called my two sons to the family negotiating table. There was a young woman called Elizabeth Eberton. Her family were drapers, brought to my attention by Sir John.

'Where do they live? Do I know them? Drapers?' I wrinkled my nose. Too much like shopkeepers.

'They may be drapers, but they are wealthy and keep a good house. Master Eberton employs men to buy and sell. He is important in the drapers' guild.' Sir John shrugged lightly. 'He is not like the Calle family. He is a master craftsman.'

Which would be acceptable. Mistress Elizabeth might be just what we needed as an addition to the family.

I turned my attention to Jonty. 'Go and visit the family. There is no point in my going if you take a dislike to the lady. Exert some charm – subtle charm, mind you, unlike your last wooing. If the family is willing and the lady attractive enough for you, then we will make progress.'

Jonty, abandoning all sense of subtlety, scowled and turned to Sir John.

'Will you go and see her for me? I am too busy.' I resisted asking him what could keep him from a visit of an hour at most. 'Tell the lady that I admire her and that if her dowry is what I believe it to be, I will willingly accept her as my wife.'

'Why cannot you go, little brother?'

'I could. But you have a more elegant turn of phrase.'

It was not a suggestion that I liked. I fixed Jonty with a stare, aware that my voice was sharp and robbed of all patience with this evasive son. 'I doubt that she will be impressed. Neither will her family.'

'A knight come to woo her for his brother? I think that she will.'

I tried another approach.

'What is her dowry?' I asked Sir John. 'Have you discovered? Is it appropriate?'

Regretfully, I sounded like Mistress Agnes, to whom a dowry meant everything.

'I think that it will be substantial,' Sir John said.

'Good.' Jonty spread his hands expansively. 'Then tell the

Ebertons that I prefer their daughter to a London lady for whom I have been offered more than six hundred marks. Tell them I have thought seriously about this London offer, but I have decided that Mistress Eberton might just suit me very well if her dowry is comparable.' I could only say that Jonty smirked. 'This is a juicy worm to act as bait for a fat carp. I am getting desperate. I must attract a wife in some manner.'

Even Sir John was speechless, until he regained his sense of order. 'You cannot begin a negotiation for a marriage with a threat.'

'It is no threat. Tell them that I might even wed Elizabeth for a lesser dowry than six hundred marks. Do you think that it will impress them?'

'No,' I said. It was an appalling idea, as if we were touting for custom.

Sir John was not willing to condemn. 'I have my doubts but I will try. Do I tell them that you have admired Mistress Elizabeth when you have seen her at worship on a Sunday?'

'You could.'

'Have you seen her?' I asked.

'No. To my knowledge I have never set eyes on her.'

I smacked my palms down on the table. My son was impossible. Sir John went off on his appointed task, returning within the morning.

'I have seen the Ebertons. I have spoken with them. I have made the acquaintance of their daughter.'

'Was she pretty?' Jonty began a cross-examination.

'Passable.'

'Did my suggestion impress them? That I would have their daughter rather than six hundred marks?'

'I'm not sure they believed me.'

We heard no more about Mistress Elizabeth Eberton. Even Jonty began to despair.

'I will wed any woman with a suitable fortune,' he announced, 'even some old thrifty ale-wife in London, if Sir John can find one.'

In a moment of exasperation I was inclined to agree. It might be the only way.

My daughter Anne fell ill. Gravely ill. Wan and without energy, she rarely left her chamber until I chivvied her into helping me at some effortless task. Her spinning of wool was listless, the quality poor. She ate and drank little. At least it was not the pestilence, but she responded to none of my dosings. I considered it to be a fever which would soon burn itself out, but Anne became paler, complaining that her head ached, until I sent her to her bed.

There were no enquiries or kind wishes from the Yelvertons.

When I hovered over her, continuing to dose her with a decoction of feverfew and honey to cure her head-ache, she turned her face away. I was becoming afraid. Would the prospect of this marriage drive her to waste away before my eyes?

Once more I was kneeling in the great cathedral in Norwich, as I had when severely troubled in my younger days, to present a most desperate petition. Then I had spurned the gold-shod feet of the Queen of Heaven in the Lady Chapel for the maternal smile and open palms of the blue-clad Blessed Virgin in a quieter place. Now I knelt at the feet of the bejewelled Queen with her austere mouth and judgemental eyes.

'Have mercy, Blessed Virgin.'

All was silent around me for it was between services. The Lady Chapel was empty. I bent my head, searching for the right words.

'I have lost one daughter to the trials of matrimony. I fear it was as much my fault as hers. Perhaps I should not have listened to Father Gloys. He has been a source of strength in past years, but I fear he has been too harsh. He is dead now, probably of a sourness of spirit. I should have held out my hands to Margery rather than ordering her from her home. And yet I feared what she would do to the family. What will become of their children, born without recognition in society? There will be many who will enjoy our failure. Thus I banished her. Did I do wrong?'

The silence seemed heavy with judgement. The Queen of Heaven's earthly husband had been a carpenter, after all. What difference between a carpenter who could probably neither read nor write, and a bailiff? The candles burned with straight flames, not even wavering in a draught. There were no shadows on the carved features of the Heavenly Queen. She was without emotion.

I shifted on my knees. Kneeling for any length of time had become a burden to me in the past year.

'I fear that I must now lose another daughter,' I said. 'My daughter Anne is sick, so severely that I fear for her life, and I can find no reason. Her skin is waxen. Her flesh wastes away. What do I do?'

I looked up into the beautiful face.

'Be merciful, Blessed Mother. Lift her into your loving arms and restore her to health. If she lives, I will dedicate myself to a pilgrimage to Our Lady of Walsingham. I will give money to the poor. I will not be critical of my sons. I promise that I will make amends with Margery, my daughter, and invite her back into her family. I vow that I will, if I have to.'

I could hear the irritation in my voice, even though I had vowed to be patient and tolerant. My voice sounded much as any mother who discovered a deep source of dissatisfaction in her children. I prayed that the Queen of Heaven would understand.

'My daughter Anne is still not wed,' I explained as if she would not know. 'It does not help the situation. I fear that her ill health is exacerbated by her fear of this marriage. There is no need to fear it, but we make no progress with it. In your mercy, Blessed Virgin, take issue with Sir John Paston, for I have failed. The Yelverton boy will find another bride if we linger, and then where will we be? Or is it the Yelvertons who are hanging back? If nothing develops, we will be back at the beginning with Anne thinking of absconding to wed John Pamping, although I no longer know where he is dwelling. I don't know what to do.'

I heard distant voices, coming closer. I did not wish to be found here.

'I suppose that I must talk to my sons again. Or to the Yelvertons. I will do it. Blessed Mother, give me strength to draw the family out of this time of indecision. It is tearing us apart.'

From the purse at my belt I drew one of the few remaining Fastolf jewels, left to my husband by Sir John Fastolf, and placed it at the feet of the Queen of Heaven. The ring of St Louis with a diamond at its centre looked small and tawdry against the wealth of gems in the hem of her gown, but it was all I had to offer as a gift in my desperation.

I stood, bowed my head, lit a candle and made to leave. Then I turned back. 'I will light a candle for the soul of Father Gloys, because my sons will be remiss in doing so.'

I lit the second candle, before adding, 'And I have given employment to Richard Calle again. At least I have done one right thing.'

CHAPTER THIRTY-FOUR

MARGERY PASTON CALLE

The Paston House in Norwich, Spring 1473

Despite my initial denial, I visited Anne after all, waiting until I knew that my mother and brothers were away from home, my brothers not in Norwich and my mother in the Cathedral. Father Gloys was dead, of nothing more memorable than old age after a life of dissension and misery. There would be no one to proclaim authority over me. I thought that I had a half-hour before we were disturbed when I presented myself at the door, and when Master Pecock opened it, I simply walked in as if I belonged there and gave an order as a daughter of the house.

'I have come to see my sister. I would be grateful if you would show me to her chamber.'

'Mistress Anne is unwell.'

'Which is why I am here. Rumour in the market says that my sister ails, although no one in this house saw fit to tell me. There is no time to exchange opinions. Take me to her.'

My courtesy was exemplary. My confidence as Mistress Calle praiseworthy. The servants must have feared for her life for they did not demur but escorted me to the chamber that I had once used and where Anne lay in bed. Her pallor and listlessness horrified me. Was she indeed close to death?

The scene was to remain illuminated in my mind, as bright as one of the pictures in the Prioress of Blackborough's missal, as Anne opened her eyes, full of despair, and looked at me. Strangely she showed no surprise that I might be pulling up a stool to sit beside her.

'What do I do, Margery?'

'You will listen to me.'

I could be nothing but bracing. To allow her to wallow in such heartbreak would do her no good.

'What is this lying abed as if you have no energy?' I asked. 'I had thought you to be made of good Paston fortitude.'

'I do not think that I am.'

'Tell me a problem that you cannot face?'

Anne did not even pause to consider. 'To be wed to a man who despises me and rails at all my family stands for.'

Of course. The young Yelverton who had been bred from the cradle to see all Pastons as the enemy after the cataclysmic falling-out over Sir John Fastolf's will.

'Is it as bad as that? I cannot believe it. He does not know you.'

'He does not want to know me.'

'But when he does, he will know that he is wrong.'

'And if he does not?'

I lifted the cup of weak beer that had been left by her bed and bade her drink, insisting when she shook her head.

'If he never sees the good in you – and I'm sure he will – then you will assuredly enjoy your own children even if you do not enjoy the father of them. Do not repine over past loves, Anne.' Putting aside the cup I leaned close and held her hands tightly in mine. 'Our affairs are not similar. Richard remained true to me, keeping step with me when all seemed lost. John Pamping is gone and will not return. Yes, I know about John Pamping. Our brother Edmund is more than happy to gossip with Richard.'

'But he wrote to me.'

I continued to be firm and lacking in sentiment. My sister must not be allowed to sink into despair.

'Writing is cheap! Words are cheap! Pamping's letter is of no value if he did nothing to see you again. Did he act on his words of love, on his promises? He is not worthy of your dedication, and you must make your own future now. Here is a marriage arranged with status and wealth. Can you not rule such a household and make it to your own liking? Did you learn nothing with the Calthorps? Of course you can do it. I am sure that you learned innumerable ways of how to manage your husband without his knowing it. Lady Calthorp must do so every day.'

She gave the slightest inclination of her head, a faintest smile as if at some sweet memory.

'Get up, Anne. Put on one of your favourite garments and enjoy the warmth of the sun on your face. The wedding is arranged. And when you are a bride in your new home, insist on appointing some of your own servants who will be loyal to you. Then you will make it your own household and feel comfortable there.'

She thought about this, and sat up, pushing her un-braided hair from her face with a listless hand.

'Yes. I will do that.'

Time was passing. I must go. I kissed her forehead, thinking that she looked less distraught, but still unsure that she would follow any of my advice.

'Will you visit me?' she asked. 'When I am wed?'

In spite of everything, Anne's innocent request made me laugh, although without much humour in it.

'Would the wife of a bailiff who struggles for work and income visit one of the Yelverton family? No, it cannot be, but I will think of you and pray for you. And perhaps we will meet when you visit Norwich. Give Yelverton an heir and he will refuse you nothing!'

Still her thoughts lingered in the past. 'I wish I could wed John Pamping.'

'Do you even know where he is?'

'No, I hear no news. My mother does not speak of him.'

'Then I will tell you, for Richard does. He is working for the Duchess of Norfolk. I would say that he has fallen on his feet after leaving the Pastons. If he will not come to you, you have to give him up.'

Still there was the brittle resentment, that I had achieved what was being denied to her. 'You did not give up Richard.'

'Because he stayed with me. He wrote to me. He came to me when I was most in need. It was Richard who petitioned the Bishop of Norwich. He would not let me go. There's the difference. John Pamping did not love you enough to ask you to exchange vows with him. He did not love you to stand with you and come to your rescue, Anne, as Richard did for me. Has he even asked after your health?'

'William Yelverton has not asked after my health either.'

'William Yelverton is a young fool who needs to be weaned away from his vindictive family. Surely you, as a Paston, can achieve that!'

At last she bent her head in acceptance.

'You do realise, do you not?' In the end I must admit it, however difficult it might be, and would not Anne be aware of it for herself? 'I am much to blame for our mother pushing you into a marriage that places status and wealth before affection. It was I who caused our mother's hard-heartedness. You have paid the penalty.'

It had struck me hard, that the scandal of my marriage would drive our mother to pursue an advantageous match for Anne with such dogged purpose, at whatever cost to her daughter's immediate happiness. In our family's eyes there must be no possibility of allowing Anne to repeat what I had done. Our mother would continue to move the chess pieces of the Paston family about on their chequered board, to ensure the best advantage, and Anne would be a pawn to be sacrificed for a Yelverton knight.

'I am so very sorry for the position I have put you in,' I said. 'I have come here to see you with love in my heart, but I deserve that you should hate me for digging this chasm into which you have been pushed.'

'But I cannot hate you,' she replied immediately. 'I must rejoice that you have found happiness with Richard. I know that you have a care for me.' She rubbed her hands over her face as if to brush away the terrors that had weighed her down, the first brisk movement I had seen in her. 'I value your advice, dear Margery, and accept it because I know that I must. I will do my best to make a good marriage with William Yelverton. I will enjoy my children and enfold them with love.'

We embraced in a final farewell, while I thought about

re-maining until my mother returned but decided it would be good policy to be gone. I had done all I could. I had sent Anne to a marriage she did not want. I prayed that the Holy Virgin, who knew what it was to love her children, would bless her with compensations.

CHAPTER THIRTY-FIVE

MARGARET MAUTBY PASTON

The Paston House in Norwich, Spring 1473

On my return from the cathedral, I went immediately to my daughter. She was no worse, and perhaps even a little better, her demeanour less frail. She had even braided her hair into tidiness. If it was my visit to the cathedral, I was grateful. Then I learned from one of the servants that the Queen of Heaven had no role in this, and it broke my heart, unless it was the Holy Mother who had guided my eldest daughter's footsteps. Margery had been to visit her sister whilst I had been away from home. Margery had spoken privately with Anne for some considerable time. It filled me with dismay that she should choose a time when I was absent, but why would she not? She would fear my rejection. Guilt warred with a return of my irritation that Margery had come to my house without my permission. I wished I had been there to see her.

I returned to Anne's room to find her dressed and sitting in the window seat despite the draughts.

'What did Margery say to you?'

Anne did not even deny the visit.

'All that you would expect a sister to say. She wished for my recovery. She told me of her joy in her children. And Richard's success in finding employment. She has a comfortable home which she rules with competence. Much as you rule yours.'

A comment that I decided to gloss over.

'Is that all?'

'She said that I will enjoy my own children even if I do not enjoy the father of them.'

Good advice, that Anne had not been willing to accept from me. So the Calle family was doing well. It dismayed me that I knew so little of Margery's married life. But I thought that Anne had censored much of what had been said. I would not question her. I was simply relieved to see an improvement.

'Do you wish she had not come?' Anne asked.

'Since she seems to have set you on the road to rising from your bed, I cannot complain.'

I ordered a bowl of rich venison soup and bread to be sent in, which Anne consumed without enthusiasm but with a determination, as if following silent orders. Whatever had been said between them had had good effect. Prayers were sometimes answered in unlikely ways.

As I was about to leave her chamber, Anne's voice stopped me.

'I do not want this marriage. I do not want Yelverton. I despise him. But I will accept it because I must.'

Maturity demanded a high price. A lesson we all must learn. On my knees before the Queen of Heaven I had promised to heal the rift with Margery. It hung over me, a dreadful cloud. I was unused to asking forgiveness, but now it would be sinful to refuse. It would no doubt be good for my soul.

The affair of Anne's marriage was still lingering with no sign of completion. Since Sir John had yet to be prompted by the Blessed Virgin, I set myself to pursue it. A discreet note to Sir William Yelverton at Rougham Manor was dispatched to enquire about the state of the negotiations. It gained a less than discreet reply, inscribed by a clerk for it was a fine and even hand.

We make no progress. We still await Sir John Paston's final settlement of Mistress Anne Paston's dowry. When that is done, we will be pleased to pursue the matter.

Until that comes about, I regret that we cannot move forward.

Blessed Virgin!

I was driven to tear the letter and cast the pieces into the fire. Despite the family celebration at Mautby, with all the expense it had entailed, nothing had come of it because my son had yet to fulfil the demands of the settlement. I disliked being made to look foolish or ignorant of family matters. The final line in the letter had set a flame to my ire:

If the idea of marriage is no longer acceptable, we will gladly look elsewhere for a bride for our son.

I disliked even more that Sir John had put me in this invidious position of having to accept discourteous correspondence from a clerk.

Anne continued to recover, slowly, but I no longer feared day to day that I might lose her. She did not care whether she was married or not but at least she responded to life about her. Meanwhile, I would take issue with Sir John. I sent for him in peremptory fashion, planning my approach.

'You wished to see me.'

Sir John's first words on his arrival from London. He was restless, begrudging me his time, refusing to sit. There were no family pleasantries to be exchanged. It did not persuade me to moderate either my demand or my tone.

'I did. Anne's marriage.'

'What about it?'

'It hasn't happened.'

His brows rose, and I would swear not through dissimulation. 'Why not?'

'Because you have not yet completed the terms of her dowry.'

'I thought it was done. I thought she would be wed and beneath Yelverton's roof by now. Why are they taking so long?'

'Because you have not completed the settlement for your sister. If I had known, I would have done it myself.' He cared so little. 'You have forgotten about it, haven't you?'

'No ... perhaps I have. I have been in Calais with Lord Hastings's great company, in the service of the Duke of Burgundy. I wrote to you and told you of Burgundy's conquest of Lorraine, but disaster on the border of Switzerland. I told you that I was not involved and unharmed.'

Which I had forgotten in my despair over Anne's health, but was not prepared to admit it. I remained as bellicose as the distant Duke of Burgundy.

'Well, now you are here. It needs to be completed. If you will not do it, then I will.' It would do no harm to ruffle him further. 'I have knowledge of a Lincoln gentleman who has offered a good marriage for Anne, if you will not approach Yelverton.'

A vague enquiry. I did not even know his name, but I would use the Lincolnshire gentleman as bait to entrap my son into action if I had to. Sir John swooped as a raptor on its prey.

'Is he wealthy?'

'Yes. Do I arrange a meeting?' I asked as ingenuous as I could manage in the face of my son's irresponsibility.

Sir John hesitated, reluctant to be drawn into yet more demands on his time. I would make it easy for him.

'If you are too taken up with Calais and Mistress Haute, I can understand that your sister's future has been put on hold.' I smiled encouragingly. 'Do I then complete the negotiation with the Yelvertons and agree the dowry?'

He almost said yes, but at the last could not endure to be supplanted by his mother. As I had known would be the case.

'No. I will complete the settlement. I will contact Yelverton immediately. And then I must return to London.'

'Of course you must. I have enjoyed this brief visit.'

I saluted his cheek. Anne would be wed at last.

'And how is Mistress Haute?' I enquired.

'Mistress Haute is in excellent health.'

How long had this involvement between them now existed? To my knowledge it was a good handful of years. Oh, in truth, on first hearing of it I had advised my son to settle his estates before undertaking matrimony, but time was passing and I was surprised by a need to meet this Court lady who had the charm to keep Sir John's affections alight through all the problems of war and treachery and Caister Castle. She must be a woman of superior will, after my own heart.

'Is it not time that you brought her to visit in Norwich?' I asked.

'When my time is my own.'

'Any news of Caister?'

'None!'

Sir John was clearly dealing with problems of his own. He would not thank me for any advice, so for once I forbore to give it. I wondered if Mistress Haute deluged him with demands and explanations. I found myself hoping that she did, and if so, I would admire her all the more for pinning my son down with an appeal to his conscience.

CHAPTER THIRTY-SIX

MISTRESS ANNE HAUTE

The Royal Court in the Palace of Westminster, July 1473

'I can tolerate it no longer.' I had to admit to my voice leaning towards shrill.

It was high summer, a time of blossom and bees and thoughts of love as the minstrels sang in the Queen's garden. A year had passed. A whole year. And we had made no progress. Sir John Paston was still prevaricating. I had never met a man who could make so many excuses in the most persuasive tones. All depended on the future of Caister Castle, of course, or the increase in rents, or his service with the Lord Hastings in Calais. Or the negotiations for his sister's marriage. I could have written his excuses for him with ease. Oh, we met, but except for exchanging words of intent and promises our marriage was no nearer completion. Sometimes his kisses revived all my old anticipation. He would arrange a priest. He would set all to rights, but he had not come to my bed again.

No priest gave us his final blessing.

No introduction of me to a home where we would live together.

No visit to his mother's home in Norwich.

Any promise of next week became next month or, it seemed, next year.

There was no substance in him or his promises.

Why did I tolerate it? Because he had touched my heart. He was handsome with wit and a lively humour. He could charm the Queen's singing-linnets from their cages. And because I was growing older and wanted a household and children of my own. If I had to wait one more week or month or year, then I would do it. My Haute family had not been showered with offers for my hand from other suitors.

Now I could wait no longer.

'What do you want from me, Mistress Anne?'

I could almost taste the edge to his voice. I must do it now or I would be chained to this fantasy for the rest of my life.

'I want this marriage formally ended. I cannot do it. You must make the proposal, Sir John.'

For the briefest of moments I could read it in his face, the recognition of what I had said, that I had given him a route which he could take to escape. The instant relief. He would happily break off the betrothal because it was the easiest path to take. Then it was hidden, supplanted by a magnificent disappointment.

Would he ever accept that we had been wrong for so long?

'I cannot believe that,' he said, still with an appeal in his voice. 'Why will you retreat now, when we have come so far?'

I would be brutal.

'Because your neglect gives me no choice. You can give thanks for it because it saves you having to make the decision.' A little curl of anger was born anew in my blood. 'I want an end to it. Now. Today. Do you agree, Sir John? I was sure that you would. I have offered you the perfect opportunity to reject me, with no blame on you. The decision was mine. The request was mine.'

'If that is what you wish.'

Even now he could not say what he truly wanted.

'I do. I want it to end fast. If you do not want me, then I have no time to waste in pursuing what is a lie. I need to find another husband.'

His expression was all compassion, as if he would act purely in my interests rather than his own.

'Then we will end it. We will agree to break our vow.'

Did he truly think that I would accept that, a statement that all was at an end? I knew the dangers in my own situation if the final severance of our vows merely rested on his word. Sadly, as my heart finally accepted, I could not trust him. Furthermore, why would he agree to my demand now? I did not know.

'I demand more than that, Sir John.' I waved away a servant who brought cups of wine. Now was not the time for toasting each other amongst the heady sylvan delights. 'I demand an annulment, granted from the Pope. Thus I will have proof that this arrangement between us is at an end.'

Arrangement. I would not call it a marriage. I had been wrong from the very beginning to do so. All my good sense had been swept aside by my yearning that this man would make an honest wife out of me.

Now he was surprised. 'Why? Why so formal? Can we not merely agree that we were mistaken in our vows, that we no longer desire to live with them? There were no witnesses, no priest.'

'It must be obvious to you, with all your legal expertise. I must emerge from this debacle with my reputation intact if I hope for a true marriage. We consummated this travesty of a marriage. I cannot have the threat of a bigamous liaison hanging over me when I seek a new husband. And neither can you, if you choose to take a new wife.'

His expressive brows rose. He had not expected this either. I could almost see him searching for an excuse. Of course he discovered one, smoothly delivered.

'I do not at present have the leisure to devote to its ending.'

'Leisure!'

'To petition the Pope is no easy matter.'

'As I am aware, but it can be done.'

'I do not have the money.'

'Then find it, Sir John. Bend your legal mind to it. Borrow the money, if necessary. It cannot be so difficult to be rid of a wife that you clearly do not want.'

'I will enquire as to the cost.'

'I would be grateful. I am sure that you already have some idea.'

His eyes slid from mine, before returning. 'It is costly. Annulment would cost the sum of one thousand ducats. I don't have it.'

'A thousand ducats? How did you know that?' Suspicion

bloomed large. 'I swear you have already looked into this possibility. Or were you just hazarding a guess?' Fury bloomed larger. The fact that I had been just as devious, discovering the cost from cousin Anthony, was of no relevance to anger with my betrothed. 'You will not escape this, Sir John.' Did he think I would go away and forget about it? 'I think two hundred ducats would do the trick, according to my cousin Earl Rivers. I have made some of my own enquiries, of course. I knew that you would make excuses. To tell me a thousand ducats is just a lie!'

'Two hundred.' Sir John considered this, in no manner disturbed by my ire. 'I don't have that amount either.'

'I think that you should make all speed in raising it. Ask your mother, or your brothers. What about Uncle William Paston? Otherwise, your reputation will suffer when I make it known that you will not put yourself out to end what should never have been in the first place.'

Without another word, Sir John turned his back on me and marched off. I thought in that moment he might have hated me, if he could ever rouse the emotion and energy to do it, for I had discovered at last the problem at the heart of this affair. Sir John enjoyed the excitement, the flattery, the company of an attractive woman. What he lacked was the willingness to undertake a selfless commitment. I suspected that this lack of responsibility to all but his acres and his own immediate pleasures would dictate the pattern of the rest of his life. To my sorrow, I could no longer be part of it. It was a cruel hurt to my pride and to my heart, but I knew that I must be strong enough to withstand any grief and press ahead for that annulment.

Cousin Elizabeth as usual made the definitive judgement when I told her.

'And about time, too,' the Queen said, then added as a parting shot: 'If I could get the King of England to wed me, you can persuade Sir John Paston to annul a marriage that neither of you appears to desire.'

How true. Marriage to a man who did not care was no longer the honeyed flower to attract this particular bee.

★

'Are you still without your annulment?' cousin Anthony asked, making his farewells before setting out for Ludlow, King Edward having appointed him Governor to the little Prince of Wales's household there. He was now High Sheriff of Carmarthen and so much involved in justice in the principality of Wales.

'Yes.'

I was in no mood to explain further.

'You will have to be more crafty-cunning, Cousin Anne.'

'He is far craftier than I,' I responded. 'He is also absent. Again.'

'Then you must hound him to earth and flush him out.'

'It seems that I must.'

In the end I enquired as to the whereabouts of Jonty and set off to waylay him at the Paston chambers in the Inns of Court. If anyone knew anything about Sir John's whereabouts, it would be his brother. The Paston chambers were pointed out to me in the labyrinth of rooms by a disinterested clerk, and I wove my way through the busy crowd of black-clad lawyers. Here, too, where the Pastons resided, there were scenes of much activity with the packing of coffers by two of their servants amidst the all-pervading reek of dust and ink and old documents. Clearly Jonty did not have much time to waste on me, awarding me the briefest of nods. For my part, I made no attempt at polite greetings.

'I wish to speak with your brother.'

'So do I, but neither one of us is likely to have our wishes fulfilled.' He barely looked up from writing some pertinent list, one hand ruffling his hair.

'Where is he?'

'In Calais.' His smile, now turned on me, was mischievous, knowing our past history. 'He always had a liking for Calais. He met some interesting women there.'

'And then abandoned them. So he has escaped me!'

'He had little choice in the matter.'

'It seems to me that Sir John always has a choice.'

Jonty took pity on me, abandoned his pen, discovered a stool that he dusted and handed to me so that I might sit. I found a space by the door, out of the path of the servants.

'Then tell me. What is all this about?' I gestured at the disarray.

313

'We are going soldiering. The King has entered into an alliance with the Duke of Burgundy against France.'

'As I am aware.'

'But are you aware that King Edward has summoned the Pastons to fight with him? Perhaps to determine our true loyalty after the Barnet episode. We are all committed, Sir John and Edmund and I and my two younger brothers, Walter and Willem. A true Paston presence. Our mother is in a frenzy of worry.'

I thought about this. 'Then why are you still here, if Sir John is not?'

'To tie up any legal matters for my mother. But chiefly to arrange a retinue and new livery for myself and Sir John.' He nodded his chin towards an untidy pile of livery garments on the floor by the door, their bright colours of white and gold and blue much muted by grime and what I thought to be dried blood. 'They were last worn at Barnet and have seen better days. Some of that blood is mine.' He discovered another stool under a pile of documents which he pushed to the floor with little respect for any importance, and came to sit beside me. 'The last I heard of Sir John, he intended to ride into Flanders to pick up a new horse and harness, and then, joining the King's forces, on to Neuss on the Rhine where Duke Charles is conducting a siege. I think he hopes to learn a few clever lessons that he can use for a siege of Caister, if it comes to that.'

'Will it come to a new siege?'

'Who knows the future? The Bishop of Winchester, despite all his promises, is as slow as a winter snail and nothing has come of the agreement. The King seems to have a renewed interest in the whole matter, when he is not negotiating with Duke Charles, of course. I know that Sir John intends to draw up a petition to give to him, setting out the whole lengthy story, all these years that the Duke of Norfolk has held it unlawfully. Sadly, I have heard that the Duke of Norfolk declared that he would as soon surrender his life as Caister Castle. It is too fine an achievement to give up. So yes, it may well come to another siege.'

'Enough of Caister.' Impatience forced me to my feet. What

use in staying now that I knew that Sir John was not even in the country? 'Is he doing anything to achieve our annulment?'

'I doubt it. Although I have to tell you that our mother wrote to him to say that she hopes he will do better with a new wife. She has given up hope for you, Mistress Haute.'

'So have I given up hope, but I need to see an end to it.'

'There is nothing I can do. All I can tell you is that he was investigating the cost of an annulment through an application to Rome some time ago. At least three years, I would say.'

So long! It horrified me that I had still been living in hope while he had been seeking out a means of escape.

'And how much will it cost him?' I asked.

'Only two hundred ducats at the most.'

'So not a thousand. Which was the sum that he quoted at me! Earl Rivers had the right of it. I have never met a man so willing to mislead and so reluctant to keep his promises as your brother! What would he intend to do? Keep me as a wife yet not a wife for ever? Don't answer that question because I am sure that you do not know the answer. Who knows how Sir John Paston's mind works? I do not.' I scowled at him. 'You look uncommonly cheerful, Master Paston, for a man about to go to war.'

Coming to stand beside me as I pulled open the door, he tilted his chin in thought. 'I have a mind to wed a most appealing lady, and I believe that she is not averse to it. When the war is over, of course.'

I would not ask. I had no more interest in the Paston matrimonial adventures. I admired his confidence and determination. His older brother had the confidence but the determination was sadly lacking. I brushed the dust from my garments and stepped outside once more into the to and fro of clerks.

'I am certain that Mistress Paston will rejoice. I wish you good fortune. More good fortune than I have had.'

He had some compassion for me in the end.

'I will send him to you when we return from Calais.'

'I would hope he would come of his own free will.'

Should I fear for his safety? In spite of everything, in spite of his infuriating intransigence over our own affair, I would not wish to hear of his death on the battlefield. It would be an easy way to secure my release, but not one that I would choose. There was even room in my heart for compassion for Mistress Margaret Paston with all her sons risking their lives and going to war. Once again, the Paston menfolk proved to be a trial to their women.

CHAPTER THIRTY-SEVEN

MARGARET MAUTBY PASTON

Framlingham Castle in Suffolk, March 1476

Elizabeth Mowbray, Lady Elizabeth Talbot by birth, newly widowed Duchess of Norfolk, clutched my hand in a death grip and howled in agony while her midwife bathed her face in lavender water, the soothing fragrance pervading the whole room.

What was I doing here, in this luxuriously appointed birthing chamber with all the curtains drawn to shut out the winter sun and the outside world at Framlingham Castle, where it was hoped that the new-born Duke of Norfolk would see the light of day? My acquaintance with the Duchess was slight and not always of the friendliest since Caister lay between us like a festering sore. It was all Jonty's doing that I was here at all. He had written to me when it seemed that the sadly bereaved lady's confinement was imminent.

> *The Duchess will be right glad to have you with her during her*
> *travails, your having survived your own pregnancies in good heart.*
> *I also think your being here would do a great good for Sir John's*
> *present difficulties, if the Duchess is inclined to be generous when*
> *her child is born. I think that you should be prepared to travel to*
> *the lady's side as soon as you hear that she has been brought to bed.*

Thus, here I was, in a spirit of compassion for the lady, suffering such an unexpected loss of her husband, and in irritation with my son. Did Jonty truly expect me to talk about the ownership of

Caister Castle as the poor woman strove to give birth? Clearly, he thought I could persuade her to sign the fortress over to us while on her childbed, the widowed Duchess exulting in my helping her to give birth to a son and heir for her recently deceased husband.

They tell me that Caister is so lightly garrisoned that a goose might walk in and take it, Jonty had continued.

My reply had been short and sharp:

But you are no goose. Stay clear. We are so close to taking it back legally. I doubt the grief-stricken Duchess will stand in your way, but I will not negotiate with her as she brings this child into the world at this sad time.

Pray for her, Jonty, as will I. And not just for the return of Caister. She has much to bear.

Jonty's reply was yet another aggravation.

You should know that Sir John has loaned the Duchess the valuable cloth of gold that he had purchased for our father's grave, until he can arrange a fitting memorial to be incised on a marble slab. He suggested that it be used for covering the Duke's body and the hearse. He expects to be well rewarded for such thoughtful generosity.

As ever, Sir John would not allow an opportunity pass him by.

Thus I was here to aid the suffering Duchess whose husband had died at only thirty-two years, although apparently in good health the previous day. Any disputes over estates could wait. I knew exactly what Jonty wanted me to do but this was women's business. It was a deep regret for me, which I never talked of to any one, that I had been absent from the birth of Margery's sons. All through my own intransigence. I would do my best for this pain-racked lady who had no demands on my friendship but needed my help. I would willingly give it.

'Will it be long now?' the Duchess asked as the pains eased and gave her a moment to collect her wits, and I once again anointed her brow with lavender, for what good it would do in her travails.

'Not too long,' I hazarded, looking across at the midwife, who scowled at me. 'Did you have a short labour with your daughter?'

The Duchess shook her head as every part of her body tensed once more and the agony resumed.

'You have had many children, Mistress Paston?' she gasped in the next pause.

'Seven. And all healthy, in spite of my sons' attempts to kill themselves on battlefields both in England and abroad,' I said encouragingly. 'Once, on Good Friday, I was brought to bed and delivered within two hours. It took everyone by surprise, including me.'

'I pray that it will be thus for me.'

It was not. It was a long-drawn-out affair that did not bode well for either mother or child.

'Do you fear for the babe?' I asked the midwife, withdrawing some distance from the bed.

'Not yet, but it is taking too long. Both are suffering.'

She was anointing her hands in wild thyme oil to aid her in easing the child into the world if the Duchess could not manage it on her own. Having done that to her satisfaction, she took from a soft package of silk a length of parchment.

'We can but try this.'

I knew what it was, of course. A birthing girdle, inscribed with blessings and invocations, as well as images of the Blessed Virgin and the Christ Child.

'Its length is of the exact height of the Virgin Mary,' she said moving to stretch it over the womb of the straining Duchess.

'I had no use for such,' I said.

'I expect that you managed quite well without, Mistress Paston, but the Duchess is not a strong woman.' Did I detect a sneer in the midwife's reply, that I could never be compared with the Duchess, not even in childbed? 'My lady inherited this holy item from her mother, and from her mother before that. It should be most efficacious in achieving an effective delivery. It has, I should tell you, been blessed by the Bishop.'

'Which one?'

I was not enamoured of the decisions of the Bishop of Norwich.

'The Archbishop of Canterbury himself, of course. Cardinal Bourchier. He will have the ear of God.'

Hoping that she was right, we prayed and administered as we could to the pain-racked lady. We could not let this child die. She needed this heir. It would be too much for the Duchess to bear, to lose husband and child within a matter of months.

And then, after a whole day and night when we truly began to give up hope of saving either mother or child, in a rush of blood and birth fluids, the babe slid into the hands of the midwife, who cut the cord, wrapped the child closely and presented it to the Duchess. It cried, but weakly. The Duchess, exhausted, seemed unaware.

'You have a son, my lady,' the midwife announced, yet she looked concerned.

'Thank God.'

The Duchess held the child, pressed her lips to its scattering of dark hair, then passed it to a waiting wet nurse to suckle.

'He is very small,' I whispered to the midwife while one of the maidservants began to cleanse her mistress and fold away the precious girdle, which, to my mind, had achieved very little.

'Born before its time, I think.'

I took the child into my arms, thinking that my own children had been far sturdier, even Willem, who had given me cause for concern. Here was so much weight on such tiny shoulders, so much authority to be grasped by those small fingers which seemed reluctant to curl around mine with any strength. All the power of the Dukes of Norfolk from the past to be wielded by this infant. I carried him back to the bed, struck by the lack of colour and the laboured breathing when the light from the candles fell on the tiny figure.

'What name will you give him, my lady?'

'John. He will be John Mowbray.'

'A good name.'

'There are enough John Pastons.' She managed to smile before her eyelids drooped into a fretful sleep, and I handed the child back to the wet nurse before sending another of the hovering servants to fetch the priest. The baby whimpered and seemed not inclined to suckle. I looked at the midwife and she at me. The priest must give the child his name as quickly as possible.

By the end of the day, the child, John Mowbray, was dead and the Duchess wept. 'I have failed,' she said. The Duchess was inconsolable.

'You must not say that.' I was bracing. It was essential that she was resilient enough to hold on to the Mowbray authority until her little daughter either wed or came of age. 'You could have done no better.'

'My husband has no heir.'

'He has a daughter.'

'Yes. My dear Anne. But she is still so young.' Her thoughts moved into a predictable pattern. 'I must find a good husband for her. He will inherit all the Mowbray acres through her blood.'

Anxiety overcame her and she wept again.

'You must rest for now. You will see what needs to be done when you have slept. We will pray for the precious soul of your child.'

A silence filled the grieving room that none of us was inclined to break. Then the Duchess, her gaze suddenly astute, touched on mine.

'You were kind to come, Mistress Paston.'

'I regret that I did no good for you, my lady. I had not the knowledge to save your boy.'

Her eyes glinted in the dimness as the maid lit more candles to push aside the shadows of death.

'Was this Sir John's doing? Did your son wish to persuade me to give you Caister as a birth gift, in gratitude for your aid?'

It was not a subject that I wished to discuss, but I could not side-step such a direct question.

'Well, it was Jonty, whom you know well. I think that was his planning, but men can be insensitive. Caister is not important. Not today.'

'Was that the only reason you came to me?'

How weary she was, and how alone with such matters of high politics to shoulder. I sat on the edge of her bed and took her hand in mine.

'No, I came because you were alone. In childbed a woman needs support, and I came to give it. It was not about Caister. When I was in your position,' I said simply, 'I would not have thanked anyone for wishing to discuss rents or manorial business with me. I will not inflict manorial possessions on you. And if my sons ask, I will tell them that it was not a matter to be discussed on such a sorrowful occasion.'

The Duchess closed her hand on mine in a remarkably strong grasp, despite the tears that stained her cheeks.

'Thank you, Mistress Paston. Your compassion touches my heart, and I will say this. I will not stand in your way. If the King wishes it, I will give you and your sons Caister Castle.'

This promise touched me deeply, almost moving me to reciprocal tears, that the rumbling clash of wills over Caister Castle had been settled by two women of unequal degree in a birthing chamber, after hours of agony and the ultimate body of a dead child.

'I am grateful.'

I said no more. It should have lightened my heart, but this was a sad day for a woman who had been called on to face too much on her own. Not all the castles, not all the comfort and luxury, not the great bed nor the tapestries, none of this could enable the Duchess to give birth to a living child, the son she so desperately needed. I should feel blessed, and thankful for my own sons, and for her promise of restitution. On that day it was difficult to feel anything but grief and loss.

The Manor of Mautby in Norfolk

Caister Castle was restored to Paston ownership, all signed and sealed.

It was done. It was achieved. Seven years of injustice put right in the blink of an eye, the scrawl of a pen. The fate of Caister Castle, for so long tottering on the edge of a precipice, was finally decided by a set of legal documents and an inquisition. King Edward allowed the Paston claim to be heard, to heal a running sore that was of no value to him in his own struggles to retain the throne. Almost seventeen years after the death of Sir John Fastolf. More than ten years after the death of my husband, John.

All was decided quite simply, in the end, by a royal signature and a heavy set of seals. Never again must the ownership of Caister Castle be challenged. It was indubitably the possession of Sir John Paston.

It was finished and the jewel in the Paston crown was ours to enjoy for ever.

It was difficult to accept, even as I ran my fingers over the critical document. Such an anti-climax, this single piece of parchment, after so many battles.

I should have rejoiced, yet I found it impossible to do so. I should have laughed, my voice raised in song, as I attended to the daily tasks in my household. Loneliness was not something I experienced often, but on that day of all being put to rights, I felt alone.

I ordered a small keg of ale to be broached for the household and bid them drink to Caster Castle and to Sir John Fastolf, who had bequeathed this foundation to our future prestige as a castle-holding family. And to the King, of course. I should have joined them in their celebrations. I could not do it, proving what they thought of me: that I was sour and unpredictable. All I felt was the absence of my husband from this greatest of achievements.

I should have been immeasurably happy. Instead, in the privacy of my chamber, I wept tears, as if my life had been emptied of all blessings.

When I had recovered my composure, I ordered a placid mare and an escort and set out to inspect the state of Caister Castle, to discover the present quality of the home bequeathed to us by my cousin Sir John Fastolf. To resurrect some memories. Who knew in what state of dereliction I might discover it? I imagined it in my mind's eye as we travelled, as I had seen it the first time I had visited many years ago when my husband John had worked for Fastolf. Over five storeys of domestic rooms, forty chambers in all, there were two halls for entertaining, a chapel, a buttery, and a pantry. And, most miraculous, as well as the bedchambers, a room with bowls, a bath and a water tank for the comfort of ablutions. The Great Hall, when I had last seen it, was festooned with tapestries, stitched with religious subjects, hunting and dancing, as well as bloody warfare. We had more than forty of them, to change the scenes as mood dictated whether we ate surrounded by dancing maidens or martyred saints.

The walls were plastered and painted. Some of the tiled floors were even furnished with tapestries. Fireplaces and garderobes were in generous supply. Many windows were large with painted glass, allowing the sun to paint coloured patterns across the floor. There were timber shutters to protect the precious glass, as well as the inmates, in case of attack.

And then there was the library. Books bequeathed to us lined the walls. They did not interest me overmuch, although I enjoyed the leather bindings, the gilding, the vivid painted pages. Such wealth had been beyond my imagining. And oh, the bedchambers with their beds under a silk canopy, with silk and velvet pillows and the bedcovers embroidered with gold.

I smiled ruefully as William Pecock chivvied me to hurry along since rain was coming. All I could think of in those early days was: how many servants would we need to employ, to keep such a vast dwelling free from dust?

Indeed, it was a jewel of a place.

Now, fearing to be faced with a stinking midden of neglect and destitution, I rode in beneath the battered outer gate on a blustery chill day that boded ill. I set myself to master the anguish of witnessing destruction, of a deliberate despoiling. The outer walls were pounded but not breached, and there had been no malicious slighting of the fortifications. What would I find inside? Dismounting, I made my familiar way into the Great Hall.

Immediately, my heart began to settle and my fears began to dissolve in utter astonishment. It was as it had ever been, even the tapestries hanging in place. The Duke of Norfolk had recognised the gem that it was, and kept all of value for himself. I went on with my investigation, into library, parlours, bedchambers. All was as I recalled, although not as cleanly kept as I would like. There were the books still on their shelves, the hangings and tapestries, the silver bowls to hold scented water. Had the Duke ever lived here? I had no idea, but he had kept the essence of it as a dwelling of strength and some luxury.

Opening a coffer here and there, I was forced to accept that some of our personal possessions had been removed. I knew that we had lost them, but it was minor loss for Sir John to have to buy a new robe or two and a pair of shoes. Then, up on the wall walk, I looked down at the moat. There were my swans, as healthy and noisy as ever, with their fluffy offspring.

'It could have been worse, mistress,' Master Pecock observed. 'The Duke could have stripped it to the bone, along with those vicious hell-bent creatures.'

'Thank you!' I breathed. Although whether to God or to the Duke of Norfolk I did not question. It removed a weight from my heart. Our inheritance remained one to be proud of. Sir John's reputation would not suffer from the restoration of a ruin to our Paston name.

CHAPTER THIRTY-EIGHT

MISTRESS ANNE HAUTE

The Royal Court in the Palace of Westminster, November 1476

We danced the familiar carole dance, joining hands, man and woman in an alternate joining; a step with the left foot, the right following to strike gently against the left with no great skill, merely some semblance of grace, the music carried by one of the dancers rather than the minstrels. It was for me as if time stood still.

'*You do not go the way I do, nor would you go that way.*' Sir John Paston had once sung as he held my hand. '*If I have great joy in my heart, do not ask whence it comes! That I love with all my heart, you know full well. Love me, my sweet blonde, love me, and I shall not love anyone but you.*'

The dance would last as long as we had the mind for it, as long as the mood took us. Once I had thought that our marriage would be the same. Now all I experienced was a sense of relief. The Court was in a celebratory mood. The war had not materialised, the Duke of Burgundy remained tied up at the Siege of Neuss, and Edward with much of the English army had returned unharmed and un-bloodied to England. There had been no great victory, but neither had there been any deaths. We sang and we danced. I welcomed new partners and encouraged light flirtations with Court gallants. Perhaps one day I would be free to be wooed again.

And there, at last, newly come to Court with victory on his brow, was Sir John Paston, looking remarkably pleased with himself. He invited me to dance the carole dance, with an unfortunate air of possessiveness, ousting my previous partner, which brought all the memories flooding back. I caught smiles on many faces. Would we be reunited or would we part? We had once more become an object of interest, of whispered gossip. I did not like it.

'Welcome, Sir John.' I took his hand in the elegantly turning chain of dancers.

'I see that you have not lost your grace when dancing, Mistress Haute. Would you believe me if I told you that I had missed your company?'

'Frankly, no, Sir John. You would always know where to find me.'

'I would,' he admitted, uncommonly laconic. 'Since March, my time has been much in demand. I have been in Calais with Lord Hastings.'

'Which would have prevented you from meeting with me, of course.'

'But now I am returned. I have to tell you that the Duke of Norfolk is dead.'

'As I am aware. Some months ago, if I recall. Was it not in June?'

'Yes, I believe it was. I sent a messenger to Caister to assert my rights.'

'And did you achieve them?'

'Indeed. I have Caister back in my possession. All was brought before the King's Council and the Lords and judges. All held that my title to it was good. I thought that the King might have an eye to Caister for himself, to give to his little son Richard, who is to be wedded to the Mowbray heiress. That was not to be. Caister is once more mine, to enjoy for the rest of my life and the lives of all future Pastons. A great achievement.'

I was past caring for Caister. I drew him from the dance, the chain reforming around us, leaving us isolated. Not one word about me or our situation in all the perambulations.

'You have your castle, which you desired above all. And yet you still have a wife, whom you would happily dispense with. Why is that? Why come to boast about Caister when you have failed to achieve what is of vital importance to me?'

'I regret...'

'What have you been doing when not engaged with Calais and Caister?'

At least he had the grace to look sheepish. 'I suffered badly from the cold when I returned home.'

'You look remarkably healthy now. In the name of the Blessed Virgin, finish this marriage before I am on my knees in the final throes of old age.'

'I promise you that I will.'

'I have had enough promises to last a lifetime.' I unfastened a little jewel that I often wore and held it out on the palm of my hand. 'Take it.'

'But it was a gift to you.'

'When you wished to woo me. You no longer do. It would be wrong of me to keep it. It is yours to give to whomsoever you wed.'

A little golden castle, all set with gems. A pointed diamond, a ruby and three pearls. Of no great intrinsic value but a pretty token to give to a lover.

Sir John closed my hand over it with his own.

'I gave it to you as an emblem of my love. Nothing has changed.'

'Everything has changed. I wish to see the annulment with the papal seal on the actual document.'

Sir John bowed, hand on heart. 'It shall be done as you wish, Mistress Anne. I promise your annulment will be achieved.'

It hurt. Oh, it hurt, but I could not allow even a murmur of softer feelings in my heart. It would only bring more pain, and I would be rid of it.

I left him. I swore that I would never dance the carole dance again, not with any man. It was far too easy to be entranced by a man with a ready tongue, a beguiling smile and a turn of foot. I would never again be so lured into what was not in my interest.

'I see Sir John is returned.'

Queen Elizabeth nodded in his direction. Sir John had discovered a new partner, who was leaning close to hear what he had to say.

'Yes.'

'And where do you stand?'

'In much the same place as I stood eight years ago when we first exchanged vows.'

She turned to watch him. I refused to give him the pleasure.

'And yet when he left you, I thought that he regarded you with such affectionate intimacy.'

'Then why did he let me go?'

'I don't think that he will ever have the energy to take on the responsibilities of a marriage, no matter how keen his appreciation of the lady. He will never do it.'

'He will certainly not do it with me!' It almost reduced me to tears. I pinned the little jewel back into the fur on the bodice of my gown. It was all I had in memory of the years of uncertainty. A jewel and a deal of experience that I would wish on no woman. Even though he had promised, I would not believe in the existence of this annulment until I held it between the palms of my own hands. Would it ever happen, if left to Sir John's initiative? I was assailed by a new wave of doubt.

CHAPTER THIRTY-NINE

MARGARET MAUTBY PASTON

The Manor of Mautby in Norfolk, February 1477

'I know the name of the woman I will wed.'

It was announced with true Jonty fanfare. He had just ridden in, bringing a blast of cold air that made the chimney smoke. I did not believe a word of it. I did not even stir myself from my chair by the fire or look up from the list of sales of malt.

'Oh, Jonty! Another fantasy? Another titled lady in London, another wealthy widow?' At least I looked up from the malt tally. 'All I ask is that you find a bride before they lower me into my grave. And if you could manage a son and heir, I would be even better pleased, for Sir John still has not settled his mind to taking a legal wife. The Paston family needs an heir.'

I was feeling low in spirit. Jonty had failed to land any of his matrimonial fish, not even a minnow. Sir John and Mistress Haute were still trapped in a marriage entanglement that had not been regularised, while my daughter Anne waited on a settlement for her Yelverton union, hating any thought of it. As for children to carry on the Paston blood. Margery now had three sons, so I had discovered, but we had still not yet stepped across the divide. Probably my fault, for they were well thought of in Norwich, and it would have been no detriment to accept this marriage after all the water under the bridge. John, William, and Richard they were my grandsons, my only grandchildren.

Pride was a terrible sin. I would be punished for it. Disappointment was an even harder emotion to carry. Who would inherit the Paston manors? What if... what if not one of my sons married and bred a Paston heir? My three younger sons were not of an age to seriously contemplate matrimony. What if my only grandchildren were named Calle and Yelverton? Eliza's children were too far distant from me even to be considered. They might be healthy and well-mannered, but they were not Pastons. It did not bear thinking of.

And then came the day in February, a cold, wet day with sleet in the wind, when all the chimneys smoked unbearably and my joints ached as if wrung by an iron hand, when Jonty descended on me in Mautby, where I had stayed for much of the winter.

Jonty flung himself down on a stool facing me, making my lists flutter with his movement. I was pleased to see him, nonetheless, despite my sense of hopelessness, and held out my hand to him. He took it and held it warmly between his own still-gloved hands. Perhaps he had seen the pain in my face before I had hidden it.

'This is no fantasy. I think she will be the perfect bride for me, and I swear she will like me. She is no fine London lady who will think me too low, nor is she a widow. You will perhaps know the family. I believe that this will be a union of true love.'

I despaired of Jonty's visions of true love. Why could he not simply wed a girl from a good family with a substantial dowry and have done with it? Love, if fortune struck, would come later. If not, as long as they could rub along together in relative comfort, then what more could a man ask? Or his bride?

'Does she have a dowry?' I asked.

I must sound like a popinjay, repeating the same question every time, but it must be asked.

While Jonty released my hand, opened the door and shouted for wine, I deliberately walked to the window to look out in the direction of Caister which was once more our own possession. I could imagine the proud towers, the strong walls, the impressive keep. Yes, it was ours, but I seemed not to have regained any enthusiasm for its cold rooms and draughty passageways. A servant brought wine while Jonty stripped off cap, gloves and travelling cloak, poured two cups and led me back to the fire to sit again.

'Tell me, then, of this perfect bride,' I encouraged, dredging up what might have been thought of as an appreciative smile.

'Mistress Margery Brews. From a very well-to-do family. A family with whom you are acquainted.'

Margery Brews. I could wish that she was not called Margery. I pushed aside any emotion caused by such an unfortunate co-incidence in the face of Jonty's enthusiasm.

'Brews is a name well known hereabouts,' I agreed carefully.

I was certainly familiar with it. Sir Thomas Brews was a Norfolk knight. But it was also a family, if I recalled accurately, with a number of daughters. Any hope that might have been reborn promptly dissipated. Jonty was only a second son, and if this girl was not the eldest, then her dowry would not be impressive.

'Have you met with this young woman?' I asked, deciding that I did not wish to destroy his pleasure too early in the proceedings.

'No.'

My irritation slipped its bonds. Another of Jonty's day dreams.

'Then how can you possibly know—'

He interrupted, eyes bright as the raindrops now spattering against the window. 'I have heard good reports from a friend of mine, who knows the family well. She is young and comely and sounds to be the perfect answer to my matrimonial problems.'

Which were legion. Primarily, he needed a manor of his own. Since he had lived in the household of the Duke of Norfolk, or in one of my properties, he needed a bride with property and income. Jonty had no resources of his own. The manor of Swainsthorpe, left to him in his father's will, had been mortgaged by Sir John to raise money to fight for Caister. I doubted that the mortgage would ever be paid and the manor reclaimed. Jonty had no home of his own unless someone came to his rescue.

'So you have never met her.'

'Not yet.'

I groaned inwardly at what already had the appearance of a hopeless case. 'Is she the eldest daughter? Is she the heiress?' I asked.

'No.'

As I thought. 'How many sisters does she have?'

'Three,' he admitted.

'And all older than Mistress Margery, I presume.'

'I believe so.'

'So her dowry, if any, will be small.'

He lifted a shoulder in a shrug.

'How old is she?'

'Not quite in her twentieth year.'

The family would be keen to find a marriage for her with a man of property. Would they drive a hard bargain, or even be willing to accept a younger son without land? Would a knightly family look at a Paston? I thought not. All in all, it did not bode well.

'Will you help me?' he asked.

'I do not see that there is much that I can do. You may not like it but I think that they will look higher than you. A man of title.'

Jonty slid from his stool to kneel before me, as he used to do as a child when he would persuade me to give him some small coin to spend in the market. He took my hands in his and kissed one, and then the other. In passing I noted how strong and broad his hands had become with adulthood. They could wield a sword or a pen. Any local family who made a marriage alliance with him would achieve an excellent bargain.

'You are my only hope,' Jonty urged. 'I need a strong negotiator on my side, one who can convince Sir Thomas Brews that I will be a husband worthy of ten knights. You have a gift of words, of clever argument. Don't refuse me in this, I beg of you.'

In spite of the overt flattery, the dramatic kneeling at my feet, I read anxiety in his face. He wanted this marriage more than any of the other hopeless ones he had promoted.

I could not turn him down. 'What do you wish me to do?'

'Arrange a visit so that we can sound out the lie of the land. Speak for me, Mother, and I will do it. I am determined.'

'Well, I suppose that you should at least meet the girl. What will you do if you find that you do not fit well together?'

'Why would we not?'

His confidence was astounding and somehow even more dispiriting. I would arrange the meeting and hope that I might like the young woman, too. But, first, I would use Pecock to discover as much as he could about the Brews family. Knowledge would give me some strength in negotiations, as I had learned so often through my life. It discouraged me that I did not have the energy to discover it for myself.

Pecock proved more than efficient. The Brews family had an excellent reputation in the town, caring of its land and tenants; a sound family, honest and peace-loving. Sir Thomas Brews had been ambitious enough to seek office and use it to the good of the community as well as for his own standing. He had a reputation as a distinguished Sheriff of Norfolk and Suffolk, as I was aware. He was a Justice of the Peace, as well as being elected to parliament on more than one occasion. I presumed that he had once been acquainted with John, for good or ill. I hoped that there had been no enmity between them. Whether he was for York or Lancaster, I did not know. I hoped that it would not be an issue.

His wife, of whom Pecock could discover nothing injurious, was, if I recalled correctly, an heiress to a sizable inheritance through her unwed brother. She was a kindly woman, by all accounts, although she did not always enjoy the best of health. I thought that I knew her by sight. My name would not be unknown to her.

They owned a number of manors, their main residence being at Topcroft, some miles south of Norwich. They were sometimes seen to worship in the Cathedral.

'No one has a bad word to say about them, mistress,' Pecock finished his report. 'Except that Sir Thomas is inclined to guard his money too well.'

'We could all be accused of that,' I replied, deep in thought.

Had Jonty at last chosen a girl who could become a Paston wife? I decided that my spirits had lifted. My confidence was not as great as it might have been, but I embarked on the campaign in good heart. Surely this could not end in another disappointment.

Dictating a letter, so that it would be in a clerkly hand, I dispatched it to Sir Thomas Brews, requesting that I and my son might visit with them at Topcroft to discuss a matter of mutual interest for his family and mine. I made no mention of a possible marriage. This was simply a friendly visit to settle an issue of field boundaries between a parcel of land under my personal ownership that ran alongside a Brews manor. Some of our tenants were in dispute. A reply came by return of my courier assuring us of a welcome.

So far so good.

Within the week, garbed to impart a strong impression of prosperity and sobriety in good quality linen and wool, Jonty and I made our way to Topcroft, a fortified manor house, substantial within its walls and corner towers. I ran my eye over the inner and outer courts, the fish ponds, and the moat which gave protection to all within. Not as large as Caister but it still announced a fair style of living for its owner. Sir Thomas Brews was a man of means.

'Speak up for me, Mother,' Jonty repeated his previous admonition. 'I do not want this opportunity to escape me.'

'I think you can speak quite well for yourself,' I said as we rode into the well-tended courtyard where servants waited to help me dismount and lead our animals towards the stables. 'It should be Sir John accompanying you, if it comes to negotiating a settlement. Too early for that, of course.'

'My brother is still waiting in London for orders to accompany Lord Hastings to Calais again. I doubt he'll put himself out.'

Which merely reinforced my own concerns.

'Jonty...' I warned as we made to follow one of the servants through the impressive doorway into a shadowy hall. All was polished, the wood gleaming and the air scented with lavender and beeswax. Dame Elizabeth Brews had commendable pride in her surroundings and her possessions, an observation that pleased me. 'Don't raise your hopes up too high. All this might come to naught.'

'I know what I want.'

'You haven't known what you have wanted any time over the past ten years!'

We were invited in, made welcome, by Dame Elizabeth Brews, to sit in a congenial atmosphere in a chamber with cushioned chairs, good lighting and a substantial fire on this wintry day, together with Sir Thomas as well as their daughters, who were all still at home, a handful of attractive young women who much resembled their fair mother. There seemed to be no urgency to wed them. Mistress Margery was the youngest, possessed of what seemed to me a demure serenity. Nothing was said about our reason for the visit. Instead, we discussed the state of trade, the settled kingdom since the King's return, the state of health of my swans, although depleted in number. We drank wine of good quality and ate hot mutton pasties redolent of high-quality spices, moving on to converse on local affairs. I introduced Jonty as my strong right arm since Sir John had taken up the sword for the campaign in France. I praised both of them, and my younger sons.

'I could not manage the Paston acres without them.'

'You must value them greatly,' Dame Elizabeth observed. 'It is our long regret that we have no son of our own. And so handsome a son, too.'

She beamed at Jonty, who smiled back.

'Thank you for the compliment, my lady. It is our mother who keeps a tight hold on all our affairs, but I have learned much from her. As I am sure that your daughters have learned much of gentility and elegance from you.'

'You are a young man with a clever tongue,' she replied, not averse to his comments.

Jonty had the honesty to appear abashed at Dame Elizabeth's praise, but not too greatly, forcing me to come to the conclusion that my son had been learning from Sir John's courtly skills. With well-balanced comments and some dignity, it seemed that he would woo the mother as well as the daughter. Moreover, Dame Elizabeth was quite prepared to be wooed, responding to the gentle gallantry with warmth, while I was cynical. If the lady had any influence over her husband, then Jonty might well win the day. But would Sir Thomas be persuaded? I decided that under the knightly robe and costly footwear there was indeed a hard-headed businessman, and the Pastons, in spite of acquiring Caister Castle once more, had suffered serious reverses. He might look elsewhere for even his youngest daughter.

When Sir Thomas and I took to an equable discussion over the disputed boundaries which could indeed easily be settled and had not required a personal intervention from me, Jonty moved to sit adjacent to the daughters. There was much chatter and laughter under the eye of Dame Elizabeth.

The whole affair was exhausting and I was pleased to leave, although I remained affable and courteous to the end. Sir Thomas and I agreed to intervene in any problem that our tenants could not solve for themselves, particularly the supervision of an area of common land to which both sides laid claim.

Jonty rode at my side with an air of satisfaction while I prepared myself for an examination worthy of the Inns of Court.

'What did you think of her?'

He was anxious to know what I thought, even though he had made up his own mind.

'A girl of some charm.'

'Will she be as practical as you, do you suppose? I need a practical wife.'

'She seemed a sensible young woman. Her mother is a woman of good sense.'

'And she is a handsome girl.'

Neat, fair, with a quiet confidence. 'I cannot disagree.'

'Do you agree that she will make me an enviable wife?'

'She may well, if we can come to some financial arrangement. As long as you are certain after actually meeting her.'

He had made up his mind. 'I am convinced.'

There it was. On one meeting where they had barely exchanged a word, and none in private.

I had watched her. She had not encouraged him, but neither had she been unaware of his admiration. The sweep of her eyelashes over dark grey eyes had hidden her appreciation, but it had been clear to me. It was a relief after his previous adventures; there was no impediment that I could see in our alliance with this distinguished family. Jonty would be an asset to them, knowing perfectly well how to conduct himself in a knightly family after living in the household of the Duke and Duchess of Norfolk. I would write again to Sir Thomas to test the lie of the matrimonial land. And then Jonty must engage his patience and wait.

All in all, it was a shame, I decided, that she had been named Margery.

CHAPTER FORTY

MARGARET MAUTBY PASTON

The Manor of Mautby in Norfolk, February 1477

As I had promised, I sent my letter to Topcroft, suggesting the possibility of a marriage. The reply was friendly enough. Sir Thomas was not reluctant to consider Jonty as a husband for Mistress Margery, but the terms, as I knew, would be difficult for both sides to agree upon.

Sir Thomas offered a dowry of a hundred pounds, a sum quite insufficient to give the couple a suitable and independent lifestyle. If he would not move on this, then our negotiations were at an end. Yet I was informed by the all-knowing Pecock that Jonty was not slow in revisiting Topcroft to pursue his wooing. It seems that he was made welcome. He came to me full of delight at his reacquaintance with Mistress Margery.

'She is everything I could hope for. We were allowed to walk in the gardens with her elder sister as chaperone. She is as pretty and sweet as a gillyflower. I shall call her Gilly.'

'Are you sure? It is very particular when there is no betrothal between you.'

'But there will be. And she will be Gilly to me.'

I glanced at him but could find no dissembling in his expression. Had he done this to save me? It would be easier than to call her Margery. It would be like Jonty to be kind-hearted, but what her parents would think I did not know.

'Well, I can hardly call her Gilly, can I?'

He touched my hand with light fingertips. Sometimes Jonty

surprised me by his quick compassion which seemed to be lacking in my other sons. 'I think it would be more comfortable for you than having to call her Margery.'

Thus Margery Brews became Gilly within the family. It seemed that the young pair had made considerable progress in coming to know each other, even though the negotiations had made no progress at all, dragging Jonty down into a well of despair, as much as he ever was. I had never seen him so downhearted; not even when we had lost Caister after all his efforts and the deaths of those under his command. I could see little hope for him if Sir Thomas would not move on the terms, but what could I do? Nothing that I could see. When my brother-in-law William decided to visit me in Mautby, it was a relief to have someone to whom I could pour out my concerns, although I was careful to guard my words. I was not as open with William as I once might have been.

I had always considered John to be the most ambitious man I had ever met. In recent years, I had changed my mind. William could completely outstrip him. And yet, if I was to discover a source of financial help for Jonty and Mistress Brews, this was the man I must win round to my way of thinking. Even so, I had warned Sir John to be aware of his uncle's threat against Paston manors which he thought should belong to him.

'He will use the law to snatch your manors out of your hands before you can even blink,' I told him in a moment of bleak honesty.

'That's the opinion of a woman who does not frequent Court and knows not the ways of men.' Sir John was sometimes inclined to be condescending, despite his own past misjudgements.

'I know the ways of William Paston far better than you!' I heard myself say.

My son smiled indulgently. 'I think you misjudge him. Leave it all to me.'

But I recalled that day, almost thirty-five years ago. I remembered it as if it were yesterday, when their father Justice William had died in London, and we had all stood together to hear the contents of the will. All the estates had been left to John, to keep everything intact, on the understanding that he would support his younger brothers and sisters and pay for their upkeep, their education and the dowry of Elizabeth. And then Mistress Agnes had stepped in. Her husband had changed his will on his deathbed, so she claimed. Manors were left to all the younger sons. As well as a sizable portion to her. No one knew of this alteration in Justice William's will except for Mistress Agnes.

John had exploded in righteous fury. To keep the family on the path to gentrification he would hold the manors and estates together as a whole. And he got his way, even to the confiscation of Justice William's bags of gold coin and items of jewellery kept in the safe supervision of the monks.

William had never forgotten, nor, I thought, forgiven. He had been robbed of his land, and would take any opportunity to claim it, particularly now that he had become an important man, counsellor and trusted adviser to the rich and powerful. The Duke of Clarence, Archbishop George Neville, the Earl of Oxford; William had had dealings with all of them. And now with the fall of the Nevilles, he was worming his way into the good offices of the Duke of Buckingham and the Dowager Duchess of Norfolk.

Here he was in my chamber. I might not trust him, but I would make use of him. I beamed at him, plied him with a second cup of ale and set to discover his opinion of a Brews marriage for Jonty.

'Jonty has his mind set on one of the Brews daughters,' I explained when William, with true lack of feeling, expressed the opinion that I was looking my years and ought to take life more gently, handing business over to my younger sons, particularly Edmund, who was still not settled in any employment. 'I'll be pleased to have her in the family if they can find enough to improve her lack of dowry. Sir Thomas is unfortunately prepared for some hard bargaining. We have not the money to be too generous. I fear it could be the end of it.'

'What's the problem? Can it not be overcome? Surely you, Margaret, can find some grounds for agreement. You were always the most managing woman of my acquaintance.'

William seemed callously unfeeling that day.

'Sir Thomas will offer only one hundred pounds. He expects us to give Jonty a manor of his own so that the young couple might live independently.'

'What does Sir John think?'

'It is difficult to know what Sir John thinks about anything at the moment. He is too taken up with the Calais expeditions and the situation with Mistress Haute, which is still slowly malingering. All I can say is that Jonty is smitten. And the young woman with him.' I frowned as I considered the young woman who was not perhaps as demure as I had at first thought. 'Dame Elizabeth Brews is become a willing advocate for her daughter, and the daughter, I believe, will put a strong case for this marriage, but sadly we get no further.'

'What about Swainsthorpe, the manor given to Jonty in his father's will? Is that not sufficient to impress Sir Thomas?'

'It might be, except that it has been mortgaged. I thought that you would have known. The sum of one hundred and twenty pounds is needed to recover it before the couple might live there and receive an income from the land.'

William grunted, straining for patience. 'Will Sir John not do it?'

'Sir John is so short of money that he has to come begging to me, to no effect. Sir Thomas is worried that if the bridal pair use up all the dowry to take back Swainsthorpe, there would be insufficient money to support them in any suitable lifestyle afterwards. They would live as beggars in their new manor.'

'What if Sir Thomas put up the cash for the mortgage as a loan to be repaid?'

'Which might work if someone was willing to take up the loan and repay it.' I smiled engagingly at him, remembering the times when we had been close enough for such a request to be effortlessly made. He had called me managing, and I would be again. 'Would you be willing to give your support to such an arrangement? I doubt you are short of a fistful of coin or two. You would get good repayment on the loan, I promise you.'

'Don't look at me. I'm not getting involved in Paston finances.'

As William shook his head, I saw a hardness in his eyes. We had had our disputes but never had we been so at odds.

'I'm sure you will think of a way, Margaret,' he continued,

smoothly enough. 'Have you no other manor you can give your son? That might be the least painful method of winning Sir Thomas round to considering a Paston for his daughter. Be generous. Do you not have something from your Mautby inheritance that would tip the agreement in your son's favour?'

I continued to smile. I would not show my cross dissatisfaction as I refilled his cup.

'Would you at least give your nephew a wedding gift?' I asked. 'A substantial one. It might impress Sir Thomas.'

'Not I, Margaret! Any gifts will have to come from you.'

There he sat, drinking my best ale, expensively clad, a worthy and wealthy man of the Court with a self-satisfied smile, but I could see that there was no moving him.

We let business slide as we ate a light dinner and William, deflecting any difficult subjects, told me of his plans to wed his two daughters, and of his regrets that he had no son to follow in his name. I was left to nod and smile at the same time as I was thinking of a way out of Jonty's impasse, wondering if I had told him too much. I did not think so. At least he had given me some advice which was worth considering. Yet, I wondered why he would not even offer a marriage gift. It was not like him to be so mean-spirited.

As he pulled on his gloves and settled his felt cap on his thinning hair, I broached a final matter where he might be useful to us.

'The affair between my son and Mistress Anne Haute has gone on long enough, William. You are a man of influence, so I hear, with friends in high places.' Nothing like a little flattery to win over a difficult man. 'I would ask you this. Use what influence you have to get the annulment before the Lord Chancellor,' I suggested, 'and we can put it to rest at last. Just think how beneficial it would be for your own reputation if you could bring the whole to a satisfactory end.'

William regarded me with sardonic amusement, but promised nothing, merely saying as he left: 'Tell Jonty that if affairs with Sir Thomas are so difficult, he should look for another bride.'

I would tell him no such thing. Or not yet, at any rate.

★

343

Jonty remained in a state of turbulence, unsettling the whole household. One moment he was certain that Mistress Brews would be his to call wife, the next, he was in a despondency from which nothing could stir him. He paced the manorial document chamber in Norwich and unburdened himself.

'I know that her affections are mine. Yet I am surrounded by difficulties. Gilly believes that I will abandon her despite my love for her and hers for me. Sir Thomas can find no more for a dowry and says why should he give more to Gilly than to his other daughters? He is as tough a negotiator as you are, Mother. As for my ever-absent brother, Sir John says that without a better dowry he will not support my venture. I had hoped for more from him. Have we not always been close?' He came to a halt and glared at me. 'While you, Mother, you are hardly more than lukewarm in your support.'

'I presume that you are speaking of money.'

'We are always speaking of money in this house. As I see it, Gilly and I will never be wed, and I will lose the one woman who has moved my heart.'

I did not mention all the rest in his flirtatious past.

'The only one who supports us is Dame Elizabeth Brews,' he continued, returning to his earlier pacing, thumping my new tapestry as he passed. 'Gilly has persuaded her to see the advantages, and she is willing to take Sir Thomas to task. She likes me. It seems that I have won Dame Elizabeth's heart.'

'I thought it was the daughter you sought,' I remarked dryly.

'But it will do no harm to win over her mother. Can you not find your way to grant me more, to give us a degree of comfort that will please Sir Thomas?'

He had my compassion but I could not, despite the touch of guilt. I suspected that Jonty had been in conversation with William. Without replying, I asked the obvious question:

'Have you told Sir John all of this?'

'I have. And I received no reply, other than to look for a different bride.'

So, both had been in conversation with their uncle. I could wish that William did not interfere. That William would keep his nose out of my Paston affairs, even though I had asked him for aid.

'Sir John speaks of one Mistress Barley. Then informs me in the next breath that she is really too young and her dowry is as insufficient as Gilly's. And then he says that he would much prefer my wedding Mistress Brews than a certain Lady Walgrave, even though Lady Walgrave sings exceptionally well with a harp. As if that would matter to me. I have no liking for the harp.'

'Then you must never consider marriage with the lady!'

At least that made him smile.

'I suppose that Mistress Brews neither plays the harp, nor sings.'

'Not to my knowledge. Although she may well. I lose all patience with my brother.'

So there was bad blood developing between my two elder sons to worry me, but for the moment I put that on one side.

'You know that I am lacking coin, Jonty, and unable to give more. Your brothers must be educated. Walter's sojourn at Oxford is expensive. He needs new clothes if he is to attract attention that will result in a lucrative post when his studies are finished. Willem is to continue his learning at Eton. It is what your father wanted. And Willem grows like a stalk of barley in spring. As for your sister, Anne's marriage to young Yelverton is still in negotiation. I have no money to spare.'

He flung himself into a chair and with a grimace pushed aside the cup of ale I had poured for him.

'All I can do is try to persuade Dame Elizabeth to work a miracle on her husband. I can see no other way. Unless Gilly and I make our own vows and force his hand.'

I was aghast at the threat. I was on my feet in an instant.

'Do not you dare!'

I heard the fury erupting in my voice and could not stop it. Jonty looked up at me, as if considering how far he could step in this direction.

'It would solve our problem.'

'Have we not had enough of this? Scandal upon scandal. I'll never forgive you if you do.'

'I see no alternative.'

I marched to stand over him, gripping his sleeve in my fist. 'Promise me, Jonty. It will bring nothing but heartache. Nothing but a terrible rift. Don't allow such to cause dissention between young Mistress Brews and her family. It would be the worst result in the world. You must not do it!'

'Very well. I will not.'

'Promise me.'

'I promise.'

But there was a set to his chin that I did not trust.

Two days later, I was still mulling over how to pay for Willem's hose and linen when Jonty strode over my Norwich threshold with his old enthusiastic bound.

'Well! Something has changed to your benefit.'

He beamed as he perched on the edge of my table, to the detriment of my neat piles of documents, and announced: 'Sir Thomas will give Margery a dowry of one hundred pounds.'

I grabbed at a stack of scrolls that were sliding to the floor, failing to secure most of them.

'But that is what he said originally. Do pick those up, Jonty, and go away.'

'Wait.' Jonty obliged and returned the scrolls to a neat arrangement, talking all the time. 'Dame Elizabeth has promised that her own father will give Gilly fifty marks on the day of our marriage. I am invited to go and stay at Topcroft and discuss a settlement. Do you know anything about it? Why Sir Thomas is suddenly become more generous?'

'I know nothing about it.'

Indeed, I felt as if I were sitting in a distant room while all developed elsewhere in the house. I did not like it.

'I thought you had discussed it with my uncle William.'

'I did, but with no outcome. He won't involve himself.' It reminded me again of William's intransigence. Something was afoot there. Something Jonty was not saying. I suspected him of some devious planning which I would not like either. 'It is your brother, as head of the family, that you have to persuade.'

Which produced an impressive scowl.

'So far, as we both know, Sir John has not become involved to any degree. I think Sir Thomas is wary of that fact.'

'And he has every right to be. Go and see Sir Thomas, and then bring the girl to visit if it comes to aught. It is in your own hands, Jonty.'

Mistress Brews did not come to Norwich or to Mautby.

I suspected that the proposed visit to Topcroft had achieved nothing. Jonty did not speak of it, and I did not question him since it became clearer by the day that the details of the settlement did not matter to either Mistress Brews or to Jonty. They wanted marriage. Neither seemed to be concerned about where they would live or how they would pay for their food and board.

Perhaps Sir Thomas expected me to continue to house Jonty. As I suppose I would have to. But it was no basis for a marriage. The fear that the pair would abscond as Margery and Calle had done continued to haunt my dreams. My waking hours were not much better. Marriage had become a subject of much speculation amongst my neighbours.

'Is Jonty wed yet, Mistress Paston?'

'Has Sir John settled his betrothal with Mistress Haute?'

'Has Sir Thomas Brews given his blessing to his daughter's marriage into your family? Or have the Pastons been rejected? How unfortunate ...'

My business seemed to be the talk of Norwich. It did not allow me a quiet life.

'Has Mistress Anne become Mistress Yelverton yet?'

It tempted me to stay at home with my doors and windows barred, as if in a siege, except that I would not. I learned the art of saying nothing but hinting at everything that was good for the Pastons.

And then ...

Despite all signs to the contrary, all was not yet lost. Sir Thomas was not as impervious to my son's acceptability as I had thought, and thus I was impressed when Sir Thomas agreed to give two hundred marks and a trousseau worth one hundred marks to his daughter as well as agreeing to give a home to the young couple under his own roof for two or three years, which would take the weight off my shoulders.

Dame Elizabeth, it appeared, had been whispering in her husband's ear.

But still nothing was finally decided.

The drip of advice from wife to husband was having no effect, just as mine to Sir John to make him support his brother in this new offer. It was time that I took a hand in it. If Dame Elizabeth was indeed determined that the marriage should take place, then we must meet. We could not go on with this endless situation with the increasing threat of Jonty taking affairs into his own hands.

It was arranged that we would meet halfway between Topcroft and Mautby.

'I forbid you to go,' Jonty said at the last minute, at his most masterful.

'Why would you forbid it? It would be to your benefit. We'll get nowhere without.'

'Because it is March and the weather atrocious. The road is flooded. What good would it do?'

But by now I was more than determined. A negotiation between Dame Elizabeth and myself would happen. 'Then arrange another meeting. Norwich would be the best choice; Dame Elizabeth can come to my house and we will eat dinner together.'

'I do not see that anything can be gained from this.'

'Then I will arrange it myself.'

If the men of our families could find no equable solution, then it was up to the women to do so. And the initiative, as ever, must be mine. All I could pray was that I was not too foolhardy in my judgements. I was not unaware of failures in my life, but that must not stop me.

But before Dame Elizabeth Brews and I could get to serious grips with the matter, with or without our menfolk, I found a need to turn my thoughts to one of my younger brood. Sir John, Jonty and Edmund all had their feet set firmly on the path to a legal future. Willem, the youngest, was still forming his character at Eton – for good or ill, since most of his communication with me seemed to be requests for money or fashionable hose. Now I had my eye set on Walter, whether he liked my plans for him or not. He would become a priest, and I would give him a benefice when his education was complete. It would be good to have a priest in the family.

Would not Walter be the perfect choice? He was the most placid and soft-spoken of all of my sons; I could imagine his slight figure in priestly garb as he both chastened and blessed his congregation, the sun shining on his chestnut hair, for he had inherited the same Mautby colouring as Anne. Perhaps one day he would become a bishop, in full clerical regalia to the glory of the family. I was full of dreams for him.

My dream of a clerical Paston was rejected out of hand. The letter I sent to the Bishop of Norwich, putting the idea before him, was returned with a brusque reply from some minion. Walter was too young.

I was not prepared to cast aside my planning. 'I doubt the Bishop ever saw my letter!' I complained to Sir John.

'Send the Bishop a gift,' Sir John advised, well versed in the road to political success.

'Of what?'

'Something that glitters. The shiner the better.'

Accepting the advice, I sent the Bishop the last of my large silver platters, only to have them returned in the same box, as if they had never been unpacked. A distinct rebuff. Not even the return of my platters raised my spirits.

'You will not be a priest,' I informed Walter when our paths next crossed, expecting disappointment.

'Good!'

My brows rose in astonishment. Walter was not usually confrontational.

'I think that I would rather not be a priest,' Walter said with an unfortunate levity as I continued to fume at the Bishop's disregard for a Paston preferment. Had Walter acquired a reputation for misbehaviour in the town, of which I was ignorant? I would not have thought it. This was the son who had inherited the dignity and erudition of his father. I scowled at him. Perhaps I should have kept a closer eye on his pastimes in the town.

'What would you wish for, then?' I asked. 'I'll not have you involved in some menial work. Or wasting time in the taverns of Norwich with your disreputable friends, doing nothing but spending my money.'

'I have no disreputable friends.' Walter smiled with unruffled amiability. 'I'll be a man of law, like my father. I have ambitions.'

I must accept that Walter would follow the rest of his brothers into the legal world. In some ways it was a relief that he had made the decision and was keen to step into the shoes of former Pastons.

I gave him a perfunctory hug, which he accepted with surprise but equanimity, and I kissed his brow.

'Then that is agreed, Walter. Look to your older brothers for guidance. I anticipate hearing of your achievements. Don't spend too much money on celebrating them.'

Perhaps, in the fullness of time, Walter would cause me less trouble than all the rest of the Pastons put together. Now to tackle the marriage of Jonty and Gilly.

CHAPTER FORTY-ONE

MARGARET MAUTBY PASTON

The Paston House in Norwich, March 1477

Dame Elizabeth and I met in what could only be called a female conspiracy.

'Does your husband know that you are here?' I asked as we sat opposite each other beside the fire, Dame Elizabeth sighing in pleasure at the heat. It had been a wet journey for both of us.

'No. Have you told your sons?'

'Not yet.'

'How untrustworthy we are becoming, Margaret.'

'I think that I have always been so when it was necessary to drive to an important conclusion, my dear Elizabeth.'

We smiled in our agreed conspiracy.

'The thing is –' I took up the crux of the matter – 'this discussion between our two houses has been the subject of gossip through the length and breadth of Norfolk now for weeks. If nothing were to come of it, how foolish would we look?'

'And neither of us would enjoy looking foolish,' she agreed.

A woman after my own heart.

'I fear that we would suffer more than you,' I said. 'A Paston can be fair game to some. Your family would be lauded for making a good escape. Besides, I dislike being gossiped about in the streets.'

'Surely we can achieve something for them.' She nodded. 'It is a good match; I am convinced of it. You have a son who will do you proud, and my daughter will make him a very capable wife. Do you know that she is skilled in the use of herbs to heal and soothe those in trouble? She will be a perfect addition to your household, as Master Jonty will be to ours. I will do what I can to work on my husband. I would not discuss finance with you, but can you offer no more to tip the balance for Sir Thomas?'

'But I think that we must discuss finance, Elizabeth,' I said. 'I know that your own father has been most generous, promising a gift on the day that they are wed. This is what I will do. If we can redeem Swainsthorpe from the mortgage on reasonable terms, I will give the manor to my son. I will also give ten marks a year from my own property at Sparham, until forty pounds is paid. Which will be six years and long enough for the young couple to become established. When I die, Jonty may have Sparham in its entirety as a jointure for Margery. I will write it into my will. Do you suppose that will persuade your husband?'

I thought that I was being more than generous.

'So I should hope,' Elizabeth Brews agreed.

We drank a cup of wine and ate dinner together in mutual satisfaction.

We parted on the best of terms.

It might have worked to the benefit of all, except that Sir Thomas wanted Sir John, as the head of the Paston family, brought into the negotiations.

'Blessed Virgin! Do we ever come to an agreement?'

I had to admit that I would have done the same in his circumstances, yet I could have told Sir Thomas that it would be of no use demanding any such thing. Sir John had no intention of giving up any of his own revenue-producing land to seal the agreement, not even for the happiness of his brother. Sir Thomas, to his eternal generosity, had gone so far as to agree to lend Jonty one hundred and twenty pounds to redeem Swainsthorpe from its mortgage, a loan to be repaid on easy terms. An excellent suggestion, if Jonty could find someone to repay the loan at twenty marks a year. It must not be paid out of the marriage money.

My suggestions to Elizabeth had taken sound root.

But in return, Sir Thomas asked Sir John to show his good will financially, too.

352

We waited. I was not hopeful. All was silent from Sir John Paston.

I wrote to him since he was not yet in Calais.

I wish to see you. Do not give me excuses. I wish to see you in Norwich before the end of the month.

Sir John arrived, none too pleased and full of argument, but neither was I too pleased with him, and would not hesitate in making my displeasure felt.

'I do not understand why you would give up your revenue from Sparham,' my son stated even before I could take him into a private chamber. 'And ultimately the manor itself. It is another attack on the entirety of Paston land, giving it to Jonty. It should have come to me on your death.'

'Only if I left it to you in my will.' I was not prepared to give way to any degree, or even to make an apology. How thoroughly selfish my son had become, and self-serving when his own interests were paramount. 'I will give it to Jonty because I see it as the only way to get this marriage to the church door. I could wish that you were as busy about it as you are about Calais. Sparham is my Mautby inheritance. It is mine to deal with as I wish.'

'If you are going to give away a manor, why not to me? You know I am in desperate need. You did not consult me about this. There has been no agreement between us. For certain I would not have agreed!'

'You have been noticeably absent from this whole event of Jonty's marriage. I do not need your agreement.'

'Sparham is the best manor you have.'

'And I have offered it to Jonty. The young couple need it. Have you no compassion for their situation?'

'I would, if I thought my brother was serious.'

'Not serious? How can you think that after all this time? I don't suppose that you will be willing to stand guarantor for Sir Thomas's loan to buy back Swainsthorpe?'

'No.'

No surprise there. I had promised myself that I would not

353

resort to hard words. I failed. My patience with my first-born was entirely at an end.

'How can you be so thoughtless of your brother's future? Sir Thomas thinks that as head of the family you should be present at the making of this settlement.'

'I will be, unless I am in Calais. Or required in London.'

Or any other excuses he could make.

'You should harvest your income better,' I found myself saying when I had promised that I would not. 'Furthermore, I think that you, as head of the family, should take on the payment of Willem's education.'

Sir John became stony-faced. 'How do I find the money for that?'

'Yet you expect me to do so.'

He turned away. Seeing the hurt there, as I might have done when he was a young boy, I tempered my next comment.

'It would be good if you could support Jonty. You were once so close.'

'Yes. He was the best friend a man could ever have.' A silence developed between us, until he turned to me and said: 'Forgive me. I will not stand in their way or complain about Sparham. It is your own choice, of course, what you do with your Mautby inheritance. I never had rights in that land, so I wish Jonty well of it.'

'That is good. We will see what we can do about this marriage. Show Sir Thomas that you have no objection to it and will accept the settlement with your blessing.'

'I will. I wish my brother well of his new wife and children.' And then, as he opened the door to leave the room that had witnessed so much emotion: 'I am sad that Jonty will forget me in his own happiness.'

His final words wrung my heart. Such a deep hurt, a loneliness, was embedded there, while I, as his mother, had failed to see it; instead, I had been single-minded in my desire to help Jonty. I sank onto a stool, resting my head against the wall behind me, despairing of my children discovering any contentment in life. Sir John needed a wife of his own, but what could I do about that? It was beyond any solving of mine.

★

April came and went in a flurry of showers. Then the heat of June, in a dense silence on the marital front. Still a terrible stalemate. Would my planning with Dame Elizbeth ever come to fruition? Would the two young people ever wed? I met Sir Thomas and Dame Elizabeth in Norwich when they travelled through to their manor of Salle.

'We must find some way forward, Sir Thomas.'

Sir Thomas, apparently of no mind to be accommodating, sat stiffly in my best chamber.

'Can we do no better?' I asked.

Sir Thomas frowned, exchanged a glance with his wife, then spread his hands in acceptance.

'Here is my best offer: I will give the young pair two hundred marks, and free board for them in my home for two or three years. And, further, I will lend one hundred and twenty pounds for your son to redeem Swainsthorpe, on condition that he can find someone to repay the loan to me so that he does not pay the loan out of the marriage money. And you, Mistress Paston, as you agreed, will contribute the manor of Swainsthorpe and ten marks a year from Sparham as a jointure for my daughter. With a promise of the whole of the manor of Sparham on your death. I think that is as generous as we can be. Do you accept it?'

Which I did, of course. Dame Elizabeth and I exchanged glances with a nod of acknowledgement. It had been a meeting with a most acceptable outcome, and not merely of a financial nature. Mistress Margery had accompanied her parents, but since our discussion had been of a legal nature, I had suggested that she spend the time with Anne in her chamber, where I had had a fire lit. It would be good for my daughter to have some female company other than my own.

While Sir Thomas and his lady were preparing to leave, I went to collect the young girl. She was sitting neatly on a stool, hands clasped, in deep conversation over the construction of some head-covering with wires and veiling. She looked up with laughter in her eyes and I knew why Jonty found her so attractive a companion.

She walked with me back to the hall, the first time that we had been alone together. I halted on the stairs, forcing her to do likewise on the step above, while it was still possible to hold an intimate conversation. I wondered how she would respond.

'I think that you hold an affection for my son.'

'I do.'

'Would it trouble you if this marriage could not be brought to a conclusion?'

Her expression remained calm as she contemplated a reply, which, when it was given, was bleak indeed.

'It would, I think, break my heart.'

'Hearts can be easily mended.'

'I expect they can. But why agree to them being broken in the first place when there is no need?'

'There are financial constraints.'

'Which I think do not compare with the strength of my wish to marry Jonty.' Her face was suddenly illuminated in a smile of pure delight. 'I love him, Mistress Paston, and have no wish to step back from a marriage that I desire more than anything in the world.'

A lady, then, of some strength of mind. 'Thank you for being so honest, Mistress Margery.'

'Jonty calls me Gilly.'

'I know he does.'

'I know why he does so, Mistress Paston. I would be happy for you to call me Gilly, too. I would not wish my name to give you painful memories.'

It touched my heart, as Jonty's kindness had in naming his betrothed.

'You have a depth of generosity, Mistress Gilly.'

'And a depth of resolution.' She leaned confidingly towards me. 'I will make your son an excellent wife, you know.' Then she continued down the stairs to where her mother and father were waiting for her with impatience.

She had impressed me more than I could have said.

★

The sticking point, apart from Sir John, who was now in Calais, was still somewhere for the young people to live. I had thought about it and had come to a conclusion that did not please me but that seemed the only possibility.

'Why will you not accept Sir Thomas's offer of board?' I asked Jonty.

'I have no wish to live under his roof.'

'You could always set up house with me,' I suggested.

'That is not what I want either.'

'Why not? Your father and I lived with your grandfather and Mistress Agnes at first.'

'And did you enjoy it?'

'No.' I could not lie.

'Family gossip says that you could not wait to rent a house of your own in Norwich to get out from under Mistress Agnes's feet.'

'Would it be better than no marriage at all?'

'I have a plan!' Jonty at his most resourceful.

'Then tell me about it. I hope that I approve.'

'You might not.' His glance was sly. 'But it might be our only hope. Behold!'

He delved into his capacious sleeve and brought out a pair of letters, both of them written in Jonty's hand. They were not addressed to me, apart from the outer cover, but to Sir Thomas and to Jonty himself. My son had come prepared for some dissimulation.

'What do I do with these?' I asked, turning the two letters over.

'Copy them into your own hand, and sign them as if they come from you.'

'I'll copy nothing until I have had time to read them. What lawyer would do that? This sounds highly devious, Jonty!'

'None who values his reputation. I'll leave you to your reading, then return to see what you think.'

Alone in the quiet chamber, I read them through.

One was to Sir Thomas, critical of his offering no more to my son than two hundred pounds, but equally condemning of Jonty, who might have misled me about what Sir Thomas had in fact promised. Perhaps indeed Sir Thomas had promised more, while Jonty had been deceitful to me? I would wish to know.

And then a shorter one addressed to Jonty himself, warning him of how dangerous it would be for him to take on any wife at all, including Mistress Brews, if he had no means with which to live. In this letter I refused my son any further help; it seemed that a parsimonious Mistress Paston was condemning the whole enterprise.

I had read them in detail before Jonty's return.

'And you want me to write, sign, and send these, as if in good faith?'

'Yes.'

'Why?'

'To prove to Sir Thomas that you can be a hard woman in a negotiation who can turn against her most beloved son rather than take on a bad deal. It will win his support for me against you. It will certainly melt the heart of Dame Elizabeth.'

'I am to paint myself as an unloving mother?'

'If necessary.'

I did not like this at all. It had a hint of trickery about it. My husband John might well have lauded it as a cunning ploy, but all I could think was that it would be wrong of me to fool Sir Thomas in this way. Was I willing to be so ruthless in this battle for Margery Brews's hand in marriage? It did not sit comfortably with me, no matter how strongly I argued the point for legitimacy before the law.

But I did it anyway.

August arrived and Jonty's cunning had had no good result, for whatever reason I had no idea. My patience had dissipated under a cloud of debts and empty coffers, finally breaking entirely under Sir John's negligence in squandering his money. Mortgaging his manor of Sporle, he owed four hundred marks against it, to be paid in three years, or the manor would be lost for ever. It was beyond my understanding that he would agree to such a contract, so much so that I warned him that I would be unwilling to leave him any property at all in my will if he could not care for it. But Sir John was in Calais again and caring for nothing but his own inclinations.

We could go on no longer with this.

Surely there was some conclusion to be drawn out of the maelstrom of the Brews marriage. To leave it to sink into oblivion would not make Jonty happy nor would it give me any satisfaction. Since no one was putting a step forward and Dame Elizabeth had taken to her bed of a fever when she reached Salle, there was no help there.

There was one possibility. It was not one I liked, but I must pray that Jonty would forgive me if all was well knotted together for him in the end. With this thought uppermost, I broke into Jonty's private domain. Where would he keep a private letter? A love letter? How often had Pastons in the past warned the recipient of a letter to burn it so that it would never fall into an unfriendly hand? Pray God that Jonty had kept any affectionate offering written to him by Gilly.

In his chamber I sat on his bed with a small coffer beside me. I lifted the lid. Mostly receipts, some scribbled notes from Sir John. One bill, unpaid, for two pairs of hose. Then I found just what I needed: three letters from Gilly. Without compunction I read through them, hoping that she might have been as clear and as passionate in her writings as she had been in her speech with me.

And there it was, a letter of true love written on the day of St Valentine.

To my most dearly beloved Valentine John Paston ...

I felt reluctant to read on but so I did, my eye falling on certain phrases, certain desires that took my breath. The hand was that of a clerk, but the signature and the Valentine heart was that of Jonty's love, without doubt. The emotion and anxieties written there were enough to melt even the coldest heart.

I am not in good health in body or in heart, nor will I be until I hear from you.

If you love me, and I truly believe you do, you will not leave me because of that. My heart commands me to love you truly above all earthly things for evermore. I would be the happiest maiden on earth if only the business might come to fruition.

Her despair was palpable on the page.

If you do not consider yourself to be satisfied, do not take the
trouble to visit any more. Rather let it be finished and never
spoken of again on condition that I may be your faithful lover and
petitioner for the duration of my life.
  By your Valentine MARGERY BREWS

Oh, the despair! I read it with much emotion. Would that John
had ever written to me in such a vein. I would not have destroyed
it, as Jonty had not put this one to the flames. I hoped that my
son appreciated the delight and the inner strength in this young
woman. I also read it with some fear. As I had learned, the lady
would not be willing to let Jonty escape her. She had no intention
of allowing him to leave her, whatever the viability of his reasoning. She loved him, she wanted him as her husband, and I would
swear that she would get him.

I arranged to meet with Sir Thomas again and travelled to Salle
with the letter in my safe-keeping.

'I think that we have both had enough of this wrangling, Sir
Thomas.' We were still facing each other in the hall of his lovely
manor. Affairs were too urgent for platitudes and comfortable
converse. 'I cannot risk our lovers running off together, and neither
can you. Making vows outside the church is not to be encouraged.
It brings nothing but trouble. I have experience of this. Do you
want it to happen?'

Sir Thomas might be as weary of this as I, but his shoulders
stiffened.

'My daughter is a well-brought-up girl who knows her duty
to her family.'

'Your daughter is a remarkably headstrong young woman. Duty
is all very well, but not when they are in the throes of love.'

Sir Thomas frowned at me. 'I trust that your son is not encouraging her...'

'Your daughter needs no encouragement.'

'I am not convinced...'

'Then perhaps this will convince you.' I took the letter from my purse and held it out. 'I suggest that you read it. It will give you a sense of the commitment between the pair.'

Sir Thomas read it. Then again. I could see what he was thinking: *My daughter would never write such a headstrong piece of disobedience to all she has been taught ...*

I did not allow him even to voice his denial.

'I am sure that you recognise the hand of one of your clerks. And presumably the signature, which would belong to Mistress Margery.'

'Yes. It is the hand of one of my clerks ...'

There – he had been forced to admit it.

'My son, too, is dutiful, but I know that I fear for the outcome if this is the level of devotion that exists between them,' I said.

'I see what you mean.'

'You should be afraid, too. There is true commitment here.' He handed the letter back. 'I think we are going to have to come to terms and allow them to be wed. My son will make her a good husband.' I remembered her own words, offered so confidingly. 'She will make him an excellent wife.'

'I expect that she will.'

'Then it is decided? You will accept my word and not wait for Sir John?'

'It is decided. Because to leave it unresolved would be to court danger.'

'Neither of us would wish to do that.'

We shook hands.

'I wish Sir John Paston was as easy to deal with, Mistress Paston.'

'So do I, Sir Thomas. So do I.'

On a chilly autumn morning with rain on the wind, Jonty and Gilly were wed at the church at Topcroft. Nothing could dampen their happiness. The young couple beamed at each other and at the whole world. They moved into the manor of Swainsthorpe and set up home there.

All promised by Sir Thomas was forthcoming while the ten marks from Sparham was my gift to them. By December, Gilly was carrying a child. I think we all heaved a sigh of relief, except

Sir John, who was still carping about paying for the education of his brother Willem. Now all I had to do was settle Anne into the Yelverton marriage with hopes that it would be even half as happy an event as her brother's alliance. No matter how many prayers I offered to the Blessed Virgin, I could not be optimistic. Her happiness must be sacrificed for family advancement. It was a thought that did not sit well with me, but it did not stop me from once more upbraiding Sir John for his dilatoriness in negotiating a settlement with the Yelvertons.

CHAPTER FORTY-TWO

MARGARET MAUTBY PASTON

Caister Castle and Rougham Manor in Norfolk, Autumn 1477

In the same year as Jonty found and wed his true love, at last my daughter became the wife of William Yelverton, by which time Anne was twenty-three years old, with a dowry which was the best we could raise in the circumstances. It was a cool wedding in spite of the sun's warmth, young Yelverton no more reconciled to his bride than Anne was to him. At least I had lived to see the marriage of this daughter under my own aegis, with prayers that it would prove to be one of some happiness.

They were wed at the church door at Mautby on a bright day that would promise good omens even if the bridegroom was prone to scowling and the bride woefully pale. Clad in their finest with a superfluity of fur and gilded lacing, the Yelvertons were out in force, standing in their own inimitable fashion aside from the Pastons. Perhaps after copious wine and ale at my expense there would be some intermingling for the good of all.

With much practice at organising such an event, from my experience of producing an array of meats and wines worthy of the royal Court to honour my husband John at his funeral, I even sacrificed one of my swans for the occasion. At least there was no need to employ barbers to ensure that the tonsures of the priests were seemly, or a glazier to take out the windows in the church to prevent a large congregation from suffering from the close heat. After the exchange of vows and a small purse of coin at the door, we processed inside to celebrate Mass. Young William led his new bride with practised grace; Anne curtsied to him with all the dignity of a new wife. All I could hope for was tolerance and a level of growing affection.

I watched my daughter with some pride, her hair brushed into a silken curtain to flow over her shoulders, as a virginal bride should be, all covered with a light gilt-edged veil, a prestigious gift from our Calthorp relatives. High waisted, full skirted, her gown of rose-pink velvet trimmed at neck and hem with pale fur, had taken much stitching; no one would find fault with her or the show we put on for this day so long in coming. Around her throat was a fine gold chain with a pearl pendant, one of the last jewels bequeathed to us by Sir John Fastolf in that contentious will. It was an ornament perfect for a young girl and so fitting that it should go to Anne. I would not think that Margery should have worn it at her wedding. This was not a time for repining over past griefs and losses.

The celebratory feast, if that is what it was, we held at Caister Castle; why not flaunt our restored grandeur? The Yelvertons must be impressed, whether they wished it or not. There were no swords drawn or use of fists and I heard no foul language; or any that was exchanged was well hidden by the troupe of raucous minstrels and mummers that Sir John employed for the day. All went off as well as could be expected between two hostile families. After the feast, the couple were led to the best bedchamber, all hung with tapestries sporting flowers and birds in a fairy woodland, where they were put to bed and liberally sprinkled with holy water by the priest. I forbade any ribaldry. Anne had enough to tolerate without crude repartee to make her blush. Nor was it mentioned by anyone present that this was the chamber in which Sir John Fastolf had breathed his last.

Then, next day, they started their journey to the Yelverton manor at Rougham, Anne now clad in russet wool, her hair neatly braided beneath a felt cap suitable for travel.

'May the Blessed Virgin journey with you,' I said, taking her aside. 'Remember this, my child. It is not a sin to be sly in managing your husband. Nor should you be a silent wife. You are a Paston daughter.'

'I will remember.'

'Make the acquaintance of the important people in your new household. The steward, the bailiff, the cook who rules the kitchens. Win them to you with fair treatment. Reward them when necessary. Their loyalty will be of use to you.'

'I will do it.'

What more could I tell her? I would not ask her about her first night as a wife. Her aura of self-possession was hard-won and I would not disturb it, watching them as they rode away until they had vanished out of sight. With them was Alice, a stalwart girl from Mautby, accompanying Anne to be her maid.

'I'll take care of her, mistress. I'll let you know if she is in any trouble,' she assured me with the stern gaze of the newly promoted, while I gave her a packet of powder ground from the testicles of a wild boar, to add to Anne's wine, to aid conception. I had never had the need for such artifice, but it was a proven procedure, according to Gilly, who appeared to have a gift for such remedies. If Anne carried a Yelverton heir quickly, she would be forgiven much.

Of course, being a woman of a managing nature, I could not resist an assessment of my own, and so, before the end of the year, not waiting for any message from Alice, I paid a visit to Anne Yelverton, as she now was, at Rougham Manor where the couple had taken up permanent residence in the family manor.

I was made welcome by my daughter in a restrained fashion as we exchanged an embrace and I kissed her cheeks. She smiled and did all that was necessary as she had been raised, with an unnervingly mature composure. Well clad in woollen cloth of a deep blue, she was confident, sternly organised with a well-run household. What she had not learned from me she certainly had from the Calthorps as she showed me around her new home with its many chambers and impressive hall, its range of kitchens and sculleries and stables, as well as a private chapel. I could not but be impressed by the wealth of carved furniture, the tapestries that covered the walls whenever we turned a corner, the embroidered hangings to make the beds private and free from draughts. Without doubt Anne had married well. Fastened at her girdle was an eye-catching rosary with carved beads and a gold crucifix. But that is where my satisfaction met a barrier.

All Anne's youthful exuberance had fled. Here was a sober matron who accepted what life had given her and was making the best of it. I was shown around their chambers as if I were a guest rather than her mother, and I was reluctant to ask, although I did when we returned to what was used as a parlour and I accepted a cup of wine. It pleased me to see that the servants treated my daughter with due deference. Anne had learned well from me.

'Are you content?' I asked when we were sitting together, alone.

'Yes.'

'Does he treat you well?'

'He does not treat me ill. I have no cause for complaint.'

Which was no answer at all. Quickly, Anne moved the conversation to a discussion of Jonty's marriage to Gilly, until William Yelverton entered the room, dressed in a heavy jerkin and boots, his fair hair hidden beneath a neat felt cap, as if he had just this moment ridden in. He bowed to me but, beyond a glance, barely acknowledged his wife.

'You are welcome, Mistress Paston. I see that Anne has offered you refreshment. We did not know that you were coming.'

'Neither did I. I was passing and had a desire to visit my daughter.'

I would not explain anything to the young man with the severe mouth and the direct, almost accusatory, stare.

'Perhaps you might send word next time, Mistress Paston. So that we might entertain you comfortably.'

'Perhaps I will, when I wish to see my daughter. I did not think that you would close the door against me, sir. Do we see you in Norwich?'

'I have not decided.' I, he said, not *we*.

Not once had he touched his wife's hand or arm, or even come to stand close to her. There was no affection here, merely an acceptance of their relationship. Guilt was a blow against my heart, but it was done. Anne must shoulder the burden of wifely duty, with all its pains, and I must support her as best I could.

'Perhaps you will bring Anne to see us at Caister Castle when my son is in residence,' I suggested, unable to obliterate the edge to my voice. 'As you know, there is good hunting and fishing in the area, which you might enjoy. Nor do I wish to lose touch with my daughter. The Pastons have always been a close-knit family.'

William looked at me, assessing my invitation, realising it would be in his best interests not to antagonise me. 'I willingly accept,' he replied, although there was no pleasure in his voice.

The visit was short after that. As I prepared to leave, William disappearing into the fastnesses of the house, Anne took hold of my arm.

'I wish that you had let me wed John Pamping.'

'Your life would not have been as comfortable.'

'My life would have been happier.'

Such bitterness could not be denied.

'You will feel better when you quicken with your first child.'

She leaned close and whispered in my ear. A time for confidences, it seemed.

'I already am.'

So the wild boar nostrum had succeeded beyond all my hopes. 'Have you told him?'

'Not yet.'

'Why not? His gratitude will know no bounds.'

'Or he will turn even further from me, if he feels that his duty to me is done.'

Any hopes I had that she and Yelverton would find some basis for affection now that they were wed were thus dissipated within half an hour of my visit. I rode away, troubled with uncertainties. Did she make the best of things? Perhaps she did, because she was a Paston.

Since I appeared to be in a travelling mood, and since one uncomfortable thought persisted in nibbling at the corner of my mind, I went to Oxnead to see Mistress Agnes, my formidable mother-in-law. Hardly had I ridden into the courtyard than she emerged from her house, in what might have been a welcome if she had managed to summon a smile.

'Margaret. What are you doing here?'

'I am come to visit you.'

'Then you should enter and we will take a cup of ale together.'

Despite her advancing years her voice still had the harsh carrying quality of her youth and her spine was as straight as a lance. It would not surprise me if she outlived us all. We sat, not quite at ease, whilst she questioned me about the Brews marriage, much as I had expected.

'Was it worth all the trouble it has caused?'

'Jonty thinks so. She is a pretty and most amenable girl. I also suspect a will of iron beneath the surface, so Jonty will have to watch his step.'

'It was not a dowry to please me. I would not have accepted it. Since you are here, you had better eat with me and stay overnight. You can tell me about my grandson's new wife. I need to know nothing more about the Yelvertons. I already know far too much about them and despise their grasping ambitions.'

Recalling all the difficulties, and not wishing to relive them, I turned the conversation into less contentious paths as we took supper and I retired to my bed through sheer weariness, not yet having broached the matter that had brought me here.

Next morning, after breaking my fast, I ordered my horse to be made ready.

'Will you not stay a few more days?' Mistress Agnes asked, which made me wonder for the first time if she lacked company other than her servants, but I would not stay.

'No, I have a mind to return to Mautby.' I could no longer put off asking. 'Has your son William spoken with you recently?'

'What about?'

'Paston manors. Inheritance matters.' I was deliberately vague.

'No. Why would he? I would discuss such affairs with Sir John.'

Her reply was clipped and instantaneous, her eyes veiled as she looked down at her clasped hands where her swollen knuckles also betrayed her age. If I could believe her, then there was nothing here to disturb me, and yet her expression had closed against me. It was an expression I knew well, so I abandoned any hope of achieving confidences here. Mistress Agnes accompanied me out to where my horse and my servants waited for me. I mounted and raised my hand in farewell. My visit here had been of no value to either of us.

'Margaret!'

I looked back. Mistress Agnes approached, looking up into my face.

'There is one thing that you should know. William has invited me to go and live with him and his family in London, in Warwick Inn.'

Now this was a surprise, and not a pleasant one. I was aware that I was holding my breath. I exhaled slowly.

'And will you go?'

'Yes. I have told him that I will. By the end of the year.'

'But why would you do that? You have lived at Oxnead for so many years. It is your jointure. Do you no longer see it as your home? And if you need a change of scene, why not go to Paston, which is part of your dowry?'

Mistress Agnes eyed me with what could only be cold cynicism. 'Perhaps I would appreciate a little comfort in my old age. And company. William has been most persuasive.'

I should just think that he had! Living under William's roof would open Mistress Agnes to a discussion of the contents of her will. We all knew that she was of the opinion that her son had been ill-treated in his inheritance of Paston lands, an opinion that William shared. William could indeed be most persuasive.

Before I could make any reply to this she had turned and walked back into the manor that had been her favoured house for as long as I could remember. She would go and live with William. I did not like that idea. I did not like it at all.

I seemed to spend my days disapproving of the thoughts and actions of one member of my family or another. Other than Jonty, all of them were capable of thwarting my plans to make Paston a great name in the county and beyond.

But this short exchange left me with another unsettling thought to accompany me as I rode home. Mistress Agnes had been lonely at Oxnead, even if she would never admit to it; a widow of many years, her children all settled within their own households, with few and infrequent visits between. Was this the fate that was awaiting me? My hand clenched on my reins, causing my mare to throw up her head and prance a little until I took her to task in soothing words. I knew that it would be so, once Edmund, Walter and Willem had flown the nest. Walter and Willem were already absent for much of the time in pursuit of their education at Oxford and Eton. There were already silences in the Paston House when evening fell, my children occupied elsewhere.

'And who will take me in, when I am old and in ill health?' I asked of no one, my heart suddenly shuddering at such an undesirable end to my life. 'The years are stalking me and I doubt my sons would welcome me beneath their roofs.'

'Mistress Paston? Is all well?' Master Pecock, riding silently behind me, as was his wont, came alongside, squinting at me as if I had lost my wits. 'Do you wish to halt and rest? We could return to Mistress Agnes, if we must.' He surveyed me as only an old retainer could. 'No need to fear for the future, I'd say. You look good enough to last for another dozen years at least, mistress.'

I shook my head and laughed at so ingenuous a comment on my appearance, although I could dredge up little amusement. I suspected that Master Pecock was older than I. He would not see his fiftieth year again. No, I was not old and neither was I in ill health.

'Thank you, William Pecock. We will go home. I think I have had enough of my family for a few days.'

CHAPTER FORTY-THREE

MISTRESS ANNE HAUTE

The Royal Court in the Palace of Westminster, December 1477

To whom did I owe my good fortune? I did not know. I would never know.

My situation appertaining to the annulment of my marriage was at last brought to the attention of the Cardinal, Thomas Bourchier, and the Lord Chamberlain. It took until August of this year before an annulment was achieved, but at last there was an end to it. Nine years of increasing hopelessness at an end. After nine years my matrimonial venture had a papal line drawn beneath it and I was free.

The cost of it! Even two hundred ducats was no mean sum. Another drain on Paston finances, but was the end to this terrible misstep between us worth the cost? I was not of a mind to be compassionate.

We made our farewells in the formality of Westminster Hall, shivering in the winter chill beneath the severe expressions of the angels carved into the hammer beams above our heads. Sir John kissed my hands, first one and then the other, as if sealing a bond, rather than applying a sword to slice through the plighting of troth that we had made with such hopefulness. That was the end of it, and I told myself that I was grateful.

Sir John was soon looking elsewhere for a marriage to a lady close to the Queen. He might reclaim more of the Fastolf estates if this venture came to pass, for rumour had it that she was a daughter of the Duchess of Somerset, an even greater catch than I.

371

I considered warning the lady of Sir John's bottomless charm and empty promises, but did not. Jealousy was not an attractive trait in any woman.

Not that I was jealous. The past was behind me and I had learned a fierce lesson about trust and hope founded on a whim and ambition. I was thirty-three years old and could not afford to wallow in the past with regrets.

Let Sir John Paston look high and take his chances. I, too, must cast my net wide for a husband who would not consider my years a hindrance to producing an heir. I could still bear a son for a man who was willing to draw up a marriage alliance with the Haute family. A supporter of York or Lancaster, it would not matter to me.

As for Sir John Paston, there was no need for me ever to set eyes on him again. No need for our paths to cross or for our feet to match steps in a dance. And if I still occasionally wore the little crenellated jewel, when in melancholy mood, who was to care but myself?

I never would make the acquaintance of Mistress Margaret Paston. I was sorry. I thought that we would have had much to say to each other.

CHAPTER FORTY-FOUR

MARGARET MAUTBY PASTON

The Paston House in Norwich, August 1479

Jonty had been smitten with love. Within two years of the happy event of their marriage, God had smitten me down in grief.

How easy it was to accept the fine health and future success of my two younger sons who had been growing up in the shadow of their elder brothers. Walter, lean-cheeked and slender, reminded me of my husband John in the fall of his hair, in the quizzical questioning of a punishment, when both he and I knew he had done wrong. Sir John had been openly disobedient, Jonty cheerfully so, Edmund the most obedient of all my sons. Walter had been mischievous and marvellously devious. Willem just the baby of the family. After surviving the rigours of childbirth and their infant years, would they not all live long lives and bring honour to the Pastons?

How sore was my heart. How cruelly grief-stricken my soul.

I expected Walter home where we would celebrate anew the conferring of his degree. He would make a name for himself, becoming a man of distinction at Court like his Uncle William. And here he was, arrived in Norwich, his legal training complete, to my maternal delight.

'Walter!'

I could not wait for him to come into the house but stepped smartly into the courtyard to take his reins. Only then did I know that something was seriously amiss. Walter's face was drained of all colour, his eyes red-rimmed. He almost fell at my feet as he was helped down from his horse, so that we took him to his bed, half carrying him, fearful that he had brought the pestilence amongst us. No pestilence, it had to be said, to my eye; no rashes or swellings at groin or neck or armpit, although the nausea and vomiting gave me such cause for concern that I sent the occupants of the house away to Mautby, except for Master Pecock and two servants to help me with the care of my suffering son. Within the week, the fever racking his body with heat and violent shivers with no remittance, he insisted on making his will.

Bathing his poor body to cool the humours and give him ease did him no good. He could not drink the draughts of wine infused with the pounded roots of Sweet Cecily. He was fading away before my horrified gaze.

A day after that meagre little will was made, Walter lay dead.

My heart was heavy with grief as I stood beside the bed, as any mother must mourn the loss of a child, and held the hand that had no life in it. He was at peace, but I was not. Yet I could not weep. How tragic that all he had in life was the manor of Cressingham, which he left to Sir John, and a flock of sheep, that he divided between Edmund, Anne and Willem. All I had to do was arrange the funeral Masses at St Peter Hungate. It gave my mind and my hands something to do, but I mourned him bitterly, unable to accept such a loss. How could a son so hale and full of life have passed from it so speedily? Twenty-three years old, and gone from us.

As I bathed and reclothed his wasted body I found myself considering the path of the Pastons for the future. Were we a family to be cursed, to die out as fast as we had made our place in Norfolk society?

'I am so sorry, John. There was nothing I could do to save him.'

Then I wept over our son.

All were gathered in church to hear Mass for the repose of Walter's soul. It was well attended by townspeople who knew the Pastons, who understood what it was to lose a son or daughter.

Kyrie, eleison.

Christe, eleison.

Kyrie, eleison.

A courier arrived at the church door. The bustle of his arrival was frowned on, the stride of his booted feet drawing attention, but he was not to be deterred. Making his way down the aisle to my side where I knelt, he knelt also.

The interruption distressed me.

'Can this not wait?'

'No, mistress.'

'But this is a Mass for my son. Surely you can give me a moment's respite from the cares of the world?'

He whispered in my ear.

'News from London, mistress, from Master William Paston.' Who I had already noticed was not present at the Mass for my son. 'Master Paston was on his way here when he received the sad tidings. He has returned to London forthwith. Mistress Agnes Paston is dead. She has asked to be buried in Whitefriars in Norwich.'

At first it meant little to me, my emotions already wrung dry. But then it became clear. Agnes was dead, too. The closing down of an era, the last of the Pastons of that generation. Another life to mourn, another burial to arrange, more Masses to say. And as if that were not enough, all in a single week, my daughter Anne had also been brought to bed with her first-born child, the Yelverton heir. It did not survive but passed into the arms of God. Nor had that been my first grandchild to leave this life. Jonty and Gilly's little son, Christopher, had not lived beyond his first year.

A year of death had been stalking us.

With hands clasped, white-knuckled, I bowed my head with the weight of too much grief, one loss so soon after the other so that I was numb with it. It made me feel old, too old to suffer any more attacks on the Paston family. For the first time in my life the intricacies of Paston business palled. I wanted no more of it.

As I walked slowly down the nave, acknowledging those who had come to mourn with us, simply because I must, I glimpsed a female figure, cloaked and hooded in the shadows by the door. Was it Margery, who would surely come to mark her brother's death? She was too distant for me to be sure, and I did not hurry my footsteps. I did not want family conversations. I simply could not tread carefully around more complex emotions. Not today. Perhaps tomorrow I would think again about stepping across the divide between Margery and I, because I could not bear to lose another child. But not today.

'Do I arrange a stone for Walter's grave?' Sir John asked, coming to walk at my shoulder.

'Do as you will,' I said.

My rejection of Paston affairs did not outlast the week.

'He has done what?'

I was supervising the packing of a coffer with the intention of visiting Anne at Rougham, to her comfort and mine, when Sir John announced the news. I slammed the lid and leaned on it in disbelief as Sir John waved the servant away. 'Repeat that, if you would.'

I should not have been surprised, but I was. At the scale of the deception, of the illegal manoeuvring. Of the speed with which he had planned and put it all into operation.

'My uncle William,' growled Sir John, 'has laid a claim to all my grandmother's properties.'

Sir John walked over to close the door after the departing servant, then lingered to allow Jonty to enter, who promptly sat on the lid of the coffer, elbows resting on his knees, his hands over his face at the prospect of yet another battle.

'He cannot legally do that,' I said. My knowledge of family inheritance was very precise.

'He has done it.' Jonty's response was clipped, if muffled. 'Why do you think that he was so keen to have the old lady live in his household for her final years? I would wager he was most persuasive when death hovered at her door.'

'Did she make a will in his favour?' I demanded.

'Yes, so he says.'

I grimaced at this. I should have expected it, his dissatisfaction festering. Had not Agnes denied any complicity in any threat that her son William might pose to us? He has not spoken to me about it, she had said, and so I had pushed my fears aside, castigating myself for my own lack of trust in my mother-in-law. And here it was, the attack on Paston acres, alive and well, at the hands of my own brother-in-law.

I became aware of Sir John addressing me.

'You knew of this, didn't you?'

'I knew of the possibility. And so did you. I warned you. But you did not listen.' I was beyond tolerance of Sir John's claim of ignorance. 'Your uncle William has a long memory, and a keen ambition. I knew of William's opinion on his lost inheritance, yes, but I hoped that we were safe. Mistress Agnes stated her intention to leave all her property to the main branch of the family, to you, in effect, in a statement witnessed by a local justice. This was years ago, while Justice William was still alive. You knew that this document existed. I remember telling you and Jonty to find it amongst all the rest of the family documents. You said that you would discover it and keep it safe, with no expense spared, just in case this issue ever arose. This agreement will give you all legal rights over your grandmother's property.'

'And so I have the document,' Sir John said. 'I know that it is legally binding.'

Fury built within me, layer upon layer, at this outrage to our land, so that I did not guard my tongue.

'Then why did you not take steps to stop your uncle from snatching your inheritance from under your nose? Can I guess? William is always willing to lend you money, so you were not going to antagonise him! You are in his debt! Did you ever warn him off? Did you ever tell him not to interfere in your grand-mother's manors?'

What point was there in my blaming Sir John? I should have known how far William would go. I should have stopped it when he invited Agnes to live with him in Warwick Inn. If Mistress Agnes was under his roof, growing old in years and in mind, what might she not be prepared to agree to? If she had stayed with me, we could have pre-empted this snatching of Paston land.

I sank into a chair and considered the effect of this news – on me, on the family.

It was a betrayal by William.

377

Agnes's lands were substantial. Her jointure was the main family house at Oxnead; her dower included Paston and the nearby manors. And then there was her inheritance from her own family as the only heir of Sir Edmund Berry: three manors, including her father's home at Horwellbury in Hertfordshire. It was a considerable amount of property.

'He cannot do it,' stated Jonty, silent until now, drawing his hands over his cheeks, as if he had made up his mind to the battle ahead.

'Not legally,' I agreed. 'But he will try, now that he has Agnes's will.'

Why had we not listened to the warnings and taken them seriously? But indeed, what could we have done?

'Would our grandmother give it all away?' Sir John asked.

'She well might!' I knew Mistress Agnes for a mischief-maker, yet still it surprised me. I looked up into his face. 'My advice, not that you will need it, is to get yourself to London and secure your inheritance through the courts before William can do any more damage. Take the document in which your grandmother promised all to you.'

'My uncle has a powerful ally in the Dowager Duchess of Norfolk.'

'Then find someone equally powerful at Court to argue the case. You might also care to remind the Dowager Duchess that she might look kindly on me for my support of her in childbed. Jonty and Edmund will deal with the manorial tenants in Norfolk.' I grasped Jonty's arm. 'Show a presence and prevent them from paying their rents to William.'

'There is pestilence in London,' Sir John said.

'Then I will pray for you. We cannot wait until the pestilence wanes. William will take every acre that Agnes has if we do not take action now.'

My sons departed on their various tasks. Oh, how I was to come to regret that advice. If only we could see the future and how our words could determine the fate of those we love.

The legal denunciation of William Paston's attempts to wrest our property from us would be dealt with by Sir John, and by

Jonty if Sir John's enthusiasm waned. Since it was in his interests to pursue it with all speed and urgency, I trusted that Sir John would fight with due diligence. But William, we soon discovered, had already pre-empted our planning, even on the occasion of his journey to Walter's funeral when he first heard of Agnes's death. Instead of returning straight to London, as the courier had told me, he had ridden to the Paston manor at Marlingford to tell the tenants that he was laying claim to them and that they should pay their rents directly to him. William had already sown some difficult seeds there, which we must quickly destroy, like taking a flail to a bed of nettles.

Sir John would take on the legal battle. I would make a more personal attack.

How could William so callously divide the Paston properties? He would know the legalities of it all, right enough; William's legal knowledge was second to none. He had no right to Mistress Agnes's dower or to her jointure, and certainly not to her own Berry family inheritance, but he could be as wily as a fox in a hen house, and twice as brutal. And as a cunning lawyer at heart, he would make it a difficult task to beat him through the courts. William knew too many powerful men and women at Court, too many with bottomless coffers.

I would go and see him. I would berate him, I would appeal to him. In the name of his dead brother, his nephews, the future of the Paston family, I would upbraid him in the name of family loyalty. Whatever needed to be done, I would do it. My suffering daughter Anne would have to wait. I must risk the threats of the pestilence and draw William back into the Paston fold.

My involvement in Paston business and Paston land was renewed.

How many times had I travelled to London? Very few. It would take me longer than a se'enight, and I considered myself too old for such jaunting. All very well to journey between Norwich and Mautby or any other of our manors; London was a daunting prospect for me. When John had been incarcerated for the third time in the Fleet, I had travelled with the purpose of healing a rift between us. When death hovered over him, shocking me with its imminence, I had travelled swiftly with a heavy heart. There was nothing to draw me to London now, except family treachery. I would go. There really was no choice for me to make. Whatever the discomforts of long days of travel, however keen my fears of pestilence that was rampant in London, I could not cast off the responsibilities that had lived with me since the day of my marriage to John Paston.

Would I be made welcome at Warwick Inn, an unexpected, uninvited guest bearing a litany of complaint? I maintained a smooth demeanour as a servant opened the great door from the inner courtyard and told me that he would inform his master that I wished to see him.

'I would be grateful if you would.'

I managed a smile. No point in antagonising my hosts before I had barely set foot on the intricately tiled floor with its plants and rare beasts. It gave me time to assess the wealth I saw around me. Not that it could compete with Caister Castle but it was as fine a town house as I could wish for, as were the inner indications of a near-bottomless purse. The Bruges tapestries. Good quality candles, wasted on this vast space. William was doing well for himself in his quest to rise in the ranks of the gentry. Remnants of the Nevilles, who had once possessed this fine house, could be detected in the coat of arms above the fireplace. There was no fire, it being August, but the air was pleasantly redolent of wood smoke and sweet herbs.

William could do nothing less than invite me to stay for the night. There had been purpose in my deliberately arriving late.

And there was William, clad in an open-fronted houppelande that fell in velvet folds to his ankles, the sleeves embroidered in gold thread, even though it was for nothing more than an evening at home. Perhaps he had donned it to impress me with his grandeur. I refused to be impressed.

'Margaret. Were we expecting you?'

'No, you were not. Will you turn me away?'

'Of course not. You are always welcome. Come in. Anne is in here. You must be weary.'

'Indeed I am. I am beyond the age of long journeying – unless the matter is urgent.'

'We are pleased that you have come to us in London, of course.'

There was no reading his expression. His smile was as insincere as mine, his words of welcome just as feigned. We both knew why I was there. I did not think that he would be in any way pleased after a half-hour of what was in my mind, but I was indeed made welcome by Lady Anne. She had never lost her sense of superior birth, yet she was gracious and friendly. I wondered if she was aware of what William was doing. I thought that she would support him whatever he was planning: Mistress Agnes's inheritance would be invaluable for the dowries of their two daughters.

'How many years has it taken you to visit me here?' William asked as he indicated that the servant should take my travelling cloak and hood.

'Perhaps too many. I had not realised that there was such a distance between us, William. And not merely of miles.'

There was a little silence, then William issued orders for cups and platters to be brought. Thus we sat by a fire and sipped and ate, exchanging news and reminiscing on the sad deaths in the family. We talked of shared grief, of Walter and the hopes I had had for him, of Agnes and her long and combative life. Of the two young babes. A sombre meeting, all in all. William could be thoughtful and compassionate. In my anger I had forgotten his care of all of the Pastons in the past.

Then there was nothing more to say except:

'Is this a business meeting, Margaret?'

'Of course. Why else would I travel this distance?'

'We both know what it is about. Can Sir John not deal with it?'

'He can, when he brings the case against you to court.' I caught the brief frown between William's brows before it was smoothed out. I kept my tone accommodating, my hands lying gently in my lap, palms open in supplication. The perfect non-confrontational guest. 'My visit is of a personal nature.'

William refilled the cups with a suave competence. He was as clever as I. The servants had long since been dispatched.

'Then I will willingly hear you.' His glance sharpened. 'Is this necessary, Margaret? You know what I have done and why I have done it. I'll not be deterred by anything you have to say. And nothing you can say will change my mind.'

'Yes, I am aware.' My tone became no less accommodating. 'On the way to Walter's funeral, so I am told, you were overtaken by a messenger to tell you of your mother's death, and so made a fast detour to Marlingford. There you told the tenants – Mistress Agnes's tenants – that you were laying claim to the manor. You told them that they must not pay their rents to Sir John, but to you. Since then, I understand that you have seized grain and wool from Marlingford. Perhaps you have also made claims on other manors belonging to your mother?'

'Yes, I have.' He had no guilt at all. 'On all of them.'

'And I know why you did it. Because you have always been aggrieved that your brother stopped you from inheriting what you thought should be yours in Justice William's will. It was not yours to inherit. Just as Mistress Agnes's property is not yours to claim, nor was it her right to dispose of it as she pleased, even if you did persuade her. Her dower and jointure properties were held only for her lifetime. Then they would revert, as you know, to the senior Paston line. To my eldest son. Not to you.'

'I was rightly aggrieved. My brother robbed me. What's more, he humiliated me in the making of his own will.'

I did not pretend to misunderstand; it was common knowledge in our family. When my husband John's will had at last been pro-bated, it had included an unpleasant surprise for William, who had counted on being named one of the executors. Why would he not be, with his knowledge of the law? But John had not named him, only myself and Sir John and Jonty. In the end my husband had not trusted his brother to keep the lands within the direct family inheritance. Another thorn in William's sensitive Paston flesh.

I slid a glance towards Lady Anne, who had kept silent so far, stitching what looked like an altar front with superlative concentration. Oh, yes. She knew all about this legal battle, both past and present. Nothing of this was new to her. She had supported William in every carefully planned step that he was taking. No doubt she had encouraged him, as a good wife should.

It crept into my mind: had I ever supported and encouraged

John in any nefarious dealings? The question of Justice William's will, of course, where I had no doubt that Mistress Agnes had lied, in the interests of herself and all her children. But there was Sir John Fastolf's will which had always had a cloud of doubt hanging over the changes that Fastolf had purportedly made on his death bed. I had stood at my husband's side, even when I had questioned his honesty. It was, I supposed, a wifely habit.

I realised that William was regarding me, waiting for my reply. Had John truly robbed him?

'My husband did all in his power to keep the Paston estates together,' I said. 'If he had not, if he had allowed Mistress Agnes to divide them between all Justice William's children, how easy would it have been for us to revert to the serfdom from which you came? And don't tell me about the line of descent from Wulfstan de Paston. I know all about that. It was as false as your claim on the Paston estates. There was no such line of descent before John and I concocted it in the Fleet prison.'

'Ha! Something I always suspected.'

'As well you might. You are no fool, William. If you had returned to serfdom, would you have wed a Beaufort then? Would they have looked twice at you, despite their fall from grace?' I sensed Lady Anne stiffen at my side, heard the click of a fine glazed cup as she placed it on the table, but I did not even glance her way. 'If it had not been for your brother John, carefully harvesting his lands and his income, you would be no one.' Now I glanced at Lady Anne, her embroidery lying idle in her lap, her expression showing mild interest. 'I think not. John paid for your education. He ensured that you had the legal training necessary. And now you repay him in this fashion. You punish his heirs in this manner.'

'Can a man not have ambition?'

'This is not ambition. It is destruction of the family. It is despicable of you.'

'You know how much land is worth.' William's gentle tolerance had now leached away. 'The Pastons have fought all their lives for it. Was the will of Fastolf genuine? Or did John manipulate it to his own advantage? If anything was raw ambition, it was that.'

'John swore that Fastolf's wishes were legal.'

'And you believed him, of course. But you are no fool either, Margaret.'

'He devoted his whole life to keep what had been left to us. But that is hardly relevant to what you have done. Were you plotting it for years, even bringing your mother to live with you last year to draw her under your influence? I doubt you enjoyed her caustic conversations while you broke your fast. But her inheritance was quite another matter, enough to tolerate her presence here. Did you stand beside her on her death bed and whisper in her ear so that she signed her will in your favour? If so, it was a despicable act!'

I could feel anger bubbling up within me however hard I tried to smooth it out.

William simply shrugged. 'I'll not step back from this, Margaret. It is an empty argument that will weary you to no ultimate result.'

'You will not step back, even at the cost of wounding me and my sons.' I made it a statement, not a question.

'If necessary. It is my right, and I'll fight it through the courts with Sir John. What's more, I will wager that I will win.' His gaze hardened, his hands clenched around the carved arms of his chair. 'I can wield far more power than you and your son, Margaret. There are lords and magnates who will stand behind me in any argument I care to present.'

'I know that you have inveigled the Dowager Duchess of Norfolk.'

'Indeed. I have long been a valued counsellor to the Dowager Duchess.'

Which was a particularly sharp blow to me, given our closeness in the birthing chamber at Framlingham when she had promised her support over Caister Castle. And here she was, turned against me. Was it possible to trust anyone when it came to matters of business? But now was not the time to step down that bitter road.

'Of course, I have many Court friends,' William continued, with appallingly smug satisfaction. 'The Duke of Buckingham. John Morton, Bishop of Ely. There are far more that I could name. And someone Sir John might wish I had not "inveigled", as you put it: Lord Hastings, with whom Sir John has served in Calais.

I trust that Sir John was not relying on Hastings's support in this little Paston matter.'

It was a horribly impressive tally of magnate power. There was no arguing that it would be a strong string to William's bow. We looked at each other, acknowledging that there was no path to agreement between us.

'You will divide the family over this, William. Is that what you want?'

'If I must, then so be it.'

I stood.

'Will you at least stay the night?' Lady Anne asked.

I looked down at her. 'So that we can continue arguing as we break our fast? I must stay, since I have nowhere else to go in London, so I will accept your kind invitation, if you wish it.'

Lady Anne rose with creditable poise to escort me to a bed-chamber, as if such heated disputes were part of everyday life at Warwick Inn. 'Of course you will not stay at a common tavern. We will not forget that we are family.'

'I will not forget. I have lost too much. It seems to me that your husband has swept such family allegiance with the dust, behind that mawkish tapestry which I have been forced to regard during our discussion. The subject of Aeneas' betrayal of Dido seems particularly apt. Although I have to say that whoever stitched Dido has given her a smirk inappropriate for a lady contemplating dying for love.'

On which cynical note I retired to the room they gave me, blind to the magnificence of the hangings and the soft luxury of the mattress, the fine silver bowl and ewer and high-quality linen: instead, I sat and thought. I had failed. Unless my sons could bring pressure to bear, the whole package of Agnes's lands would go to William. How could I ever have thought that he would listen to me? Of course he would not. He enjoyed power and would not step back. I could not see his claim ever being overturned.

The next morning, we broke our fast, few words being spoken, and I prepared to depart in a cool atmosphere. All would hang on the strength of Sir John's case driven through the courts. Thus I made my farewells. William, to my relief, had gone out into the city, but Lady Anne wished me a brief God Speed, retiring as soon as I was mounted. There was nothing to say between us anyway.

But there, riding in beneath the arch into the courtyard, was a familiar figure. Sir John, arriving to accost his uncle. I pulled my mare to a halt and waited for him to come abreast. He was dressed with precision, and frowning.

'What are you doing here?' he asked.

'The same as you, I imagine.'

'And you travelled all this way? God's Blood, Mother!'

He was disbelieving. And perhaps rightly so. I was low in spirits and not prepared to argue too vociferously.

'As you see,' was all I would say. 'This is a dangerous situation and it would not pay me to sit at home with my hands in my lap. And I warn you that William is not here. He is out on business. You can guess what that might be.'

'Then I will return when he is at home.'

'If you wish to reason with him, don't bother practising impressive legalistic phrases. I have used up all my arguments and all my patience.'

His frown had still not dispersed. Indeed, I thought that he looked unusually weary. 'You should have left it to me. Uncle William has no legal standing in his case. And I have influential friends, too. Lord Hastings will stand for me.'

I grabbed hold of his hanging sleeve and pulled him closer, even as his horse edged away.

'Don't rely on Hastings…'

'Why not? I have to rely on someone! Lord Hastings owes me for my support in his Calais campaigns. Why should I not make use of him?'

'Because I think you will find he has given his support to your crafty uncle! He might have no loyalty to you if you call on him.'

Into the courtyard rode William on a fine bay to make of us an unfriendly trio.

'Is your mother telling you that all is hopeless?' he asked, his smile full of malice.

'Nothing is *hopeless* before the law, Uncle.'

I left them to disagree loudly, my heart sunk low. Sometimes hopeless was the only possible word to apply, as any thoughts I might have nurtured of a reconciliation with Margery after so many years. They were beyond imagining.

And yet still I hoped...

CHAPTER FORTY-FIVE

MARGERY PASTON CALLE

The Market Place of Tombland in Norwich, September 1479

'Mistress Calle.'

It was a voice I recognised instantly. A voice I had not heard for ten years except at a distance in the market place, engaged in buying some commodity, when I had deliberately walked away, unable to risk a new level of rejection if my mother turned her back on me. How agonising it was to be pulled in two directions; to fear the embarrassment of a very public rebuttal, balanced by a desire to walk up to her and say:

'I am your daughter. Did we not once love one another? Is there no common ground between us where we could stand and talk?'

This morning, there was no doubting the timbre, the tone of command from the Paston Captainess. Even though Richard had been working for her, there had been no social contact between myself and my family. Richard was trusted but I, strangely, had remained a pariah. Not that I had done anything to remedy the situation. It was fear that kept me silent and distant even though I was a wife and mother in my own right. Even though, as a mother of three sons, I now had a clearer vision of why my mother had fought so strongly for the security of the Paston family, albeit at the expense of my happiness. Would I not do the same if I thought my children would suffer from any ill-made choices? Experience had given me a clearer sight so that now, on hearing her voice,

I turned. It was my mother who had hacked at the thick ice between us.

'Mistress Calle.'

I took a step towards her.

She had not called me Margery. I would have given the world to hear that. On the other hand, she had never called out my married name before. I thought that perhaps on this day she had lain in wait, although why I could not guess. It must have hurt her pride to address me as such. For the briefest of moments my own pride made me consider walking on, but she was my mother, these children who were with me and my maid were her own flesh and blood. Should they not know their Paston grandmother? For their sakes rather than mine I remained facing her. And for Richard, who had done well in the renewed Paston employment.

I said nothing. I drew no closer. All I could remember was Father Gloys, passing on her cruel denial to me. I was not welcome. And her final words to me in the Bishop's chamber when there had been the possibility of reconciliation.

You have made your decision. You must make what you can of your new life. Do not come to me for aid if all falls awry.

How could I have forgotten?

'Good day, Mother.'

She gave a brisk nod. 'Margery.' At last she had spoken my name. 'It behoves me to speak with you. I thought that you should know.'

'Yes?'

Oh, I was unforgiving.

'There have been deaths in the family.'

I waited. I watched my mother, taking in her appearance as I would never have done in the past, but now I was an adult and owed her nothing but the occasion of my birth. She was pale and drawn, her face strained with new lines beside her eyes and across her brow despite the close-fitting gown beneath her cloak and soft heart-shaped headdress that spoke of her prosperity. I knew from Richard that she had been ill. Had she sent for me? No, she had not, so I had not risked being sent away again. She had no need of me since she had soon recovered and was robust enough to be seen in the town.

Was I hard-hearted? Yes, I was. Did I feel any guilt? In the dark hours before dawn, yes, I did, but it did not send me to direct my steps to Elm Hill and knock on the Paston door. My mother was often at Mautby and I did not go there either. So I waited.

'Mistress Agnes has died. Your grandmother. It was not unexpected at her age.'

Did she believe that Richard did not keep me well informed of the happenings within the family? I knew that she had died in London. I said nothing.

'I thought that you should know.'

'She lived a good life, even if she was never satisfied,' I observed coldly. 'Mistress Agnes was driven by conflict and greed. Did she mention me in her will? Did she send any parting affections to me or to my children?'

How harsh I sounded. I remembered my grandmother's denunciation as clearly as I recalled my mother's rejection.

'No.'

'Then it is no concern of mine. But I thank you for the news.'

'You are become a hard woman, Margery.'

Yes. A woman. I was not the girl who had left the Paston house. I had confidence now, experience as a respected townswoman of Norwich.

'Hard? And who made me so? Mistress Agnes had no love for me when last we met. Her sentiments echoed yours.'

My mother shook her head. I saw her gloved fingers tighten together.

'You should know that your brother Walter is also dead.'

'I am sorry for that. You must mourn his passing.'

I knew that he had been ill and had been brought home to be cared for but to no avail. He was so young. There was grief in her face, but I would not allow it to soften my feelings. She would not know that Richard had told me of Walter's sad passing, or that I had been in the congregation, well shrouded in black, thus well hidden, when the Masses had been said for his soul. I had made my own mourning for him.

'And your sister Anne—' she said.

For the first time I allowed emotion to rule. 'No! Not dead!'

It shook my composure. Surely not. She was low in spirits when we had last spoken, but since then she had become Mistress Yelverton, offering a comfortable life even if not one imbued with contentment or happiness. I was certain that Richard had heard no talk of her death.

'No, no. She had a child who has sadly died, but your sister will return to health. I thought you should know. And I should thank you.'

'For what?'

'I know that you visited her when she was ill. She found your advice helpful. I wish that you had still been there with her when I returned.'

'Do you? I think your memory plays tricks on you, Mistress Paston.' I knew nothing of compassion on that morning. 'I dared not risk it. You should know that. Why would I willingly give myself over to a repeat of earlier humiliations?'

For the first time in my life, I saw my mother flush with what just might have been embarrassment, or regret, and I was drawn back in my memory to that visit that I had organised to see my sick sister. Her undesired marriage had come to fruition, but how tragic that her child had died. My mother's next words drew me out of my sorrow, but deep into another one.

'And I expect that your husband told you that Jonty and his wife lost their young son Christopher last year.'

'Yes. I am aware. At least I know that Jonty will be a comfort to his wife. Does Anne find any degree of happiness with William Yelverton?'

I had not intended to ask, but I needed to know.

'It is a marriage of tolerance,' my mother stated, lips thinned. 'No better, no worse than for many women. If you have found happiness with Richard Calle, I must be grateful and regret that I stood in your path.' She would say no more; indeed, such a confession had astonished me.

My heart ached for Anne, alone in an unloving marriage, losing a child who might have brought her much compensation in love and dependence. And Jonty, too, who had wed a woman he adored, but lost their first child. I had wept alone at home when Richard had told me. I had held my own sons close.

'It has been a great grief in my heart,' my mother added. 'To lose such young children has been an unutterable anguish for me.'

'I am sorry.'

Never did I recall my mother expressing such emotion to me. Her sorrow must be raw indeed. It was in my mind to step forward and take her hands in mine in comfort, but still the shadows of the past stood between us and I could not.

A silence developed as the noise of the town continued around us. Death was so close to all of us. No Paston grandchildren except for the illegitimate daughter of Sir John. And my children. Is that what had pre-empted my mother's willingness to speak with me? That her only grandchildren were mine with Richard Calle?

'These are your children,' she said. 'They look in robust health.'

I called them together, indicating that my maid should approach. 'Yes. They are raised with care and love.'

Three sons, John and William, the babe Richard in the arms of my maid.

'It pleases me that you have such comfort for your later years.' Lifting a hand, my mother lightly touched Richard's hair where it curled from under his little cap. 'I would say that this child has a look of a Paston.'

'I cannot agree. His hair is as fair as Richard's.'

'His nose and chin have the determination of a Paston.'

She looked about to say something more, then did not, the lines of age and worry deeply engraved on her face. Neither did I speak, even in farewell, even when my mother began to walk away in the direction of the Paston house. She walked stiffly. Yes, she was growing old.

Then as the street opened into the market place she stopped, walked back.

'We have valued the work of Richard Calle in recent years.'

'I am sorry that you could not have valued him as my husband ten years ago.'

'I think, now that you have children of your own, that you would understand...'

'I do not understand why you could not accept the judgement of the Bishop of Norwich. Was I not your daughter? Was I not deserving of forgiveness?'

'I find it difficult.'

'I was barred from the house. Was it the cleric, full of religious condemnation of any who had committed a sin? Or was it the woman in her fine wool and pleated veils who had employed him? You are my mother, but the Paston inheritance meant more to you than my happiness.'

Richard would condemn me for my harsh words. It was not in me to forgive, even though I had so accused my mother. I must make penance on my knees, but there was too much water under this particular bridge, like the River Wensum in flood, battering against the pillars of Bishop Bridge, to allow for true reconciliation.

And yet...

Knowing the trials of her life, the authority she had often been called upon to wield alone, I was, it seemed in the end, not without compassion. Beneath the severe expression I recognised the features of the woman I had once loved and who had loved me.

A moment of decision.

I took the hand of my eldest son and drew him forward, to stand in front of me, my hands on his shoulders.

'This is John, my first-born. I called him after my father.'

She looked at him, her features smoothing out a little.

'It is a good name. And an honour to be named for such a good man.'

'So I thought.'

'Even if another John in the family further complicates matters.' She looked at me, the faintest smile in her eyes. She held out her hand. I took hold of it. It was warm and steady around mine.

It was a reconciliation of sorts. There was a softening in my heart after all; the terrible shadows of the past began to thin and break to reveal a brightness as if a light could at last shine through. Perhaps we could now meet with equanimity. I could begin to look ahead with a confidence that I had not felt for many a year. I decided to make my own step forward. I knew what would do it.

'Tell me how you fare with Caister Castle,' I enquired, although I knew the answer because Richard had told me. 'I think that you must be rejoicing at the outcome.'

My mother's face softened in what might have been pride in me. 'Once a Paston, always a Paston. Of course I will tell you. It is good to see that you have not lost the Paston nose for news ...'

She drew me with her so that as we walked towards the cathedral we began to converse, as any two women of respectable households might. She would not come to my house, but we had both taken steps to heal a most grievous wound. I felt a softness grow around my heart, a desire to help our reconciliation further.

'Do your swans thrive?' I asked.

'They do indeed.' There was nothing false in my mother's smile. 'Safe from the fox, and from my sons, who see them as a necessary part of a feast.'

I returned the smile. One day, if the Blessed Virgin permitted, we would be close as mother and daughter again.

CHAPTER FORTY-SIX

MARGARET MAUTBY PASTON

The Manor of Mautby in Norfolk, November 1479

No! No, it could not be! The news struck me hard, a physical blow to my heart.

All the nagging worries of my days faded into insignificance as I retreated into my chapel, ordering William Pecock to see that I was left alone. Taking even a single breath seemed so difficult. I could not weep. I could not think beyond one single name as I fell to my knees before the sparsely furnished altar.

Sir John Paston would never find his way to Paston. He would never intimidate or persuade our tenants into paying their rents to him.

My son, my difficult, sometimes belligerent, often guilty of prevarication, always self-indulgent, but most well-beloved son, Sir John Paston was dead. Sir John Paston had passed from this life on the fifteenth day of November when I had been involved in nothing more important than learning more about the family of this unknown woman who was too old a bride for Willem, with too many dependants. The pestilence in London had tracked him down and robbed my son of his life.

Was the fault mine? I had ordered him to London to deal with his Uncle William. If I had not sent him to this hotbed of disease, he would still be alive. If only we could unmake our choices.

'Go and arrange to bring him home,' I told a silent Jonty, emerging from the chapel, before shutting myself into my chamber where I sat and contemplated the view beyond my window, without seeing it.

Jonty's muffled advice echoed through the closed door.

'Do not let the blame lie on your shoulders, Mother. Sir John would have gone to London without your command. Besides, he could equally have contracted the pestilence here in Norwich.'

Children died in their early years so often, taken with fevers and illness before they had gained their full strength, but to lose a son who had not reached his fortieth year was a cruelty I had never anticipated. His health had always been so good, his life full of activity. But his death was fast. Such was the pestilence, to take a man so full of life before I could even hear of his illness. I had not had the time to travel to London to dose him. The last time I had seen him was in the courtyard at William's residence, Warwick Inn, where he was cross and argumentative but most assuredly alive.

What had I said to him on that final meeting? Would he know that, in spite of all the vicissitudes, he was my beloved son? I feared that I had said nothing of affection.

Mired in sorrow, I waited for Jonty to come home with my son's body. We would bury him at Bromholm where his father lay, and I would pay for a headstone to mark his achievements. I would ensure that they both had a memorial worthy of them. I would not place it into the hands of another, but do it myself.

My thoughts moved on, as ever back to affairs of business, as my thoughts always did. The pestilence had begun to make itself felt even in Norwich. Jonty had sent Gilly out to Swainsthorpe. Willem was considering marriage to a woman of thirty years with children of her own which did not seem to me the ideal match for him. Our tenants at Paston were causing me much distress, claiming that they did not know who should be their lord since Mistress Agnes had, disastrously for the strength of the Paston inheritance, transferred her possession of the manor of Paston to William. Our tenants were complaining loudly that they had seen neither hide nor hair of Sir John for months, and so would willingly pay their rents to William. If Sir John could not get himself to Paston, the opinionated tenants would not pay at all, and all would be lost. If Sir John...

But then of what importance was all this in the face of Sir John's death?

Sir John had no son, no heir, only an illegitimate daughter whom I had never met. For the first time I wished his marriage to Mistress Haute had become real. How careless he had been with his future.

Jonty was now head of the Paston family. Jonty, with his pretty wife and the opportunity to have many Paston children to strengthen the family. He did not have the same Court connections as Sir John, nor even the same exuberance, but maturity had given him a steady hand on the reins and a clear vision. The Pastons would flourish under his care. They must flourish. I was certain that the Court connections would ensue.

It did not matter now. Nothing was of any importance.

My first-born son was dead.

The days passed so slowly while I waited for Jonty, anticipating a letter to tell me that he had left London, bringing his brother home. The house was clouded in sorrow as the household waited, and I was clad in black. I recalled the extravagant preparations I had made for my husband John's return. The guests, the food, the preponderance of clerics and choristers to honour the dead. Knowing that I must put similar plans in place for my son, I considered sending for Richard Calle who had been my mainstay in those days before we buried my husband.

I had not the energy that I once had. My years had drained me of it. The weight of it all pressed me down into sorrow so that I could barely stand. I must arrange Masses for the dead, open discussion with Bromholm Priory, discuss ale and meats for those who would come to pay their respects. Had my son actually made a will? I had no knowledge of it. Perhaps I would talk to Calle, after all.

And then there was no need for me to do any of this.

It is all done, Jonty wrote to me.

Sir John had been buried, with all speed, in the Carmelite

Priory of the White Friars near the Thames. He had stated it in his will, Jonty said. He was already buried before Jonty reached London.

Then I wept at last. How could he have been so thoughtless of his Paston roots in Norfolk, so thoughtless of my grief at his passing? I had been prevented from mourning him as he deserved to be mourned.

I have much more to write but my empty head will not let me remember it.

Jonty's words of loss for a brother who had been so close to him all his life.

Thoughts which echoed my own.

You must come home too, I wrote to Jonty. *I cannot lose another son to the pestilence in London. You are needed here.*

Nor could I afford to be weary and retiring, for Mistress Agnes had placed her hand on the Paston inheritance from beyond the grave, leaving in her will her property to her son William in recompense for what she considered he had lost. A new battle must commence. William had staked his claim on these Paston acres, sending in his own people to oust ours; it was a battle that we could not allow him to win.

CHAPTER FORTY-SEVEN

MISTRESS ANNE HAUTE

The Royal Court in the Palace of Westminster, November 1479

Sir John Paston, my one-time lover and betrothed, was dead.

Such a cataclysmic wounding for me, yet this small event seemed to touch on no one else's life to any real degree. It was barely mentioned other than a passing comment of regret for the death of a man of good legal experience. The royal Court was existing in a spirit of optimism. Warwick was dead on the battlefield at Barnet. Edward of Lancaster, too, had met his end at Tewkesbury. The royal brother Clarence had been executed for treason, and Henry Tudor was in exile. King Edward became smilingly indolent, gaining flesh as he no longer needed to don his armour. Elizabeth accepted his affairs with women of the Court or the tavern. She was in no position to object, so she became complacent, secure in her position with two sons as heirs to the throne.

Sir John, for all his boundless optimism, all his hopes, had never been on anything but the periphery of Court politics, merely one of the gifted exponents of chivalric skills in the tournaments, and even advancing age had put a stop to that. My lord Hastings would miss him, of course, as a member of his retinue when campaigning, but even that had waned and England was at peace. The attractiveness and glamour of Sir John's well-clad person and his skill in argument would be missed but they were such nebulous qualities in a Court where power-brokering around the King was pre-eminent. For me, my commitment to Sir John Paston was already over. The annulment was mine. It should have been a time of relief, of rejoicing, of looking forward. I was thirty-five years old, still with much pleasure to anticipate in my life. But there was no joy in me, only an emptiness when the Court met to witness the marriage of Richard, Duke of York, second son of Elizabeth and Edward, and the little Mowbray heiress. What were my hopes for a husband and a child to warm my heart? There were enough Court events and intrigues to fill my days, but my nights were long and lonely, stretching into the distance.

But that was not important. Sir John Paston was dead. There would be no more future days and nights for him to enjoy or despair over. When the news came to me, it was written by the hand of someone who knew that I would care, even though all was well over between us. There was no signature.

On the fifteenth day of November, Sir John Paston had died after the briefest of sojourns in London. I read the short, bleak lines. At first, I did not believe it. He was thirty-seven years old, too young to meet death. But there was pestilence about in the city and it had struck him down. I presumed that his body would be returned at his mother's request to Norwich and then buried in the sacred ground of Bromholm Priory beside his father. Sir John had often spoken of Bromholm, that he had not fulfilled his promise and duty to his family to complete his father's tomb. Perhaps both would be given effigies now.

I sat quietly for a little while, letting my thoughts roam with honesty. There was no enmity in me. We had had the opportunity to be wed and make our own family, and we had squandered it. Too little affection, too much self-interest from Sir John, although I had not been innocent. My lack of patience with him had made me quarrelsome in the end, but who could be patient with a man who promised a glittering future on the palm of one hand, then snatched it away with the other, with vivid excuses and remarkable indecision?

The value of my royal connections was insufficient for him in the end.

Had we ever truly loved each other? Had I loved him?

Perhaps I was too selfish to truly love. I had wanted a husband and a household, my own security with a man who could bring me security and esteem. Sir John Paston had proved to be a man of inestimable appeal, even on his first days at Court when we were both young and impressionable. A man with whom it had been a pleasure to spend time, but unutterably self-serving. He enjoyed the company of women as long as he had no debt towards them, loving the excitement of the chase rather than the ultimate capture. Sir John had always enjoyed hunting almost as much as the tournament. The chase was everything. In that moment of discovery of his death I wished that he had been willing to pursue me to a church door and a priest's blessing.

I traced his name written in the letter with my fingers, again and again, as if it would bring him to life in my presence. Yes, I had loved him, in spite of everything. Why not admit it? I would never forget him, or the part he had played in my life, to the day of my own death, but was forced to admit that I had failed to anchor him into the idea of marriage with me.

Then the thought came to me that perhaps he never would have married. He had brothers who would wed and provide Paston heirs for the future. Even though he could wed a wife and leave her at home while he made his life at Court or in campaigns across the sea, I did not think that he would.

I would pray for his soul when we met for prayers after supper.

Then came another letter. By the same hand, I was told that Sir John would be buried, with all speed, in the Carmelite Priory of the White Friars near the Thames. He had no desire for his earthly remains to be returned to Norwich. And I would go. There had been enough between us for me to wish to pay my final respects.

It was the smallest of gatherings in the church of the sprawling Priory. I was clad in black and veiled, calling no attention to my presence, as I looked round, able to count the number of mourners on the fingers of my two hands, two of whom were monks in their white cloaks. The pestilence deterred many from attending such events. I felt sorrow that Sir John's passing should happen with so little acknowledgement. There were no members of the Paston family, not even his brother Jonty, but there was another darkly clad woman I did not know, accompanied by a young girl. His mistress and her daughter, I presumed. And there were some legal associates, their heads bent in seemly respect. There was no one from the Court.

I stood at the back, wrapped in my veils and my own reverence as the priest spoke the words that would commit Sir John to God's grace, thrusting aside the resentment that here was a child of his body, with dark hair and dark eyes, with another woman. He had never given me that blessing to warm me in the winter days of my isolation.

Afterwards, I stood beside the vault where his body was interred and still lacked an engraved stone. I could not claim to be grief-stricken, but the memories came thick and fast, some bittersweet, some kindly, some infuriating, as I gently touched the little brooch that I still had though seldom wore, but which I wore today. A golden castle set with gems, which he had refused to take back when finally we parted company. It all seemed a long time ago now, when he had first given it to me as a sign of his love; eleven years since we had flirted and danced and lived in hope in Calais. So much time wasted on what came to nothing. It was a salutary warning of how fleeting life could be.

I stood with my hands folded with not a little regret in the end. What would they say of him? He had compromised and slid his way through a legal morass, but he had kept Caister Castle and some of the Fastolf lands. He had won the heart of a woman of the Court, then let her slip through his fingers. He had a daughter who was not blessed with legitimacy but who might remember him with affection.

He would be remembered.

What would they say of me in later years? Would anyone remember me, the woman of the Court who had loved and struggled and come away with nothing but a bruised heart and wounded pride? For the first time true sorrow touched me, and loneliness, and I wept behind my veils until one of the friars approached.

'Can I be of assistance to you, mistress? Did you know Sir John? Shall I pray with you?'

I wiped my tears with my fingers. Did I weep for myself or for Sir John, whose voice I would never hear again? There were no answers for me in my heart, only a desolation that was as black and deep as the vault into which they had lowered his body.

'No, but my thanks,' I murmured. 'I have done with praying. And I have done with weeping.'

My glimpse of happiness had all been an illusion, a fantasy created by a troupe of Court mummers. I walked out alone into the winter cold, into a future I could not envisage, a woman made tragic by circumstance. But I would not invite pity. I would remember Sir John until the day of my death, but I must search for a new path, a new fulfilment, as any abandoned woman must.

CHAPTER FORTY-EIGHT

MARGERY PASTON CALLE

The Calle House in Norwich, Spring 1480

The air of my bedchamber was ice cold against my face, so cold that I could barely breathe, yet my skin was as hot as the fires of hell in the doom paintings in the cathedral. I burned with it, unable to find any comfort. The bed covers clung to me, wrapping me around like a shroud as I tossed and turned.

And then, it seemed to me within a moment, I was cold, so cold that I shivered and shook.

'Drink this.'

It was Richard who pressed a cup against my lips. I shook my head. I could not drink.

Then it was a woman's voice and I recognised her, the healer who had come to me when I gave birth to my sons. She bathed my limbs, which gave me some relief.

'My whole body aches,' I croaked. 'Can you stop it aching?'

I sounded in my own mind like a child asking for a miracle, but I was adult enough to know that this affliction would not quickly depart from me. It had been in the town for some weeks. It was dangerous. But I was strong and healthy. Richard would save me.

I heard voices in the distance and strained to hear them.

'She is getting weaker.'

'Is it what we fear?'

'Sweating sickness.'

I called out, although my voice sounded as weak as my limbs.

'Let me see my sons. I wish to see my children.'

But they would not.

'You are not strong enough, Mistress Calle. It is best if they do not trouble you. Not yet. Perhaps tomorrow.'

Did time pass? Did I ever reach tomorrow? I could not tell, day or night seemed the same to me, broken only by the bells from the cathedral and Carrow Priory, and all the rest of the panoply of the churches of Norwich. I could not eat. The tinctures dried my mouth unbearably. The sharp perfume of rosemary and the softer aroma of lavender made my head ache. The pain that racked my whole body was greater than any I recalled, even than the agonies of childbirth.

'Richard...' I whispered.

Immediately he was there with me. He must have been sitting in the shadows. He held my hand, and I felt the brush of his lips against my forehead.

'Lie still.'

I felt the blessing of a cool damp cloth against my throat.

'My neck hurts. My shoulders. It is so difficult to breathe.'

'All will be well. Will not the Blessed Virgin look down on you with mercy?'

In the dim light I saw him make the sign of the cross on his breast.

'Stay with me, Richard,' I managed to say. 'Don't leave me.'

'I will never leave you. Are you not the love of my life?'

'As you are mine,' I sighed. 'I regret nothing in our life together...'

I tried to tighten my hold on his wrist. 'Richard...'

'What can I do for you, dear heart?'

I knew what I wanted, but now how to put it into words?

'Tell my mother... I want my mother to know.'

'I will do it.'

But there was really nothing that he could do. My mother had cast me off. The room was empty and I drifted into a place where there were no footholds, day merging into night, for how long I had no conception. When I opened my eyes again there was a candle beside my bed. Outlined in the glow was a figure. Was this the Blessed Virgin come to succour me in my pain?

'Margery...'

I blinked, and then I knew, even when my breath laboured in my chest.

'Mother...'

'I have come to you. Rest now.' Her hand closed around mine. So secure, so firm. I heard the soft click of her rosary beads in the folds of her skirt.

'It pleases me that you have come here.' I tried to smile but found it difficult.

'How could I not when my daughter was in such need?'

When she sat on the edge of my bed, I felt tears on my cheeks. I saw a glint on hers too.

'Will you stay?'

'Yes, I will stay.'

I thought for a moment about what was important to me. 'Is Richard here, too?'

'Yes, he is. We will both stay with you. As long as you have need of us.'

I drifted again but now the sea was calm, a soft benevolent light beckoning me onwards. I grasped my mother's hand as if I would never let it go.

CHAPTER FORTY-NINE

MARGARET MAUTBY PASTON

The Manor of Mautby in Norfolk, Spring 1480

Death. Grief. Loss and longing.

How I was afflicted in those few short winter months when the days were dark and the nights long with little sun to raise my spirits. So too was my heart dark with fears and forebodings. Three children now gone from this earth, their years so short, so much promise destroyed by the touch of that fell hand. Disease could strike when eyes were closed, backs were turned, minds occupied with the business of living. There was no earthly remedy for some ailments.

The words repeated themselves again and again in my mind. Sir John Paston dead. Walter Paston dead. Margery Paston dead. Or Margery Calle, as I should accept her. As I should have accepted years ago.

I shut myself in my chamber, my loss too deep, too agonising for tears, refusing food and visitors. Who would I wish to see? So many came to our door in Norwich to express their compassion. I could not tolerate it. Grief was a pain in my chest that could not be dislodged, not even by prayer. In all my life I had not wept, nor did I in those days. How long did I remain there, shut away, my household, like a beached fishing boat on the coast, left without my hands on the sail or tiller? Never had I been so careless of my dignity, my authority, my central role in the Paston family.

Until one morning when I awoke to loud voices in the house and unwanted activity. There was laughter, and running footsteps. I sat up, my solitary mourning momentarily forgotten. The servants were stirring and, if the levity was as uncontrolled as it sounded, they had too little to do with their time. There were matters for me to attend to. My mourning must be set aside.

'I am a woman of infinite resource.'

I spoke aloud, the familiar refrain when I was in trouble, the dust motes in the air shimmering with my breath. The cleaning of this chamber needed my attention as well. I clothed myself with care, braided my hair beneath a plain linen coif and descended to the kitchens, to call my servants to appropriate behaviour, pointing to each in turn as they sprang to their feet at my entrance.

To Master Pecock: 'You go forthwith to the market and purchase what is necessary to feed us all this day. Don't be cheated over the cost. I will wish to see the tally when you return.' To one of the kitchen maids: 'You take yourself to the dairy. The cheese will not make itself.' And then the young girl who had come to us recently: 'You take a cloth and a bucket. I wish to see not one trace of dust in any room. I swear that there are spiders infesting the bed curtains.' And then to anyone who was left: 'Will someone remove these kittens from under my feet...'

I had been away too long. If I counted up the years of my life, they now totalled fifty-eight, I was old enough, perhaps, to step back from business dealings and to leave them to the next generation. I would not. My age was not a matter for anyone's discussion. The household was once more under my sway.

CHAPTER FIFTY

MARGARET MAUTBY PASTON

The Paston House in Norwich, December 1482

We were breaking our fast, I in desultory fashion, Jonty and Gilly with good appetite. I took a final sip of ale, my decision made. The years were passing by, three since the shock of the death of Sir John, which had almost robbed me of my spirit. However uneasy it made me feel, this was the day to do it.

I stood, leaning my weight on the table, but gently so that my company would not comment. My legs felt weak, my back sore, but there was no reason why anyone should know other than myself. Gilly had been staying with me to sample what Norwich had to offer in the purchase of cloth and shoes; now Jonty had come to collect her and take her home to Caister where they were enjoying life with their young family. The voices of the infants William and Elizabeth were shrill in the chambers above our heads.

Once I had valued Caister as a symbol of Paston power. I still did but I had no wish to live there. Too noisy for me with a young family always under my feet. Nor did I appreciate the vast chambers and constant draughts. Mautby and the Paston house in Norwich, with their more intimate rooms and fewer long corridors to walk down to break my fast or retire to bed, were far more to my taste.

We were in the season of Advent. We might have been looking ahead to celebrating the birth of the Christ Child, as undoubtedly Jonty and Gilly were, but there was no celebration in my heart unless I tried very hard.

'You look tired, Mother.' Jonty was keen to leave, chivvying Gilly to finish the dish of preserved plums that she was savouring. 'In fact, I would say that you look ill.'

Jonty had noticed. He had sharp eyes and was rarely tactful these days. Gilly nudged him with her foot, much as I used to nudge my husband John in the old days.

'Thank you, Jonty,' I replied dryly, straightening my spine as if I had no difficulty in doing so. 'I am merely tired. I slept poorly last night. The cockerel next door, waking with the first glimpse of light, did not help.'

'I could ring its neck for you, if you wish, before I go.'

'Perhaps not.'

I smiled. I was ill.

'What he means is, Mistress Margaret, perhaps it would be good to lie down for a little. A rest before dinner, even if not now. We can stay, if you wish. One more day would make no difference.' Gilly directed a wifely glare at Jonty. 'Would it?'

As ever, Gilly was a young woman of rare solicitousness. She was a dear girl, a true daughter to me, if sometimes a bracing presence, even with her sorrow for the loss of her baby Christopher. Since his untimely passing from life, they had had two more children and perhaps hoped for more. It was a pleasure to watch her managing my wilful son, making me smile through my pain. I suspected that she also managed me, but her touch was light and I enjoyed the company of her joyful optimism even though it was sometimes overpowering. Now all I needed was calm and thoughtfulness.

'I have only just risen from my bed,' I said. 'Besides, I have a task to do this morning.'

They exchanged glances.

'Surely it is nothing that cannot wait, Mother.' Jonty was still adamant.

'It cannot.'

'Can you not send a servant?' suggested Gilly.

'This is something that needs to be written.'

'I could write it for you,' Jonty offered, 'if it is so urgent. Or even Gilly, if it is something you do not want me to see.'

'No.' I leaned gently on Jonty's shoulder as I walked past him.

'Gilly's writing is even worse than mine. I will do it myself. I will be in the business chamber. I would be grateful if you do not disturb me.'

'I will bring you a cup of ale in an hour, if that would please you,' Gilly offered.

'It would. Thank you. Although perhaps not infused with some overpowering concoction from the herb garden.' Gilly had gained a reputation for her knowledge and use of herbs in healing and giving comfort, practising on her family whether they wished it or not. 'But I think that you should leave this morning, or Jonty will wear a hole in the tiles. Pecock will care for my needs.'

I walked slowly, carefully, to the chamber where all the Paston legal life was stored. All the scrolls and documents of the manors that had kept me busy, often in a state of terrible anxiety or despondency, since my marriage so many years ago. I selected the one I wanted, discovered a pen and sent Pecock, whose joints were now probably as painful as mine, to mix a pot of ink. Ignoring his perennial grumbling, I sat, a whole sheet of paper with just a few lines written across the top, pen in hand, and thought.

This was the will that I had started four years ago in May of the year 1478, when my health had begun to suffer. It was time to complete it and add my signature with our priest as witness. Reluctant as I was to accept my declining years, I was being forced to do so. The humiliation of it, having to ask permission three years ago from the Bishop of Norfolk to hear Mass in my own private chapel in my home. Had I not attended church regularly all my life? Some days now it was too far for me to walk to St Peter Hungate, a mere few steps for a young woman. And even if I did, if the priest was not there, of what value was that to me? It would be better if I stayed at home and knelt to make my own prayers. It would give the gossipers of Norwich something to entertain themselves with as they met over their platters and cups.

That was four years ago. Since then, Jonty and I had continued to hold on to the Paston acres, deflecting William's attempted depletions, even though raids on our mills and molestation of Jonty's men became commonplace. Oxnead and other Paston manors changed hands with troubling regularity, until Jonty persuaded the

Bishop of Ely to stand beside us. With such authority on our side from the Bishop as well as the Lord Chamberlain, William decided on the wisdom of a temporary retreat. How long this would last, I could not fathom, but now, as I had told Jonty, I was tired, not just my body but my mind too. I was sixty years old and although I did not seek death I feared that its shadow was creeping up on me.

I dipped the pen into the ink but still did not write.

It was all the deaths that had brought me low. So many. So many loved ones. I did not need to list them on the paper before me. It would have been a waste; and did I not know them all by name? Did I not remember them nightly in my prayers? What terrible years these had been for death in the family. It wore my heart out. As did my worries about Anne, who had emerged from her sorrows to become a true Paston and a confident manager of the Yelverton household. Perhaps also of William Yelverton, if he did but know it, although they still had no living children to give them pride in their heirs. I never asked her about her state of happiness. What would I gain from that? I would not stir up harsh memories for my daughter.

Briefly I considered Mistress Anne Haute who had vanished from our lives. I had never met her, and Jonty had not kept the connection. I had the generosity to hope that she had found a man to wed her and give her a family. Life was always tolerable when surrounded by family. I smiled. Even when they drove me to distraction.

I looked at what I had written. There were items to add now, bequests to make.

I applied my pen to the paper, but the ink was almost dry. When I dipped again, it splattered. For so important a document I must accept that someone must write at my dictation. Oh, I wished for Father Gloys, whom in spite of all his faults I could trust to keep a still tongue in his head, although Jonty did not regret his death.

Or Master Calle. I prayed that Margery had been aware of my hand around hers as she slipped away from me and those who should have cared better for her.

There was only one step that I could now take, and I would take it.

I walked to the door, making no attempt to disguise my painful steps, and raised my voice to summon our priest. He was young but had a good hand and was discreet. He would finish it for me, to settle all my earthly affairs.

And then I must send Edmund out to visit two of our manors in dispute with his uncle William. They belonged to Jonty, and they must be reminded of that. I might be writing my will, but I was not dead yet.

So I dictated my wishes and it was written. I signed it, added my seal. Then I added the date 1482. Thus, it was done to my satisfaction.

Then I smiled a little.

And if it was not written completely to my satisfaction, then I could add to it as I wished; it was my choice to make. Had it not always been my choice to make as a Paston woman? My smile broadened. To whom in my family would I bequeath my most valuable possessions? They would just have to wait in anticipation, until my will was read.

Pray the Lord have mercy on my soul in the making of it.

Later in the morning, a knock on my chamber door announced Richard Calle. My ailments were not so severe that I would not receive him, as efficient and as composed as ever, although perhaps the lines beside his eyes were deeper than they had been, his mouth less inclined to curve into a smile. Nor would it on this occasion. His news brought no cause for joy.

'I could not find Master Jonty, so I must give the bad news to you, mistress.'

'When did you ever not? Tell me, then, Richard. Is it William Paston's doing?'

'I fear so. He has occupied your manors at Oxnead and Paston, claiming them for his own through Mistress Agnes's will. Master Jonty must take it in hand.'

I nodded. 'I will tell him.' Another weight on my heart, but nothing unusual in William's rapacious campaign. It was now beyond my capacity to deal with it, however much I might like to ride to Oxnead and order William's men out. Perhaps Gilly would like to take on that role of Paston Captainess.

After a discussion of rents and the cost of grain, business complete, Master Calle turned to leave, until, on an impulse, I stopped him.

'Will you bring the boys to visit me, Richard? They are my grandsons.'

He hesitated. For a painful moment I thought he would deny me.

'Of course. Margery would have wished it.' He bowed and stepped again towards the door, then looked back over his shoulder. 'I have no regrets, Mistress Margaret, only that your daughter is now lost to me. She was my heart's gleam, brighter in my life than any sunbeam.'

'I know it,' I admitted. I, too, hesitated. 'If you would take my advice, Richard, wed again if you find a woman who will be a good wife to you and mother to your children. Don't let heartbreak or a life of perpetual mourning stand in your way. Life is long and we are but creatures who need comfort.'

He did not reply. Perhaps he even shook his head as he closed the door quietly behind him. I hoped that he would ponder on it. He was still a young man. Life was too long for loneliness.

CHAPTER FIFTY-ONE

ELIZABETH PASTON BROWNE

Betchworth Castle in Surrey, October 1483

The clamour of combat came to me from the distant corner of the inner bailey. I was not disturbed by the shouts, by the clash of sword against sword; it was almost a daily occurrence since George had returned home. But when I made my way towards it, my mind was not at ease as it usually was.

There were two figures, stripped down to tunics and hose, engaged in what appeared to be mortal combat. George my husband and Matthew our son, thoroughly enjoying a hand-to-hand battle, in spite of the groans and bellows of instruction from George and the heat of the autumn sunshine. For their safety they both wore brigandines banded with thin plates of metal: Matthew had donned an elderly sallet with many dints in the crown and a pair of metal gauntlets that had seen better days; George made do with a close-helm, the visor lifted. He clearly lived in no fear of Matthew's ability to wound him, although our son's tenacity was admirable.

My daughter Mary sat and watched the cut and thrust, adding her voice, often in unladylike manner. Not a serious bout but a useful manly exercise with swords. I sat on the steps beside her although my daughter was inclined to sulk at being thwarted in spending too much money on the enticing wares of the Canterbury pedlar who had just departed.

'Who do you think will win?' I asked with experience of winning her smile back into evidence.

'My father,' she said promptly.

'It might be Matthew.'

'If it is, he will never let us forget it!'

'And of course we will praise him,' I agreed. 'Because for Matthew to beat your father into submission would be a momentous feat.'

Mary laughed, so our earlier dispute was healed, while in front of us the battle raged. I admired George's skill and Matthew's enthusiasm, wincing at the blows, but at the same time allowed my mind to run over what the pedlar had gossiped about. It had been disturbing, although I had been of a mind to reject it. What was there to trouble me? All was at peace in the country. Our new king was recently crowned to great acclaim. Not the young boy Edward, first-born son of King Edward IV, as we might have expected. Instead, the crown was placed on the clever and experienced brow of the royal brother Richard, Duke of Gloucester, as King Richard III.

I could find no fault with it. Why would it bring any change to my new life, which was one of contentment? The Pastons, the Poynings, the Brownes, had all been staunch Yorkists, the Brownes at least since Tewkesbury, when it was in their interests to change allegiances. If one closed one's mind to the absence of the two young princes, King Richard would rule the country well and with authority, keeping the peace so that we might prosper. A man with a reputation for strong government in the north and with an army at his back was the best man to take hold of the reins. A child-king presented problems, as we had learned. Ambitious magnates simply saw the opportunity to feather their own nests. There was no need for me to look beyond our gates, other than to wonder if my Paston relatives were keeping their heads down to stay out of trouble. Margaret would have the family well in hand, although she must miss Sir John, as any mother would mourn the death of a first-born son. I recalled his energetic visits to me, with some sadness at such a loss to us. I imagined that Jonty would step admirably into his shoes.

As I watched George step aside to allow Matthew an effective clout that sent up dust from his brigandine, I could not believe my happiness. It came to me as I opened my eyes at dawn. It was still at my side when I retired at night. And George was with me, the creator of that inner joy.

I had not enjoyed what the pedlar had imparted. It had made my heart race to such an extent that, after the mock-battle, sending Matthew off to rid himself of sweat and dust, I dragged George into the relative peace of one of the empty stalls in the stable.

'Thank you,' I said.

For what?'

'For allowing Matthew a victorious blow at the end.'

George laughed. 'He deserved it. He will make a worthy knight. He begins to wear me out. But you did not bring me in here to tell me that.'

He might have pulled me towards him but I sidestepped the embrace.

'Only when you are cleaner than you are now. But this is it. Tell me what is occurring,' I demanded. 'A pedlar has just passed through.'

George's expression was suddenly unreadable as he applied a snatched-up length of hessian to his face and hair, adding more dust and straw.

'And did you beggar me with what you bought?' he asked.

'I bought moderately, although Mary was much taken with a silver-latched purse stitched with pearls. I dissuaded her.' I snatched the hessian from him. 'Do we pull up our drawbridge and post look-outs on the battlements, this week or next?'

'Why should we?' He took the cloth back again and reapplied it to his hair.

'The pedlar said that there was to be an uprising against King Richard. Is that true?'

George grimaced. 'It may be so. Rumours of treason abound. But then there are always rumours.'

'Who?' I asked when he let his hands fall and I read a faint element of worry on his face, however much he might try to hide it. 'You may as well tell me now.'

'Then I will. But come with me, I am thirsty.'

He took my hand and led me out in the direction of the

kitchen where he was supplied with a cup of ale. We dragged two stools into a corner where we could talk without eavesdroppers. By now, as I picked spikes of straw from his hair, the worry had become gloom.

'Believe it or not, it's King Richard's closest and most powerful ally, his cousin Henry Stafford, Duke of Buckingham. He has made the astonishing decision to organise a rising in the name of Henry Tudor.'

'And who is this Henry Tudor,' I asked, not being as well versed in Court politics as George had become.

George's gloom deepened. 'A man who has a stronger Lancastrian claim to the throne than most, through his mother, Lady Margaret Beaufort, and her broad streak of royal blood. The blood of the Beaufort children of old John of Gaunt still carries its claim to the English crown. At the moment Henry Tudor is in exile in Brittany. I imagine our king hopes that he stays there.'

I absorbed this for a moment or two, taking George's cup to take a sip before he drank it all. It still did not explain the core of this rumour.

'Why would the Duke of Buckingham do that?' I asked in disbelief. 'Why would he give his allegiance to this exiled Tudor?'

Buckingham had indeed been one of the closest and most powerful allies of our new king.

George considered, a frown on his brows as if he too found it beyond belief. 'Who's to know? Did he not get what he was hoping for in power and wealth from Richard? It may be, but whatever the cause, there is rebellion afoot.'

'Will it be dangerous?' I asked, although I was not greatly concerned for our own situation.

Whatever the Duke of Buckingham chose to do would be dealt with most effectively by the King, and by the end of the year peace would be restored. I presumed that if the uprising would be centred on the Stafford fortress in Brecon, the rebels would be chiefly his Welsh tenants. No concern of mine. I was already planning to celebrate the Feast of the Christ Child with a visit from my Poynings son Edward and his new wife, Isabel. We had made an excellent match for Edward with this daughter of Sir

John Scott, Marshal of Calais, a man with considerable influence in Kent, where many of George's manors lay alongside Edward's own still-disputed Poynings lands. The young couple seemed content enough in this politically negotiated marriage, with sufficient affection to bind them together.

Beside me, George's brow was now creased in thought.

'Dangerous? Who's to know the answer to that either? It will all depend on how much support Buckingham can drum up. The whispers say that it will begin on St Luke's Day – the eighteenth day of October – in Kent. The Kentish men plan to attack London from the south-east, drawing Richard's attention in that direction as men of the West Country, swelled by Buckingham's Welsh army crossing the Severn, and Henry Tudor's force of Breton mercenaries landing in Devon, will move in from the west. With Richard's attention on Kent, they will fall on him, catching him unawares, and bring down the might of their combined dissatisfaction upon him.'

It all sounded to be well developed in the planning.

'And will this happen?'

'It is rumoured,' he replied carefully. One thought struck me like a hammer blow.

'George!' He slid a glance across to me, an amazingly bland expression that might hide all his thoughts. He was a master at dissembling when he chose. 'Why is it that you know so much about this insurrection that might be mere rumour? Where has the news come from?' I had been aware of no couriers.

'My brother Anthony.'

It sounded innocent enough. But there again, here before me, was Sir George Browne, knighted at Tewkesbury, thus a knight of the body of Edward IV, Sir George, who had carried one of the King's banners at the royal funeral. Here was a loyal Yorkist who knew all the details of an imminent insurrection. Was there treason in him? I remembered Cade's rebellion in Kent, when Robert Poynings had supported it and ended incarcerated, lucky to escape without an axe applied to his neck. It had ended as a bloody affair. Would this be the same? I knew that in the summer months after the death of King Edward, George and other local landowners had met together to discuss the restoration of his sons and freedom for his wife and daughters from sanctuary. Suddenly nothing was as clear as I had believed, and I felt a familiar ripple of fear begin to grow beneath my heart and snatch at my breath.

How much was George not telling me? It would be like him not to worry me.

'Is Anthony certain of this?' I queried. Anthony, George's younger brother, was a frequent visitor, a young man of much intelligence and wit whose company I had grown to like. Built in the image of his brother with a strong body and a shock of dark hair, he had a chatty tongue, bringing news from outside.

'He seems so.'

'Will your own tenants in Kent be involved?' I asked, my tone still as innocent as George's.

'Some will,' he said. 'Show me a Kentish man who is not willing to join rebellion and uprising. A more argumentative rabble when they see an opening to pursue what they believe to be their own rights I have never met.'

I could not let it drop. 'Will it involve *you*?'

He shook his head. 'No need to worry, Eliza. You'll not see me riding out to war.'

It put my mind at ease. There would be no treason in this household. In June, Richard's coronation had been a triumph, after which he had been well received all around the country, particularly in the north. I doubted that, in the face of such popularity, Buckingham would attract too much attention, even in Kent, even from the recalcitrant Kentish populace.

And yet...

There was some coming and going to the castle, messengers who rode in like the wind, then rode out without stopping to take more than a bite and a cup of ale. They were not introduced to me unless I was in the vicinity when they arrived. Wearing no livery, no distinguishing marks, they had speech with George of a private nature.

'Who are they?'

'Couriers. Estate business.'

'Nothing to do with this rising, of course.'

'Nothing like that.'

I thought his refusal to meet my eye ambiguous, but it was outside my remit. He was comforting, placing an arm around my shoulders when he suspected an argument developing between us.

'I understand your concerns, Eliza. Robert lost his life on a battlefield. I have risked mine once. I have no intention of so risking it a second time.'

It was all I needed to restore my contentment, even when the surprising number of visitors continued at our door in the coming weeks. Including one I did recognise and welcomed into my home, Anthony Browne, George's brother. No, it did not trouble me, and my thoughts were given a gentler turn when Edward and Isabel descended on us long before they were expected.

Beware contentment. Beware happiness. Suddenly, it was like a strange recurrence of past events: the men of my household turning over their pieces of armour, their weapons, the vestments and horse armour that had last been used by George at Tewkesbury. George stood in the midst of these various pieces of military equipment in the armoury at Betchworth, my son Edward holding up a gambeson that had seen better days, Anthony inspecting the blade of a once-fine sword that needed the attention of our blacksmith.

The noise and raised voices arrested me. I walked in on them. So preoccupied were they that, for a time, they did not even notice me.

'What are you doing?'

How many women asked their menfolk such a question in these unquiet days?

I read the guilt on Edward's face despite his being adult and governor of his own actions at twenty-four years. Anthony was uncommonly unconcerned at my appearance. I fixed a stare on my husband.

Not again. My blood had chilled, my mouth suddenly as dry as a chalk-stream in drought. Surely they were not preparing for battle? George had said that he would not fight. The old fears returned, as strong as ever. I could not cheerfully wave them off to war as I had once done with Robert, expecting him to return home unscathed. I had done it once with George before Tewkesbury. I could not do so again. At that moment I felt the urge to shriek my rejection of such a plan, making my denial echo from the roof beams. Instead, I dragged my thoughts into sensible array, remembering George's promises.

Besides, to which battle would they march? Was not their loyalty to King Richard unquestionable? Surely it was not this rebellion that had caught George's interest? Was not George content with how things now were? I had not thought that he would be swayed by the rebelliousness of the Kentish men, or by Buckingham's whims. And as for my son, he would surely not.

'Is this a piece of housekeeping?' I asked, as calm as if this were a weekly event.

My husband and my son looked at each other. Anthony continued to run his palm over the obviously blunt blade.

'Yes, in a manner of speaking,' George replied, returning a sword to the side of its companions beside the hearth which had not seen a fire for some months.

'You are going to fight?'

He turned to face me, his expression one of resignation that he must tell the truth.

'Yes. We are going to fight.'

How could I not presume that it would be for the King to put down the Kentish rebels? George was Sheriff of Kent. It was in his interests to preserve peace in the King's name.

'Where is Richard?' I asked. 'Where is the King's army?'

George walked towards me and took my hand. Straightaway I knew the answer.

'We will not be fighting for the King, Eliza. It is not Richard that we will be joining.'

'Who then will you fight for?'

I thought that I had misunderstood him. Would he fight perhaps under the banner of the Duke of Norfolk, one of the King's most fervent allies? I held to that idea until all was lost in George's regretful expression. Oh, no. I had not misunderstood at all.

'We will join the revolt of the Duke of Buckingham. We will lead the rising in Kent against the King.'

'But why?'

'I think that our new king fears my past closeness to King Edward and to his direct heirs, the two young lads. I have already been dismissed from the Surrey bench of justices,' George explained. 'I think that it will not be the last step taken against me. It may be better if I pre-empt it with an attack.' He paused, then added, 'I believe there are others with a stronger claim to the crown than the man who wears it today.'

I did not know any of this, I had no idea of the direction of his thoughts on the competing royal rights of the sons of Edward IV or of Henry Tudor himself. He had not told me. Were all men so secretive? I snatched my hand away, unable to accept what I was hearing. This was nonsense. There would be no good outcome in it.

'Edward!' I stared at my errant son. 'Not you, too!'

'Yes,' he replied with a terrible crispness. 'I am convinced that I should. That we should.'

At least he did not tell me not to worry.

'Have you told Isabel?'

'Not yet.'

'When will you tell her? When you ride through the gate with your liveried force behind you? Are you also going to tell her not to worry?'

'No, but I will. And neither should you.'

'Don't worry?' I rounded on George. 'I lost one husband at St Albans. I have no wish to lose another. Or a son. Why are the men of Kent so convinced that they must join this rebellion?'

Edward remained determined under fire, full of his convictions.

'Some have strong connections with the Woodvilles. Some support the Beauforts, which will bring them into league with Henry Tudor. The Kentish gentry are all hand in glove, and I will join them to bring Tudor home from exile. I doubt there will be a full-scale battle. We will support Henry Tudor, who will come in Buckingham's wake and take the throne.'

'Your father would never have done this. He died for York and yet you would cast yourself into the unknown Tudor camp.'

'Times change, Mother.'

What could I say? Nothing would make any difference. All I could do was watch as they prepared to depart, and worry, as all women would when their menfolk went to war. All I could do was stand at the door. And pray, and keep my two younger children safe at home. They would come home safely. If I prayed enough, they would return home.

'Don't take risks,' I said.

'I must,' George confirmed. 'I will lead the Kentish men. If that entails a risk, then I will take it.'

'I don't understand why you have to become involved at all! Or you!' I swung to face Edward again. Both of them would know of my disfavour, but all I could see was their preoccupation with what lay ahead for them. 'Very well, I accept that you must go. But you will not take Matthew as your squire.'

Our son was fourteen years and of the opinion that he should not be left behind.

'No,' George agreed. 'Matthew will stay here.'

I embraced and kissed them both at the end, remembering that when George returned from Tewkesbury we had met in the middle of the Thames, the water lapping around my feet. How long ago that was. How unimportant, and yet it was a memory that brought me a brief moment of joy as they rode to war, clad impressively in the best armour they could muster, the banners of Poynings and Browne announcing their allegiances, Matthew given orders to remain behind to protect the castle and the womenfolk. Isabel and I watched until they were out of sight. I could not pretend that George was not riding into danger.

'Where will this end?' asked Isabel.

'I know not.'

The night before he left me, climbing into bed at my side, George put into my hands a Book of Hours, little larger than my palm and beautifully bound in gilded leather.

'A peace offering?' I asked, my heart already heavy with fore-boding.

'It is a precious thing, owned by my mother and her mother before her. I had forgotten it,' George admitted, 'and found it wrapped in leather in the corner of a coffer. You should have it. It may give you comfort when you feel bereft. I don't know how often I will be able to send you a message or a courier. Or even how long it will be before we can get this insurrection off the ground. You must stay strong.'

'Pastons always stay strong.'

'I know that they do.' His smile was strained. 'Pray for me, Eliza.'

'I will pray for you.'

As George dressed for battle, I held the book with its jewelled clasp and fragile pages as if it were an object of great mystery and would keep him safe. I clasped it to me as if it were a holy icon as he rode away after a tender leaving of exchanged kisses and embraces.

During the coming days, into weeks, I turned the pages, studying the vividly drawn initial letters and the plates of sacred images in the calendar. It was indeed a precious object. Yet how often, as I turned the pages, did I not see the masterpieces of the craftsman who had created it? Instead, how often did I see the events in my own mind superimposed on the pages, as if telling me of what was happening beyond the walls of my well-defended castle?

This was how my days passed through that terrible month of October, gleaning information where I could, both gossip and informed reporting, painting it with my imagination when the detail was sparse, imagining the events that were far from me but might have such a bearing on my life. I turned the pages in my real Book of Hours, bright pictures of harvesting, of picking apples, of women weaving and gossiping, but I saw instead the bloody progress of this insurrection against the crowned and anointed King Richard, as if my mind's eye dictated what my eyes might see of the brutal reality of war. Armies and bright banners, chivalric soldiers laid waste in a gruesome winnowing.

What would be the future? What would be the final picture?

I did not know. I could not, dare not, envisage it. Anger now fired my fears. Why had they gone, to involve themselves in so unpredictable a project with a man not known for insurrection? What had made them leap from York to Tudor? There had been nothing I could do to stop them, but the guilt lay heavily on me. Sometimes Isabel sat with me, waiting as I did.

'Does it give you no comfort?' she asked. 'You often read your Book of Hours.'

'None. None at all.'

Silence wrapped us around. All news was muffled. It was as if the whole realm was waiting. Henry Tudor had sailed for England, braving autumn storms, but although he might have landed in Dorset, he sensed that all was not well and retired back to the French coast to fight another day. Meanwhile, attainders were passed against King Richard's enemies. Many fled to Brittany, others remained to pay the high price of treachery.

Still no news.

The silence became ominous.

I dared not open the Book of Hours again.

A man rode slowly up to our gates at Betchworth Castle. Even before he reached us Isabel and I were standing on the gatehouse walk, leaning between the crenellations, holding our breath. Matthew was at my side, and his eyesight was better than mine.

'It is not my father. It is not Edward.'

I ran down, Isabel following close at my heels, as the gate was open and he rode in. Matthew was already there when I called out to our visitor.

'Anthony!'

Weary and dishevelled, with little similarity to the man who had ridden out with the two I loved most in this world, he was accompanied by a squire but no escort. He wore no insignia to draw attention to his family name. I forced myself not to question him before he had dismounted. For a long moment he stooped, hands on his thighs as he drew in a deep breath. Then he straightened and looked up.

'I have come to beg refuge from you.'

'And that you shall have.'

I did not even think about it, but walked forward to take his arm and draw him forward. Why would he not tell me what he knew I must need to know?

'Anthony!' I all but shook him.

'It all collapsed into disaster. Buckingham is betrayed and executed. We are being hunted.' His voice croaked with the dust of the road.

My patience was at an end. 'Never mind that. Where is your brother?'

'Hiding with a loyal friend in Maidstone.'

'Blessed Virgin!' The faintest hint of relief touched me. 'Will he be safe there?'

'Yes, until we can get him away. There are orders for his arrest as the leader of the rebel force.'

I had not known that he would be so pre-eminent.

'What about Edward? By the Virgin, Anthony! Do you wish me to die of anxiety?'

His face grey with fatigue, he drew his hands down his cheeks, smudging the dust.

'In God's name, I know not.'

I could feel Isabel trembling at my side.

'Is he dead?'

'I don't know.'

'So you will not know if he is taken prisoner?'

'No.'

'And what of you?' I tried to be compassionate, even as I struggled to keep my mind clear in this deluge of fear.

'They will arrest me, too, if they get their hands on me. That's why I am here...'

At least they were all alive, as far as we could tell. I began to breathe again. So, at my side, did Isabel.

'Come and rest. Then you will tell me all.'

'They'll come here,' Anthony apologised later, when he had eaten and drunk. 'I am sorry I have put you in danger, but I had nowhere else to go.'

427

It confirmed what I knew would happen, that the King's supporters would soon be at our gate, yet I could not turn him away. For George's sake, and for his own, for he had been a good friend, I took him in and prayed that Edward, too, would make his way home.

Was there time to send Matthew and my daughter Mary elsewhere? But where would I send them? Briefly, I wondered where my Paston family stood in this threat to their much-cherished law and order, then pushed it aside. There was nothing to be gained by my worrying about the Pastons. They would fend for themselves in their inimitable self-absorbed style.

CHAPTER FIFTY-TWO

ELIZABETH PASTON BROWNE

Betchworth Castle in Surrey, October 1483

We closed our gates and drew up our drawbridge after all, and waited.

'Allow no one to enter unless it is our own lord,' I ordered. 'Or Master Edward, of course. Gossip to no one.'

Perhaps the royal troops would find easier meat and leave us alone if they could round up enough of the traitors before they went to ground. But they came anyway, early in the morning, soldiers loyal to the King, retainers of the Duke of Norfolk with his banners bright in the clear autumn light, riding along the track to the castle. They would think to discover George. But here was Antony...

'Hide him,' I ordered Isabel, standing once again on the highest viewpoint of my gatehouse.

'Where?' She looked distraught.

'We have planned for this eventuality,' I said as calmly as I could. 'You know what we agreed.'

'Of course.' She blinked as if coming to her senses. 'I know what to do.'

While she went to organise the hiding, all brisk efficiency, despite her earlier panic, I gathered Matthew and Mary. 'What do you say if a soldier asks you if you have seen your father?'

'We say no,' Matthew replied promptly, seeing nothing but the excitement of the moment.

'What do you say, daughter?' I asked Mary who, at twelve years, was really too young for such terrors but must play her part.

'I say no.'

'Good. What do you say if you are asked if your uncle Anthony Browne has been here?'

'No!' they chorused.

'And have you seen your brother, Edward Poynings?'

'No.'

'That is very good. We have not seen any one of them.'

'Even though Uncle Anthony is hiding in—' Mary said.

'Hush!' I silenced her. 'Even though. If the soldiers find him, they will chop off his head.' A desperate thought but it was all I could do, to put fear in them. 'You must guard your tongues. We are quite safe and we will not be harmed.' I caught the slide of immature anxieties in Mary's eye. 'On some occasions it is acceptable to lie, my daughter. This is one of them. God will assuredly forgive you.'

Now I must face the enemy whom I could both see and hear, loudly demanding to be admitted.

'We have come to arrest your husband, the traitor, Sir George Browne.'

Once again, I was leaning through the crenellations of the gatehouse. I looked down at the captain of the little force while he looked up at me. He was polite enough to doff his cap and nod his head in semblance of a polite greeting.

'My husband is not here.'

The politeness died a sudden death.

'Open the gates, mistress. I would not willingly call you a liar, but we will search for ourselves.'

'And if I do not open my gates?'

'We await a larger force with cannon. They could be here by tomorrow. I doubt you are prepared for a siege.'

Of course we were not. Did I believe him? I could not afford to take the risk. I gave the order, because to refuse would be too dangerous. They were chillingly courteous when they entered.

'With your permission we will search, mistress.'

430

'My husband is not here.'

Which, of course, was true. They would read no deceit in my face. Yet they searched, with Isabel returned to my side, the children too.

'You will find me in the chapel,' I informed the captain, 'where I will pray for the safety of all concerned.'

'Better that you pray for mercy from King Richard,' he growled but did not insist on accompanying me.

'Is he safe?' I murmured as the soldiers departed to carry out their orders and we knelt before the altar.

'I know not, but I have tried,' Isabel replied. 'They will have to desecrate the altar to find him.'

The captain returned after a good half-hour of increasing tensions as they combed the vast array of chambers and storerooms of the castle. Their search of the chapel around us was desultory as we knelt in silence, hands clasped, eyes closed in prayer, hardly daring to breathe. The children did not even shuffle. Then the captain was standing over me.

'Dame Elizabeth Browne.'

I looked up, brows raised in haughty query that he should interrupt me at my prayers, but he was unperturbed.

'We cannot find him, mistress, but that does not mean that he will not return here to take refuge. Have you heard from him?'

I stood, genuflected to the altar with bowed head, and turned to him. Would they investigate the incised carvings in so sacred a place? Anthony was secure behind the reredos, not ten feet from where we were conversing, where the space was just large enough to take a grown man. A tapestry of the Crucifixion of Christ completed his holy confinement.

'No, sir. Sir George may be dead, for all I know.'

'So he has not fled abroad.'

'Not to my knowledge. It is, of course, possible. You are wasting your time here, sir.'

He had not asked the children. Thank God he had not asked them. Hardly had the thought entered my mind than he pointed at Matthew, who, to his credit, did not shrink back.

'Are you Sir George's son?'

431

'Yes, sir.'

'Come with me.'

He took Matthew's forearm in a firm grip and drew him to his side, walking out into the courtyard where most of his troop was already mounted. Pushing Matthew to one of his soldiers he gave the order.

'Take this lad up with you.'

'No. You must not!' Seeing what was intended, I ran forward but was held back. The curve of the captain's mouth was not a pleasant one.

'We have here a useful hostage. When you see him, tell your husband that if he wishes to see his heir alive again, then he will hand himself in.'

'But I cannot tell him. He is not here!'

'When he comes, as he assuredly will. We will keep the boy under surveillance in Maidstone. We have a secure prison there, fit for the offspring of traitors.'

There was nothing I could do. My son was already hauled up to sit before the soldier; his face was pale but his composure was admirable as we continued to play out the terrible repercussions of insurrection.

'Don't worry, mistress.' The captain saluted. 'I'll keep him safe.'

'Be brave,' I adjured my son, when I was struggling for my own courage.

'I will. Tell my father I will never bring his name into disrepute.'

They turned to ride from the castle, Matthew straining to look back.

And there was Anthony come from the chapel, having extricated himself from behind the reredos, sword in hand. His eyes were wild, his hair and clothes begrimed, but he strode purposefully to the captain and cast his sword to the ground at his feet.

'I think that it is me that you want.'

The captain surveyed him from head to foot.

'I surmise that you are Anthony Browne.'

'I am Sir George's brother. Take me, not the boy.'

For one long moment I thought that they would take both. It was clearly in the soldier's mind. Then: 'Better a man than a child.

I should commend your honesty.' His eye slid to me. 'He was well hid for we found no trace.'

They took him away.

Did I plead for his release? I did not because I knew it would be to no avail. Did I write to my Paston family for help? I did not. If any such letter were intercepted, my treason would spread like wildfire into the Paston household, making them punishable also. I must deal with this alone.

At least they left Matthew with me. But what to do next? I could not sit at Betchworth Castle, letting the days pass, with no attempt from me to mount a rescue.

Allington Castle in Kent

It was my decision to make. I was subject to intense terror at what I had come to do, and what I would find here. I was not even certain that my visit would be permitted. I asked advice from no one. Margaret would tell me to just get on with it; she had visited her husband John in the Fleet prison without any second thought. But John had not been imprisoned for treason. George had a sentence of death hanging over him. I had to come here.

'I wish to see my husband, Sir George Browne. It would please me if you would take me to him. I have travelled some distance.'

Issuing this demand, I dismounted from my horse in the court-yard of Allington Castle, built on the banks of the River Medway, just outside the town of Maidstone. It was more a fortified manor than a castle, and much neglected so that parts were in disrepair, but it was being used to house some of the rebels from the up-rising. If Edward was also here, then I would be able to rid my heart of two fears.

The captain, slouching in the doorway, cup of ale in hand, did not even bother to scowl. He turned to walk away, back into the shelter of the guardhouse, for the wind was keen. He obviously did not see me, a woman wrapped around in heavy cloak and hood, as a person of any importance, not even worthy of his notice. 'I have no permission to allow visits to the prisoners,' he said.

'Do I look as if I could arrange an escape?' I raised my voice. 'I have come to see my husband. What will it take for me to achieve this?'

He barely halted, looking back over his shoulder.

'What's it worth?'

'How much value do you place on your compassion?'

Seeing the chance of some personal gain in this, his face slightly flushed with what I hoped might be embarrassment, he returned. There was some haggling, undertaken by the captain of my escort, before coin changed hands and I was shown down a draughty passageway to a locked door. There were rats.

'How long?' I asked.

He tilted his chin. 'Half an hour. Longer will cost more.'

'Half an hour and not a minute less.'

My heart beat so loudly that I could barely think, much less bargain. He unlocked the door, pushed it ajar, and I walked in, hearing it locked behind me.

It was no dungeon but neither did it have any semblance of comfort. The castle was as neglected inside as it was out with November cold and damp rising from the stone floor. There was no fire to recompense for the draughts that rattled the shuttered windows. But there was George, my beloved George, perched on the stone window seat so that he might look out to freedom beyond the river. He was wrapped in a thin coverlet from the bed, but visibly shuddering.

'Eliza!'

A mix of shock and despair, not the affection I had hoped for.

'Who did you expect?'

'No one. And not you! You should not be here.'

'Of course I should, after all my efforts. It took me no little time to discover you.'

He had risen, clearly unharmed, except for fading bruises along one cheekbone, and took me in his arms, the coverlet sliding to the floor. Beneath my embrace his body felt spare and his face was gaunt.

'Thank God you have come anyway.'

There was the affection, there was the love as his kisses moved

434

softly over my face, acknowledging the danger of his position but making the most of this one moment of reconciliation after so many weeks. I took a step back, pushing his hair from his forehead. It immediately fell forwards again in rank disarray.

'You look hungry.'

'I am.' He grimaced. 'The food is sparse and not worth the eating. The water in short supply, to drink or to wash with. I must stink of prison.'

We stood silently for a time, hands clasped. How hard it was to speak when all conversation seemed worthless behind this locked door.

'How do I get you out?' I asked eventually.

'I doubt that you can. They have yet to decide what to do with me and the rest of the rebels they managed to capture.'

'I am afraid.'

I had not intended to say it, but I did.

'Don't be. King Richard may decide to win us all back to the fold. Mind you, I'll not go willingly.'

'If you won't, he will not be magnanimous. Anthony was taken. They came for you, to Betchworth Castle, where Anthony had sought shelter with us. He gave himself up so that they would not take Matthew. I don't think that he is here.'

'What of Edward?' George murmured.

We kept our voices low, for fear of ears at the door.

'I don't know. All I could discover was that you were betrayed and had been taken prisoner. So here I am.' From the leather satchel I had brought I took out a book of French poetry, a flask of mead and two mutton pasties. 'I could think of nothing else to bring you that could be carried without drawing attention. I dared not bring a weapon.'

He laughed at the strange combination of offerings.

'All I need is yourself, and your love.'

He had taken hold of my hands once again.

'You have that, as always.'

We sat together on the bed with the mutton pasties and the book pushed aside, savouring every minute. What to say in a half-hour that might be the last for many months, even years?

435

'Will they take you to London?' I asked as the minutes passed and George drank the mead.

'I doubt it. I might have to pay a heavy fine, but they will probably let me go. Our lands might well be attainted, of course – just when I had got them back.'

'We will deal with that. Matthew and Mary are stalwart companions and Isabel, of course, when she is not worried sick.' I turned within his arms to face him. 'I am so sorry that all you hoped for was betrayed.'

His face was drawn and his eyes bleak with memory.

'It all came to nothing. Richard's hold on the throne is even stronger.' I watched as the regrets flickered over his features. 'What is your Paston family doing?'

'Keeping its collective head down at Caistor, I expect. My family knows what is best for its survival.'

'I seem to have stabbed mine in the back with my own knife,' George growled.

The sound of footsteps approached.

'Our time is run out,' I murmured. 'Should I find the Duke of Norfolk and plead for your release? Do I ask Jonty for help?'

'No, dear heart.' There was an urgency about him now. 'Norfolk'll not even give you the time of day, and I think this is beyond the Pastons' clever tongues. Go home. Go back to Betchworth. You can do no good here. It may be that Edward will come to Betchworth when he can, and you should be there to welcome him and arrange his escape.'

The key rattled in the lock.

'We have had so little time together,' I said, my lips against his hair.

'When this is over, we will have all the time in the world,' George promised.

The captain was standing at the door, indicating with a jerk of his chin.

I whispered: 'Always believe that my thoughts and prayers are with you.'

'They will give me strength. It was a fortunate day when Eliza Poynings fell in the dust at my feet.'

436

'I have never regretted it for a moment.' Then I remembered, searching in the safe confinement of my sleeve. 'I have brought this back to you. You will need solace, without company; a solace that poetry may not give you. Bring it back to me when you are free again.'

I pressed my lips against the jewelled clasp of the Book of Hours. George took it and pressed his lips where mine had rested.

'I promise.'

Thus the little book exchanged hands once more, with promise and hope. And then I was shown out, turning for a final glimpse of him, his outline a halo lit by the winter sun through the window, before the door was once more locked.

'Is there a man called Edward Poynings here?' I asked as I retraced my footsteps, scattering the rats once more.

'No Poynings, to my knowledge.'

My worries were as keen as ever.

Leaving more coin for George's care, I rode home, tears chill like iced rain on my cheeks. I doubted that the money would go further than the captain's pockets except to be spent on ale.

'Don't worry, mistress,' were his final words to me. 'It costs too much to keep them here. They'll release him, see if they don't.'

'Yes, of course, they will.'

I cursed them for their treatment of him. I cursed the followers of York and Lancaster alike. Even as I prayed that George would be released and restored to me, it was in my heart that it would take a miracle to achieve it. I was all out of miracles.

CHAPTER FIFTY-THREE

ELIZABETH PASTON BROWNE

Betchworth Castle in Surrey, December 1483

How does a woman discover that her husband is dead? I learned about Robert's demise on the battlefield at St Albans from his squire, who had been with him and seen him hacked down in battle. This time, well into the season of Advent, it was from the lips of a royal herald, sent to inform the widow that Sir George Browne was dead and his estates confiscate. Clad in his bright regalia, all delivered in a flat tone, it was as if the royal official's words meant nothing to me as they flitted through my mind. I had to struggle to hold on to each one, to make them have a meaning for me as a whole. If it was any consolation to me, news of George's death had been sufficiently important to merit the dispatching of a royal herald to his widow. It was no consolation at all.

I knew what the royal messenger would tell me, even before he opened his mouth.

'I am here today, mistress, to inform you that Sir George Browne has paid the ultimate price of insurrection with a traitor's death.'

As cold as winter. Did he truly need to read it from the document, heavy with seals? As cold as was my blood in my veins.

Matthew stood with me, my hands curved over his shoulders, even when he flinched as my fingers dug in. And Isabel had come to join me, too, dreading any mention of Edward. I could barely absorb the enormity of this appalling death, my heart thudding at the extent of my loss, yet to my inner pride, my composure was supreme.

'Where did he die?' I asked.

'On Tower Hill,' the herald replied as if surprised that I did not know.

'Then he was executed. At the will of King Richard.' I made it a statement.

'Yes, mistress, on the third day of December. As the leader of the Kentish traitors who rose up against their rightful king, parliament condemned him under an Act of Attainder. A trial was held in Westminster Hall.'

'Were all the rebels so punished?'

'No, mistress. Only the leaders, such as Sir George Browne, were brought to trial.'

A very speedy one, I presumed inconsequentially. I had heard no noise of it, or even his removal from Maidstone. I did not ask where his body might be. The herald supplied me with some of the news with relish. George's head has been displayed on one of the gates into London. I breathed deeply to quell the rising nausea, turning my mind into less painful paths because I could not tolerate imagining such a terrible end to the life of so good a man.

'Am I being dispossessed? Are my children dispossessed?'

How many times would this happen to me?

'It may be good policy, mistress, to be prepared to move from here when the King grants the Browne estates to a new loyal owner. Perhaps you should return to your own family.'

To him there was no difference between losing an estate and losing a husband. To me it was everything. Later I could not remember what I said to him. Even if I made any sense. I supplied him with bread and ale, for he was not my enemy, and sent him on his way to deliver his devastating burden to some other unsuspecting family. It was not his fault that his news was the worst it could possibly be.

'What of Anthony Browne?' I asked as he prepared to ride out.

'I know nothing of him. He still lives, to my knowledge. Although if I had my way—'

I interrupted him. 'And Edward Poynings?'

He shrugged. 'I know not. You seem to have a veritable nest of traitors here, mistress, if I might say.'

He could say whatever he wished. It had no impact on my stone-like heart. Matthew fled to his own place of isolation, to mourn in private, while I knelt in the chapel, but there was no comfort. Not for any of us.

Except for me there was one tiny spark. The herald had given me a book.

'I was told that this was to be returned to you, mistress.'

It was brusquely done, but how compassionate, for he could have sold it to his own benefit or prised out the jewels on the cover. I opened the clasp and then the cover, and there was the little Book of Hours with my name inscribed on the first page.

'It belongs to you, mistress.'

'Yes,' I said. 'It does.'

George had written my name – *Elizabeth Paston Browne, Betchworth Castle* – in his mother's book so that it might find its way back to me. I pressed my lips to the spot where our lips had touched, so many weeks ago when we had made our farewell and our promises. He had not forgotten me, and I would not forget him.

When this is over, we will have all the time in the world.

How wrong we had been. We had no time at all. The traitor's axe had robbed us of it. How could I mourn such a loss? It still had no meaning for me. How could I believe that my worst fears had been brought to my door? I would never see George Browne again.

I forced myself to think clearly, to accept what must be accepted, as I considered the best words to use to tell Mary that her father was dead, another pain that was as sharp as a knife in my side. Where was Edward? I feared that he was dead, too. How could a woman tolerate such pain? I did not think that I could. For a long moment I closed my eyes to block out the world around me that had brought me such agony.

Then I opened them again.

Even in the midst of my anxieties, I had a mind to make a visit. A visit that was long overdue.

CHAPTER FIFTY-FOUR

MARGARET MAUTBY PASTON

The Paston House in Norwich, December 1483

The woman who stood on my threshold was a ghost from the past, one that shivered over my skin in a moment of uncertain disbelief, that became sharp and clear-cut when she smiled.

'Elizabeth!'

'Meg!'

No one had called me Meg for years. It stirred my turgid emotions so that I held out my arms and she stepped into them, all the troubles of my heart strangely soothed. I laughed softly, interested that joy and pleasure had not entirely abandoned me as pain and advancing years claimed me.

'You are right welcome, Elizabeth,' I said against her cheek.

'Am I no longer Eliza to you?'

'Of course you are. It is so many years...'

'Why have we been apart for so long?'

Our lives had moved in such different directions but once we had been as close as true sisters, sharing the trials and tribulations of young women who failed or succeeded in achieving an acceptable marriage. While Sir George had joined the Buckingham rebellion, Jonty had considered three options: to join the rebellion, to fight for the King when summoned to do so by the Duke of Norfolk, or to sit tight and do neither. To my relief Jonty had chosen the latter, and so we had weathered the storm better than most.

'Come in. Come in where we will not be disturbed.' Taking her hand I pulled her into the parlour, dark with the winter light;

I was astonished at how delighted I was to see her. 'What are you doing in Norwich?'

'Come to see you.'

'Why?'

She lifted her shoulder in a little shrug, as if she needed to make an excuse. 'To talk about the past.'

'How we have aged.'

We regarded each other, noting, but accepting, the signs of the passage of time. Skin had lost its lustre, hands were no longer fit to attract attention with jewelled rings, greying hair was best hid within a coif or soft cap. And yet there was such life within our grasp, our desire to tell old stories.

'I see that you are not so old that you cannot still control your household,' Eliza said.

The maids had been sent running for wine and to mend the fire for our comfort.

We talked. We talked of our lives, our sons, our hopes. Our happiness in marriage and grief as we became widows and our children died too early. Of Eliza's fervent hope that her son would survive, for she knew not where he might be. Of the hardship brought by ownership of property – for Eliza, inheritance from both husbands still hung in the balance. We would not give up. We would fight to secure what was ours. Perhaps our eyes glittered with unshed tears in the firelight as the room dimmed even more towards evening. It was a moment of warmth for both of us to be able to talk freely, accepting that we would not be judged. It drew me into talking of my daughters, a weight that dragged at my heart.

'We value our sons who fight battles and win cases in the law courts, but I have spent my life worrying about my daughters. Does not every family? A good marriage is essential if we are to preserve our social status. One false step, one unfortunate marriage, and we become figures of ridicule and common gossip, the family tumbling down the ladder into the gutter. Margery and Anne challenged me and I think I did not always treat them kindly and with understanding,' I confessed as I looked back over the years.

Eliza's smile was wry with remembrance. 'I swear you did not beat them.'

'I did not. But no, I was not always kind. Distance makes me see it with more clarity. It was as if Margery tore the careful weaving of my Paston tapestry from my loom and ripped it into shreds. All my plans for her marriage! To wed the bailiff was more than I could bear. Sometimes I am weighed down with such guilt. I should never have listened to Father Gloys, but a priest is a powerful adversary when fighting the battle against sin. I should have loved Margery first, and condemned her in a gentler frame of mind. And now she is dead.'

Eliza leaned forward and touched my hand with a gentleness I rarely received from my close family. Perhaps they thought I did not need it. Perhaps, a lowering thought, they decided I did not deserve it. Eliza's gesture wrung my heart.

'Was Margery happy? In the end?'

'I think so. Her three sons gave her great joy. But no thanks to me.' I pleated the wool of my skirt as if it were the most important task in the world. 'We had a reconciliation of sorts. I should have done it years ago.'

'And Anne?'

'Is desperately unhappy. I can do nothing to help her, only pray for a child to give her contentment.' I looked away from her. 'We will not weep.'

'No, we will not weep, but we are allowed to be a little regretful.'

I smiled ruefully. 'You made a fine life, Eliza. I could not have hoped for better for you.'

'Nor I.' She sighed. 'As long as Edward returns. Some days I am without hope.'

I stood, refilled her cup and bent stiffly to kiss her brow. 'Will you stay?'

'I will, I will see Jonty and his bride.'

'You will enjoy Gilly.' I lifted my chin. 'Here they are—'

There echoed sounds of an arrival in the house, urging us to stand, clutching each other's ageing hands for just one moment before company would force us to act with more dignity.

443

'I have made my will,' I whispered.

'I would love to read it!'

'It is not for anyone's eyes until I am dead!' I found myself making a confession, which I had not intended. 'There has been much heartbreak and heart-searching in my life, but I think that I would do the same again,' I said. 'I made mistakes, yet how could I have allowed my daughters free rein, to make the worst of choices? I upheld my duty to the family to the end. The Paston name is held in high regard in this town. That is what they will say of me when I am gone from this earth.'

'We will not consider such an eventuality, dear Meg!' Eliza's smile was a bright gleam in the shadows. 'We both know the meaning of victory and defeat. I have lost two husbands, to my utter regret, but I will fight to my death to keep the inheritance of my children intact.'

How I had missed such close companionship with a woman of my family, the easy discourse, the exchange of private feelings.

'You must definitely stay and eat with us,' I said. 'We will make it a celebration. I will even sacrifice one of my swans for the event.'

Eliza's eyes shone with long-forgotten humour. 'Excellent. How could I refuse? Do not all Paston women rise admirably to the occasion?'

'They do,' I agreed. 'But don't tell Jonty that. He still believes that he rules the roost. He has no idea how strong a will Gilly has!'

I did not condemn a swan to the roasting spit. Of course I did not. This was no celebration, Jonty and Gilly wisely leaving us alone, merely a sharing of simple platters between two women of some age and much experience while memories were relit to be laughed at and cried over. It could not have been better.

CHAPTER FIFTY-FIVE

ELIZABETH PASTON BROWNE

Betchworth Castle in Surrey, January 1484

It was in the dark cold of a January night, too cold, it seemed, for frost or snow, when the barn owl flew ghost-like in the courtyard. On such a night, after I had returned from Norwich, Edward rode up to my gatehouse, that was probably no longer my gatehouse. Recognised by my guards, he entered as silently as a mouse aware of the hunting owls. I was awakened. I had long since abandoned my Book of Hours, hiding the pictures, fearing what my mind would imagine in them. Fear of blood and death troubled my days and nights. By the time I came down the stairs, my son was sitting at a rough chestnut table in the kitchen, spooning up a bowl of thick venison broth as if he had not had a square meal in a month. A heel of coarse bread was half-eaten beside him. It was such a mundane occurrence that for a moment it took my breath.

Edward was alive. My son had returned to me. He was here under my protection, eating my meat. My cook, inclined to be irritable when wakened, had been quick to see my son's need. I smiled my thanks as he left us alone.

I sat, choosing a stool across the board from Edward, determined not to overwhelm him with all the emotion that had swept over me, knowing that he was not dead. He would not thank me for weeping over him. A thought came to me. I should have woken Isabel; I should send for Isabel now. It was her right to be here and it would soothe her own fears, but not yet, only after I had obtained some hard facts, before any strong feelings were allowed to hold sway. My son was sitting here before me; filthy and dishevelled, as if he had been living in a ditch, leaner in the face than he had been, but indubitably alive, wiping crumbs from his mouth with the back of his hand.

'Edward.'

His smile, oh, so familiar, was crooked, his lips cracked from the cold, as he licked his fingers. 'I am not dead.'

'Thank God.'

The smile had quickly vanished to be replaced by a harsh reality. All his dreams, whatever they had been, that had taken him to join the men of Kent, had died a cruel death. His face was engraved with lines of which I had no recollection, the youthful vibrancy was gone and I mourned it. But he was here. His father Robert had never returned from war.

Oh Robert, I am so sorry. You would not want this for your son. He has lost his lands and now his dreams. I do not know what I can do for him.

I touched Edward's hand that rested on the table, his fingers curved around the cup of ale as one of the servants, aroused from bed, brought a platter of cold roast meat and placed it before him.

'Are you injured?'

I stretched out to touch an abrasion on his forehead but he flinched away.

'No. It is nothing.' I knew that I must not fuss over him. 'You know that Sir George is dead.'

It was a brutal way to break it if I did not know, but needs must.

'Yes. I know.' Determinedly, deliberately, I gave no reaction. 'I have been told.'

'Did you see him?'

'Yes. They let me see him in Maidstone. For which I will be everlastingly grateful, although I cursed them at the time.'

Edward laughed softly. 'I might have known that you would insist on seeing him.' Then the bright emotion died in an instant and his explanation was savagely brief. 'We fled when there was no hope and Buckingham was taken. Some were caught and rounded up. Some, I think, managed to get to France. Sir George was captured and met his end on Tower Hill. Something my own father escaped after Cade's rebellion.'

'Yes.'

The old numbness returned. Robert's early adventures had been a tale much told in our household when he had fought with Jack Cade, ending up imprisoned, but granted a pardon and his life. No such good fortune for George Browne. I felt Edward's eyes on my face and looked up. There was an anxiety there, that I would not be able to withstand the news he brought.

'Don't worry,' I said, swallowing against any further emotion. 'I will not weep. I knew of George's execution. I have wept all my tears for now, and I will not inflict them on you.'

Edward nodded in silent understanding. 'Sir George probably saved my life. Did you know? Of course you would not.' Edward had pushed aside the platter now. 'Sir George gave me his better horse and told me to save my own skin. He said he would meet up with me here – and with you. He was coming home. We tried to stay together but we were separated. And then I could do nothing to save him. The forces loyal to the King under the Duke of Norfolk were too strong and we did not have the numbers to resist.' He was silent for a long moment. 'It was badly planned. Too many of the local magnates remained loyal to the King. We started the rebellion too early. We should have waited until Buckingham came closer to London, but then that would never have happened anyway. With Buckingham's death.'

I saw the despair, heard it in his merciless summing up. He was far away, reliving the blood and death of an insurrection that went so badly wrong. And I had been wrong. Tears tracked down my cheeks, at the suffering of these brave men. George had sacrificed himself for my son. He might have put himself in harm's way so that my son could escape and live. How would I ever know the answer to that? How would I not weep?

'Sir George took refuge in Maidstone, but someone spoke against him,' he said at last. 'He was arrested and then there was no hope.'

The silence engulfed us again, broken only by the intermittent crackle of the fire that had been stirred into life and the rustle of my own sleeves as I wiped away the tears.

'What has happened to Anthony?' Edward asked.

'I do not know. He was taken from refuge here.'

A small voice interrupted. 'He saved me from being taken away by the soldiers.' Matthew had crept in.

'You should not be here,' I admonished. 'You should be in bed.'

'Let him stay. Is he not part of the story of this disastrous revolt?'

Edward's smile was bitter indeed while I told him of Anthony's brief stay with us, hiding him behind the altar, and the outcome while Edward made room for Matthew on the settle beside him and handed him a piece of bread.

'All I can tell you is that Anthony is not dead,' Edward reassured me. 'George was the only Kentish man to meet the axe, as the leader.'

It was not much of a reassurance.

Matthew broke the dread silence. 'Did you fight beside my father?'

'I did. He was a brave man. As I have just told your mother, he probably saved my life. He gave me his horse.'

'But he is dead.'

Raw anguish pushed itself into the room, for Matthew and for me.

'Yes, he is dead but with an honourable name. Now it is for you to carry it on. To stand for yourself as the heir and for your sister. Your mother will be beside you.'

Edward's smile was barely a twist of his mouth, but it was nonetheless a smile to encourage my son.

'Was it very bad, Edward?' I asked.

'Yes. Very bad.' He did not try to hide it. 'Norfolk's forces gave no quarter. But then we would not have expected it.'

'What have you done since?' I asked, to bring him back to me, to dispel some of the bloody images that clearly haunted him. 'You look half starved.'

He gulped down another mouthful of ale. 'Not so, although my armour sits loosely on me. What have I been doing? Keeping one step ahead of Norfolk's men. I moved from one friendly house to the next, mostly under cover of darkness. I dared not stay long in one place although I discovered plenty of friends. Nor could I send you a message. Too dangerous. Buckingham thought he knew his friends but one of them betrayed him. It was his servant Ralph Bannister, a man whom he had known and trusted since childhood. Trust has its limitations. Bannister informed the King's men and Buckingham was picked up and taken to Salisbury – and I am sure that you know the rest. I could not risk staying under a strange roof or putting them in danger, so I made my way here. They will be searching for me. The parliament that condemned Sir George attainted me as a traitor, and my remaining estates are confiscate.'

What could I say? Any comment that came into my head was of no value. If he was caught, he would be executed. All our property was stripped away. I gave my son the only reassurance that leapt into my mind.

'I will hide you here. You will be safe. Our people will not betray you.'

I made to rise, to make preparations, to warn the servants.

'No, I have other plans.' He took hold of my wrists to hold me still, pulling me back to my place. 'I cannot sit idly by and watch for royal troops approaching. I was willing to fight for a cause. I think that cause is not yet dead but will be taken up for the House of Lancaster by Henry Tudor. I will give my allegiance to him.'

I was not convinced. I wound my hands around his, holding tight, as if I would keep him here by physical force. How could I accept that he would go to war again? How could any mother send her son to fight with her blessing?

'I cannot let you leave and live the life of a homeless vagrant, always on the watch for those who will take you prisoner. I cannot do that, to worry every day from dawn to dusk that you might be hacked down on sight or given an execution without trial, by some local lord who is keen to impress the King.'

But Edward released his hands from mine.

'I cannot stay, Mother. It would be unforgivable if you or Sir George's children suffered more in my name.' He ruffled Matthew's hair. 'They will come looking for me, of course. I came only to eat a good meal,' he turned to grin at the servant who was still hovering, 'and to reassure you that I am still alive. I need money and clothes. Don't ask me to stay. I will only disobey you.'

The grin was turned on me, lightening the engraved lines that had marred his youth. I would not ask again what he had suffered.

'Where will you go?' I asked instead, recognising his father's strength of will. Of course, he had plans.

'To Brittany. I will cast my lot in with Henry Tudor.'

It was not a surprise to me. I must be thankful that he had come here first before taking ship. How long would he be lost to me? How was it possible to lose so much that I loved?

'I don't think that I can bear it,' I said with harsh honesty.

'Yes, you can. You are a Paston by blood. You can withstand any hurt that fate throws at you. Better that I work to return from the safety of Brittany than risk a certain arrest and execution if I remain here.'

I was not convinced. 'But that might mean a lifetime of exile.'

'Not so. I think Tudor will return before too long, and I will come with him. Why wait and allow King Richard to become entrenched with strong support? Better to attack and meld together all those dissatisfied with his reign and his claim to the throne. It may be one year, it may be two, but I do not see myself living across the water for ever.'

So confident, without any evidence whatsoever that Tudor would return. Edward had thought and planned in those days when his life was under threat. I could not stand in his way.

'Then you must go with my blessing, and in the safe keeping of the Blessed Virgin.' Pragmatic to the last, I called on all my Paston reserves when I had been given an ultimatum by the son who held my heart in his hands. 'How will I know what you are doing?' It seemed that I was destined to live as if my son were truly dead.

'I will get word. But you must wait in patience. Don't move out of this place, whatever you do. The Browne estates may be attainted, but don't move until you have to. Until you have a siege on your doorstep.'

'I will not. I have faced this before. I will cling to these estates with all my power.' I dredged up all the courage to which I could lay claim. 'If I fail, I may have to take refuge under a Paston roof again. I would not seek that, although I doubt Jonty and his wife, or even my brother William, would turn me away. Margaret would certainly take me in.' We faced each other in the shadowed reaches of my kitchen. 'God keep you safe, my son.'

'And you.'

I gave him all the money I could find and my blessing and sent him off to find his fortune in Brittany with Henry Tudor, knowing that he might never return.

'Stay tonight at least. Sleep at ease in your own bed. Make your peace with your wife, who will be more than sorry to see you go.'

'I will. But I will be gone on the morrow before you rise from your own bed.'

He kissed my hands, my cheeks, where tears had begun to fall once more. Then I sent for Isabel and left them alone. Isabel would be the one to wave him farewell. Meanwhile, I sat in my chamber, awake, waiting. How could I have slept? Eventually I heard him go, the hooves of his horse clattering on the bridge then disappearing into the coming dawn. With no one to see or comfort me, I wept inconsolably. I seemed to have wept more in these past weeks than in the whole of my life.

I remained isolated at Betchworth in the coming months, but I was not without a purpose. Edward had considered me well up to this task. I would not relinquish all without a fight, although the odds had grown against me. Edward had been attainted in absentia.

To whom should I turn? There were no doubts in my mind. My man of business, loyal John Dane, who had been with me since the years of my first widowhood. Old now and spare but as incisive as ever in his thinking. I would trust him with my life, and Edward's.

'What can be achieved from all of this?' I asked him when he travelled down to Betchworth to talk with me. 'What is the best that we can achieve?'

'Your own security, and some land that will keep you with income until we see what the future might hold.'

'Until Edward can return.'

'Yes. We will hold on to that hope. We will seek to have your jointure manors in Kent and Sussex restored to you. You can leave it to me, mistress.'

'Will it matter that my husband is executed and my son attainted? It is a heavy pall of treason hanging over us.'

'But you are an innocent widow with young children to support. I think that King Richard will not be without compassion.'

'I wish that I was as assured as you appear to be. I think that he might execute the lot of us.'

But I stopped weeping. Of what value were tears? Time enough, if I never saw Edward again. Meanwhile, I turned a stoic face to the future.

Resilience.

That was all that was demanded from me.

It was the word that I would have engraved on my tombstone.

CHAPTER FIFTY-SIX

MARGERY (GILLY) BREWS PASTON

The Manor of Mautby in Norfolk, November 1484

It seemed to me that the Paston households would never be the same again; admirable enough in their smooth running, but like a cunningly wrought mosaic, fatally damaged, with the most important tessera missing from the centre.

Mistress Margaret Mautby Paston was dead on the fourth day of November in the year 1484 after an envious life-span of sixty-two years. The woman who had held together the Paston family, who had fought and striven, who had been recognised far and wide as the Paston Captainess, had passed from this earth. What a space she would leave in our family, in the families of Norfolk.

The task was now mine, to take the weight onto my shoulders. Would I be as capable? I considered my inheritance, both good and bad, as we travelled to Mautby when the news reached us. I lacked the same skills in matters of business as Mistress Margaret had at her fingertips, but I could learn. I hoped that I might have more tolerance of my children than Margaret had sometimes shown for hers. All in all, Mistress Margaret had striven for justice; I trusted that I could do the same.

'What are you thinking?' Jonty grumbled as the blustery wind whipped his cloak and stirred his horse into an uneasy canter which he controlled with a curse and a firm hand.

'That I will never live up to your mother's standards,' I said, struggling to keep up with him, pushing my little mare with my heels.

Jonty grimaced. 'Argumentative, combative, not always easy to live with? I would say that might be a blessing for both of us.'

'Yet I will speak for her,' I said. 'Your mother welcomed me into the family with true affection. You cannot argue against it.'

'Nor will I.' His expression softened. 'She recognised the perfect wife for me when I told her that my love for you was an intransigent thing. My mother barely knew my father when she wed him, but by the end she accepted that love holds a marriage together, strengthens it. God's Blood! Why could my mother not die in the height of summer? This is poor travelling weather!'

'We will travel together. Love will bind us, whatever the future will bring.'

My words were scattered like leaves in the wind, unheard, but it did not matter. I knew them to be a great truth, and so would Jonty as the years passed.

We stood by the bed in her chamber at Mautby: Mistress Margaret, her hands folded on the embroidered bedcover, the lines on her thin face smoothed out, her hair neatly confined in a linen coif, looked at peace now for perhaps the first time in years.

'You and I are the head of this family now,' said Jonty.

'Does it feel a burden to you?' I asked, interested to know.

He shook his head without hesitation. 'No. My mother has been ailing for some time, even though she might have been reluctant to admit it, and since Sir John's death it has been my burden to carry. Besides, I have you at my right hand to help and guide me. And to scold.' He stretched and touched my hand across the body.

'I will scold when necessary,' I agreed.

Furthermore, I would take over the record from those very capable hands, because it needed to be written. She would not approve, of course. Mistress Margaret never approved of any woman stepping into her shoes, but now the decision was mine. Besides, my writing was better than hers, more well formed, whatever she said. Jonty placed gentle fingers against his mother's cheek and bowed his head.

'And now to business.'

He wasted no time, but that was the Paston way. Within minutes

Jonty and I sat facing each other, a scarred table between us, wit-ness of much business both good and bad over the years, and now on it a document of some weight. John spread out the separate pages. Without interruption, I left him to read through it. His reading was quicker than mine. Sometimes he smiled, then there was a frown, and even a guffaw of laughter.

'Well, she left nothing to chance,' he said, clearly marvelling at the detail of what his mother had written.

'Did you know of it?'

'No. She could have a strong secretive streak in her when she wished. She has been adding to this for years, looking at the change in hand.'

He turned the pages towards me but I shook my head, even though I enjoyed his willingness to include me. I might read it later, but now I would leave it to his logistical mind.

'Will she be buried in Norwich? Or at Bromholm next to your father?'

'Neither.' John actually laughed aloud, although he touched the signature and seal with some kindly reverence. 'My mother is returning to her ancestors. She fought like a cat for her kittens to safeguard the Pastons, but she never forgot that she came from a family of far more pre-eminence. She never forgot her ancestors of good birth. She decided that she would be amongst those ancestors to be buried, not the Pastons.' He looked at me. 'Should I feel slighted by this?'

I shook my head. 'Your mother loved you dearly, even if she rarely told you. It is her choice where she will be laid to rest.'

'Listen to this.' John translated the instructions into his own words. 'My mother will be buried in the south aisle of Mautby church. She has made a clear note of the stone which will mark her grave and must be completed within a year.' He smiled again but it was bittersweet, for it roused a memory of his beloved brother as well as his mother. 'She had bitter memories of my father's unfinished tomb since Sir John was always too busy to complete it. It's disgraceful. I think it might still be incomplete.'

'Perhaps you should go and look. We will both go.'

'Yes. Meanwhile, my mother has put this charge of arranging her resting place on me.'

He read on.

'There are many individual bequests, as you would expect. It will please the family.'

'Who has got the swans?' I asked. I really did not want them.

'Not us! Listen! My brother Edmund has been the fortunate recipient.' Edmund had at last settled into marriage and legal work, enhancing the Paston name. 'Our mother has willed him some silver plate and a feather bed and a small income from her lands. For his wife Catherine there is a fine purple girdle and assorted kitchenware. Not something that will fill her with joy. But listen to this: Edmund's son, her grandson, Robert, gets her swans!'

'I hope he values them. They take enough looking after and keeping safe from the fox.'

With a huff of breath, Jonty continued, running his finger down the page. 'Anne will receive some of the silver plate, too, only small stuff since, if I recall correctly, the large pieces were sold or given as bribes. Anne has also been left a girdle, a primer, enamelled silver beads, a bed and again an assortment of pots and pans.' He ran his finger on down the page. 'For my brother Willem, the rest of the small silver plate items, a feather bed and one hundred marks so that he might buy as much land as may be had for the money. She is generous indeed.'

He paused for a long moment, his finger stilled again.

'Now here's what I did not expect. She has left ten marks for the daughter of Constance Reynforth.'

Of course. Sir John's illegitimate daughter.

'She was family, I suppose.'

'And my mother could be surprisingly generous, even when she claimed that she had no coin to keep the wolf from the door.' He paused. 'Well, now!'

'What is it?' Now I was peering at the document, wishing that he would make haste rather than offering tantalising glimpses.

'This is even more surprising, but indeed I am right glad. There is twenty pounds for John, Margery and Calle's eldest son.'

'Oh …' I thought about that. 'I think it an excellent decision. Do you suppose that she regretted the rift at the end?'

'Who's to know? Perhaps this is to show that she had forgiven Margery's defiance after all these years.'

'I am sorry that Margery is not alive to hear it from her mother's lips. May she rest in peace.'

John proceeded to rush through the rest. Gifts for Mistress Margaret's servants, her religious and charitable donations, bequests to churches on her own manors. And then her tenants, who were to receive a few pence each. And, finally, the sad inmates of the leper houses at the gates of Norwich and Yarmouth.

Jonty sat back. I leaned forward, for I had seen what he had done.

'What about you? What about us? You have not mentioned us.'

Jonty's smile was soft with pleasure.

'All the Paston estates come to me.'

I nodded. 'As it should be.'

He stretched his arms above his head as if shuffling off relief, then folded them across his chest in a masterful manner.

'She has left no complications, for which I am heartily relieved. All the Paston and Mautby acres and what is left of the Fastolf inheritance is now consolidated in my ownership. I also have the silver-gilt standing cup I have always admired, and the six silver goblets. And for you, Mistress Gilly, you have not been forgotten, for I swear that she loved you as much as do I. Her Mass book and altar cloths and silver vessels to hold bread and wine at the Eucharist. And there are one hundred marks for our children, William and Elizabeth. I am named as chief executor to divide all that is left between her living children.'

We sat in silence for a little time, the final document of Margaret's long and turbulent life lying between us.

'I suppose that you must get on with it,' I said.

'I suppose that I must.'

On a day when the stone slabs in the churchyard were thick with frost, Mistress Margaret Mautby Paston was laid to rest, as she had made perfectly clear in her will, in the south aisle of the church at Mautby, the last heir of the Mautby line of which she was so proud. On her grave was to be engraved the Mautby arms, in pride of place in the centre, impaled with those of her ancestors and present family, shown to a lesser degree: Paston, Berney, Loveyn and Beauchamp.

'Can it all be done in a year?' I whispered to Jonty as the coffin was lowered into the vault, impressed by the number and rank of people who had come to express their own apparent sorrow and farewells.

'The stone to mark the grave can be, but not the rest of it,' Jonty growled. 'My mother has said that the aisle where her tomb will lie is to be newly roofed, newly leaded, with new glass in the windows. Not only that, but the walls must be heightened to allow more light and space to accommodate her grave. Can you imagine? It will take much work.'

'Which will be yours to arrange, I suppose. To the combined glory of the church and of Mistress Margaret.' A thought crossed my mind. 'Did your mother leave a bequest to pay for all of this? Or did she leave it to your sense of duty?'

'Of course,' he replied, his gaze on the twelve men, her poorest tenants, who at Mistress Margaret's behest, stood around the coffin, clothed in white with white hoods, and torches lit. I considered it a true gesture of Mistress Margaret to be escorted to her grave in such extravagant style. 'She left money for the rebuilding, and I am to receive the sum of ten pounds for my troubles. But it must be my groaning coffers that pay for Masses for her soul for seven years. Such a sting in the tail should not surprise me.'

'The church of Mautby will remember her name for ever.'

'I think that everyone in Norwich will remember her name, with or without an escutcheon. She was not a woman to cower in a corner.'

The interment of Mistress Margaret was as serene and as dignified as befitted her in life. I thought that she would have been highly satisfied. When all else was forgotten under the weight of years, the church here at Mautby would recall her name with reverence. Exactly as she had planned. She would be triumphant at the prospect. With a gentle hand, in passing, I stroked the head of one of the little carved griffins on the end of a pew, unable to repress a smile at this choice of a Paston symbol with its powerful claws and strong wings. Was not a griffin renowned as a protector of its young and its wealth? So had Margaret Mautby Paston been throughout her long life. It was my intention to be carved in the same image.

Blessings given and received, Jonty and I walked out into the churchyard where the ground was still frost-hard and the rooks huddled silently in their roost in the elms. While Jonty discussed money and escutcheons with the priest, I allowed my thoughts to wander, then focus. A little breath of wind had stirred, lifting the edges of my veil. Suddenly it was as if Mistress Margaret herself stood beside me. I knew exactly what she would be saying, claiming my attention with her sharp eyes and caustic expressions. There were things for me to do. It was as if she was inscribing the list on the top of the tomb slab in front of where we stood.

Make sure that you visit Anne, who still has no child to take her mind off her ills. Do not allow her to forget that she is a Paston with a will of her own. Yelverton may not be enamoured of the Pastons, but he has given her rank and security. What more could a bride ask for? Then there is Jonty's uncle William, still refusing to loosen his grip on Paston estates which do not belong to him. Use some feminine charm on him if Jonty cannot cleave his ambitions in two with a sword. Send him one of your noxious ointments to ease the pain in his sore hip. It might improve his temper.

I found myself smiling, inappropriate as it was at an interment. I would indeed send him my ointment, a rare mixing of bacon fat with grease from a neutered boar, pounded with wax and incense as well as ground wheat and rye grain, all spread on a piece of thin leather and applied to the afflicted part twice daily...

Do not forget Elizabeth, Mistress Margaret was saying, drawing my attention back in a manner with which I was completely familiar. *She is another Paston who has escaped from the fold and needs succour. She will benefit from advice if her son Edward does not return. She will miss him dreadfully but will never ask for help.*

As for your increasingly-slippery-Uncle-William-by-marriage, Jonty will need no reminding because he is well aware of the continuing problem.

459

William still wants to get his hands on any Paston manor that is weakly defended. Don't let him do it. It is high time that he came to terms with his losses. Might you cultivate William's Beaufort wife? She seems a woman of good sense. Most informed decisions in a household have the woman's fingerprints all over them.

'Well, that will keep me occupied for the next decade,' I murmured.

It was as if Margaret inhaled sharply at my side as she pronounced:.

If you wish to be Dame Margery Paston, enjoying damask and velvet and gem-studded collars nestling in the fur at your neck, or a clever wire and gauze veil construction for a hennin, then you must encourage Jonty to seek Court promotion. Why not a knighthood?

Why not indeed? I would enjoy silk and jewels.

Keep a contact with Richard Calle. I did ill by him. He was a good husband to Margery and their children have a claim on you, even though Calle is remarried. Mistress Anne Haute is sadly lost to us. Not that she was ever one of us, which I now regret.

I sighed a little. 'Is that all?'

I would be happy if you make sure that Edmund's little son gives sufficient care to my swans. Do not expect Jonty to keep a weather eye on all that needs to be woven into the new Paston tapestry. He won't do it. Men rarely do. You will be the one to spin and weave with all the skill you have.

With a shower of melting frost from the tree above my head, I sensed that I was alone again. Margaret had completed her instructions, having placed them all on my shoulders. What a weight of responsibility they would be. Nor was I particularly gifted at weaving and spinning. What was Mistress Margaret's favourite statement when faced with impossible odds?

'I am a woman of infinite resource.'

It would become mine. I would take on the responsibility for future Pastons, and not merely through a sense of duty. Mistress Margaret would be proud of me. I repeated the statement aloud.

'What is it? Who are you talking to?' Jonty, stepping through the grass, his shoes crunching, to stand at my side, did not wait for my answer, nor would I wish to explain that I was conversing with

460

Mistress Margaret's shade. 'All is finished here, except for serving warm ale to the mourners to thaw them out. Dear Gilly, you look most severe and contemplative.'

'I have been thinking,' I said.

Jonty slid a glance in my direction and pulled my hand comfortably through his arm.

'Then you had better tell me.'

'Perhaps we should be John and Margery now, since you are head of the family. Now that we must adopt a life of honourable propriety and staid behaviour, should our given names not reflect it?'

Transferring his arm to around my shoulders to pull me even closer, Jonty laughed, another most unsuitable expression of joy for a funereal gathering. It scattered the rooks from their roosts.

'Of what good would that be? Everyone knows us as Jonty and Gilly. Thus we will stay, Mistress Gilly.'

'So we will, Master Jonty.'

I watched as a thought passed across his face, and was not altogether surprised when he remarked in all seriousness, 'Until, perhaps, I receive a knighthood; then I might reconsider...'

A knighthood indeed. A little frisson of delight shivered along my arms. Had I not always known that Jonty was as ambitious as the rest of the Pastons? And in truth I would enjoy becoming Dame Margery, to the admiration of our Norfolk neighbours. I linked my fingers persuasively with Jonty's.

'When you become a knight, Master Jonty, I will expect you to buy me a velvet tippet and a jewelled collar, suitable for Court celebrations.'

'I will, Mistress Gilly, if it be not too costly.'

I smiled at his reaction to any overt extravagance. He would conveniently forget, of course. But I would assuredly remind him.

ACKNOWLEDGEMENTS

I have so many acknowledgements to make, and so many thanks to give:

To all at Orion Publishing who have made me so welcome in my new home.

To Charlotte Mursell, my editor, for her words of wisdom and endless patience when editing *A Marriage of Fortune*.

And to the whole splendid Orion Publishing team: Lucy Brem, Katie Moss, Frankie Banks and Paul Stark, who have launched the Paston women into the world.

For Jane Judd, my agent, who continues to give me her friendship, her support and her advice through all the intricacies of the publishing world, as well as giving me the first review of my new book. I am very appreciative.

To all at Orphans Press who maintain my website and my newsletter, and come to my aid with all the technical knowledge that I do not have.

And finally, all my thanks to the Paston women, and their menfolk too. For their inspirational writing in their letters, full of all the minutia of 15th century family life: unwanted advice, family disputes, shopping lists, love affairs, warfare, victories and heartbreak. They are the true heroines behind *A Marriage of Fortune*.

CREDITS

Anne O'Brien and Orion Fiction would like to thank everyone at Orion who worked on the publication of *A Marriage of Fortune* in the UK.

Editorial
Charlotte Mursell
Lucy Brem

Copyeditor
Marian Reid

Proofreader
Linda Joyce

Marketing
Katie Moss

Audio
Paul Stark
Jake Alderson

Contracts
Anne Goddard
Dan Herron
Ellie Bowker

Design
Nick Shah
Charlotte Abrams-Simpson
Joanna Ridley

Editorial Management
Charlie Panayiotou
Jane Hughes
Bartley Shaw
Tamara Morriss

Finance
Jasdip Nandra
Nick Gibson
Sue Baker

Publicity
Frankie Banks

Production
Ruth Sharvell

Sales
Jen Wilson
Esther Waters
Victoria Laws
Toluwalope Ayo-Ajala
Rachael Hum
Anna Egelstaff
Sinead White
Georgina Cutler

Operations
Jo Jacobs
Sharon Willis